The Daybringer · Book I

Beneath the Vault of Stars

Blake Goulette

Brightest Stars Publishing Co.

ISBN-13: 978-1-7346505-0-1

Cover image and book design by Blake Goulette

Printed and bound in USA

Published by Brightest Stars Publishing Co.
520 Gooseberry Dr
Holly Springs, North Carolina 27540
USA

Visit www.blakegoulette.com

For Mary, William, and Nathaniel—
Zhi usmawin erume ib zhàyahal

CONTENTS

PART I.

CONTENTS

PART II.

Part I.

CHAPTER I

On the Way to the Pump

KALAS STRUGGLED TO KEEP UP WITH HIS FATHER, Tàran, as they crossed the desert. Dead roots and black stones reached up from the sandy ground and harried his every step. Tàran seemed to bound over the trail, avoiding each obstacle with preternatural ability. Unable to maintain his father's winged pace, Kalas stopped and clung to his shovel for support.

"Father, I need a minute," he panted. A few steps ahead, Tàran stopped moving, too, his silhouette a stout patch of black against the faintest hints of rose.

"How do you do it?" wheezed Kalas as he gestured at the terrain.

Tàran laughed, not unkindly. "It doesn't happen overnight, boy! Takes time, I reckon: after all these Sevens, I just know how to miss every rock. Someday, you will, too. I'm sure of it."

Kalas grunted, unconvinced. He stood, and the pair continued on their way.

"I know we're not taking the Pump Road, but what road is this?" asked Kalas. Though it would be a few minutes before the premier sun ascended above the horizon, in its reflected light Kalas wondered at the unfamiliar terrain and its unique geology.

"Since today's your second Seven, I thought we'd do things a little differently," Tàran smiled. "It's a much longer trip—why we had to stay in tents the last few nights—but, as you'll see in just a bit, it's much more impressive, too!

"And besides, there've been reports that something's fouling the water. The Ruins Road—what we're on now, though it's not much of a road anymore—leads to an old path down into the Empty Sea. From there, we'll follow the Ilswàr about a league, league and a half until we reach the Pump."

"The Ruins Road?" prodded Kalas.

"No one uses it anymore, but a long time ago, when the Empty Sea had another name, there was a great city along its shores. Kësharan. You can still see the remains of some of its piers."

"What happened to it?"

"I have no idea. Something bad, though, I think: most stories only mention it in passing. I think I read something about it in one of your grandfather's books? Or maybe I heard about it from Tsharak? Like I said, it was a long time ago. Anyway, we'll be there in a league or so."

They walked in relative silence, broken only by the rhythmic crunch of gravel beneath their feet. Soon, fragments of paving stone dotted the widening road, and Kalas tried to picture it as it must have looked in centuries past.

"Kësharan," nodded Tàran, noting Kalas' distraction. "We'll reach its outer walls in less than a mile; the old shoreline just after that."

The sun—the first sun—sliced the waning darkness with a thin strip of silver. Kalas stumbled, dropped his shovel and clutched his head. For a moment, his world turned white and soundless; then, subtle hints of *music* rose up within his mind. Without warning, the music swelled to orchestral proportions and danced across his synapses. Time seemed to slow. Kalas fell, struggling to make sense of the enlivened aural energy that arced all around and within him.

Father! he tried to scream. He wasn't sure if he'd actually made any sound.

"Boy?" Tàran turned and raised an eyebrow.

Kalas didn't hear him. The music stopped, its last reverberations mere echoes. He remained where he'd fallen, pressed his hands against his eyes, and let his head swing in time to the receding sound.

"Boy!" repeated Tàran, offering him a rough hand.

Slowly, Kalas lowered his arms. He blinked and looked around as though he'd forgotten where he was before he noticed his father.

"What…what was that?" he wondered, accepting Tàran's aid.

"You hurt yourself?"

"No, I don't think so. That music though: what was that from?"

"Music?" Kalas, still holding his father's arm, felt it stiffen for the briefest instant. "I don't know what you're talking about, boy: I didn't hear anything."

"You didn't hear those…I don't know, *chimes,* I guess?"

"Chimes? Out here?" Tàran's forced laughter didn't reach his eyes. "No, boy, I didn't hear anything. You feeling all right?"

"Yeah, I'm fine, I just—" He raised a finger to his upper lip and wiped at something wet.

"You sure?" demanded Tàran, pointing at Kalas' bloody nose.

"Yes, I'm sure, Father. See? It stopped already."

Kalas *knew* Tàran wanted to take him home. His head throbbed, but it wasn't anything he couldn't endure. And while Kalas really wanted to see the ancient ruins, his primary desire was not to disappoint his father.

With a knowing sigh, Tàran decided, "If anything happens to you, I'll never hear the end of it from your mother." The leathery skin around his eyes crinkled as he winked at his co-conspirator. "Come on then, boy: we've still got a way to go before we reach the Pump, and with both suns in the sky, traveling will be difficult."

Kalas returned his father's smile, retrieved his shovel, and as they set out again, he mumbled, *"Tàfayan."*

Tàran slowed down and cocked his head: "What was that?"

"Tàfayan," repeated Kalas. *"Nalënahwu,* the Premier Sun."

"That's…what I thought you said…" he muttered, quickening his pace. Changing the subject, he added, "Anyway, I almost *hope* we find something in the River. If we don't, then it's probably something wrong with the Pump, and it could be weeks, maybe months before someone figures it out."

Soon, the spires of Kësharan rose up behind a vast wall. Kalas gasped, enchanted by the interplay of jewel-toned colors glinting from rooftops in the sun's waxing light. Through crumbled gates and broken stones, he let his gaze follow the few remaining towers into the sky. Drawn, he took a step toward the largest opening.

"The Plains Gate—what's left of it, at least," nodded Tàran. He joined Kalas and continued, "The busiest gate when Kësharan was a thriving metropolis. At least, that's what Tsharak claims."

"That crazy old man who's always telling those stories?"

"I wouldn't call him crazy, but…yes. He knows more about Lohwàlar, its surroundings, and its history than anyone else, I'd wager. Strange as he is—strange as his *stories* are—there's something honest about him. Who do you think told me about the Ruins Road in the first place?"

As they walked through the remains of Kësharan's shadowed colonnades and weathered porticoes, Kalas saw its decay was much more advanced than he'd assumed, as though the city had suffered violent tragedy. Shattered fragments of crystal-paned windows and sculpture littered the streets. Several buildings were missing huge sections: others had collapsed completely. They altered course several times, avoiding canted and broken pillars and statuary, and exited the city onto an immense platform. Kalas peered over its edge and struggled against a wave of vertigo. The surface on which they stood was hundreds of feet above the earth, somehow still supported by brittle-looking pilings.

"Watch yourself, boy!" warned Tàran, grabbing his son's arm and leading him away from the ledge. Loose stones hurtled into the chasm. "Come, this way."

The pair reentered the city, where Tàran led Kalas through another maze of avenues marked with faded chalk blazes that deposited them just outside the wall at the foot of a small hill.

"There's a trail here that leads down into the canyon. From there, it's a few miles to the Pump. We've made good time, so we'll rest a minute. Drink some water: you don't want to—"

Again, Kalas' mind filled with music as everything around him —time included—seemed to smear. This time, however, he thought he saw *shapes* within the music. When it passed, the second sun was above the horizon, warming the first sun's argent light with a soft, golden glow. Tàran's mouth was moving, too slowly, until time snapped back into place.

"—drated," he finished. His eyebrow arched, he regarded Kalas for a moment.

"It happened again, didn't it?" he accused.

"Did you hear it?" asked Kalas, his enthusiasm bare.

Tàran shook his head and pointed to his son's nose. "No, boy, I didn't." Kalas wiped away another bloody streak. "If this keeps up, I'm taking you home. And I don't—"

"Father, I'm fine! I promise!" Kalas protested, squinting against the dull pounding between his temples. "If...if it gets worse, I'll tell you! I promise! Please don't make me go home!"

Tàran remained silent. With a huff—and a hint of pride—he conceded, "I admire your determination, boy. I do. And it's your second Seven: you're not a child anymore. If you say you're fine, fair enough. Still, I am your father…"

"I'm fine, Father. Really," Kalas assured him. He picked up his pack, cinched its straps, and gestured toward the hilltop, beyond which lie the rim of the Empty Sea.

2.

Kalas peered out over a vast gorge, its opposite edge obscured by haze. Beneath him, birds soared on updrafts toward points unknown. An immense and ancient forest, its treetops rippling in the warm, rising air, spread out across the floor of the canyon. Obscured by the forest's canopy, occasional specks of reflected sunlight glimmered across the meandering surface of the Rumilswàr, a stitch of silver thread sewn into the very fabric of the earth.

What Tàran called a trail, Kalas discovered, was little more than a series of thin switchbacks and rough hand- and footholds carved into the slope of the cliff. Another slight suggestion of dizziness upset Kalas' equilibrium. He closed his eyes for a moment: when he opened them, the sensation had passed.

"It's almost a quarter mile straight down," Tàran explained. "It's more like a league, maybe less, for us. It'll take an hour or two to reach the bottom; after that, it's still quite a hike to the river. Just watch your step. You'll be fine."

They reached the ground without incident. Kalas, panting, noticed his father seemed a little breathless, too.

"That's the worst of it," said Tàran, recovered. Kalas, seated on a tree-shaded rock, nodded. "It's downhill—if only slightly—from here to the Pump. It's another three or four miles, but they're easy miles. Especially compared to that! You ready?"

"Now I know why we usually take the Pump Road!" he nodded. Kalas picked up his shovel, and, ignoring his headache as best he could, followed his father along an almost invisible path between the trees.

As the forest deepened, the suns-light weakened and the air grew cooler. It wasn't long before he could make out the gentle rush of the Rumilswàr somewhere ahead of them. Myriad woodland creatures chattered within the shadows. Songbirds chirped and flit from branch to branch. After a while, Tàran and Kalas reached the river.

Animal tracks dotted its serpentine banks. Where its waters frothed and tumbled over rocks, Kalas saw rainbows shimmer in the spray. A bit downstream, the rapids lessened, dissolved into powerless whorls and eddies carried away by the exhausted current. They walked, fording the river's many curves along their way.

"Well," surveyed Tàran, "at least this part of the Ilswàr looks all right. We should keep working our way upriver, make sure everything's okay."

Without warning, the sky darkened and the air turned amber. Just as suddenly, the animal sounds ceased. Kalas looked up at a writhing mass of purple clouds, ripe with hints of fire. Before he could ask his father what was happening, a sizzling fork of orange energy split the sky, wormed its way into a tree, and, for a fraction of a second, disappeared—the tree seemed to *glow* as it exploded with a searing flash. Kalas ducked as a sizable branch sailed over his head; Tàran dived for cover as another whistled through the space where he'd been standing.

"What's going on?" Kalas yelled, his voice swallowed by wind that had risen out of nowhere.

Tàran took a step toward him and bellowed. *"Ilâegsal!* Back! Toward the cliffs! *Hwer!* Now!" With an anxious shove, he prodded Kalas, who stumbled and dropped his shovel. He knelt to retrieve it.

"Forget it! Just go!"

Kalas obeyed and crossed the knee-deep river with moderate difficulty. Tàran helped him over its bank and continued, "Quickly! Shelter! Look for shelter! A cave! A ledge! Anything!"

Tàran scanned his surroundings, saw nothing satisfactory, and, with a curse, dropped his pack and rifled through its contents. He withdrew a bundle of poles and skins which the mounting wind ripped from his hands.

"*Bethru, al neshrëthu!*" he swore.

"Father! Look!" shouted Kalas. A gust had pushed aside just enough cover for the young man to notice an outcropping under which they could find shelter.

"Well done, boy! Well done!" cheered Tàran as he grabbed his pack and followed his son into safety.

"Toward the back," he urged. When he was satisfied they were safe, he sat.

"What's going on?" demanded Kalas, shivering.

"Just wait," breathed Tàran. "Listen."

At first, Kalas heard nothing—not even the wind, which had already died. Then, a series of faint *tink, tink, tinks,* each followed by a hiss of steam, broke the stillness. With abandon, the sky opened up.

"The rain that hungers," said Tàran. "We should be safe here. *Should* be." Thunder boomed, underscoring his doubt.

Above them, the clouds hurled themselves in torrents to the ground as occasional lightning bolts stabbed at the earth. Kalas and his father waited, silent as the storm unleashed its fearsome rage.

3.

"The rain-that-hungers?" asked Kalas when the downpour stopped.

"Hungry rain. Rainfire. Falling fire. It's rare, and you do *not* want to get caught in it. If you hadn't spotted this place, we'd have had to hope this tent would have been enough." Tàran patted his pack.

"Why? It's just rain, right?"

Tàran surveyed the forest. Deeming it safe, he suggested, "Look around."

"It's the forest," Kalas muttered. "Same as before."

"Look a little closer," encouraged Tàran.

Kalas looked again. He was about to repeat himself when he noticed thick, white smoke swirling among the trees, rising in some places and spilling over the pocked ground in others. Many of the trees looked like they'd been burned: some still smoldered, glowing with subtle embers. The suns, shining down through cloudless sky, glinted from something near the river's edge. Kalas picked his way toward it, knelt to retrieve it, and held up the smoking remains of his shovel. Its metal blade, gleaming mere moments ago, was now pitted with rough, black indentations, ragged where the rainfire had eaten it.

"Not 'just rain,'" noted Tàran, who'd joined Kalas. "No one knows what causes it, but those purple clouds? that orange sky? That's a sure sign it's coming. This, though: this is the worst I've ever seen."

"I'm sorry about the shovel," said Kalas.

"Well," he said, his eyes smiling, "I'm sure Gandhan can have Zhalera make us a new one…"

Kalas blushed and looked away. Something seemingly out of place caught his attention.

"Father, what kind of rock is that?" he asked, pointing toward the formation under which they'd sheltered. The storm had burned away most of the vines and mosses covering it; now, it appeared milky white, almost pearlescent. A thin, straight line, beginning somewhere within the cliff, bisected its perfect symmetry; another rose perpendicular from the first and followed its contours until it was no longer visible. Unlike the surrounding exposed faces, it bore no trace of the hungry rain's destructive touch.

"I don't know," Tàran marveled. "I've never seen anything like it."

Kalas approached it and reached up and ran his fingers over its surface.

"It's so smooth! Feels like some kind of metal!" he exclaimed, turning to Tàran.

Two wholly unnatural sounds—*beep beep*—emanated from deep within the canyon's wall. A wash of rich blue light spilled over him, over everything, then faded, leaving a weak yellow aura in its stead.

"What was that?!" shouted Tàran. Kalas withdrew his hand and stepped back. After a brief, rising whine, two more pulses of light —green this time—illuminated an intricate network of fine lines beneath the object's exterior, its *skin,* then disappeared. The object turned opaque, again resembling nothing more than a curious part of the rocky face.

"I have no idea," said Kalas, and he took a step toward the thing.

"Don't touch it!" ordered Tàran. Kalas froze, mid-stride, then lowered his outstretched hand.

"Don't…don't touch it," he repeated. "I don't…I don't *trust* it."

"But Father—!"

"Not today, boy. The storm's already delayed us. And I want to check your grandfather's books. Do some research. Maybe someday, when we have more time, we'll come back…"

Tàran rubbed his temples. He slumped as though burdened by an invisible weight.

"Father?" asked Kalas.

"I'm fine, boy. Fine. Storm's over: let's keep moving.

Without another word, Tàran searched for a path, found one,

and started upriver. Kalas watched him. With one last glance at the overhang, he followed after his father.

The next mile passed with relative insignificance; however, at midday, when the suns met at the top of the sky, Kalas screamed, pressed his hands flat against his ears, and collapsed.

"Kalas!" shouted Tàran as his son's eyes rolled up within their sockets.

"Kalas!"

4.

Otherworldly music swelled along an infinite staff, created shapes of hope and promise as every note erupted in showers of wonder. The shapes assumed colors representing every facet of visible light, collided with and cascaded over one another like serpent-tongues of flame. Intersecting harmonies wove themselves into a seamless fabric of exultant melody that wrapped itself around Kalas' mind and surrounded his thoughts with hints of purpose. The aural power swept through him on a river-like course, and, both outside *and* within himself, he glimpsed his world from a thousand simultaneous perspectives.

The music ceased; the shapes and colors fled; and Kalas, groggy, heard sobbing.

"So…so beautiful!" he wept, and realized *he* was the one crying. He wiped his eyes and blinked them a time or two as he tried to remember his surroundings. He was on his back, his head cradled in Tàran's shaking and knotted arms.

"Father?" he said.

"I've got you, son. I've got you," Tàran comforted as he batted at his own uncharacteristic tears. With a trembling hand, he wiped away smears of blood that had trickled from Kalas' nose and ears.

"What…what happened?"

"For almost half an hour, you—it doesn't matter," soothed Tàran. "He told us this day would come, but…I've got you now. I've got you."

His voice cracked. Pent-up tension poured out of him in wracking waves as he wrapped his burly frame around his son and held him close—so very close—to his heart.

5.

Kalas removed himself from his father's protective embrace, stood, and reeled from a throbbing rush of blood within his temples.

"You okay?" asked Tàran. Kalas nodded. Delicately.

"Good. Pick up your pack: we're going home."

"But Father! I—"

"Enough, boy! I can't—you can't—This is no time to argue! Your mother'll probably flay me alive as it is!"

"But—!"

Tàran held up a palm and glared at Kalas.

"Yes, Father," he acquiesced. He shouldered his pack and did his best to ignore the hammer-like pounding in his head while Tàran supervised.

"Ready? Let's go."

"Help! Help!"

Tàran stiffened, cocked his head, and looked around. His eyebrow raised, he glanced at Kalas.

"Did you—"

"No, but I—"

"Somebody! Please, help!" came the nasal voice again. Closer this time, and more panicked.

"That almost sounds like Dzharëth," said Kalas.

"Ëlbodh's boy?" wondered Tàran.

"Yeah, that's right"

"Ëlbodh was on rotation to tend the Pump. Makes sense he'd have his boy with him."

"I thought the Pump was still a few miles upriver?"

"It is," admitted Tàran, puzzled. "Anyway, come on!"

Tàran started toward the voice. Kalas followed, stifling an outcry as his head protested.

The forest thinned as they progressed, giving way to splotches of dead and dying trees. The cries for help increased in volume and hysteria. As the pair crested a small hill, a gangling gray shape collided with Tàran and knocked him to the ground. He absorbed the impact, rolled with it, and sprung lightly to his feet in one fluid motion. The haggard figure remained where it had fallen, quivering. Tàran looked toward Kalas—

Dzharëth?

—who nodded.

"Dzharëth," said Tàran, reaching out a hand and placing it on the boy's shoulder.

He and Kalas recoiled as Dzharëth screamed, jumped to his feet and clawed at his chest.

His clothes, reduced to thin strips in places, were soaked through with something dark. Red and white flecks of dried blood and spittle clung to the coarse hairs surrounding his mouth; his eyes, wide and unfocused, scanned everything. He whined, gathered himself, and screamed again: "Help!"

"Dzharëth!" shouted Kalas. *"Dzharëth!"*

The figure raised his arms in a protective gesture.

As though expecting a blow.

When nothing happened, Dzharëth lowered his arms. His eyes had snapped into focus. He wiped his mouth and worked his jaw. As though perceiving his surroundings for the first time, he whimpered, "Kalas? Tàran?! *Erume dàbiras nir!*"

"Dzharëth, what happened? Whose blood is this? Where's Ëlbodh?" asked Tàran.

"Oh! Father! The *ilâegsal!* He's hurt—badly! Come! Quickly! *Quickly!*"

With a rough shove, he sprinted away from them, his tattered clothing whipping in his wake.

"Help!" he shouted again.

"Boy, tell the truth: are you okay?" demanded Tàran.

Kalas squeezed his eyes for a moment. "I'm fine, Father," he insisted. Tàran's furrowed brow belied his disbelief.

"It's not like we have a choice," he muttered. To Kalas, he instructed: "Go home. Find a healer. Tell him Ëlbodh was wounded in a rainfire storm. Tell him to get here as fast as he can: the Pump Road is probably the quickest route.

"Take only what you need. After you've sent a healer, find another one: tell him about…your head today. And stay with him."

"But Father, I—"

"Mark my words, boy: *stay with him!* Now, go! I don't think Ëlbodh has a lot of time! *Hwer!* Be swift!"

CHAPTER II

Under a Shooting Star

KALAS GRABBED A POUCH OF DRIED MEAT AND A WA-terskin from his pack and raced along the path leading to the Pump Road. Every footstep wracked his throbbing skull.

What's that noise? The Pump sounds awful! he noted as he rushed past the side trail that lead to its guts. He moved with such speed, such purpose, that he ignored anything not directly in his path.

At the base of the cliff, he allowed himself only a moment before ascending, grateful that the Pump Road was considerably less steep than the Ruins Road. When he hauled himself over the canyon's edge, he panted for a moment, clutched at his head, and threw up. Immediately, he felt better, his head clearer. His stomach gurgled, and he remembered the dried meat. After washing it down with a swallow from his waterskin, he kept going.

In less time than he'd anticipated, Kalas reached the sand-strewn outskirts of Lohwàlar. He paused for a sip of water, then sped the remainder of the rough way toward the clerics' Sanctuary.

Inside and out of breath, Kalas staggered toward a small dais, grabbed at the young secretary's robe, and rasped, "Cleric!" Annoyed, the young man removed Kalas' hand, smoothed his robe, and, with reproach, disappeared into the building's dim interior.

One of the oldest surviving structures in Lohwàlar—and once a temple, the Sanctuary building's architecture evoked thoughts of what the town's ancient past might have looked like. Vast stone walls, flecked with minerals and flanking broad corridors, sparkled in the torchlight. As he waited, Kalas felt his pulse slow, his focus sharpen, though the pain in his head remained. He became all too aware of the stink of his own sweat, mingled with vomit. Underneath those odors, however, ran a faint metallic component.

"That would be blood, no doubt," suggested a deep, rich voice from somewhere behind him. He whirled and faced the voice's owner, draped in robes and wrinkles. Most of his features were obscured by prodigious eyebrows and a gleaming white beard that flowed across his chest, rippling like water with every breath. His bald, dark brown pate reflected torchlight; his green eyes seemed to radiate some kind of energy—or maybe it was just the old man's crows' feet. Still, there was something peculiar about the cleric. Kalas was too curious to consider his appearance further:

"Blood? What? Wait, how—?"

"You're at the Sanctuary, child!" The old man smiled, his eyes flickering like the torches in the mid-afternoon breezes that filtered through its hallways. "An olfactory curiosity, I'm sure, the ability to discern various odors. Useful most of the time, though it certainly has its downside! I noticed the dried blood on your face, and, well, come along: we'll get you patched right up."

The old man beckoned Kalas to follow him, and he did, for a step or two, before remembering his purpose.

"No, I'm not here for me! I'm here for Ëlbodh, Dzharëth's father! They were working out in the Empty Sea, and the *ilâegsal*—"

"Rainfire! All right, child, allow me a moment to collect my things, and we'll be off!"

"Please hurry!" urged Kalas, and this time he did follow the old man into a small cloister off the main corridor.

The cleric wrapped the traditional leather pouches around his upper arms, then looked about the room. Searching. Thinking. He waggled a finger, nodded, and reached beneath a counter and withdrew a few small bottles, a bowl, and other items. With practiced care, he mixed his ingredients in varying proportions, squinting as the concoction's fumes assaulted his senses.

"The downside," he coughed with a wink. "And the name's Falthwën, young…?"

"Kalas, sir," he answered. Falthwën's smile broadened.

"Tell me, young Kalas, what were you doing in the Empty Sea? That's not exactly the safest place for a child."

"Today's my second Seven," said Kalas, bristling. "I was helping my father, Tàran, with the Pump. At least, that's what we were supposed to be doing before we found them."

"Your second Seven!" exclaimed Falthwën, and spared a glance at the young man. The cleric's thoughts seemed to trail off, or perhaps complete some side journey as he once again turned them toward his work. Kalas watched, rapt, as the old man, with deftness that belied his aged appearance, withdrew a gleaming instrument, small and intricate, from within the folds of his silver-threaded robe and stirred the mixture, humming softly as he worked. A faint luminescence seemed to rise above the bowl's contents.

That's the tune! thought Kalas. *That's the sound I heard!*

"That song! Where did you—"

"All right, we're ready!" he said as he poured his potion into an empty vial. He slipped it into a pocket sewn into one of his arm pouches. After slinging a stout bag over his shoulder, he grabbed a pair of staffs and tossed one to Kalas.

"Let's go!"

"Yes, sir," said Kalas as the pair exited the small room. Something unremembered tickled the back of his mind, but, compelled, he followed the old man's hurried pace.

2.

"We'll take the Pump Road," said Falthwën. Kalas nodded as though the cleric required his approval. "It's…this way, yes?"

"That's right, sir," Kalas nodded again. "Just came from there."

"It's been…a long, long while since I've been in Lohwàlar," noted Falthwën. "Glad to see I haven't forgotten everything!"

"You're not from here: I didn't think I recognized you, and, well, I thought I knew everyone in town. So where are you from?" wondered Kalas.

"No, I'm not from here, although I've visited often. Last time was probably long before you were born."

"You still haven't told me where you're from. Your accent: are you from Tarular? In the North? I've never met anyone from Tarular."

"Not Tarular, young Kalas. Let's just say I'm from…beyond many sands."

"'Beyond many sands'? What does that even mean?"

"It means let's talk about something else," finished Falthwën. "The second sun will set in a little while: if we move quickly, I think we can reach the Empty Sea before it does."

Focused, the pair traveled in relative silence. Occasionally, Falthwën would pause and tilt his head, as if listening for something; then, without comment, he'd continue.

"Why do you keep doing that?" Kalas asked the next time the old man stopped.

"Doing what?" he said, resuming his pace.

"You keep stopping and listening—for what, I don't know. I don't hear anything, and I thought we were in a hurry!"

Falthwën nodded without making eye contact. Instead, he followed the second sun through a thin string of nascent clouds as its edge intersected the horizon.

"Well?" demanded Kalas. "Aren't you going t—"

Again, the world around him dissolved into a whirl of light and color as music swelled and ebbed into and out of existence. In his mind, the chimes acquired spatial coordinates; the melodies seemed to rise and fall and whip past him, too quick to be analyzed or deconstructed. In front of him, the swirls swooped and turned and gave way to a luminous bloom of penetrating green light.

It looks like health, thought Kalas—

—and in that moment, the chimes fell silent. The colors flashed white and faded into his present reality. Falthwën stood above him. Observed him, his eyes dancing in the sun's waning light.

"Everything all right?" He waved his staff at Kalas' face even as the young man felt the warmth of his own blood on his upper lip. He stood—only then realizing he'd fallen—and wiped it away. The last vestiges of green were slow to dissipate: the old cleric seemed wreathed in emerald. The pressure emanating from every direction within his head increased, making the simple act of seeing painful.

"I…my father told me to stay in town, to find a healer and tell him about…about this. It's never happened before! I mean, sure, I've had a nosebleed a time or two, a headache, maybe, but nothing like this. And then there's—"

"And your head?" wondered Falthwën. Kalas realized he was massaging his temples again. "Here," said Falthwën as he rummaged around in his pockets. He produced a small, translucent green lozenge and tossed it to Kalas, who regarded it with curious suspicion.

"That'll help, but only if you put it in your mouth!" laughed the cleric. He appraised Kalas' condition and, apparently satisfied, nodded and said, "All right, you'll be fine. Let's be on our way."

Falthwën turned and resumed walking. Kalas shrugged and popped the medicine into his mouth. A cold wave of innervating energy swept through him, starting from his tongue, swelling within his mind and traveling the length of his entire body. He gasped as the ever-present throb behind his eyes disappeared. The element tucked into his cheek began to melt, taking with it the fatigue of the day.

"What was *that?*" said Kalas, amazed.

"Better?" asked Falthwën.

"Yes, but—"

"Excellent! If memory serves, the Pump isn't more than a few miles from here." He looked around again, nodded again, and started down the subtly sloping road. Kalas, frustrated with the cleric's reticence, considered leaving Falthwën to his own devices and returning to the Sanctuary.

That's what Father would want, he affirmed; however, his curiosity overwhelmed him and he rushed to catch up to the old man.

3.

Although longer, the Pump Road's subtler slope allowed Kalas and Falthwën to reach the floor of the Empty Sea with greater speed than Kalas thought probable. Years of feet, hooves, and wheels had compacted its surface, presenting a somewhat smoother journey than the rough trail along the Ruins Road. In a short time, the pair reached a crossroads and a crumbling archway bearing traces of delicate scrollwork, worn by time and weather. Beyond, buried in the earth behind the cliff face, the ancient Pump whirred and clicked, its gears and assemblies struggling to irrigate the land surrounding distant Lohwàlar.

"You were on your way to the Pump, yes?" asked Falthwën. Kalas nodded.

"Then we head downriver, to the northeast! Come!"

They turned, passed beneath the archway, and, with the Rumilswàr on their left, quickened their pace. The Pump, historically much quieter, produced a noise that increased in volume. Again, something in its rumbling cadence seemed off to Kalas. Atonal. Although he'd only been to the Pump a few times with his father, he remembered its workings sounding like a kind of music; now, he thought of the orchestra that played in the town's Crescent during the last festival: he remembered how one of the less skilled percussionists weaved in and out of time with the rest of the band and tainted its overall harmony.

"That's not how it's supposed to sound," said Kalas.

"I noticed that, too," agreed Falthwën. "Though more pressing matters attend us. When there's time, tell your father: I suspect he'll know what to do."

A short distance later, the road turned sharply to the right, around a protrusion of rock. Almost immediately, the discordant banging of the Pump dwindled to a dull series of clunks and thuds. Once past the Pump, the road's poor condition more closely resembled that of the Ruins Road. After another rough mile and an intersection they almost missed in the deepening shadows, the pair reached Tàran, Dzharëth, and Ëlbodh.

"Healer! Over here!" shouted Kalas' father.

Falthwën stepped into the small clearing in which Tàran stood over Ëlbodh, whom he'd draped with skins from his pack. Dzharëth huddled nearby, whimpering again.

"Healer! *Zhi Ilun dàbiras nir!* Ëlbodh is hurt. Badly. And I don't—"

Tàran noticed his son hadn't remained in town. His eyes darkened as he continued: "I don't think it was just the rainfire."

Falthwën nodded toward Dzharëth. "And him?"

"Dzharëth. Ëlbodh's boy. He's…I think something's wrong with him. Wouldn't know what."

Falthwën nodded again and removed the skins covering the

wounded man. Kalas gasped.

Ëlbodh's face—what remained of it—was pocked much like Kalas' shovel. One of his eyes dangled from its socket, perhaps staring sightlessly through the jagged hole that used to be his cheek. The chill in the late day air must have roused him from unconsciousness, because after a series of shallow breaths, he stirred: his remaining eye blinked once or twice before widening to its uttermost. Ëlbodh raised his arms—revealing ragged, parallel scrapes, dark with clotted blood—and screamed.

Not from pain, thought Kalas. From fear. *But fear of what?*

Vitreous seeped from his ruptured eyeball. Fresh blood oozed and dribbled from his opened cheek as his scream decayed into a choked gurgle. His arms fell limp, his staring eye snapped shut, and, for a moment, the world seemed to wait, silent.

"So much…so much redness," murmured Dzharëth, who had drawn up beside Kalas without a sound. Kalas flinched, unsettled by his friend. Tàran seemed not to have noticed him, either.

"Is…is he dead?" said Kalas.

Falthwën had already knelt and produced the unguent he'd prepared back at the Sanctuary. With the same thin silver instrument, he stirred it briefly, and, with his finger, applied it to Ëlbodh's wounds, humming to himself as he did. Maybe it was a trick of the light, but Kalas thought he saw that same subtle glow he'd seen earlier in Falthwën's alcove. Neither Dzharëth nor his father seemed to notice.

"Not dead, child. Not yet, anyway, though I can't say with certainty for how long." To Tàran he added: "Come, let's get him back to the Sanctuary. I've done what I can for him out here."

Falthwën and Tàran fashioned a litter from the cleric's staffs and a thin sheet from his bag. With care, they lifted Ëlbodh onto it. He whimpered for a moment, then remained silent. His breathing slowed and his breaths deepened: Falthwën's potion seemed to be working its magic.

"Kalas," commanded Tàran, "You and Dzharëth: run ahead of us. This time, *obey:* tell the clerics we're coming!"

Kalas nodded once. He turned to Dzharëth and said "Let's go!" as he patted him on the shoulder.

Dzharëth's head lolled back and forth for a moment, his eyes unfocused again.

"Let's *go!*" Kalas repeated, snapping his fingers mere inches from Dzharëth's face.

"I…right, the Sanctuary. The clerics. Of course," he mumbled. Stiff and numb, he followed Kalas.

4.

The second sun had almost set, spreading long, dark shadow-fingers across the blur of gray and brown the forest had become. They hurried, and soon, the subtle drone of the Pump's inner workings pressed against Kalas' senses. For the last mile or so, neither Dzharëth nor most of the woodland fauna had made a sound, and Kalas lost count of the times he'd thought for sure the disturbed young man had strayed from the path. Each time, however, Dzharëth was close behind, his former stiffness gone, his steps impossibly quiet atop the twigs and gravel.

They stepped through the ancient archway and into the crossroads, the noise of the Pump again a cacophonic bass line underneath the infrequent twilight sounds all around them. As they started up the slope of the road, the last slice of the silver sun crept behind the world, and again, the now-familiar music blossomed in Kalas' mind like a violent flower. Petals of raw energy unfolded from its center and wrapped around his thoughts in fronds of ripening power as myriad tunes climbed and crashed over themselves, intermingled with one another, and resolved into a solitary chord. Then the white sensation of heat receded and blew away like wisps of cloud with the Song's last reverberations.

Kalas staggered and stumbled as the shapes of rock and cliff and road reappeared. Whether the effect of Falthwën's lozenge lingered, he couldn't say: he just knew his headache only seemed a touch more intense than before. He wiped at his nose—no blood this time—and closed his eyes for a moment.

"I don't suppose you heard that, did you?" he said as he turned to Dzharëth.

Dzharëth was gone.

"Dzharëth?" Kalas called.

No answer.

"Dzharëth!" he repeated. Louder.

He surveyed the area for some sign of his friend. None existed. He thought of looking for him, then decided getting help for Ëlbodh was his priority. He started walking again, looking up the gradual incline toward the miles-distant rise he hoped to reach soon. Against a flat yellow plate of sky, he thought he saw the shifting lope of a shadowy figure, gaunt and clothed in tatters.

5.

He ran now. The moon hung low in the sky behind him, dull pink and stippling the desert as its reflected light fell, wearied, through the smattering of clouds that had gathered during the afternoon. In his haste, he tripped over a stray rock or branch. He sat for a moment and massaged his temples. And shivered: the sands only held the suns' heat while they were shining; now, in the dark, cold wind oozed, languid, through the air and dragged itself across Kalas' sweat-beaded skin. He stood, picked his way along the road for a while, then ran some more, keeping an eye out for Dzharëth.

The wind moved with an unpredictable syncopation: sometimes beside him, sometimes in front of him. Sometimes not at all. On occasion, he glimpsed in his peripheral vision what looked like—or at least gave the impression of—a pair of gleaming yellow eyes, but whenever he turned to be sure, they were gone. Maybe they'd never been there in the first place.

"Dzharëth," he called out from time to time, never receiving (nor expecting, he realized) an answer.

Maybe he's already at the Sanctuary, he hoped.

He reached the broken cobblestones leading into Lohwàlar sooner than he thought he would. He paused to catch his breath before making his way toward the Sanctuary through the town's spiraling streets.

"*Âu!*" he began, addressing the still-annoyed man at the dais. "My father, Tàran, and the cleric Falthwën will be here soon: they're carrying Ëlbodh—Hwena's husband, Dzharëth's—has Dzharëth been here? No? Dzharëth's father. There was a…a rainfire storm out near the Pump! Ëlbodh was caught in it! Please, he—they need your help!"

The secretary's annoyance evaporated as he nodded and trod a pedal beneath his desk. From somewhere behind him, Kalas heard a series of chimes and thought for a moment he was hearing the music again. Instead, an older cleric emerged from around a corner. She raised an eyebrow toward the secretary, who pointed at Kalas.

"Someone's injured?" she inquired.

"Yes!" he answered. "Falthwën and my father should be here soon, from the Pump Road. They're carrying Ëlbodh, Dzharëth's father. Got caught in a rainfire storm!"

The cleric nodded and signaled for a stretcher and a lantern.

"*Ilâegsal,*" she clucked. "Horrible curse. Come!"

• • •

They retraced Kalas' steps, her lantern casting dancing shadows all around them. A handful of townsfolk noticed them and whispered to one another. Soon, a small crowd formed and followed the pair. Kalas' mother, Màla, was among them.

"Kalas? Son, is that you?" she wondered.

"Mother? Mother!" he said, and let the crowd flow around him until she reached him. Màla hugged him and buried his face in her steely tresses.

"Is Tàran—is your father—?"

"No, Mother, he's fine: it's Ëlbodh, Dzharëth's father. Rainfire!"

She squeezed him too tightly, then relaxed her grip and held him at arm's length, surveying him—no, assessing him.

"What about you, child? What are those streaks on your face? Are you—?"

"Mother, I'm fine. I'm fine! Father's fine, too!"

She held him close again. He could feel her fear slip away like a heavy cloak falling from her shoulders. She released him, took his hands, and smiled, an expression of relief tainted with concern.

"You stay with the cleric. With your father. I'll…I'll find Hwena. She should know."

Kalas squeezed his mother's hands, then turned and ran to catch up with the swelling crowd. It didn't take him long. They'd reached the edge of town when a pinprick of greasy, yellow-orange light appeared in the distance, bobbing and swaying as it grew nearer. He was sure it had to be someone other than Falthwën and his father: it didn't seem possible they'd be here already, given their burden. Somehow, though, here they were. Tàran had suspended a lantern from a tent pole strapped to Ëlbodh's litter. The silver stitching in Falthwën's robes glittered in its rays. Two sturdy townsfolk stepped forward and traded places with the wearied pair and rushed the injured man toward the Sanctuary.

"I can't believe how quickly we got here!" Tàran said to Falthwën, who made a show of wiping his brow, his expression grim.

"Vàyana," said Falthwën, addressing the cleric. "We don't have much time."

The old man bowed his head. So did the woman called Vàyana. Together, they began a low, almost inaudible conversation. *A prayer,* Kalas realized. The lantern's brightness seemed to swell, though it might have been the moon, now high above the earth. With their prayer complete, the clerics retreated toward the Sanctuary. A cloud drifted overhead: the lights waned. The solemnity of the crowd's tones fell away as its members exchanged questions and suggestions. Kalas tuned them out and approached Tàran.

"I saw Mother, on my way back here. She went to see Hwena. How…how is Ëlbodh?" he asked.

Tàran mopped his own brow with a scrap of cloth and shivered. For a moment, he said nothing, then: "You heard the healer, boy. What was his name again?"

"Falthwën."

"Falthwën? Wonder how long he's been in town. Seems to know his business, at least."

Tàran thought for a moment, then shrugged.

"Anyway," he said, returning to the subject, "I'll tell you what, boy: in all my Sevens, I've never seen the hungry rain eat a man's face like that. That was a bad storm, sure, but his eye? his cheek? those marks on his arms? Looked like something clawed at him. Some kind of animal. Maybe the same thing that spooked his boy. Did he stay at the Sanctuary when you got back to town?"

"Dzharëth: he ran…I lost him on the way up the road. I…I stopped—just for a minute, I think, and when I looked up, he was gone. I thought he was on his way to the Sanctuary, but no one there had seen him. Maybe he went home? I hope he's all right."

"So do I, boy. So do I. I'm sorry this is how you had to spend your second Seven."

Kalas smiled: he'd forgotten today was his birthday.

"But it's not over yet! Come on, let's go home."

Somewhere in the darkness, beyond the reach of the lantern's glow, something bayed at the moon, pearlescent pink like bone.

6.

Màla clung to her husband's neck and refused to let go. They stood there, entwined, until Kalas returned from putting away his tools. Only then did his mother pull away, gracing her husband with a simple peck on the lips. Kalas smirked as subtle roses bloomed within his father's already suns-burned cheeks. Màla turned to her son and said, *"Vamëhath dàbiras nir,* Kalas."

"Thank you, Mother. I'll remember it, that's for sure!" He paused, not quite sure how to phrase his question, so he just asked: "How was Hwena? Was Dzharëth there?"

Màla shook her head.

"I walked her to the Sanctuary. I offered to stay with her, but the clerics promised to take care of her and told me I should go. They brought Ëlbodh in as I was leaving. I've never heard screams like that," she shuddered. "I hope I never do again."

In the dim light, his mother's years seemed more pronounced, the silver in her hair more drab.

"And no, Dzharëth wasn't there. Was he caught in the storm, too?"

"No," said Kalas, and he told her the story.

"When we passed the Pump," he added, now addressing Tàran, "we noticed something wrong, something in the sounds it made. The cleric said you'd know what to do."

"I'd have to hear them for myself, but how would a healer from

30

—where did he say he was from? 'Beyond many sands,' you say? Hmmph! How would he know anything about Lohwàlar's Pump? About *me?*"

A sharp rap on the door interrupted them. Màla's head snapped up, and she smiled at her son as she disappeared into the small anteroom. Muffled voices slid around the thick, mud-mortared stone walls, and it was Kalas' turn to blush as he recognized them.

"*Fan ávam dàbiras nir,* my boy!" exclaimed Gandhan. His daughter, Zhalera, stepped up from behind him.

"*Dàbirëthu ávam,* Kalas! Here, I made you something." She held out a small wooden box.

"Thank you," replied Kalas. He took the box and opened it.

Gandhan was Lohwàlar's preeminent blacksmith, and, much to his delight, for the year since her second Seven, Zhalera had been his apprentice. Gandhan often boasted about his daughter's skill with anvil and hammer, and as Kalas took hold of the small metal blade nestled within the straw-padded box, he could see—could *feel*—the substance of Gandhan's pride. He examined his present, admiring its every curve and corner as its edge glinted in the room's soft light. In his hand, its weight felt perfect, its balance precise.

Zhalera, mistaking his awe for something else, apologized: "I know it's not much, and the box—I made that, too—isn't very pretty, but I—"

"No," corrected Kalas. "It's…it's perfect. This is *perfect.*" Zhalera smiled and looked at her feet.

"Thank you."

He tucked the knife into his belt and stepped forward and hugged her. She returned the gesture: suddenly self-aware, Kalas stepped back, the burn in his cheeks even more pronounced.

"You really like it?" she asked.

"I love it," he confirmed. The color in Zhalera's heat-tanned face deepened, matching that in Kalas'. Gandhan laughed.

"I knew you would, my boy! I told you he would, didn't I, *Âsru-fin*—Firebird?" he bellowed, tousling his daughter's raven hair.

"If you'll excuse me," interjected Màla, "I still need to prepare the meal. There was some excitement, as you've probably heard." She disappeared behind a curtain of animal skins.

"Yes, Ëlbodh!" said Gandhan. "Tell me, Tàran: what happened?"

As Kalas' father began his tale, the young man left for the anteroom and pulled an old cloak from its peg. He stepped out into the bracing night air, breathed deep, and stared up at the star-filled sky.

"Going somewhere?" said Zhalera, surprising Kalas.

"I thought…I thought I might go for a walk while Mother cooks," he said as he turned around. "Try to clear my head. I keep seeing Ëlbodh: his face ripped apart, his eye just hanging there, and I can't get it out of my mind."

Zhalera took his hand and massaged the webbing between his thumb and index finger. Her high cheekbones shone in the moonlight; her tawny eyes glinted gold in its waxing radiance. A slight gust displaced a length of dark, shimmering hair that had been tucked behind her ear. She smoothed it back and asked, "Would you like some company?"

"You know what? I would." His former reserve overcome, he wrapped his fingers around hers, marveling at the paradox of callused elegance and delicate strength therein.

Hand-in-hand they walked, silent except for the crunch of dirt beneath their feet. They stopped when Kalas realized the town's flickering lights had thinned out behind them. Together, they stared up at the stars and all their myriad colors; at the iridescent halo that ringed the moon. Together, they wondered why the stars came in so many different sizes; why one in particular, high above them, fell across the night with an undulating gleam. It trailed vibrant, crimson light as it sped across the sky and disappeared.

"They say it's a good sign," said Zhalera, nodding at the spectacle. She shivered. Embarrassed that he hadn't thought to do it sooner, Kalas removed his cloak and draped it across her shoulders. She leaned into him, filling his senses with a mingled fragrance of smoke and flowers, and suddenly, the cold had no power over him.

After a while, though it pained him, he suggested they make their way home.

"Mother's gotta be done with supper by now," he said. "Still…I think I could stay out here all night with y—"

He hadn't even heard the creature's approach as it launched itself from a high rock, sailed into him, and splayed him on the ground.

"Kalas!" Zhalera screamed.

Stunned, it took Kalas a moment to collect himself. He shook his head and dived out of the way as the hulking black mass came at him again, missing him by mere inches. Its breath, hot and stinking of old meat, condensed in a fetid film on his neck. He leapt to his feet and squared himself with his assailant.

"Zhalera, *hwer!*" he shouted, never taking his eyes away from the thing in front of him.

It panted, thick gobbets of red saliva dripping from its fangs and matting its fur. Its yellow eyes bored into Kalas, sized him up, and, with practiced intent, it circled him. Kalas matched its movements, unsure of what to do. It appeared to be some kind of wolf. Kalas had never seen one, but his father had told him about them: none of his tales had made then out to be so big, so *hungry.* With its ears folded back against its skull and its teeth bared and glistening, it coiled itself like a spring and unwound with a growl. Again, Kalas hit dirt, rocks and roots digging into his spine as the wolf-thing snarled and snapped.

"Get away from him!" Zhalera yelled. She hit the monster with a rock, then another, and another, none with any effect.

"Go!" Kalas repeated, and he cried out as the wolf's claws opened up his chest.

"I said get away from him!" sobbed Zhalera, her voice cracking. She stepped forward and hurled the largest rock she could. It smacked the side of the wolf's head, which the beast whipped around as it finally seemed to notice her. It growled again, the sound a fearful blend of rage, hurt, and hate that almost sounded like words, and it stepped toward Zhalera. She stepped back—and tripped. As she fell, the wolf advanced.

No, thought Kalas.

No.

And unbidden, the music—the force that had been locked within him since the rising of the suns, found an outlet. The darkness shriveled, split like a scrap of old black paper as Kalas' flesh erupted in a blaze of power, a philharmonic conducted in energy and light.

He shouted something—words he'd never heard before—and held up a hand, and the wolf howled as something arced across the air gap between its hide and Kalas' outstretched palm. It skittered as though physically struck. The creature hesitated for a moment —only a moment—then went for Kalas.

The moment was enough. Kalas withdrew Zhalera's birthday present from his belt: in one fluid motion, he plunged it into the wolf's chest, hit bone, and stepped—almost danced—to the side. It howled again, more in fury than in pain, and wrenched the knife from Kalas' hand. He could sense its desire to come at him yet again, but with its life leaking onto the ground, it limped into the night, which had begun to knit itself whole. The light that had consumed him receded, and Kalas fell to his knees. Blood poured from his wounds, and his vision swam as hot pain groped at his body with greedy fingers. Something made a sound, not unlike his name shouted through a bowl of oil. He thought he heard the rush of footsteps fast approaching.

"Kalas!" Zhalera screamed again.

"Âsrufin?" he managed before the entirety of his existence snapped black.

CHAPTER III.

After a Deep Sleep

A SHAPE SHIFTED AT THE EDGE OF HIS PERCEPTION, LIKE someone or something moving subtly through a not-quite light-less room. He called out to the sound of voices whispering all around him: immediately, they ceased, their conversation unresolved, the substance of their discussion lost. A flash of silver stabbed him in the mind, and suddenly, a wash of muted, swirling colors rose up from unknown depths. He called out again—a name culled from some distant…dream? memory?—and the colors seemed to pause before coalescing into another vaguely familiar shape: a shape of curves and lines flecked with topaz; a shape that blinked away as a strand of singular notes percolated through his senses. A pinprick of light appeared at the center of the darkness. It hovered for a moment; then, with impossible speed, it rushed upon him and—

Kalas closed his eyes, only to realize they *had been* closed as the ivory warmth of suns-light splashed across his face. He sat upright —or tried to, at least: he cried out at the sudden fire sizzling in his chest.

"Kalas!" gasped Màla from his bedside, her look of worry replaced with one of joy.

"Mother?" he said, his throat scratchy. He cleared it, winced at its dryness, and tried again: "Mother, what's going on?"

"I thought you were…we didn't know if you'd…"

"Mother? What's going on? Where am I?"

"You're at the Sanctuary. You were hurt: a wolf, Zhalera said, when she dragged you home."

"A wolf?!" He let his head sway from side to side: his memories, he discovered, had jagged edges that felt like shards of glass as he tried to sort them, tried to make sense of how he ended up in the Sanctuary.

"She said it attacked you! She yelled for it to leave you alone: she threw rocks at it until it turned on her. She said she fell down, hit her head, and when she woke up, the wolf had run off and you were bleeding."

"Zhalera! Is she all right?"

"She's fine, dear, she's fine: the clerics released her after a day."

"A day? Wait—what is today? How long have I been asleep?"

"Four days, child."

Kalas let the shock roll over him. Màla tugged on a cord beside his bed, and soon, as the tinkle of chimes diminished, a cleric —Vàyana, he remembered—appeared beside his mother.

"You're awake!" she beamed. She gave Màla's shoulder a reassuring squeeze. She checked his vitals, nodded here and there and arched an eyebrow every once in a while.

"Tell me, young man: what's the last thing you remember?"

Kalas started to speak, then frowned.

"The storm. Ëlbodh. A cleric I'd never met—Falthwën, I think. I remember Zhalera's gift and going for a walk. We saw a falling star—red and really bright. We were on our way home, and then, well...?"

When he mentioned Ëlbodh's name, Vàyana and his mother exchanged glances. Kalas wanted to ask if Dzharëth's father was going to be all right, but the cleric spoke before he could: "Very good, then. If you'll excuse me, I believe Falthwën would like to have a word."

"Mother, is Ëlbodh going to be all right?" he ventured when Vàyana disappeared.

"Your father came to see you, just yesterday, back in town on an errand! He'll be—"

"Mother?"

Màla didn't say anything, and Kalas had his answer.

"I'm sorry, son. I know he was your friend's father." She patted his hand. The caustic fire at the edges of his wounds had leached into the surrounding tissue as an ache that throbbed in time with his heartbeat.

"How is Dzharëth?" Kalas asked. At that moment, Falthwën entered the room.

"Young Kalas! *Shâu* Màla," he grinned. "It's good to see you awake! I'll tell the truth: I was worried—all of us were worried for a while, but here you are! You have a formidable constitution, child!" He smiled as he spoke, but his words betrayed a subtext Kalas couldn't quite decode.

"I know you've spoken with Vàyana, but, if you'd be willing to humor an old man: please, tell me what happened the night of your second Seven."

Kalas recounted the experience as best he could. Falthwën listened, his focus intense. The deep green in his eyes flashed in the afternoon suns when Kalas mentioned the wolf.

"I didn't think they were that big," Kalas said when prompted.

"Most aren't," Falthwën agreed. "And most don't wantonly attack people. Not without the rest of their pack. Please: go on."

Kalas finished his story. The cleric thanked him with a nod. After a silent moment, he removed the dressing from Kalas' chest and examined the lacerations. He poked. He prodded. Kalas winced. Falthwën pulled from his robe a small pouch filled with leaves —or petals, maybe: something with a bouquet that tickled Kalas' memory. He poured them into a small bowl filled with clear oil. As he stirred the ingredients with his silver implement, the fragrance intensified. He hummed, softly, and Kalas thought he knew the melody. The cleric reached out to spread the mixture over the young man's injuries, and Kalas noticed he wore a matte gray ring of hammered metal he'd overlooked the day—no, the *four* days—before. It was large, almost gaudy, and set with a number of different gemstones. Then the ointment hit his skin with a crisp shock: he sucked in a breath as his eyes widened. His aches dissolved into numbness, and Kalas exhaled, suddenly very tired.

"Rest now," whispered Falthwën, who turned to speak with Màla as Kalas closed his heavy eyes.

"I'll be leaving Lohwàlar tomorrow. Vàyana, I'm sorry for the short notice—I have…some errands I need to attend to. Madam Màla, should anything—*anything*—about Kalas' condition concern you, by all means, return with him to the Sanctuary. But I'm confident he's on the mend.

"Where are you going?" asked Kalas. "Your hometown?"

Falthwën smiled. "Not so far as that…" He paused, then continued: "You're an inquisitive young man—I like that—and I'd like to ask a favor of you: While I'm away, would you train that curious mind of yours on anything…odd you might notice?"

"Odd? I'm not sure what you're getting at, but sure, of course. What should I do if I see something?"

"Just take mental notes." He glanced at Màla, whose expression hardened at Falthwën's suggestion, and added, "That's it. Should anything unusual crop up in Lohwàlar, remember, but be wary. I want to see you when I return—shouldn't be more than a few days at most, and you can tell me about anything untoward. Is that… acceptable?"

He looked at Kalas as he spoke, but his tone, his body language made it clear he was asking Màla for permission. Kalas understood and shifted his own gaze toward his mother.

"I…you'll just observe? Yes, that's acceptable."

"Excellent! Thank you. Both of you. Now, however, I must pack. Vàyana, walk with me: a word, please…"

2.

A day later, the Sanctuary released Kalas. Vàyana was most impressed with how quickly the wolf's claw marks, wide maroon canyons when he'd arrived, had narrowed and turned a vibrant pink.

"Falthwën believes this kind of wolf has poisoned claws, so even though things are looking good on the outside, it might be another day or two before it's wise to return to work. Here, he left these vials for Kalas: their contents should help with any pain," she said as she discharged him.

As Màla walked him home, Kalas asked if they might stop by Gandhan's smithy.

"I…I need a new shovel, Mother. The rainfire destroyed the other, and, well…"

"A new shovel? Anything else?" Màla smirked. Kalas cheeks, though still pale, grew flushed.

"It's not so far out of our way, and I'm sure…*Gandhan* would like to see you're all right. And sell you a shovel, of course."

"Gandhan? I—yeah, I mean, of course."

When they reached the smithy, turbulent waves of heat rolled from its open doors. The sound of bellows breathing and hammers clanging echoed through the street.

"Gandhan?" Kalas shouted into the dim interior. "Mister Gandhan?"

"Master Kalas! I'm so glad you're awake!" roared the giant

blacksmith, stepping onto the sidewalk and blinking as his eyes adjusted. He brushed the sweat away from his brow and continued: "I'm not ashamed to admit I was as worried for you as I would have been for my own child! Zhalera told me what she remembered, right up until she—Oho! But you're not here to see *me*, are you?" Gandhan winked as he slapped Kalas on the shoulder with one of his callused paws. The young man tried not to wince, but Gandhan noticed all the same.

"Oh! I'm sorry, my boy! I just—hey, wait here one moment, let me get Zhalera! Zhalera!" he bellowed as he disappeared into the back rooms.

"Oh? So this *is* a social call? I thought we were here to buy a shovel?" Màla feigned bewilderment. "Yet you didn't say one word about Gandhan's wares."

"I…uh…I mean, he didn't even let me speak! I was just about to ask him! I was! I'll—Mister Gandhan! I need to buy a shovel!"

Gandhan reappeared at the doorway, once again wiping his brow. He paused as if he didn't understand Kalas' statement, then laughed until tears streamed down his ruddy cheeks.

"You don't need to buy a shovel, my boy!"

"What? Yes, I do: the rainfire ate through my—"

"Let me rephrase: You cannot *buy* a shovel because I will not *sell* you a shovel. I will *give* you a shovel. I'll give you seven shovels! All the shovels in the world! I can never repay you for saving my only daughter!"

Kalas didn't know what to say. The subtle fire in his cheeks swelled through no fault of the furnaces nearby.

"Father, I finished—Oh! Hello, Kalas!"

"Hi, Zhalera! I wanted to—uh, I wanted to buy a shovel from your father! But I really—I mean, I wanted to see how you were doing! I remember you fell, and the wolf thing turned toward you…"

Without glancing at Màla or her father—who smirked at one another, Zhalera wrapped her arms around Kalas and squeezed. His wounds screamed, but he didn't care.

"I'm doing great!" she said as she relaxed her embrace. Against his will, he gasped, his face contorting with pain.

"Kalas? What's wrong?"

"I'm fine, I—*Ahhh!*"

"You're not 'fine,' child," corrected Màla. "You just got—I need to get you home. Here, drink this." She fished one of the vials from her pocket, uncapped it, and pressed it into Kalas' hand. He accepted it without protest and downed its contents. Almost instantly, his singing injury, once an anthem, became a lullaby. His eyes felt heavy, too.

"That's...okay, Mother, that sounds like a good idea."

"Gandhan, Zhalera," she nodded as she ducked beneath Kalas' arm and struggled to support him.

"Firebird, mind the smithy until I return!" said Gandhan as he lifted Kalas to his feet and gestured for Màla to lead them. "Won't be gone long!"

3.

"And here we are," huffed the blacksmith as he lowered Kalas onto the bed. The boy had drifted in and out of wakefulness while Gandhan carried him the remainder of the way home.

"Thank you, Gandhan," said Màla.

"Until he's well, and until Tàran returns from his shift, should you need *anything*, I *insist* you let me and Zhalera know."

"I'm well now," mumbled Kalas, who hadn't quite fallen asleep. Whatever the cleric's medicine contained, it had worked wonders, and despite wisps of mental fog, Kalas felt much better. Well enough to attempt to stand. He probably would have reached his feet—if only for a moment—had Gandhan not restrained him.

The large man laughed, gently, as Màla said, "No, you're not, no matter how insistent you are."

"Really, Mother, I'm fine! And I've been in bed almost a week!"

"So what's one more afternoon?" she countered.

"But what about Father? He's at the Pump, right? I'll bet he needs my help. I'll bet he—"

"You might be looking better, maybe even feeling better," Màla interrupted, "but Vàyana told us the wolf's claws were poisonous. No, I didn't think they had poisonous claws, either, but I'm no cleric."

"Listen to your mother, my boy!" advised Gandhan as he released Kalas. "Màla, I should be getting back. Tàran finishes his shift tonight, yes?"

"Yes, of course. Thank you." She looked at Kalas, who really *did* look better, and added, "And please, if your plans allow, we'd like you and your daughter to return for supper this evening. Celebrate some *good* news for a change."

"Of course!"

Gandhan took his leave. When he was gone, Kalas attempted to stand again, but Màla held him with her gaze.

"Mother, what if Father needs my help? What if…what if that wolf is still out there?"

"Kalas, please. Rest. Your father will be home soon. And maybe tonight, no one will get caught in a rainfire storm or mauled by poison-clawed wolves or—"

She stopped, closed her eyes, and continued with a gentler tone: "Please, Kalas. Your father's been tending the Pump on and off since even Gandhan was a child. He's not out there alone, and he knows how to take care of himself. It would mean a lot to me to know you're safe.

"And," she said, her voice not much more than a whisper, "Tàran told me. About your…nosebleeds." She looked down.

Kalas cocked his wobbly head and the room swam; reflexively, he touched his upper lip.

"My…what? Nosebleeds?"

"Never mind, son. He'll be home before long. So will Gandhan and Zhalera. You could use—no, you *need* the rest."

Kalas wanted to argue, but nausea bubbled up from somewhere in his gut. Instead, he agreed. Màla stood to leave and closed the curtain behind her.

I'll just wait a few minutes, then—

He fell asleep before he could even finish the thought.

And he dreamed.

4.

He saw the Empty Sea, no longer empty, and for an instant he thought he knew its name. It was dark, the moon a glistening, purple boil on the skin of night. Its glow stained the water like blood; its cratered reflection twisted in the subtle motion of the waves. A figure, silhouetted in the moon's lurid aura, rose from the sea. Kalas thought it was a man at first, until it crouched and opened its sickly yellow eyes. It growled, and in the dream the sound was speech, though he didn't understand the words. The wolf stood, towered above him on its haunches, and several similar creatures climbed from the blood-like waters. *Its pack,* Kalas realized. Each seemed to stare through him, their jaundiced gazes focused on something behind him. Nothing moved except the waves.

As one, the pack howled and sprang forward. Kalas braced himself, squeezed his eyes shut, and waited for the impact that never came. When he opened his eyes, he was alone, standing in a lush, green field dotted with a vast array of wildflowers. A solitary sun beamed bright and clear from above a crystal sky. He lowered his arms and looked around. Nothing looked familiar. Without preface, thick black clouds rolled across the sky and blotted out the sun. With a violent crack, the wolves appeared in mid-leap, and Kalas couldn't help marveling at their grace. Ropes of muscle concealed beneath taut black coats propelled them across the landscape, their paws chewing through the grasses that wilted in their polluted wake.

Iridescent fire tumbled within the clouds, snaking just beneath their surfaces. Soundless, the burgeoning force tore the sky to ribbons, split itself into tongues of varying hue that slashed the darkness and consumed the wolves one at a time, flashing from within them and leaving nothing but skeletal shapes of ash that soon scattered in the rising wind. One of the tongues seemed to pause, to hover for a moment before it turned toward Kalas. Above him, in the cloudless wasteland of the sky, something fearsome roared with a voice like thunder, and Kalas felt his heart melt. The fire bore down on him. He raised his hands against a deafening hollow rush as heat and light surrounded him, and he was in his room, his bed sheets soaked with sweat.

It was late in the day. The suns had almost set, and Màla had placed a lighted candle in the sconce for him. In its quivering flame, Kalas saw the motionless outline of a figure robed in peculiar garments and seated at the foot of his bed. His breath caught in his lungs. After a long, tense moment, he exhaled, and his visitor turned: where its face should have been there was only light. The shape swelled and unraveled in a whirlwind of sparks. Indecipherable words poured like many waters from its nonexistent mouth and pressed against Kalas with the force of a hailstorm. One phrase took shape—*fan kal nir!* The music from days past intruded upon his thoughts and shifted toward a dark and foreboding key. Behind an intangible plane of sound, the wash of light dimmed. Decayed. Peeled away like old paint. Something waited within that exposed darkness. Kalas felt it—immense and *wrong*—reach for him. He screamed and raised his arms and he was in his room, his bed sheets soaked with sweat.

5.

"Kalas?" said Màla, softly. "Kalas? Are you awake?"

"Mother?" he said as she shook his head to clear away the mental ambiguity plaguing his thoughts. "Mother, were you…was someone in here?"

"I heard you cry out. I brought another of the cleric's vials."

"No, Mother, I'm fine. Just a bad dream. That last vial still seems to be working, because I really do feel fine."

"Then why don't you get some more rest then while I prepare the meal."

"Can I help with anything?"

"No."

"What about the water? There's no way you've been to the well this afternoon!"

"Kalas, rest. It won't take me that long to draw the water."

"Mother, will you please let me do this one thing? The well is in town, with plenty of people nearby, and I'm two Sevens now!"

Màla wanted to protest, but instead, she sighed.

"All right then, child, if you're so insistent, fetch the water: go straight there and come straight back! You might be two Sevens, but you're still my only son! But before you go anywhere, make sure you put out the light!"

"I won't! And I will! I promise!" said Kalas He stood, tested his balance, and puffed out the sconce beside his bed.

Although he was in much better condition than when he first arrived home, the fact that the pain in his chest had lessened seemed to amplify the aching soreness in the rest of his body. After a few rough minutes, however, the stiffness in his muscles disappeared. Soon, he reached the well, where Rül, one of his friends, was also drawing water.

"Hi, Rül," said Kalas as he lowered his empty buckets. "Something wrong with the water at the farm?"

Rül, a few years older than Kalas and built like an ox, looked up and smiled, amazed.

"Kalas! *Ëth hashrafi—lushà paro!* I heard—well, *everyone* heard about what happened! Out on the farm, sometimes we'll hear *rudzhínme*—little wolves—in the fields at night, but they've always kept their distance. We've never seen one as big as the one Zhalera told us about! What was it like?"

An image raced across Kalas' thoughts, collided with the remembered impact of a small knife digging into bone, and in his mind's eye, the wolf was on him until a blast of white light consumed the entirety of his existence—then the image was gone.

"It was…it was terrible."

"Oh, right," said Rül, wincing at Kalas' pained expression. "Uh, they say Dzharëth's still missing. So is his mother. You were one of the last people—maybe *the* last—to see him. What do you think happened?"

"He's missing? But I…no, that was *five* days ago, wasn't it?" said Kalas, somewhat shocked. "Hwena, too?"

"I'll tell you what, Kalas: not too long ago, maybe a few weeks back, Dzharëth and his father were out at the farm, and Dzharëth was acting…well, weird, I guess. I mean, sure, he's always been a little bleak about things, pretty dark sometimes, but this time he was more intense, more…I don't know, just *off.* And jumpy. Almost like he was scared of something. *Everything.*"

"He was acting that way when we…when Father and I found Ëlbodh, too. I thought he was just in shock. But you said this was a few weeks ago?"

"Yeah, they'd come all the way out to buy a few goats. I don't know why they didn't just wait until market like everyone else. I don't know what they needed three goats for, either, but Father was just happy for the sales, y'know?"

"Three goats! That must've been expensive. Wait—you said Hwena's missing, too?"

"Yeah, everyone says she disappeared the night after Ëlbodh died. No trace. And now Father's acting all weird about it—he's even more paranoid than usual! That's why I came into town for water: I just needed a break from his ranting…"

"What's going on in this town?" mused Kalas, mostly to himself. "These things just don't happen in Lohwàlar!"

"No idea, *sàyahal.* No idea. But hey, as strange as Father's acting, I do need to get home, and I have a long walk ahead of me! Good to see you up and about!"

First, Ëlbodh; then, the wolf. The strange new healer. The attack. Dzharëth. Hwena, Kalas listed as he looped his buckets over the staff across his shoulders and started home. *Strange things are—*

He'd been so lost in thought he didn't see Tsharak until after he'd bumped into him and sloshed some of his water onto the old man's cloak.

"Oh! *Aswanthalu!* I'm so sorry! I didn't see you there!"

Tsharak was Lohwàlar's oldest inhabitant. That's what everyone said, anyway. Most people said he wasn't quite right in the head, that his uncounted years had taken an unkind toll. Here, however, staring into his knowing, ochre eyes, Kalas saw keenness and clarity of purpose.

The old man returned Kalas' gaze…and smiled.

"Master Kalas! You're looking quite well, given all that's happened in the last few days!"

Fine wisps of his suns-bleached hair stirred in the rising evening wind. The suns would set soon, and the changing temperatures usually brought subtle breezes. Tsharak removed his damp outer garment to wring it dry. His bare arms, though indisputably those of an older man, seemed impossibly taut with muscles that shifted smoothly as he wrung his cloak. Atop his right hand, almost lost between the folds in its wrinkled skin, Kalas saw what appeared to be a series of irregularly sized circles. At first, he thought they were merely age spots, but the closer he looked, the more they resembled tattoos.

"Those marks on your hand," said Kalas.

"Ah, you can see those, can you?" said Tsharak as he stopped. There was a touch of surprise in his voice. Or maybe it wasn't surprise but something else. "Most people…don't seem to notice them."

"I'm sorry, I didn't mean to—"

"Nothing to be sorry for, my boy!" he chuckled as he looked toward the remaining sun as it sought *Miryan*, its companion —*Ilmazhasahwu*, the Beloved Sun—beneath the horizon. Kalas looked, too, and as it disappeared, Tsharak hummed a tune Kalas had heard before, a tune that reminded him of Falthwën's song. A tune he realized Tsharak wasn't actually humming: as he listened, he realized the music sprouted from within his own mind. He reached up, touched the skin beneath his nose, and found himself surprised when he suffered neither nosebleed nor headache.

"Were you—?"

He looked to Tsharak, whom he now realized had been watching *him*, anticipating his reaction. The spots on his hand, greenish-black moments ago, now seemed to shimmer as the last rays of Nalënahwu faded from view.

Tsharak smiled as he raised his right hand, examined the markings across its back as if seeing something new in them, then turned it over and absentmindedly massaged the old tattoo.

"A word of advice, Master Kalas," said Tsharak as the mirth in his smile shifted toward severity. "Be wary. The world is...*gilded*. Particularly here in Lohwàlar, it would seem.

"*Seem!* That's it, exactly! Things here—things the world over, under, and above—aren't always as they *seem*. Do well, and remember that."

The winds, gentle before, gained intensity, scooped up fragments of dust and gravel and whipped them through the air.

"Gilded? I don't understand!" said Kalas as he tried to shield his face from the bolstering gusts.

"When this gilt is stripped away, will what's revealed be for our good? or for our doom?" the old man wondered aloud.

With one final push, the winds, spent, descended toward their former, gentler selves.

Tsharak had disappeared.

6.

"Kalas! Your father's home!" Tàran stood beside Màla, his face lined with worry. And pride.

"How are you feeling, boy?" he asked as he helped Kalas with the water buckets. "I see not even wolves can keep you down for long!"

"I'm fine, Father. It still hurts, but not like it did before."

"Good! That's good!" he smiled. "I knew you'd be all right: you're a tough one, I'll give you that!"

"So what was wrong with the Pump?" Kalas asked. He sat, tried to hide his fatigue and winced as the wounds along his chest reminded him of their presence.

"Broken gear," Tàran said. "Me and Azhëk—that's right, Halbën's uncle—spent almost a whole day trying to find out exactly what was going on. Finally found this gear in an ancient filtering sub-assembly: off-axis, missing a few teeth, and banging around.

We disengaged the assembly and brought the gear to Gandhan. Something about it seemed familiar, so I looked through your grandfather's old books and found what looked like an instruction manual. Brought that to Gandhan, too. He built us a new gear—I looked in on you while he worked, but I didn't want to wake you. The next day—yesterday—we hooked everything back up. Pump sounded almost perfect. That whole assembly probably hadn't been touched in a heavy handful of Sevens.

"Once we got the gear off, Azhëk found what he thought was a door. Said it looked like it'd been built into the earth. Of course he wanted to see what was behind it—just like you would, I reckon. I told him to leave it alone, said we were in the middle of fixing the Pump: the manual didn't mention any door, and I didn't want him breaking something else! He didn't listen. Banged on the door a few times, said it was hot to the touch, but gave up when he couldn't get it open.

"Anyway, took us nearly a week just to get the Pump working again. I'm glad to be home tonight, boy. Glad to see you're all right."

Kalas listened, rapt, while Tàran told his story. His father seemed to read his thoughts and added, "Door wouldn't open, remember? Locked or rusted shut." Kalas opened his mouth to say something, then closed it and nodded, resigned.

"That all sounds terribly interesting," smirked Màla, "but I think I'll wait for our guests in the great room." Tàran laughed and followed her, motioning for Kalas to do the same.

Gandhan and Zhalera arrived not much later. With one coarse, meaty hand, the huge smith thrust a gleaming new shovel, freshly oiled, toward Kalas; with the other, he slapped the boy across his shoulder and apologized again as Kalas recoiled. Zhalera just hugged him (gently, this time), her warmth and fragrance lingering in his thoughts.

"I didn't mean to squeeze so tightly before! It's just...I mean... It's so good to see you up and around," she explained, and Kalas realized she was still holding his hands.

"And none too soon," rumbled Gandhan, "after what happened to Ëlbodh and all! To think that a wild animal could just sneak right into the Sanctuary, slice a man to bits, and get out before anyone could do anything! And now his boy is missing, and it's—"

"What do you mean?" Kalas asked, puzzled. Gandhan blanched as he glanced at Màla, who stood looking at the ground. "I thought it was the rainfire that, well, you know..."

"It was more than that, boy, but never mind right now," said Tàran. To Màla, he suggested, *"Follirín,* why don't we stay out of your way and let you finish up in the kitchen?" She agreed and parted company.

"I thought he knew," Gandhan mumbled, his voice small.

"It's a small town. No secret lasts forever."

"What happened to Dzharëth?" Kalas wondered aloud.

"Seems you're the last person who saw him," Tàran sighed. "No one's seen hide nor hair of him since Ëlbodh was attacked."

"The wolf?" said Kalas.

"The wolf," nodded Tàran. "Given recent events, that seems most likely. I'm sorry, boy."

"And what about Hwena?" Kalas added. "I talked to Rül at the well, and he said she's missing, too?"

Silence.

After a moment, Tàran said, "She's...not missing anymore."

Kalas understood his tone. After another moment, he whispered, "What happened?"

Tàran hesitated, gathered his thoughts and, at last, said, "The night after that *rudzhún* attacked you and Zhalera, someone heard Ëlbodh scream. When she got there, he'd been torn apart and the room stank of rotting meat. Another healer said a huge beast was running through the halls, like it was searching for something—or someone. Some of the braver people—or the dumber—armed themselves with whatever they could find and worked their way through the Sanctuary. There was a small shockwave, and soon after, the creature ran past them and got away.

"A few of them headed for Ëlbodh's house to give Hwena the news, but when they got there, the door had been ripped from its hinges, the inside was a mess, and that familiar stink was still in the air. There was no trace of Hwena or her boy.

"The townsfolk set up a perimeter, had groups here and there keeping an eye on things, but as far as anyone knows, they hadn't been seen since then. Until tonight, when they found Hwena's body somewhere near the Southwest Cracks."

Though horrified, Kalas couldn't help wondering: "In the canyon, near the Pump, when we found Ëlbodh, Dzharëth didn't seem like himself. I thought he was just scared, but when I talked to Rül earlier, he said a few weeks ago, he'd been acting strange then, too. Said Ëlbodh bought three goats. Couldn't wait until market.

"What if Ëlbodh knew something was after him? after his family? Something like a *rudzhyún?* That might explain Dzharëth's behavior. Might explain why Ëlbodh bought three goats, too…"

Tàran risked a glance over his shoulder and into the kitchen where Màla, Kalas noted, pretended not to listen.

"I reckon that makes sense," said Tàran as he shifted his gaze toward the floor.

"But why not tell someone?" posed Gandhan. "Why go it alone? Surely he knows any number of townsfolk would have been more than happy to help!"

"Maybe he didn't want to be a burden," offered Tàran, and Kalas sensed he didn't really believe his own suggestion.

"I don't recall Ëlbodh ever being too shy to ask for help," scoffed Gandhan.

"Well, looks like now we'll never know," Tàran dismissed.

"Did they find Dzharëth?" asked Kalas.

Tàran shook his head.

"The Southwest Cracks, you said?"

Tàran nodded.

"Something on your mind, boy?"

"I—no, I was just curious," he finished, recalling Tsharak's odd words.

The four figures in the great room remained silent a while longer, lost in thought, until Kalas' father said, "Gandhan, I have an idea I'd like to talk to you about. Oh—boy, Zhalera: I reckon you'll be so kind as to stay indoors tonight?"

It wasn't a question.

"Yes, Father," Kalas answered. He shivered as the small flames heating the room flickered.

Tàran and Gandhan wandered into a small study filled with musty codices and scrolls—artifacts bequeathed to Tàran by his father, Wodram—and Kalas and Zhalera were alone.

"Dzharëth. Gone," murmured Kalas. "He was acting strange, but after what had just happened to his father, I thought it was just shock. I should have gone after him, but I..."

"You can't blame yourself, Kalas," soothed Zhalera as she took his arm and led him to a well-worn couch where they both sat. "If you hadn't come straight to town, Ëlbodh might have never made it back to the Sanctuary."

"A lot of good it did him."

"At least Hwena got a chance to say good-bye!"

"And now she's gone, too," he said.

"You were unconscious, doing your very best not to die, Kalas! It's tragic, but it's not your fault!" she chided.

He fell silent, stared into the great room's hearth, and let his tension melt away.

"I'm sorry I lost your birthday present," Kalas said after a while.

"Well…I won't hold it against you!" Zhalera smiled. "That's *not* how I imagined you'd use it! Maybe this is a little gruesome to admit, but I wish I could have seen it in action. How did it all happen?"

Kalas told her what he knew.

"I'm sorry, I wish I could remember more, but I'm not exaggerating when I say your knife saved both our lives that night!"

Zhalera took his hand and squeezed it. "No weapon can save a life unless it's wielded by a brave soul: *you* saved our lives, Kalas. The knife was just an instrument."

"It…it was a perfect *instrument*," he said. She kissed him on the cheek, and the warmth that spread across his face and into his bones chased away the chill creeping into the evening air.

"I've still got a lot to learn, but some day, I'll make you an even better knife," she smiled as she squeezed his hand again. "Or maybe, after Father's taught me how, a sword!"

After they ate, Ghandan said, "It's a good idea, Tàran." He pushed his empty plate away, leaned back in his chair, and dabbed at the corners of his mouth. "Sàrush should have set his personal feelings aside and sent an envoy right away. *Should have,* but I know as well as you do—better, really—how out-of-character that would have been! I'd be happy to speak to him—and maybe a few others —about requesting a garrison from Ïsriba."

"I never made it past the Chief Magistrate's secretary: do you think he'll listen to you? I mean, well, given…*things…*"

Gandhan looked down at the table and closed his eyes for a moment.

"Ferïn's death—*o shelu fie ith nir*—gave us an unfortunate foothold on a patch of common ground. I know, I know: you'd think he'd hate me for 'stealing' his daughter from him, or maybe I'd hate him for thinking me beneath her station. but somehow, we ended up understanding each other a little better. Not a lot, I'll admit, but a little. I'll speak to Sàrush. He'll listen to me."

Tàran inclined his head. "I hope you're right."

"Of course, even if *he* listens to me, there's still the queen-regent to persuade."

"Let tomorrow take care of itself, old friend."

Chapter IV

At the Bottom of the Southwest Cracks

"Now just calm down, sir, and wait your turn!" said Sàrush from behind the Council Hall's rostrum to the man in the crowd.

"'*Wait my turn*'? Why don't you say that to the townsfolk who died—*died!*—trying to protect Lohwàlar! If you respected your people half as much as you *drool* all over the queen—*regent*, I'll remind you!—there's a good chance those men and women would still be alive!"

"That's hardly fair!" whined Sàrush. The paunchy figure in front of the assemblage, glistening with a sheen of sweat, dabbed at the back of his neck with a cloth. Fear, mingled with condescension (and, it seemed, derision), haunted his flitting stare.

"It's true!" shouted a woman. "My husband was just a weaver! A kind and gentle man who knew nothing of fighting! That didn't stop him from stepping up! And now he's dead! If you'd only done what Tàran suggested *a week ago,* none of this—"

"And what did Mister Tàran suggest? If he'd come to see me—"

"He did go to see you!" charged Màla, stepping forward from Taran's side. "And you hid behind your secretary!"

Kalas couldn't remember a time he'd seen his mother so angry. Except it wasn't anger. Not really. It was sorrow over her neighbors' deaths. Tàran placed a hand upon her shoulder, gently drew her toward himself and whispered something in her ear. Though still upset, she held her peace and glared at Sàrush.

Màla had tapped into the general ethos of the crowd, however: nearly everyone voiced his or her frustration with Sàrush's leadership, some more forcefully than others. Only a handful mumbled half-hearted words in his defense. Even his embarrassed wife, Tshama, seemed unable—or unwilling—to acknowledge her floundering husband.

Gandhan, sitting not too far from Kalas, had remained silent; now, however, he stood and raised his considerable arms above the nascent mob, and with a voice to match he boomed, "People! Friends! A moment, please!"

The blacksmith was well-respected enough that people granted his request. The grumbling subsided—though it never disappeared completely—and Gandhan cleared his throat.

"I know many of you gathered here tonight have lost loved ones. Family. Friends. And although it was Sevens ago and the circumstances were different, I've lost someone, too. Many of you knew Ferïn. My bride. *Sàrush's* daughter. Knew her and loved her. I'd be lying if I said time has made her loss any less painful.

"And speaking of time, unless we make better use of it than casting blame at one another, it's probable that more of us will suffer between the teeth of that *rudzhegu*—what else could it be?—that prowls the outskirts of Lohwàlar."

Whispers rose at the mention of a *rudzhegu*. Before they got out of hand, Gandhan continued: "Tonight, Sàrush will finalize his list of those he's appointed to make our case in person before the queen-regent of Ïsriba. A list I'm sure he's been most keenly refining all the while. Would that be fair to say, Chief Magistrate?"

Tshama's resolute disinterest faltered as she regarded Gandhan with a look of gratitude. He caught her eye and nodded, just a little.

"Ah, yes! Of course! Why, thank you for reminding me, Gandhan, my son! I should have said something earlier, and perhaps all of this ugliness might have been avoided!" He, too, extended his silent thanks to his son-in-law.

"And, *perhaps,* had I been allowed to see you, we could have avoided even more," added Tàran, now standing and sweeping his arm across the pained and angry faces of the townsfolk. "But here we are, nonetheless. If you and the town elders need volunteers for the journey to Ïsriba, consider this my application."

A few others stood as well; more, however, remained seated, deeming the problem facing the town suddenly less important. Ïs-riba was leagues and leagues from Lohwàlar, a rough, weeks-long journey fraught with perils of its own.

"I think I'd rather face a devil-wolf," someone whispered. Murmurs of assent followed.

Màla grabbed at Tàran's cloak and dragged him down to his seat. Before she gave voice to the thoughts writ across her face, Tàran said, "Sàrush has no interest in sending me to Ïsriba, *follirín!* He has too much pride to be outdone by an old crosspatch like me, and there's no way he'll go himself, no matter how much he wants the queen-regent's attention."

"You'd better be right," she warned, "because you are *not* going! Not with what's been happening in town! You remember what… what *he* told us! I know you do!"

"Told you what?" Kalas asked. He couldn't help overhearing his parents' discussion.

"Now is not the time, nor the place!" breathed Màla, and Tàran nodded.

"Nothing to worry about, boy: your mother's just reminding me of something."

He glanced at Gandhan, who responded with a subtle wink before returning to his discourse with Sàrush and some of the presumptive volunteers.

"Looks like things are winding down here," he finished. "Sàrush has enough volunteers, I reckon. Let's head home."

2.

Long weeks passed while Lohwàlar's citizens waited for the delegation to return from Ïsriba. Hopefully with an army. A platoon at the very least. Tàran's prediction proved true: although he made a subtle show of insisting he be permitted to journey to the capital, Sàrush made an equal show of expressing his regret that more than enough able-bodied men, all much younger than Tàran, had already begun their preparations. Kalas had begged his father to let him volunteer, but, as expected, his parents objected. Strongly.

"No," said Tàran and Màla together, as though sharing the singular thought between their two minds. The mingled ice and steel in their tone proved clear enough for Kalas to grasp immediately. Wisely, he chose not to press the matter.

To pass the time, Tàran brought Kalas into his study. The smell of tanned hides, dried pages, and various inks lent a weighty air to the room's modest confines. Stacks of leather-bound books filled one corner; shelves containing scrolls occupied another; throughout, random leaves had been tucked here or there, all surrounding a small, cluttered stone table which served as a desk. So unlike Tàran, the room's disarray more accurately reflected Wodram's personality, Kalas' grandfather. Very rarely had Tàran permitted him to enter —every last item was irreplaceable, if perhaps nothing more than an unremarkable curiosity to the casual observer (according to Wodram). Kalas had never met his grandfather, but his parents had told him stories.

"Always wondered how he found anything in here," mused Tàran as he took a deep breath. "You know, your grandfather thought I'd take over his work someday...."

"Why didn't you?" asked Kalas.

Tàran thought for a moment, smiled, and shrugged. "Don't know, boy. That was a long while ago. Probably the Pump, though. Everyone works their shift, and some are better at it than others, but for some reason I just seemed to *understand* it, I guess. As much as Wodram loved his books, would have loved to see me follow in his footsteps, he knew I was better with my hands.

"Anyway, the Pump takes up most of my time: not a lot of opportunity to go through all this stuff your grandfather left behind."

"Yeah, it...it doesn't really look like *you,*" agreed Kalas. Tàran laughed.

"No, boy, it does not. In fact, other than me poking around looking for that 'manual,' I reckon this place looks almost exactly like it did before Wodram passed away."

"So what are we looking for? I can't remember the last time I was in here. It smells amazing!"

"Your grandfather would've loved to hear you say that! But with the Pump up and running again, and with the delegation on its way to Ïsriba, it just makes sense to keep close to home. I thought we could use the time to look through Wodram's papers—well, I guess *my* papers, see if we could learn anything about that strange metal shape we saw in the wall of the Empty Sea."

"Does that mean I can come in here now?" Kalas gasped. "Does that mean I can go through all these books? scrolls? drawings?"

"So long as I'm with you, but yes: you're two Sevens now."

Tàran flushed as he took in Kalas' awed expression.

"Well," he finished, "you know about as much as I do about where your grandfather kept things; that is to say: nothing. Where do you want to start? Pick a corner."

3.

For hours, neither spoke more than a few words as they pored over the collected works of hundreds—maybe thousands—of forgotten authors. In between pages here or there, or rolled up in a scroll, one of Wodram's notes would spill out: a cross-reference, an inference, a recipe for some kind of dessert.

As Kalas' eyes raced from line to line, he found he was most interested in the occasional images and drawings scattered throughout the works. Some were Wodram's, according to Tàran, but many were not. In what looked like the oldest manuscripts, Kalas noted repeated woodcuts and other renderings that depicted immense, lion-like creatures; others hinted at wolf-like beings. If he closed his eyes, in his mind he could see them leap from the pages and assume the shapes in his nightmares.

"Father," he asked, after discovering an ancient work that featured armies of such creatures arrayed for battle. "What do these drawings mean? Why is that…I guess it looks like a lion? Why is it holding a sword? And these wolves: are they *rudzhegume?*"

"Hmm? Let me see that," said Tàran, his curiosity piqued.

Kalas handed him the codex.

"I tried to read some of it, but the words don't make sense. Can you read it?"

Tàran said nothing at first: instead, he examined the musty pages as dust from uncounted centuries spiraled upward. Kalas noted his jaw tense when he reached one of the battle scenes; still, he remained silent. After a long, drawn out moment, he closed the book and answered, "Afraid not, boy. I don't recognize it, either."

"What do you think it's about?" insisted Kalas.

"Looks like a battle, based on these images. These here: these look like skydogs—*zhàrudzhme*, another word for *rudzhegume*. Do they…does this look anything like what attacked you?"

"A little," confessed Kalas, "Maybe bigger. I only remember bits and pieces."

"Well, let's set this volume aside. There's bound to be someone —somewhere—who can make sense of it."

For some reason, Kalas thought about Tsharak, his piercing gaze, and the Song shared between them.

"But we still haven't found any mention of that shape in the canyon. Might not be anything, but there's still a lot to look through. What do you say, boy? Tired of all this yet?"

"No!" said Kalas. "I mean, if it's all right, I'd like to keep looking."

Tàran nodded. "I knew you would. Good! All right, let's see what we can find."

"Hey, what's this?" said Kalas after a few mostly silent hours. He held up a translucent, light blue object, almost as thin as a leaf of paper but smoother. Sturdier. One edge had been jammed against something, and the ensuing crease had turned milky white. The markings it bore on one side represented people in odd costume performing obscure tasks; on the other, though faded, Kalas thought the artwork resembled, if vaguely, the thing in the rock face. He handed it to Tàran.

"What's it made from? I've never seen a material like that!"

"Neither have I, boy. It's not paper. Not skin or metal, either. Seems pretty flexible. I wonder where Wodram found this? Guess we'll never know."

He curved the leaf of strange media and rotated it, curious about how the object seemed to consume the room's faint light and send it racing along threadlike courses within itself rather than simply reflect it.

"Anyway," Tàran continued, "on this side, I see what you're thinking, and I agree. Shame we can't make out the rest of this faded part. Were there any more pieces like it?"

"None that I saw. It was stuck behind an old book. But I guess you could say that about everything in here!"

Tàran chuckled. "Too true, boy! Too true. I'll tell you what, though: let's rest from this for now. I might be nearing eleven Sevens, but all this sitting cooped up indoors takes a greater toll than getting outside! You seem to be doing well yourself: how do your wounds feel?"

"I'm fine, Father! Look! The scars have almost disappeared!" Kalas stood, arched his back, and stretched his arms. Tàran observed him for a quiet, uncomfortable moment.

"And…your head?"

"My what?"

"No nosebleeds since your birthday—none your mother or I have noticed, at least. How about…what did you say it sounded like? *Chimes?* Have you heard any *chimes* since then?"

Be wary.

"Chimes? No, Father, I—not exactly…"

The world is gilded.

"All right," confessed Kalas, "what I mean is that I haven't heard anything exactly like that since my birthday, but I have heard—no, not *heard*, but *sensed*, I guess—the song. But now it's more like I'm aware of it without it giving me headaches. Or nosebleeds. And I wasn't lying: I'm fine!"

"I believe you, boy," nodded Tàran. "I appreciate your honesty. So I'll ask you one more question: what's at the Southwest Cracks?"

Kalas hesitated before he answered. "Dzharëth and I used to explore the caves there, thought of it as our 'hideout.' Other than the two of us, I don't think anyone's been there in years.

"What if that's where he ran after we found his father? If that's where they found Dzharëth's mother…What if the wolf got him, too—"

An image leapt across his vision: a single frame culled from a recent dream in which liquid darkness, pierced with two sickly yellow eyes, rose up against a bloodstained moon.

"—or what if it's something worse?"

Tàran stroked his chin and scratched behind an ear while he stared intently at the corner of the desk. Suddenly weary, he sighed.

"The Empty Sea's too far away today, but how about if we take a walk to the Southwest Cracks?"

Kalas felt the blood drain from his face and pool somewhere within his pounding chest. Tàran noticed, and Kalas bristled at the change in his father's expression, embarrassed at his trepidation.

"Yeah, let's do that," insisted Kalas as he did his best to ignore his baser thoughts.

"You sure, boy?"

"Of course. When do we leave?"

"Now. Wait for me in the anteroom: let me put together a few things, then we'll be off."

4.

The Southwest Cracks lie just outside Lohwàlar's southern-most boundary, about half an hour's brisk walk from Kalas' house. Dunes rose and fell, obscuring and revealing ancient sands-blown rock formations, most supporting needle-rich cacti or scrub. A carrion bird glided overhead, banked, and circled toward some distant point. Soon, the pair reached a shallow gulch; on its far side, wind-sculpted sand- and limestones stood sentry over the soulless desert, reflecting suns-light from their varnished sides. Kalas pointed his father toward an almost hidden footpath at the base of a large boulder.

"Right through there," he said as he hopped down into the channel.

"I haven't been here in years! Sevens, even," mused Tàran. "Oh, my friends and I used to explore these rocks, too, boy. A long, long time ago."

The setting suns had parted ways some time ago; now, Miryan —the second sun—disappeared in a ruddy haze. From the back of Kalas' mind, the Song—ever-present, he realized—thrust itself toward his conscious thoughts. Curious, he looked around, not sure what he expected to see until the Beloved Sun's last rays glinted from an object half-buried in the sand.

"Wait, Father, I thought I saw something," he said as he ran the one hundred or so feet toward the spot. When he reached it, he froze.

"Boy?" wondered Tàran as Kalas gasped.

Kalas stooped, retrieved the item from the desert floor, and walked with a sober pace toward his father.

"Well?"

He said nothing, simply held what he'd discovered for his father to see.

It was Tàran's turn to gasp.

"That looks a lot like the knife Zhalera made for your birthday."

"It *is* that knife," said Kalas as he turned it over in his hands. "There's no mistaking it! But how did it get out here? We're nowhere near where that thing attacked us!"

The knife still bore traces of the animal's blood, now black with age. Kalas scraped at them until they flaked away. Tàran reached beneath his cloak and produced a blade of his own: not quite a sword, but longer than a typical dagger.

"Maybe not, boy, but keep that knife ready! It saved you once, and even though I hope I'm was wrong, it may have to save you again. Soon."

"What are you talking about?"

"For right now, just be ready. Show me where you think Dzharëth would have hidden himself."

"Father? All right, it's this way…"

A few minutes' walk through the labyrinthine rocks brought them to a small opening, not much more than a crevice.

"Through there," said Kalas. He caught a faint waft of rotting meat and tightened his grip on his weapon. "Earlier in the day, the suns shine through holes in the roof: even then, it's pretty dim, but at this hour, I don't know if we'll be able to see inside."

"We will be," said Tàran as he dropped the pack he'd been carrying. He snagged a pair of torches, handed them to Kalas, and struck his long dagger against a chunk of flint. After two strikes they had fire.

"Better call for him, boy, see if he's in there," suggested Tàran, now standing in front of Kalas.

"Dzharëth?" he shouted.

No answer.

"Maybe he's not here? *Dzharëth?*" he called again.

Nothing.

"I don't think—wait!"

Tàran heard it, too: something within the shadows moved. Someone in the darkness groaned.

"Dzharëth? Dzharëth, come on out! We need to get you back to town! Your—we—you really need to see a cleric."

Movement inside the cave stopped. Who- or whatever waited within held its breath. Tried to, at least: the effort spawned another groan, more pained than the last.

"Come on out, Dzharëth. You need help!"

"Go away," wept Dzharëth.

"We can't do that, boy," said Tàran. In his peripheral vision, Kalas noted his father's knuckles, white on the hilt of his weapon.

"I don't…I don't want to," he mumbled. Without conviction.

"Dzharëth, we're coming in," said Kalas, and before Tàran could protest, he was through the narrow doorway.

Kalas' flickering torch cast strange new shadows across the walls, framing Dzharëth's emaciated form in its weak orange light. The fetor of rot clung to Kalas' nostrils and he fought not to gag. Bones—some small, some surprisingly large: all recent—littered the cave floor. Recovering himself, Kalas stepped closer. Tàran followed close behind. In the light of both torches, Dzharëth's plight revealed itself more fully.

His eyes, now sunken and lined with red, had a yellowish sheen; he was naked, and his skin appeared raw and loose and bore a peculiar livid tracery. Patches of his stringy black hair were missing, and as he shifted his weight, something vile suppurated from a thin, vertical slit high on his chest.

"I don't want to...hurt..."

"You're hurt? We know, Dzharëth. C'mon, we'll—"

"That's not what he means, boy," growled Tàran. "Get back here. Now."

"What else could he mean? Look at him! He's in bad shape, Father! Looks like something attacked him, too! We have to get him help!"

"He's in bad shape all right, but I'm telling you, boy...Look, you're right: something *did* attack him, but not what you think. Not *how* you think. Please: *get back here!*"

Kalas turned toward his father, regarded him with a quizzical look, but once he grasped the fear in his eyes, he obeyed.

"Father?"

Tàran said nothing else, but kept his eyes on Dzharëth.

"No more goats!"

Goats?!

"I don't want to go back—I can't! After I...I killed...My father. My mother!"

"What are you talking about?" said Kalas.

"But not before I tried—I *tried!*—to kill you!"

"What are you talking about?!"

Dzharëth stood. It took more effort than it should have, and once he reached his feet, he staggered and braced himself against the wall. When he'd first spoken, his voice had the same high-pitched quality Kalas remembered, but with every syllable, it changed, became more guttural, gravelly, and *dark.*

"I watched you from the shadows while you ran, *Nëshritilkursh!* I waited, in darkness, for the opportunity. And when it came, I moved—but too slowly!"

Dzharëth made an enraged gesture toward the seeping wound between his pectoral muscles.

"I knew you were one of *hers*—we can always tell!—but I had no idea how much *power* you hide behind that unassuming guise!"

"Power? What are you talking about? Dzharëth, talk to me! What's happening!"

"He's gone, boy," consoled Tàran. "I'm sorry: your friend is gone. That's—"

"Kalas!" said a weak, nasal voice with Dzharëth's crooked mouth. The figure lost its balance and landed on its knees. "Kalas! I'm sorry! I tried to fight—I tried! But it's too—it's—*Aaagh!*"

Whatever the last vestiges of Dzharëth's old self tried to say drowned in a viscous black sludge that poured suddenly from his mouth, his eyes, ears, and nose. His limbs spasmed, wrenched free from their sockets, and split his sallow skin, spilling more of the oily filth and leaking smoke the color of unpolished jet. Its gurgles became howls—Kalas shivered; something discordant reverberated through the chamber—as its insides twisted and it somehow knit its broken bones into an all too familiar shape.

This time, it stood on two feet, like a man, though it had to stoop to fit within the small cave. It stepped toward Kalas and held him for a moment with its jaundiced gaze. Before the boy could move, a streak of silver whistled past his ear and Tàran's blade plunged into the beast's chest just to the left of its other wound.

"*Run, boy!*" shouted Tàran. "Dzharëth" lunged for them, but he was already weak, and his new injury slowed him down. He fell, hit the ground with a palpable thud as Kalas and his father scrambled for the exit.

And they ran.

5.

Out of breath, they stopped once they'd retreated past the small arroyo. Dzharëth hadn't followed them: Kalas didn't care why not.

Maybe he's…No! Never mind!

The remaining sun hung low in the sky, and soon, it would join its partner behind the horizon.

"What happened to Dzharëth?" said Kalas between wheezes. Tàran held up a hand, allowed his heart to slow before responding.

"That, boy, was a *zhàrudzh*. A *rudzhegu*."

"They're *real?!*"

"Most people today like to pretend they're not, but, well, what do you think?"

Kalas said nothing while he tried to comprehend what had just happened to his friend. Tàran watched him think, then continued: "You've heard the stories, I'm sure. Your mother and I probably used them as a warning a time or two: but they're not just stories.

"That woodcut you found, with the battle: from what I remember—Tsharak knows more, I'm sure—long ago, before the world held the shape it holds today, something happened, something terrible, and the boundary between material and immaterial blurred.

"*Zhàfàrokme*—another kind of spirit-being—fought against the *zhàrudzhme*. The odd thing is that to this day, no one remembers why. No one knows who won. For all I know, those armies might still be at war with one another.

"There's more, but I'm not sure if it's…safe to reveal it. Not yet. I…your mother and I made a promise to someone a long, long time ago…"

Kalas considered his father's words. He ached to hear more, but he remained quiet—for a moment.

"Father, Dzharëth said something about *power*. I don't know what he was talking about, but then again, I don't remember what happened that night. Do you know what he meant?"

"Son," said Tàran, using that rare appellation, "I have my suspicions, but to explain would require that I break that promise. I have to ask you to trust me right now: when the time is right, when it's safe, I'll tell you a story—a *true* story—that I've wanted to tell you ever since you became a part of our lives. Will you do that? Will you trust me?"

Without hesitation, Kalas nodded: "I will. I do, Father."

Tàran smiled even as his shoulders sagged, like he was shifting the weight of an unbearable burden. His father's eyes bored into him as rough hands swallowed one of Kalas' and shook it, grateful.

"Thank you, boy."

"What will we tell people about Dzharëth?" asked Kalas once they'd resumed their trek. In a few minutes, the barrens would give way to the outskirts of Lohwàlar. "I mean, we can't just tell people, 'Hey, my friend killed his parents—tried to kill us—and, oh yeah, he's a wolf monster,' can we?"

"No, I don't suppose the townsfolk would react well to that, even if it is the truth. For now, we'll let everyone know we saw a *rudzhegu* near the Southwest Cracks, that they should stay away from there. *That* is the truth, and Ëlbodh and Hwena—and Dzharëth—are dead. It's over now, and there's nothing to be gained from soiling their memories."

"He was my friend for a long time. He wasn't always like that —he wasn't always one of those things, was he?" said Kalas, after a moment's thought.

"No, boy, I don't think so. In the stories I remember, the *rudzh-egume* were heavenlies at one time. Now, they can't come and go like the *elume:* they need a different way to interact with the material world. So they use someone's *body,* bound to the immaterial through one's *kelâ*—one's *soul.* At least, that's what I've heard. I don't know for sure."

"What if one comes for me? For my *kelâ?*"

Tàran nodded, acknowledging Kalas' concern, but answered, "In all my Sevens, Dzharëth is the only *zhàrudzh* I've ever seen or heard of, but more than that, even though no one knows for sure how the spirits 'choose' their *tethers,* most of what I've heard hints that it's not a one-way decision."

"You mean Dzharëth *asked* for this?!"

"Not exactly, boy. Evil is subtle, and like I said, no one knows for sure how it all works. Least of all me! But again, it's over now. Your friend—no, that *creature!*—was in bad shape when we found him, and I put a dagger through his chest. I don't imagine we'll be seeing Dzharëth again."

Chapter V

Within the Wall of the Empty Sea

Tàran spread the word: *Avoid the Southwest Cracks!* He told the town he and Kalas had dispatched a large wolf haunting the area: the creature most likely responsible for Ëlbodh's, Hwena's, and, he added, Dzharëth's deaths. This news tickled people's ears for a day or two, but soon after, the Ïsriba delegation returned, and it seemed everyone's interest tacked toward the travelers and their new companions. As the party entered the Crescent, choked with people, Sàrush, beaming, cleared his throat and prepared his remarks. From a not-too-distant balcony, Kalas and Zhalera watched the procession.

"How many people did Sàrush send out?" she asked.

"Seven, I thought," said Kalas, straining to count the arrivals.

"That's what I thought, but it looks like there's maybe, what? twelve people altogether? I thought Sàrush said Ïsriba would send an army!"

"It's still strange to me you don't call him *Grandfather*," Kalas opined. "Maybe because I never knew mine?"

"If Sàrush were *your* grandfather, it wouldn't seem strange at all," she growled. Kalas dropped it.

"Well, maybe seven or eight soldiers is enough. I mean, I think Father and I might have put an end to the recent attacks."

"I still can't believe it was Dzharëth!" exclaimed Zhalera.

"It wasn't. Not really," defended Kalas. He thought of the wretched figure's twisting form, its stench and frothing putrescence. "Not anymore, at least. You should have seen it—No! I mean, no, you shouldn't have!—but the way it…*changed*, the way it broke itself apart and put itself back together!"

Kalas shuddered at the memory.

"I am glad I found the knife you made for me," he finished. He'd cleaned and oiled it so that it shined; now, as he held it out to her again, the suns-light danced along its razor-fine edge.

"Me too," she smiled.

The pair watched as the spectacle unfolded beneath them. Eight lightly armored men, all astride powerful-looking war horses, seemed to fill the Crescent, dwarfing the four remaining townsfolk who escorted them. The riders' armor—naught but a few well-secured plates connected with shimmering green leather straps—gleamed in the few places where wind had blown away the dust. At their sides hung swords in scabbards constructed of the same green leather. Each wore a headpiece that appeared ill-suited for desert climes, although at some point they'd added veils to hold the sand at bay.

At first, Kalas and Zhalera only caught fragments of the conversation, but it wasn't long before Sàrush's voice swelled with ire, making it impossible *not* to hear.

"Eight men? *Eight* men?!" roared the magistrate. He cast a withering glance at the delegation. "Did these men—where are the others? Did they fail to make known the severity of our circumstances? That a *rudzhegu*—yes, a wolf demon!—has been murdering our people without the slightest provocation?

"Because I *know* the queen would have sent her very best warriors had these *fools* acquitted themselves with any measure of propriety!"

Before the "fools" could react, one of the soldiers—their superior, Kalas guessed—barked a condescending laugh. From atop his destrier, the formidable (and most heavily-armored) figure peered down at the magistrate. Most of his men began to chuckle, too, but from his vantage point, Kalas noticed one man taking in his new surroundings, gauging the particulars of his environment. He seemed little interested in the worsening conversation.

"Queen Ësfàyami refused even to see your envoy—the half that survived the journey, that is!" the imposing man exulted as he removed his veil. His voice, pitched high with an oddly musical quality, dripped with perverse glee as he delivered his retort.

"But most of these men, these *dhëmme*—children—have never stepped beyond Ïsriba's illustrious gates, and it seems as though breathing that rarefied air for so long has made them soft. *Weak.* Why, their operational readiness rates somewhere south of pathetic! What better way to burn away the chaff than to march them through lesser frontiers like…what do you call this place? *Lohwàlar?* Bah! If a few weeks in this desolate waste, shoulder to shoulder among their inferiors, should prove insufficient motivation for improvement, then maybe they're more suited for a life of…whatever it is you do around here: they'll stay behind while the rest of us return to civilization!"

Addressing his men, he added: "Ladies? What will it be? An unhappy existence in this blasted desert? Or a name for yourselves after we've delivered the blighted denizens of Lohwàlar from this… *zhàrudzh?*"

"By your word, Commander Valderïk!" said six of the remaining men, making no attempt to camouflage their snide chuckles: the seventh, whom Kalas thought looked much older than the others, continued assessing everything around him in silence.

"That Valderïk sounds like a little girl!" Zhalera whispered with a giggle. Kalas nodded even as he bristled at the commander's pomposity.

Sàrush seemed at a loss for words. From the balcony, Kalas watched the magistrate's color drain from his face, only to darken with embarrassed rage before he managed to collect himself and say in his most diplomatic tone, "Should that be the case, then Lohwàlar welcomes you and your men and looks forward to improving your perception of our admittedly modest estate. Commander Valderïk, if you will permit us the privilege of escorting your company to the garrison?"

"So they do have manners here in these nether regions!" the commander declaimed with an unexpected nod. "Very well... Sàrush, was it? Show us to our quarters!"

The seven trotted after the magistrate; the eighth, however, lingered a moment longer. He casually raised his head in Kalas' and Zhalera's direction, clearly well aware of their presence ever since entering the Crescent. He locked eyes with the young man, and although most of his face was still veiled, his gaze sparkled with some indescribable quality wholly unlike that of his compatriots. As his mount canted toward their balcony, he smiled and touched the side of his headpiece in what appeared to be a salute of some kind. Just loud enough for the two of them to hear, he said, *"Lushà vam, sàme."*

"Good day, friends?" repeated Kalas. "What do you make of that?"

"C'mon, let's ask him!" suggested Zhalera. She grabbed Kalas' hand and led him toward the street, but by the time they reached its cobbled surface, the curious stranger had disappeared.

2.

Instead of ushering in a sense of security, the people of Lohwàlar experienced a rising contempt for their *Poyïsriba* "saviors." The first day, a pair of soldiers made a show of scouting the surrounding area, but within a few hours, they returned, visibly exhausted, and, when questioned about the brevity of their expedition, claimed they needed to compare their observations with prior records. Moments later, however, passersby noted loud snores emanating from within the garrison. The next day, and the days after, weren't much different.

"Waste of resources," most townsfolk grumbled. "Dirtying our water and eating all our food! Whining about everything the whole time!"

For the most part, Kalas shared the peoples' unflattering appraisal of the *Poyïsriba* detachment with one exception: for days, he'd done his best to learn what he could about the man who'd spoken to him and Zhalera. Something about his demeanor resonated with the young man. Kalas tried to follow him whenever he left the garrison, tried to observe him when he explored the town, but he had the distinct impression that any information he gleaned was a gift, that the man permitted Kalas to learn only what he was willing to share about himself, and that proved to be almost nothing.

His name was *Shosafin*, but more often than not, when the other soldiers thought he was out of earshot, they called him *Ilbardhën* —the *Fortunate One*. Kalas understood they intended it as an insult, but Shosafin seemed indifferent to the epithet.

His comings and goings were frequent and increasingly secretive; soon, Kalas found he was unable to keep up with Shosafin's movements.

"He's like a ghost," Kalas remarked one afternoon as he trucked another load of fuel for Gandhan's smithy.

With the Pump in good repair, Tàran—and Kalas, by extension —had more time to explore Wodram's collection for clues about the object in the Empty Sea. Gandhan, however, had other plans for the young man: in his customary unsubtle manner, he insisted he could *really* use an able-bodied young man to handle sundry tasks around the place. "I'm pretty busy," he'd said, "so whoever it is would probably spend a lot of time with my *apprentice...*" Kalas accepted the position without question.

"A ghost?" repeated Zhalera.

"Yeah, a ghost: he's there one moment, gone the next, and when I think I know what's going on, he shows up from some other direction, like he's letting me know that *he* knows I'm watching him. Trying to, anyway." He finished his task and wiped his brow as another wave of heat washed over him.

"Why *are* you watching him? Do you think he's up to something?"

"No, not that—well, nothing bad, anyway. He's just so unlike the other soldiers. And he spoke to us—and not like we're just children. Yes, I know all he said was 'good day,' but...I don't know, I can't really put it into words. Just curious, I guess."

"And I love that about you, Kalas, but it sounds like if this Shosafin wants you to know something, he'll tell you."

"You're probably right," sighed Kalas. "And I suppose Father and I might make better progress if I were more focused on our *other* task."

"That metal thing?"

"If it *is* metal, but yeah, that part of the canyon. We haven't found much of anything in Grandfather's old collection. Not yet, at least. I don't know, sometimes I think we should just go back and take another look at it."

"I've never been to the Empty Sea," hinted Zhalera. "I've heard about it, sure, but I'd love to see it someday."

"You would? Do you think Gandhan would let you come with me? Uh, *us*, I mean? Father and me? It would probably take a couple of days to check things out, but it'd be great if you could be there!"

"Yeah? All right, I'll ask him! When are you planning on

going?"

"Tomorrow! I mean, I'll have to check with Father, but I think he'd welcome the opportunity to get away from all those books and papers. Oh—would that be enough advance notice for your father? If not, maybe in a day or two?"

"Father's not happy about his services being conscripted for those 'ungrateful *Poyïsriba mafame.*' Not when there are *Lohwàlar-rinme* who could really use his help. I think he'd prefer I were somewhere else. I think he'd prefer *he* were somewhere else, too!"

"Talk to your father: I'll talk to mine. If they agree, I'll see you tomorrow before the suns rise!"

3.

"Kalas, let's go!" said Tàran as he jostled the boy's shoulder. Still sleepy, he sat up and rubbed his eyes. He thought he smelled flowers and—

"Gandhan and Zhalera are waiting! Your mother's got breakfast ready: get dressed and eat quickly. I'm hopeful we can reach the canyon wall before the second sun breaches the horizon."

In seconds, Kalas dressed and entered the home's modest dining room. Gandhan and Zhalera were already seated, enjoying the breakfast of eggs, hominy, and strips of cured meat Màla had prepared. He sat across from Zhalera and bade them good morning as he devoured his own meal.

"Thank you, Mother," he managed between mouthfuls.

When everyone had finished and cleared the table, Tàran whispered something to his bride, embraced her for a moment before placing a brief kiss on her forehead, then turned toward the assembled party.

"Everyone ready?"

"*Hish!*" said Kalas and Zhalera in unison.

"*Hish!*" said Gandhan.

"Gandhan? You're coming with us?" wondered Tàran.

"Swords only need so much sharpening, friend! I think those silly *Ïsribarinme* can go a day or two without wasting my time! But truthfully, when Zhalera told me what you and Kalas discovered, I knew I just had to see it for myself! All that refined metal, from the description, buried under how much rock? Multicolored lights without fire? Almost enough to make Tsharak's tales sound plausible!"

*Things the world over, under, and above aren't always as they seem…*Kalas remembered.

"I brought gear and provisions for Zhalera and myself. Won't be in the way at all! So yes, it sounds like we're all ready!"

Tàran smiled. "We'll be fortunate to have you with us, friend." He turned to Màla one more time, said, "*Follirín, mën al paresëthu,*" and ushered everyone into the chill morning, lightless except for the dull glow of the waning moon.

As they traveled along the Pump Road, Gandhan surprised Kalas with his dexterity and stamina: that someone so large should move with such ease seemed peculiar to him until he thought about what a busy day at the smithy must be like—the constancy of motion and exertion had forged Zhalera's father into a human machine, much like he forged his metals into everything from swords to shovels. Zhalera, too, had little difficulty with Tàran's pace; unlike her father, she moved with an altogether different grace, lithe and nimble. What surprised Kalas most, however, was his own improved endurance as he stepped almost as lightly as his father.

The first sun's silvery light had just begun to touch what few clouds dotted the deep blue sky when a familiar sound insinuated its chords within Kalas' thoughts. He paused as it transitioned into his conscious mind, then took an extra step to catch up with Zhalera.

"You all right?" she asked him.

"Yeah, just…I was just thinking about something."

Other than a slight pressure, a strange impression of cognitive *fullness,* the worst effects the Song once wrought never came.

"Kalas, tell me again what it's like! The trees? The animals?" she said, her voice charged with anticipation.

"When we reach the edge of the Empty Sea, look down: it'll be like looking at the desert through green-tinted glass, except it's not sand, it's leaves from trees that are hundreds of feet tall, maybe hundreds of years old—or older. If the wind is right, you'll smell sap and resin: the fir trees are my favorite.

"It's colder inside the canyon, darker, too, but getting down there takes a while. The trail is narrow, and even though it's also hundreds of years old, it's a good idea to watch for falling rocks.

"Sometimes we see animals on either side of the trail—birds, squirrels, things like that. Sometimes we don't see anything except tracks—if even that. Oh, one time, years ago, we saw a bear, but that was really early in the morning.

"And you didn't ask, but there's the River, too. In some places, it seems more like a stream, but Father tells me not that long ago, it was still too deep to ford—and it still is in lots of places. He also tells me according to Tsharak—yeah, *that* Tsharak!—when *he* was a boy, it was too deep and too broad to swim across! But I don't know if that's true! I mean, sure, the trees along the river banks look younger than the others, but even they have to be dozens of Sevens, and there's no way Tsharak's *that* old! In any case, seeing the River close up like that, putting your hands in it…it's amazing! Pretty soon, you won't have to take my word for it: we're almost there!"

• • •

"It's…it's nothing like the picture I had in my mind," said Zhalera once they reached the lip of the canyon and paused for a brief rest. "It's so much…*more!* I mean, it's everything you said it was, but actually *being* here is something else entirely!"

"Just wait until we're at the bottom looking up! But first, the fun part," grinned Kalas as he wiped away tiny beads of sweat. The second sun had risen, and with it the temperature.

When everyone had eaten a light snack and drunk from their waterskins, Tàran signaled it was time to pack up and begin descending into the Empty Sea.

"Watch your step, you two; boy, watch *your* step, too!"

The path, worn and well-traveled as it was, proved unsettling to Gandhan, laden with his packs and a large iron hammer tucked into his belt: although the road had room to spare, his movements soon consisted of cautious sidles, and Kalas could read fear in the huge man's eyes. The smith said nothing, however, just continued working his way down. His awkward pace wasn't much of a hindrance: this terrain required calculated steps regardless of what form they took.

"You're doing great, sir," whispered Kalas. "Not much more of this before we reach flatter ground."

"Is it that obvious?"

"Not really," Kalas winked. "You look like how I used to feel, but you're doing great."

"I just didn't realize I was so s—that this height would have such an effect on me! I guess in Lohwàlar, the ground is just… *right there*, not thousands of feet beneath you! I hope we reach the bottom soon—but not *too* soon!"

As he moved, his foot struck a loose rock and sent it hurtling into the emptiness a mere step in front of him. It bounced against the cliff with a series of solid thuds on its way down. Gandhan closed his eyes, took a few deep breaths, and inched his way forward.

"This had better be worth it," he warned with a smile.

"It will be, sir! It will be!"

4.

Even both suns near their zenith only blunted the shadows of the canyon floor with their shafts of gold and silver. High overhead, what began the morning as whimsical bits of bright white fluff had become foreboding gray sheets of cloud, static in the sky above them. The diffuse light, scattered here and there amid the imperfect silence, implied a solemn atmosphere even though birds still chirped and insects still buzzed. An arboreal creature leapt its way through the higher branches of the immediate forest, drawing Kalas' eyes skyward.

"Father, those clouds…"

Tàran followed his gaze and understood.

"Wrong kind of clouds. Wrong color sky. I reckon there's little chance of rainfire today. Still, it's always good to know what's around you!"

"Even so," interjected Gandhan, "will these skins *really* protect us from *ilâegsal?*"

His relief at having reached the canyon floor had been palpable, and even Zhalera had teased him about it with a loving smirk. The smith had unshouldered his pack for a new waterskin, but now, he held up a tanned hide and ran its peculiar surface through his thickly callused fingers.

"They use some special chemical cocktail during the tanning process. I never learned the particulars, but it's some combination of minerals and plant oils that resists both the rain's heat and hunger. I've had to rely on such shelters in the past: they don't last forever —that's why I pack extra, even though they're heavy—but they do the trick.

85

"But from here, it's a couple leagues, if memory serves, to that weird thing with the noises and the colored lights. We're making good time: let's keep up the pace."

It had been a mile or two since they'd passed the old stone archway. Here, the River was broader than it was from the Ruins Road approach, and Kalas delighted in Zhalera's unvarnished awe. Some of the clouds above had burned away as the suns began to separate: just enough to illuminate the forest's splendor with rare clarity. They approached a small waterfall, and the suns' beams split apart in its soft haze, revealing all the myriad colors comprising everyday white light.

"Now I understand why you love coming out here with your father!" said Zhalera. "This place is beautiful! Just *beautiful!*"

Kalas nodded as she reached a hand into the mist and marveled at how much cooler the air was, how *clean* it smelled as they breathed its tangy, resinous fragrance.

The forest thinned out as they kept walking. Thick stands dwindled to just a few trees here and there, bearing scars from the rainfire's ill effects. Kalas recognized the side trail where they'd discovered Ëlbodh. He shivered even though the waterfall's chill was miles behind them. Tàran spared a brief look through the subtle breach amid the coppice that marked the trailhead but showed no signs of slowing down nor stopping.

They chewed through the remaining mile with little ceremony. A few deer—a piebald doe and two bespeckled fawns—darted across their path. Delighted, Zhalera squealed at the sight.

"Did you see that?!" she whispered—loudly.

Kalas nodded with a smile, enlivened by the unadorned joy that danced across her features.

"We often see deer down here. All right, *I've* only seen them a couple times myself, but Father's seen them a bunch. Says they're still wary of humans."

Before he could say more, something snapped just off to the right. Kalas glanced over his shoulder, then spun around.

"Gandhan!" he shouted as a hulking shape bore down on the smith.

Gandhan heard the noise, too. He dropped his packs and held his hammer in a wary fist.

The forest writhed and churned as a huge buck crashed through the trees and into Zhalera's father; dipped his massive, many-tined rack; and tossed Gandhan through the air, tearing his outer garment in the process. It stamped the ground and snorted, jetting spumes of steam from its nostrils while red flickered in its eyes. Disoriented, it paused long enough for Gandhan to gain his feet. The blacksmith, enraged, raised his hammer and charged the beast, but the creature side-stepped him, checked him with its hindquarters, and thundered into the woods, snorting all the way.

"Do they always do that?" grumbled Gandhan as he picked himself up again and brushed away the dirt.

"That's the first I've seen of it," Tàran remarked, concerned.

"Did you see its eyes?" said Kalas. "They were *red*. I think it might have been sick."

"Father! Are you all right!" Zhalera cried, rushing to Gandhan's side.

"I'm fine, just fine, Âsrufin," he insisted. He played his finger through the fresh rip from the deer's antlers and added: "My shirt, not so much!"

"It's possible we just surprised him, but I think you're right, boy," said Tàran, addressing his son's suggestion. "I've never known any of the deer in these woods—what little of it I've explored—to act that way. But we're here. Just around that bend."

5.

Most of the immediate forest seemed to have recovered from the falling fire with greater speed than Kalas would have deemed possible. Only a few weeks had passed since the storm, but new growth had already reclaimed vast portions of the blackened scene. So vigorous had its renaissance been that Kalas had to spend a few moments rediscovering the shape's location. The air, however, had acquired an unpleasant flavor, its prior cleanness now soured.

"There, behind those trees," he said as he hurried toward it.

All four worked together to prune away the flora that obscured the object. When it was clear, Gandhan ran his hands over its etiolated surface, knocked a time or two at various points as he tried to make sense of the experience.

"You were right, my boy!" he laughed as he continued his tactile examination. "This is worth it! I'll be honest: I wasn't expecting something so huge! But where are the lights? the noises? You've got a sharp eye, Kalas. I don't think I would have noticed it had I been here that day."

Tàran watched, kept his distance, and removed the translucency from his pack and examined it while the others explored the area.

"I just touched it, like what you're doing now, and there were lights and sounds. Right here, like this..."

Kalas came alongside Zhalera's father and ran his fingers over the object's surface in the same place as before, and again, something about it suggested *skin,* like something more wondrous lay hidden behind its unassuming façade.

Beep beep!

Subtle vibrations emanated from deep within the canyon wall in tandem with a subsonic hum that rose to audible frequencies. The object—the *artifact*—shed its opacity as vibrant blue luminescence intensified along unnatural, perpendicular courses and snaked its way through a network of *subcutaneous* corridors.

"That sound!" shouted Zhalera, covering her ears. Gandhan and Tàran did the same.

"Let go, boy!" shouted Kalas' father. "Let go!"

"It's all right," he protested. "Just a little more…"

"Kalas, please!" Zhalera said, concurring with Tàran.

"Just—"

The noise surpassed the threshold of human hearing as the vibrations amplified, became tremors. Fragments of rock sheared away from the cliff, striking the artifact and sliding toward the ground. Though its corona still shone blue, the tracery of light glowed white and spread to nearly every surface. A falling chunk of stone smashed into Kalas' arm, breaking his contact with the object. The lights faded before winking out entirely. The rising whine and the tremors ceased as the thing resumed prior appearance.

"Wait! No!" said Kalas. Ignoring the hurt in his arm, he touched the object again.

No hum, no lights this time: rather, some force seemed to punch out from the artifact's surface, sending him sailing through the air and sprawling into the dirt. He felt his body convulse, heard shouts of concern, but for a moment, he couldn't control his limbs as every muscle contracted at once. Tàran's wiry strength and Gandhan's powerful arms lifted him to his feet while Zhalera's gentle hands cupped his cheeks and turned his face toward hers.

"Are you all right? Kalas! *Kalas!* Can you hear me?!"

"I'm fine," he said, appreciating the warmth of her touch. "Just a little sore."

The two men released their grip on him, although Tàran held on a bit longer.

"Looked like you got yourself kicked by a mule, boy," he said, still assessing his condition.

"Felt like it, too!" Kalas agreed. "I mean, okay, I've never actually been kicked by a mule, but I imagine it's probably just as unpleasant!"

"I told you I don't trust it," Tàran reminded him. "Even after all the shaking, why'd you reach for it again?"

Kalas opened his mouth to explain, but realized he had no explanation. Puzzled, he thought for a moment before answering: "I really don't know. I just wanted to get inside and—"

"Get inside the cliff?" interrupted Gandhan.

"No, not inside the cliff! Inside that *thing*, that…that *artifact*."

"'Artifact'?" Zhalera interjected. "What do you mean?"

"Think about it," Kalas said, turning toward his father. "That sheet of…*not-paper* we found: the one with those lines and drawings. *Someone* knew—knows?—about this thing."

He retrieved the leaf his father had dropped.

"But how do you know it has an 'inside'?" she insisted.

"I…don't. I don't *know*, it just…well, touch it—not where I did! —and tell me what you think."

Zhalera hesitated for a moment, looked to her father, who shrugged—*I wouldn't do it, but it's your choice*—then approached the object and ran a trembling hand across its surface.

No lights. No quakes. Nothing out of the ordinary.

"It feels like metal, but it's *not* metal," she said after a few seconds. "Not exactly. I can't really explain it. I can't tell if it has an inside, though."

She knocked twice, then withdrew her hand without incident. Gandhan and Tàran, tense, both relaxed.

"When I touched it—both times—I kept thinking it was like a *skin*, like an outer covering. You all saw those lights, right? The shapes? The lines they followed? Have you ever known anything in nature to have such symmetry, such perfect angles?"

"Certain rocks tend to split along their cleavage in predictable patterns," offered Gandhan, unconvinced but still unsure.

Tàran coughed, spat, and rooted through his pack.

"Whatever it is, we still have tomorrow to figure it out. Boy: help me with this shelter."

Suddenly fatigued, he slumped as he untangled guylines, skins, and poles. He shook it off and continued his work. Everyone else emptied their packs, too, and soon they had a four-person structure in place.

"Father, are you feeling all right?" asked Kalas when the others were out of earshot.

"I'm fine, boy, I'm…A little tired, maybe," he confessed—something he *never* did. "I'm sure I'll be all right after a good night's sleep."

Gandhan built a small ring with some of the stone fragments littering the ground, dug a pit for some of the unburned wood nearby, and lit a small fire. Kalas hadn't realized how cold the canyon had become since the suns passed over its towering walls. Though their stronger rays had dimmed, it would still be some time before the fire was their only source of light. Tàran prepared supper: cured meat; biscuit-like bread; a significant block of cheese; and dried *golfrasme,* an apple-like fruit with a tart citrus flavor.

Zhalera shivered and tried to ignore the dwindling temperature. Kalas got up, grabbed a blanket, and wrapped it around her shoulders as he sat down beside her.

"Thanks," she smiled and leaned into him.

Seated around the fire, they took turns examining the translucent sheet and discussing their thoughts about the "artifact," as Kalas called it, and what else the cliff might contain. Gandhan suggested they attempt to break it free of the surrounding cliff, said he had some tools that might help, though he had other, more powerful means back at his shop. Tàran emphasized his disdain for the thing: he said he had a strange feeling about it, same as when they'd first discovered it.

"Gives me a headache," he groused.

"Well," said Gandhan after piling more wood on the fire, "both suns have almost set, and the more I think about it, I'll admit I'd like to see what else is in there: Kalas, your curiosity is infectious! But it can wait until morning."

"That it can," agreed Tàran. He stood, massaged his temples, and said goodnight as he shambled into the tent. Gandhan remained outside with Kalas and his daughter. They traded stories for a while before he also retired, and Kalas and Zhalera were alone. On their backs atop their shared blanket, they looked up at the sky, at every pinprick of light that stretched from one end of the canyon to the other.

When the first sun followed the second sun into darkness, Kalas heard the Song again. It was different this time: major and minor chords vying for dominance.

"What are you thinking about?" Zhalera asked him. "You've got that look on your face again," and took his hand, and he realized he'd been lost in concentration, wrapped up in the contrasting melodies that somehow retained a measure of holistic unity.

"Zhalera, do you ever hear music…in your head? Not like remembering something you've heard in the past, but something taking place within your own mind? I'm probably not explaining it very well."

"No, I don't think so," she said. "Do you hear something now? Do you think it's because of that thing inside the cliff?"

"I do hear something now, but I don't think it has anything to do with that artifact. A few weeks ago, on my second Seven, I heard it for the first time. But it wasn't just *hearing*, no, it was something more—*much* more. I thought my head was gonna explode! Father wanted to take me home, but I told him I was fine. And I thought I was, too.

"Anyway, I heard it more than a few times that day: always the same song, but always a little different. Like different instruments, or variations on a theme. I don't know. Gave me nosebleeds whenever it would start up. But that night with the wolf—with Dzharëth —something changed. When I woke up, the song was still there, but at the back of my mind. It still comes and goes: sometimes it's louder—more *present*, I guess, but it's always there."

"What does it sound like?" Zhalera wondered.

"There's so much going on with it, it's hard to say! Melodies on top melodies; motifs that seem to contradict one another at first, only to resolve as part of some amazing chorus. Overall, it sounds… *hopeful*. I can't really explain how or why. Not the whole thing, not all the time—there's fear, there's doubt, and there's uncertainty —but underneath every strain, there's *hope*."

Chapter VI

At the Center of Lohwàlar's Crescent

"Looks like there are words written here, but I can't make them out. Tàran, can you read them?"

Gandhan stepped down from the ever-growing pile of rubble where part of the cliff face used to be. He'd woken early, before the first sun had risen, and started hammering away at the rock. The noise had roused everyone else, and soon, bit by bit, they'd unearthed more of the artifact.

"I can't," confessed Tàran after examining the strange markings the blacksmith had discovered and comparing them with the translucency. "I'm not sure if they're words or just pictures. Maybe after some breakfast, we'll be able to make better sense of it."

As they ate their breakfast in relative silence, save for the sounds of the forest waking around them, Kalas couldn't shake the sensation that something—or perhaps some*one*—was watching them, observing them from some nearby vantage point. He paused with a handful of *golfras* bread halfway to his mouth, cocked his head, closed his eyes, and listened.

"Boy?" said Tàran after observing him a while.

"Is it the song?" Zhalera, seated beside him, whispered.

"No, it's not that, it's…probably nothing. An animal, maybe. I don't know, I just felt like something was watching us."

"Not that bedeviled deer?!" growled Gandhan as he retrieved

his hammer.

"No, I don't think so. Like I said, probably just an animal sniffing at our breakfast." Kalas shrugged and popped the morsel into his mouth.

When everyone finished eating, Tàran took another look at the symbols Gandhan discovered. The first sun, having risen high enough above the horizon, cast its rays against the opposing wall of the canyon, which reflected them onto the work area surrounding the artifact. The gray-white metal warmed when hit with Tàfayan's silver beams and radiated its welcome heat. Kalas extinguished their small fire with rocks and sand and joined his father.

"I still don't know what they mean, but some of these markings look like those on this *not-paper* the boy and I found in Wodram's old study. I'm not—"

Without warning, Tàran doubled over, coughed, and spat blood.

"Father!" shouted Kalas as he struggled to support the old man. Gandhan, for all his size, proved quicker, and propped him up until the fit passed.

"Well, friend?" asked the smith, his eyebrows arched, once Tàran had recovered. "Should we call it a day? Get you back to Lohwàlar? The Sanctuary, maybe?"

"Nothing so drastic as that!" scoffed Tàran. "Just let me rest a bit: I'll be fine! I might be old enough to be your father, but I reckon I've got a few more Sevens in me all the same!"

"All right, if you say so," Gandhan deferred. "Holler if you need anything…"

"Father, now you tell *me* the truth," demanded Kalas once Zhalera's father resumed his work. "What's going on? Ever since we got here, you've been, well, you haven't been yourself. Are you ill?"

"No, boy, I'm fine. It's this…this *artifact* of yours. I told you we'd come back here when we had the time, and here we are, but I still don't trust this thing. It's more than the lights and sounds. Tell me: don't you feel the *wrongness* in what we've uncovered? Maybe the Creator buried it beneath the earth and sea for a reason.

"Anyway, give me some time—and some distance from this thing—and I'll be just fine. I swear. Just…please, don't tell your mother!"

Kalas smiled despite his concern. He sat down beside his father, who eased himself onto a bed of skins.

"Boy?" Tàran said when Kalas remained next to him. "I'll rest easier if you're out there doing what we came here to do! The sooner you're done, the sooner we're out of here, and I don't need you babysitting me!"

"Okay, Father, but if you need anything—"

"I won't, but I'll let you know. Now go!"

Kalas winced as Tàran endured another coughing fit.

"I'm all right! I said go!" he laughed in a wholly unconvincing manner.

2.

"I don't know, my boy: this…whatever it is seems to stretch deep into the rock. It's amazing, that's for sure: doesn't chip or scratch, bend or break—doesn't do *anything* when I hit it with my hammer! And I haven't seen any lights since yesterday. Even after running my hand all along the length we've uncovered.

"And there's Tàran. I know he won't let us pack it in on his account, but you and I both know he needs to get to the Sanctuary, see a cleric. This heap's not going anywhere. Why don't we call it a day and get your father back to town?"

Kalas wanted to protest, but he knew Gandhan was right. The three of them had been excavating the area all morning; soon, both suns, now touching, would separate. Regardless of Tàran's condition, they'd need to start back before long.

"You're right," he admitted. "Before we pack up, can I just take another look at the parts we've uncovered?"

"Of course," Gandhan said. "Zhalera! Let's get our things together. We'll take the tent apart last…"

Kalas stepped up to the "words" Gandhan had found earlier, looked them over and compared them again with the shapes and symbols scattered across the odd medium he'd discovered in his grandfather's study. Everything…printed? painted? on the revealed portion of the object remained indecipherable.

What are you saying? he wondered as he reached for one of the pictograms, then another, tracing their lines with his outstretched finger.

Something inside the artifact clicked, and one of the icons started glowing a muted blue; something whirred beneath its skin, and the luminescent shape began to pulse. Slowly, at first; then, as Kalas simply stared, transfixed, its rate and intensity increased. The whirring noise became a familiar whine as the now-vibrant blue light shifted toward violet, then crimson.

"What did you do, Kalas?" said Zhalera as she jogged toward him.

"Nothing! I mean, I just touched it!"

"It's getting faster! And louder!" she observed.

"Yeah. I don't like it," said Kalas as he tapped at the other shapes.

"Then *why are you still messing with it?!*"

"I know, I know! Just wait a minute!"

Zhalera said nothing with her voice, but Kalas couldn't drown out the discomfort in her body language as he stared at the network of lights that had begun leaching into the surrounding surfaces of the artifact. He could hear internal elements shifting position with faint creaks and groans. Thin black lines appeared, like those he'd seen when he'd first discovered the object, and spread out along its contours.

C'mon! he chided himself. *Think!*

He stared at the translucent item from Wodram's collection and tried to unlock whatever secrets its shapes contained by force of will. He glanced at the artifact again, now generating heat from something more than reflected suns-light—*lots* of heat.

"Well, Kalas?" demanded Zhalera at last. He scanned the *not-paper* again, his eyes darting back and forth between its contents and the artifact.

"All right, all right!" he mumbled as he pressed three symbols in quick succession.

"Nothing happened!" Zhalera said and clutched his arm.

"I know! I—"

The heat dissipated, the lights faded, and the whirring stopped. The black lines seemed to melt together, and a faint punch of bright red light, accompanied by two noises of different pitch and duration —*beeeeep BOOP!*—signaled an end to the excitement.

"How did you—?" she began.

"I didn't! But this *not-paper...*"

All the commotion woke Tàran; he and Gandhan finished packing up the shelter in time to observe Kalas' frenzied poking and prodding.

"You about done, boy?" sighed Tàran.

"Yes, Father," Kalas answered, abashed.

"Let's get home. Should reach Lohwàlar before suns-down."

Without another word, Kalas nodded, shouldered his pack, and took his place in line.

Kalas thought his father might be right about the object and his proximity to it: as they put some distance between the two, Tàran's pace quickened, his coughing ceased, and, although as gruff as ever, his spirits seemed much improved.

They reached the canyon's rim shortly after the second sun disappeared. No crazed deer attacked them, and aside from an unshakable sensation of a presence on the cusp of Kalas' perception, nothing untoward interfered with their return. Gandhan ascended with much less hesitation (though Kalas still heard him curse the slope more than once), and as he pulled himself onto flatter ground, he wheezed his satisfaction that the worst of the trip was behind him. Tàran laughed, his former malaise naught but a memory.

Conversation trended toward the afternoon's excitement: Gandhan, Zhalera, and Kalas voiced their conjecture about the artifact's provenance, its possible purposes, but Tàran kept his peace.

"It has to be some kind of machine," insisted Gandhan. "but I have no idea how it generates those lights, those sounds, nor why anyone might have built it! Who knows? Maybe it's *magic!*"

"*Magic,* Father?" Zhalera pretended to scold him. "I thought you knew better than that! But what about that metal it was covered with? It's not iron or steel, not bronze or brass. Kalas, I think you're right: the way those lights were *under* its...what did you call it? *Skin?* There has to be some kind of system *inside* the thing, maybe levers and pulleys? I don't know what it could be for, either. What do you think?"

Kalas kept quiet for a while, long enough for Zhalera to repeat the question.

"I...don't know," he finally answered. *Maybe there* is *magic in the world. Maybe it's not the myth we've all been taught...And maybe it's not all benevolent...*

He thought about how the object affected his father, how being near it seemed to drain him. He shuddered in disgust and said, "It's not important, anyway. Probably better to forget it's even there. Wouldn't surprise me if it were buried for a reason."

At the front of the line, Tàran grunted his agreement.

"Really?" said Zhalera, surprised and somewhat confused. "Wow, all right. Not what I was expecting from you. I thought you said you had to get inside the thing?"

"I know, but maybe I was just talking nonsense. Caught up in the moment, I guess," he deflected. In hushed tones, he continued, "And the way it made Father sick? No, I think I'm done with it. Whatever it is. Whatever it might have been."

"Buried," repeated Gandhan, thinking out loud. "I'll be the first to admit I'm not an authority in all things geological, but I know a fair amount, and the way the sand- and mudstones were layered around the artifact? Well, I don't think the thing was *buried* so much as it was *already there* when the canyon was formed!

"But anyway, whatever it's made of is like nothing I've ever seen. Whether it's been dozens or hundreds of Sevens, no metal, no alloy I know could have survived such exposure in such prime condition. If we could break it apart, find a way to work it, just imagine what we could create with it! Plowshares that never rust! Swords that never lose their edge!"

"Blacksmiths who beg for bread in the Crescent!" muttered Tàran. "After everyone has their new, magic tools that never corrode, never blunt, what'll be left for you to do, old friend?"

Both Kalas and Zhalera laughed at Gandhan's sudden change in expression.

"Maybe you're right, my boy," he said. "Maybe we'll just leave that thing right where we found it."

3.

In relative silence, punctuated by rare bursts of small talk, the quartet made its way across the dimming desert until the faint lights of Lohwàlar dotted their horizon. Tonight, the usual evening breezes seemed otherwise occupied, and the unmoving air had a thick, stifling quality about it. The second sun had disappeared some time ago; now, the first sun prepared to complete its course, paving the way for the solitary moon. Kalas had always thought it strange that the first sun to rise was also the last sun to set. In school, an instructor had repeated the familiar story: The first sun battled and overcame the darkness, making it safe for the second sun to rise; after a time, the path of the celestial conflict traveled elsewhere, and the first sun gave chase, always ensuring the darkness would never touch the second sun as it followed the first through the heavens.

As they entered town, more than a few people regarded them with curious glances: still more bore expressions of unvarnished terror.

"What's going on?" Gandhan wondered aloud.

Kalas thought the townsfolk held a morbid interest in him, and, to a lesser degree, his father, judging from the way they regarded them. He spotted Rül and asked him, "Why is everyone looking at us like that?"

"It's Dzharëth!" hissed Rül as he backed away. "He's at the Crescent, demanding you and your father come out and face him! He looks terrible, like he's half-dead. Or worse! He's already wounded a few men who've tried to help him. Couple of those soldiers, too. Kalas, I thought your father said he was dead?"

"We thought he was," agreed Kalas.

"Gandhan, Zhalera," said Tàran. "Would you please look in on Màla? Perhaps it would be best if she stayed with you for a while?"

"Tàran?"

"Please. And keep your hammer ready, old friend."

"Kalas, what's happening?" said Zhalera, gripping his arm tightly.

"I thought he was dead," Kalas mumbled. "No, Dzharëth *is*

dead: what's waiting for us is that *zhàrudzh* that wears his skin. Zhalera, please, go with your father: protect my mother—protect yourselves!"

"Of course," finished Gandhan, and he and Zhalera disappeared into the shadows.

"Boy: you have the girl's birthday present with you?"

"Always."

"Keep it close. Let's go."

Tàran dropped his pack in the street. Kalas did the same. Side by side, at the center of a growing crowd, they turned toward the Crescent. Kalas kept a sure grip on his knife and tried to remember the *power* the wolf-monster had mentioned. Somewhere above them, a shape whistled through the night.

"There you are!" cackled Dzharëth as Tàran and Kalas entered the Crescent.

Kalas thought Rül's description had been generous: if the figure was still naked, it was hard to tell, so filthy was his jaundiced skin. Almost every inch of him was wrapped in tatters of what looked like cloth, but Kalas knew to be strips of rotting flesh. His hair, patchy under the Cracks, had all but disappeared: what remained was a tangled stringy mess, clumped in wads of that unnatural oily substance. And his eyes, once a faint shade of hazel, were so bloodshot the whites appeared deep red, almost black, and his greenish-brown irises flashed scarlet.

Not too far from the animated remains of Dzharëth's form lay a handful of wounded or unconscious bodies. One of them, a soldier, raised himself to a sitting position and clutched his head. Upon observing the creature still there, he promptly fainted. Pretended to, at least.

"Dzharëth, these people have done nothing to you. Let them alone: your quarrel is with me," soothed Tàran.

"With you? Perhaps—if only because of that *freak* you call your son!"

"Father?" whispered Kalas.

"He has *no idea*, does he?" teased the monster. "Ha! I should have known! Oh, things make so much sense now! But still…"

"Dzharëth—whatever your name is—please…"

"The next time you throw a dagger at someone, old man, make sure he's *dead!*"

With a flick of his wrist, the *zhàrudzh* produced Tàran's long dagger. For a moment, it glinted in the moonlight; then, in the next, the weapon sailed through the space between the creature's withered fingers and Tàran's forehead, where it buried itself to the hilt.

Kalas' father didn't even have time to look up: his eyes remained focused on Dzharëth as his head snapped back and carried the rest of his body with it. He toppled to the ground before Kalas could reach him.

"FATHER!" howled Kalas as he cradled Tàran's head.

His body was still warm, his eyes—not afraid, but wary—still stared straight ahead. The blade had sunk so deep and with such force there was hardly any blood, just a thin red rivulet trickling from the old man's half-open mouth.

"Father! Please!" demanded Kalas of Tàran's lifeless corpse.

Dzharëth laughed, a high, nasal sound that descended in pitch until it acquired that gravelly, guttural quality from before. Rather than breaking apart like the last time, the creature knelt, hunched, and flexed its arms as though retreating within itself; then, with an almost subvocal roar, the last vestiges of Dzharëth flew apart in oily shreds that dissolved into black breaths of sour smoke. The crowd scattered in a cacophonic blur of shouts and screams: the soldier pretending to be knocked out bolted for the garrison.

The monster continued its haunting laughter and clawed its way through the frantic mob. Kalas wiped his eyes, readied his knife, and was about to stand when a pair of thin hands stayed his own.

"Let me go!" he demanded and looked up at Tsharak.

He tried to break the old man's grip, but his aged sinews held remarkable strength.

"Now is *not* the time!" Tsharak hissed.

"But my *father!*" he wept.

Before the old man could respond, several shapes seemed to crack the heavens and streak through the sky: balls of sickly yellow-white light smacked the earth with unimaginable force, sending sheets of dirt skyward and creating immense, smoking craters. As the smoke dissipated, Kalas realized each "ball" was in fact another *zhàrudzh:* each one grabbed and clawed at anyone unfortunate enough to cross its path. Above, more pestilent lights raced earthward.

4.

"What's all this, then?" bellowed Valderïk's lilting voice as he cantered into the Crescent. His horse reared and whinnied, desperate to be anywhere but here, it seemed to Kalas. The soldier who disappeared earlier hid behind him, along with most of the *Poyïsriba* detachment. Like their commander's steed, none appreciated the situation thrust upon them. Valderïk locked eyes with the wolf that had been Dzharëth.

"Oho! So you *do* exist!" he exulted even as he struggled to rein in his horse. To his men, he charged: "To arms, *temme!* To arms! *Revehwa ihi kàsh! Shelu i ikinihath!* And victory to Her Majesty, the queen!"

With a sharp kick to his destrier's ribs, he thundered into the creature's path, nearly trampling the hapless villagers in his way.

The skydog snarled as the commander, sword raised, bore down on him. Before Valderïk could strike, his would-be quarry moved with unexpected grace and speed and wrenched the soldier's arm from its socket. Kalas winced as the warrior tried to swing his useless limb at the place where the wolf had been and dropped his sword.

Several other *rudzhegume* engaged the remaining soldiers, some of whom expended valiant effort: the first attempted to parry a blow and ended up with a hole where his heart once beat.

"I surrender!" shouted another as he threw his battle-axe to the ground. Some of the others followed his example; one or two continued their well-intentioned but ineffective exertions—all for nothing: the dogs descended on them en masse. As they screamed, one tried to run, but gained only a few yards before a living shadow consumed him, a feeble hint of light extinguished by an overwhelming darkness. When every soldier had been devoured, the pack scattered, tasted the air in search of fresh prey and loped after anyone whose scent piqued its macabre interest. The people screamed, confused, their terror mere seasoning for the wolves' feast. Yet amid all the shrieking, Kalas thought he heard pained *zhàrudzhme* yelps and barks mingled therein.

"Well met, fiend!" cried Valderïk, having turned his mount with his remaining hand. He released the reins and tumbled from his saddle, retrieving another, shorter sword in the process. With the flat of its blade, he smacked his horse's flanks: freed from the commander's sway, it bolted from the scene.

The commander's lost his mind! noted Kalas, still held by Tsharak's grasp.

Dzharëth cocked his head and swiveled toward the crazed warrior.

"That's it, demon! The first blow goes to you; now, let's really test your mettle!"

Valderïk advanced with measured steps, assessed the monster's stance, the situation's probabilities, and adjusted his approach. Dzharëth followed suit and adapted to the commander's movements. With feints and half-thrusts, Valderïk closed the distance, springing back with surprising lightness when the beast lashed out.

There is *more to him than bluster,* Kalas had to admit.

Finding an opening, the commander lunged and buried his short sword into the monster's leg. Before he could pull back and strike another blow, Dzharëth twisted, shifted his weight, and ripped the blade from Valderïk's hand. With a wet tearing noise, he wrenched it free and hurled it like a missile at the soldier's head.

Valderïk had anticipated the move, however, and before the weapon could impale him, he rolled, retrieved his longsword, and swung it with all his remaining might at the wolf's injured limb, where it sank into bone and remained fast. Dzharëth roared with pain and fell to his knees as smoke and slime spurted from the wound.

"His heart!" Kalas shouted: *"Aim for his heart!"*

Valderïk gave no indication he'd heard the boy's cries, but he let go of his immobile sword and pummeled the monster's chest with his gauntleted fist. For a moment, his strikes seemed to weaken it —but only for a moment: its eyes rippled with pain—

That's not pain: that's rage, Kalas noted.

—and Dzharëth placed one huge, stinking paw against the commander's neck and squeezed, lifted him off the ground, and staggered to his feet.

Zhi âsru—tayitimu! it *thought* at Valderïk with such malice that both Kalas and Tsharak somehow *heard* its curse and recoiled.

"I'll see you there!" laughed the commander as the wolf snapped his neck. Without ceremony, it tossed Valderïk's lifeless body aside and turned again to Kalas.

"Now we'll end this 'prophecy' nonsense once for all," it smoldered as it stepped toward the boy.

"No!" insisted Tsharak and released his vise-like grip on Kalas' hands. He stood between the boy and the wolf, and at first, Kalas thought the wizened old man intended to *fight* the beast; instead, he raised his arms in an entreating pose and bowed his head.

"Your prayers are useless, *ëth dzhasturún!*"

It raised its poisoned claws and struck, but before its blow connected, that subtle whisper Kalas had heard time and again manifested as a whirling blur that proved to be Ilbardhën, the soldier who'd addressed him days earlier. With a quick maneuver, Shosafin placed his weapon between Tsharak and the wolf, and with little more than a subtle ring, the creature's fast descending arm passed through the warrior's extended blade. Dzharëth barked in pain as it cradled the stump where his forearm used to be.

Above the Crescent, borne upon the music of ethereal instruments, twisted forks of green-white light tore apart the darkness and arced across the sky, scenting the air with an acrid tang and stabbing at the shadows.

"No! *No!*" mumbled Dzharëth, his eyes raised. Somewhere close by, a blast of verdant power snaked its way toward the ground: one of the skydogs howled in fear as the earth erupted in a bloom of cleansing energy. Thunder pealed, and Kalas sensed vibrations in the air, a tangible *hum* that reverberated right through him.

"Go! *Hwer!*" Tsharak yelled at the boy and nodded his thanks to his savior. "Màla!"

"Mother!" remembered Kalas. He looked at Dzharëth. At Shosafin.

Covered with dust and cuts and scrapes from what must have been prior encounters—the source of those yelps, perhaps?—Shosafin panted but maintained his composure. He spared two glances: one for the wolf; one for Kalas.

"*Hwer, sà!*" he insisted as he readied for the creature's next attack. Kalas nodded and obeyed, the clash of steel and the screams of townsfolk echoing in his wake.

5.

He raced through Lohwàlar's empty streets, wrestling with bouts of tears and fits of rage and praying Gandhan and Zhalera had reached Màla before the skydogs: if they were after *him*, as "Dzharëth" suggested…

That freak *you call your son!*

Kalas refused to follow that line of thought, redoubled his speed until he reached the open door to his house.

"Mother?!" he shouted. "Mother?!"

"Kalas!" answered Zhalera from the great room. He sighed, relieved, and only then recognized the now-familiar reek mingled with the odor of burning flesh.

"Zhalera!" he began as he rushed toward the sound of her voice. "Where's my mother? Where's your—?"

"Kalas, I'm so sorry," sobbed Zhalera as she held Màla to her breast. Beside her lay an immense sword stained with black. It looked familiar, but Kalas' thoughts were elsewhere.

All around them, fresh blood and viscous filth spattered the walls. Kalas looked down and saw Gandhan's hammer, chipped and caked with matted fur; just beyond, he saw Gandhan himself, torn open and spilled onto the floor, his outstretched arm a wreck of shredded muscle, the lacerated remnants of his face a mask of rage. Beside his corpse smoldered what could only be the empty hide of one of the *zhàrudzhme,* as if something had vaporized its bones and innards.

Zhalera, seated in a spreading pool of Màla's blood, comforted the injured woman as best she could. Kalas' mother breathed in shallow gasps, each labored breath a punctuated surrender toward her end.

"Kalas," she wheezed, beckoning him, but he was already there.

"I'm here, Mother," he said, choking back tears and squeezing her hand.

"Kalas, there's so much we should have told you, so much you need to know! We thought we'd have more time, but the wolves… Your father: he's dead, too, isn't he?"

Kalas nodded through tears he could no longer keep at bay. Màla coughed blood.

"Before I follow him, I have to tell you: In our youth, your father and I couldn't conceive; our Sevens came and went without such a blessing. We'd given up hope, accepted it as best we could, until one day, a stranger appeared—I mean *appeared*: one moment your father and I were alone; the next, a man who hadn't been there… *just was.*

"'*Ilëntharasme!*' he said, 'Behold: your son!' There was light— such bright, white light!—and suddenly he held you in his arms! He handed you to us—Oh! How your father cried! He told us about a prophecy from 'before the world was cracked;' he told us you had a destiny, how one day you would—"

"Prophecy? Mother, we need to get the clerics—the wolf's poisonous claws—"

She coughed again, cried out this time.

"There's no time! And there's so much more to tell, my son— *and you* are *my son!*—The stranger instructed us not to reveal your secret until the appointed time: your second Seven. That music you hear: the stranger told us about the Song, that on the day it rived your mind, you would begin to understand your place, your purpose in the coming storm."

Màla paused and tried to catch her breath. Couldn't.

"I'm sorry, son, that we kept all this from you, that our attempt to keep you safe has left you unprepared! Forgive us, please! And know this: despite our failure, we love you—we will *forever* love you!—more than you will ever understand, more than I could ever tell you had I all the time in the world!

"Kalas, *pïn sashin zhi dàbirafime ar shir zhenda, zhi uskathin* ëth *nir*—of all the blessings we have received, *you* are the greatest!"

With her free hand, Màla, trembling, reached for Kalas' face and caressed its familiar contours. She smiled, and Kalas, amazed, saw resplendent joy in her dying features. One final exhalation wrest itself from her lungs: it seemed to hover for a moment before resuming its ultimate ascent. Kalas caught her hand as it fell.

"Forgive? You don't—of course I forgive you! Mother?! Mother! No, *please! Please, no...*" he whispered as he pressed her lifeless palm against his cheek.

Zhalera said nothing; instead, she leaned into Kalas, wrapped her free and shaking arm around his shoulder. He did the same, and for as long as they could, they held each other while they cried, ignored the world outside and let it fall apart around them.

III

Chapter VII

In Rooms Below
the Ancient Temple

"KALAS, WHAT DO WE DO?" SAID ZHALERA, AFTER A long, shared silence, occasionally interrupted with grief-stricken tears.

"I...I don't know," he responded, numb, his mother's already-cold hand still in his.

A gust of night wind blew through the open door, swirled around the room and mingled the smells of putrescence and blood before whipping away through a huge, sparking hole in the roof. Kalas hadn't noticed it until now. He shivered, and as he looked away from the patch of stars framed within what remained of the ceiling, he saw Gandhan again, just as motionless as his mother.

"Zhalera, I'm sorry," offered Kalas as he pulled her close. More tears from both of them.

He released his mother's hand, stifled fresh sobs as he realized he would never hold nor be held by it again.

"Good-bye, Mother," he whispered as he caressed her eyelids and helped them close for the last time.

Together, he and Zhalera helped each other stand. Together, in the thready torchlight, they helped each other to the same well-worn couch they'd shared not too long ago. It had been overturned in the attack; after righting it, they sat, surrounded by semidarkness and the sound of the wind.

"Your father," Kalas began. "If we hadn't gone to the Empty Sea, maybe—"

"Just *stop it,*" said Zhalera, her tone a blend of sorrow and anger, and Kalas understood.

"I'm sorry," he repeated.

"Before Mother died, we had a chance to come to terms with it: her illness gave us that, at least, but Father…"

"Something we have in common, I guess," said Kalas, unsure if he should have said anything.

"Tàran? Oh, Kalas! On the same day!"

"Dzharëth," he nodded. "It was fast—too fast—but after…this, maybe it's better. Zhalera, what happened here? I mean, you don't have to talk about it if you don't want to."

"No, it's all right. I feel like if I don't talk about it now, I never will. When you left for the Crescent, Father came straight here, but he told me to go home and get the sword—right, the one above the mantel, so I did.

"There was a rush of wind, of fire—by the time I got back, Father was fighting one of those things—it looked just like the one that attacked us, maybe bigger. Màla was already on the ground, bleeding. I thought Father was putting up a good fight—I even thought he would win!—but then it grabbed his arm and just… Kalas, it was like skinning a rabbit!

"That's when the wolf-thing went for his face. I tried to get there, but I was too slow: I swung Father's sword at it, but it just slapped it away, *laughed,* and backhanded me. I went flying and dropped the sword. It came at me, and I thought I was dead, but then the strangest thing happened! I've never seen anything like it! There was thunder, and a bolt of lightning came through the roof, right where that monster was standing! It was so bright I couldn't see what happened next, but after a second, maybe, the wolf thing was gone—nothing but a pile of skin!

"It wasn't like regular lightning: no, this had a *thickness* about it, maybe as wide as a barrel. It had a green glow around it, too, and the only thing it seemed to touch was that wolf. I'd probably be dead if it hadn't hit when it did.

"I ran to check on Màla, but I could tell it was bad. Really bad. I didn't know what to do, but that's when you came in. Kalas…"

"The *Ïsribarinme* are dead—all but one, I think," Kalas said after wiping away the latest spate of tears. "Commander Valderïk, for all his bluster, actually put up a good fight, but Dzharëth got him, too. Would've gotten me first if Tsharak hadn't stopped me from doing something stupid."

"Tsharak?"

"Yeah, he just showed up out of nowhere, after Father…I was going to, I don't know, stab Dzharëth, like before, with your birthday present. I hadn't really thought it through. But Tsharak grabbed me—he's surprisingly strong!

"Then Shosafin showed up. He'd been following us, I think. Even into the canyon, maybe. He cut off Dzharëth's arm. There was some of that green lightning in the Crescent, too, but that's when I ran for here."

"Your mother said something about a prophecy," Zhalera reminded him.

"So did Dzharëth," added Kalas. "I have no idea what he meant."

"Really? Prophecy, hmm? I wonder if anyone knows what she was talking about," she mused.

"I think I know someone who might."

2.

Having covered their parents' remains, Kalas and Zhalera gathered a few items into a pack and prepared to venture outside. Neither had noticed much since the thunder and lightning had ceased: just the wind, bearing the occasional lamentation from some other hapless *Lohwàlarrin.*

"I guess it's safe?" said Kalas, unconvinced but unwilling to remain indoors.

"I guess we'll find out soon enough," Zhalera whispered, her father's sword and scabbard slung across her back.

They waited another moment; then, Zhalera's hand in one of his and his knife in the other, Kalas held his breath and stepped into the darkness.

Here, the wind blew colder, striking Kalas' face with an occasional grain of sand. The first few times, he flinched.

"Just dust," he muttered when he felt Zhalera tense.

At first, Lohwàlar looked much the same, but it felt wholly different. Soon, they crossed paths with other townsfolk tending to their injuries, their murdered loved ones. As their path brought them toward more populated regions, however, they realized the *zhàrudzhme* had wrought substantial destruction on their town. Its few clerics were making their rounds: helping where they could, consoling where they must. Kalas thought he recognized one of them and called out.

"Kalas? *Zhi halum erume ágazhalu,* you're alive!" Vàyana marveled as she turned and rushed toward him. Without reserve, she embraced him and wept as though he was—and always had been —more than a former patient: a close friend; a nephew, perhaps.

"We thought the *zhàrudzhme* had found you, put an end to the —to your life! I'm so thankful we were wrong!"

"Vàyana, my mother, my father—Zhalera's father: they're—"

"I can tend to them right away! Just—"

"They're dead, Vàyana."

"Oh!" she gasped at last as her bronze features cycled through confusion, shock, and sympathy. "Master Kalas, I'm…You've been through so much already, and yet there's so much…Here, come with me." She beckoned him to follow as she retrieved her lantern.

Kalas looked to Zhalera, who regarded the cleric with curious surprise. She squeezed his hand, and together, they allowed Vàyana to lead them through the bereaved and wounded masses. She paused now and again to speak with and offer sympathy and suggestions to the survivors.

She's leading us toward the Crescent, Kalas realized, and his steps faltered. Vàyana sensed his hesitation.

"Master Kalas?"

"The Crescent is where Dzharëth—no, the *rudzhegu*—killed my father. I don't…Right now I can't…"

"I didn't know, I'm sorry. It's all right: we can go around," she said as she gripped his free hand in both of hers, gave a gentle squeeze, and let it go. Some quality in her touch reminded him most cruelly of his mother's. He blinked away would-be tears, and he and Zhalera continued following the cleric through more naked misery than Kalas had ever seen.

"We're not hurt: we don't need anything from the Sanctuary," said Kalas once he realized where Vàyana was leading them. "Look, thank you for your concern, but I think Zhalera and I need to figure out what's next for us on our own."

"But we're not going to the Sanctuary," Vàyana countered. "Not…exactly."

"No?"

The cleric seemed to wrestle with some thought, some further explanation that hesitated on the tip of her tongue. She suppressed it and said, "You'll see."

"See what?" said a familiar voice.

"Tsharak! Shosafin!" said Kalas as the wearied pair stepped into view, no longer hidden in the lantern's shadows. He threw himself at the old man and wrapped his arms around his neck. "Then the *rudzhegu* didn't get you?"

"Not because it didn't try," Shosafin said with a rueful smile.

"What happened? Please tell me that *nëshras egu* is dead!"

"Not dead, just *runshethas*—unskinned." interrupted Tsharak. "In all my Sevens, I've never known a mortal to kill an *egu* in such a way that it remained thus; rather, on occasion—like tonight— someone might be fortunate enough to separate an *egu* from its material form. That ends the immediate threat, but in time—some- times moments, sometimes millennia—that same *egu* will acquire a new tether, eat away at its *kelâ* like acid until nothing remains, and achieve our plane once again."

Shosafin laughed, and something in his skeptical mien coaxed an impatient sigh from the old man, who ignored him.

"Tell me, Kalas: Màla? Is she all right?"

Zhalera stepped forward and told her part of the story, omit- ting the details of Màla's last words with her son; Kalas, however, explained as best he could his mother's inchoate revelation.

"Dzharëth said something about a prophecy, too, and the only person in Lohwàlar I can think of who might have any idea what she was talking about is you. I mean, Father is—*was*—always telling me stories he learned from you: as strange as they were, he always believed there was something honest about you."

"You could learn a lot from this young man," Tsharak said to Shosafin. To the boy, he continued: "Your intuition serves you well, Master Kalas—"

"*Âu* Tsharak, is this the best place for this?" said Vàyana with a hint of nervousness in her voice.

"Not at all, of course. Continue on your way, cleric: Ilbardhën and I will join you. In fact, I believe we're headed for the same place —and for the same reasons."

3.

The crowd thickened and the townsfolk' wretched cries intensified as Vàyana led them all toward the Sanctuary. Kalas couldn't believe how much hurt and damage the skydogs had caused in such a short time. He saw his friend Halbën with one arm wrapped around his mother's neck, the other bent at an anatomically impossible angle. Several other friends and their family members mobbed the streets in search of help, of an explanation: *what did Lohwàlar do to deserve this?!*

"I thought you said we weren't going to the Sanctuary," said Zhalera, giving voice to Kalas' unspoken thoughts as the five of them approached its ancient stone façade.

Uncounted centuries had weathered its exterior so severely that a casual observer might have overlooked its eclectic architecture, its collective design choices that spanned generations: wind-driven sands had ground sharper features into rounded vestiges of former detail. Still, even in the darkness the structure's *presence* weighed on Kalas' thoughts. The Sanctuary's carved and columned entrance, especially when contrasted with the utilitarian buildings on either side, evoked thoughts of a more resplendent era, a time when Lohwàlar might have been rich and green rather than sparse and beige. Veins of crystalline mineraloids sparkled in Vàyana's light as an orderly saw her and created an opening in the sea of people for her party to cross.

"Not *to* it—*through* it." said Tsharak.

"Oh? Uh, all right then…"

119

• • •

Inside the Sanctuary's walls, the din seemed less raucous, though the press of bodies remained ever present. Somehow, people seemed to move out of their way at just the right moment, providing an unimpeded path toward…wherever Vàyana was leading them.

"Not the Sanctuary?" Kalas whispered to Zhalera, who giggled despite—or because of—her nerves.

"This way," said the cleric as she led them through an unfamiliar section of the structure, little-used, Kalas guessed, since its service as a temple long ago. Here, the voices disappeared, and in silence they approached an ancient stone staircase, a cantilevered spiral polished smooth from millennia of footsteps, now mostly blanketed with dust.

"A moment," she whispered, then bowed her head.

Like she did the night we found Ëlbodh, Kalas noted.

Tsharak bowed his head as well, and while neither spoke, the boy thought he sensed something, an ephemeral impression that disappeared when both raised their heads. Vàyana looked at Tsharak, nodded, and started down the stairs, the muffled brush of her leather-soled shoes almost imperceptible in the stillness.

Kalas counted every narrow, reverberant step—*one, two… ninety-seven, ninety-eight*—

"We're here," said the cleric as she lit several torches, which guttered for a moment before spilling soft yellow-orange light and casting star-like shadows across the small chamber in which they found themselves.

More polyhedral than round, the lights revealed myriad friezes carved into each face of the stone walls surrounding them. Opposite the last stair, a vast door, wood and banded with iron, blocked their way. At least twice as tall as a man, it had no hinges, no visible lock, and Kalas wondered if perhaps it wasn't really a door at all. Shosafin must have had the same thought: he freed one of the torches from its sconce, approached the door, and played the light over its surface.

"Looks like this door hasn't been used in dozens—maybe hundreds—of Sevens," he remarked.

"What do these symbols say?" Kalas asked Tsharak.

"What makes you think I would know?"

"I…well, you're the…I mean, everyone says there's no one… who knows Lohwàlar's history as well as you do." Kalas answered, doing his best not to make an issue of the old—the *ancient* man's unknown Sevens.

"And everyone says you're the oldest person in Lohwàlar," added Zhalera with a bemused glance at Kalas.

"Ha!" he laughed, and even in the torches' faint illumination, they saw the crinkles around his now-glittering eyes deepen. "I like you, miss! Kalas, *you* could learn a lot from this young woman! Anyway, I'm sure you've heard the stories; now, let me tell you the truth."

4.

He gestured at the imagery etched into the walls, beginning with the facet to the immediate right of the door.

"Nearly one hundred twenty-eight Sevens ago, in the port city of Kësharan—"

"Kësharan? I thought we were talking about Lohwàlar?" interrupted Kalas.

"Perhaps you'd prefer to tell the tale?"

"Uh, no, I…I'm sorry. Please, go on."

"Kësharan was a beautiful place. Still is, in some ways, and from a distance, but no matter. As I was saying, many Sevens ago, *zhàrudzhme* fell like fiery stones from heaven upon the city in the

121

same way they fell upon Lohwàlar tonight. With similar results. 'The Night of Falling Skies' we called it. No one knows why, nor what they were looking for, but my mother had her suspicions, and—"

"Wait! I'm sorry, but your mother? Almost *nine hundred* years ago?" Kalas blurted. Zhalera elbowed him in the ribs. Tsharak smiled, shook his head, and continued.

"—and hid me underneath the city in an abandoned cistern while up above, everything burned. I heard thunder even from my hiding place, but not much else. It was just after my first Seven, and I didn't know what to do.

"I don't know how long I was down there: days, I think. Scared to move, to breathe, until I heard someone coming down. By then I was so hungry, so weak, that I didn't care who—or what—it was, so I called out, and a man appeared.

"At first I thought I was hallucinating, that I was so out of it I thought I saw a wreath of green-white light shimmering all around him. I learned later—*much* later—that no, I saw what I saw. He knelt, helped me to my feet, and placed his hands on my shoulders. I'll never forget those piercing eyes, or the way he looked into mine, like he was searching for something. He smiled—there was sadness in his face—and said *something*. I don't remember the exact words, but I felt a kind of energy leave his fingertips—just a light vibration; then, I felt something welling up from inside myself, triggered by his touch...

"I blacked out...or fell asleep. I don't know, but when I woke, I—*we*—were in one of the intact buildings. Alone in Kësharan: there were no other survivors. He'd made a small fire and prepared some kind of food. I didn't ask what it was—didn't care, I was so hungry! I ate, and when I'd finished, he made my darkest fears come true: he told me the city was dead. Except for me, all its inhabitants —my mother, my father—were gone.

"'There's magic in your blood, child,' he said. 'Hiding for now, but it's there. Someday, Tsharak, you'll understand.' I didn't remember telling him my name. Found out later I never did.

"'I have to be somewhere else soon. I can't take you with me, but I can take you to a place where you'll be cared for, where you can be part of a family. Of course, you don't have to come with me: you can stay here, if you'd like, though it would break my heart. It's your choice.'

"That's when he brought me to Lohwàlar. Back then, everything was green here! Tall trees, thick grasses, and the Ilswàr running strong through what's now the Lower Quarter. He was right about me becoming part of a family, too: 'In time, that *eruseranà*, that star-magic in your blood, will manifest itself—how, I can't say; when it does, though, be…*discerning*. Be wary. Protect this family —*your* family—from other powers that would visit destruction upon them.'

"Then he was gone. Right away, though, my new family comforted me as best they could, integrated me into their lives, and by the time my second Seven came and went, I'd almost forgotten I hadn't been born to them. They—most of the townsfolk back then —were members of the *Randa pïni Sharumilël*—the Order of the Emerald. They believed the *eru* Sharuyan, delegated his powers by the Creator, ensured the health of their crops and their forests, and beyond that door is where they gathered, twice a year, to express their thanks.

"Tens of Sevens came and went, and over time, crops failed, the forests died, and the town's namesake river dried up. Mercifully, my parents had died long before all that, but Sharuyan's devotees grew fewer and fewer in number until almost none remained. This temple—these lower parts now—was mostly abandoned. So was the town: famine, blight, and drought killed scores of people. Survivors stored the bodies in the levels above us, hoping, I think, to get the *erudas* attention.

"Then someone discovered the Pump. To this day, no one knows exactly where it came from, how it got down into the Empty Sea, nor what its original purpose was. Some people thought Sharuyan or some other *eru*—maybe even *elume*—caused it to be there. Most didn't care once they discovered one thing the *Machine* could do —what people called the Pump at first—was move water from the River: after a few years of some genuinely creative engineering, the *Lohwàlarrinme* brought water back to their town. Not a lot—not enough to be the agrarian society it used to be, but enough for its people to survive. Of course, the effort resulted in a lot of injuries: we were used to working the soil, not the rocks beneath it; we were trying to understand technologies we'd never encountered before. What few *ilrandame* remained started using this temple as a make-shift hospital: the tradition continues to this day.

"Remember, this was generations after everything dried up: those who knew anything of Lohwàlar's former abundance only knew what they'd heard through stories. It was already ancient history to them. For a while, I tried to set the record straight, but almost no one believed me, and to be fair, why would they? It's all pretty unbelievable. Still, I told my stories, trusting that one day, they'd find an audience who'd recognize them as truth.

"These markings tell the same story: Lohwàlar's history. This symbol represents the Machine—the Pump; over here, this block describes the Night of Falling Skies, visible even from here so many Sevens ago…

"And here: this sequence, running through every block—sometimes subtle, sometimes less so—describes a portion of the prophecy that brings us here tonight."

Tsharak paced around the room while recounting his tale, pointing here and there with impassioned gestures as he moved. Kalas listened, rapt; still, Shosafin's bearing belied his unswayed amusement.

"You don't buy it, do you?" the young man asked the soldier.

"Nine hundred years old?" Shosafin said, after a while. "No, friend, I'm not persuaded. It's a good story, sure, and I think Tsharak believes it himself, but there's just no way it's true. How many people do you know who've lived more than fourteen or fifteen sevens?"

"We're free to believe or disbelieve as we choose: the truth requires no one's approval," Tsharak interjected.

"I won't argue that point, but all you've provided is your own say-so. No corroborating evidence. If I told you I was a ball of twine before I left Ïsriba, would you believe me? You wouldn't. Nor should you! I'm simply reserving judgment."

"As is your right," deferred Tsharak.

"How long do you think he'll be?" Vàyana whispered to the old man, waking Kalas in the process. He'd fallen asleep with his head on Zhalera's lap; she'd rested hers on his side. For a moment, he thought the cleric's voice was his mother's.

It had been…actually, Kalas had no idea how long it had been since they'd reached the door in front of them. The torches guttered as invisible wind from some unknown source danced across their flames. He shivered and startled Zhalera awake. Kalas sat up and wrapped an arm around her.

"I thought he would have been here by now," Tsharak confessed. "Still, he wrote his name in the sky…Shouldn't be much longer."

"Expecting someone?" added Shosafin, still seated against a wall with his eyes closed, somehow alert even while at rest.

At that moment, bright, green-white light leached from behind the door's edges, gained intensity, and shined with such brilliance that Kalas had to shield his eyes. The others did likewise until a coarse grating sound echoed across the chamber. Despite the oppressive effulgence, every eye turned toward the door.

It shattered. Smoldering sticks of wood and glowing clouds of dust sailed through space; somehow, no one was hurt, and as quickly as it appeared, the brightness dissipated. From within the inner room a figure staggered into the torchlight.

He held a familiar-looking staff, and in the places where his outer garment wasn't scorched Kalas glimpsed hints of sparkling silver. The visitor panted. Collapsed. Tsharak and Vàyana rushed to his aid and helped him into a seated position.

Hey! That's—!

"Falthwën!" cried Tsharak. "We saw *Sharuyandas Âsru* in the sky…"

"You're hurt!" shouted Vàyana as she began tending his wounds as best she could. "What happened? How did you get here?"

"That," said the injured cleric, "is a long story."

5.

"When the boy first led me into the Empty Sea, when I first came face to face with his friend Dzharëth, I had my suspicions," Falthwën began after a few minutes of rest, "but the tether was imperfect. Incomplete. Hard to discern. After he attacked Kalas, that's when I was sure the *zhàrudzhme* had returned. Kalas, Zhalera —all of you: forgive me. I had hoped to spare Lohwàlar the fate of Kësharan…I failed."

"What happened?" Vàyana repeated in hushed tones, more awestruck than accusatory.

"I intended to consult with my colleagues, to ascertain the ebb and flow of the celestial tides and their potential intersection with the prophecies, but I never made it that far: soon after departing Lohwàlar, I was waylaid by a band of *ekume,* and—"

"*Ekume?*" interrupted Kalas.

"Lightless stars. Harbingers of darkness. Low servants of *Ilnëshras*, the Accursèd One."

"*Ilnëshras?*" Zhalera repeated.

"Chief among the *elume,* once, although that was a long, long time ago. And *elume* are—"

"'Messengers.' 'Warriors.' 'The will-bearers of Ilun,'" said Kalas. "According to the stories, at least…"

Falthwën smiled. "Yes, exactly. Now, where was I…Oh! Yes, the *ekume*…I'd be their prisoner even today had not a like-minded colleague discovered my predicament: she, too, was concerned about the rising darkness; she, too, sought answers, which is how she and I crossed paths. That was two days ago.

"With her help, I escaped, and we confirmed one another's fears. Knowing others had sensed the same thing, I returned to Lohwàlar with all speed, but my wounds required patience. Tsharak, I believe Sharuyan heard your petition: I saw his fire in the sky not too long ago!"

"So he must have," nodded Tsharak. Kalas watched the ancient figure arch an eyebrow as he addressed the cleric, who seemed not to see it.

Did I miss something? he wondered as he looked back at Falthwën.

"If only he'd been able to send his forks of flame sooner…Nonetheless, Tsharak: how would you gauge the extent of the wolves' destruction?"

"It's bad, but it could have been much worse: it will take Sevens to rebuild, but at least enough men and women survived to undertake such an enterprise, and having lived roughly seven lifetimes here, I'm confident they—*we*—have the fortitude to get it done."

"Very good. Vàyana: casualties?"

"Several dead, many more wounded, but not as many as one might have anticipated. Kalas lost both his parents; Zhalera, her father…"

"You never answered her question," said Shosafin, who'd just returned from a cursory examination of the inner chamber. He'd been listening to the back-and-forth from the shadows from which he now emerged. "*How* did you get here?' she asked you. The door was sealed, and there are no other passages within that larger room. I'll confess: you've surprised me, and I'm not one who's easily surprised."

"Magic," said Falthwën with a dismissive half-smile.

"Magic, you say? All right, then: keep your secrets."

"If he says magic, he means magic," defended Tsharak, still silently assessing the bald old healer.

"Does he now? What makes you so confident?"

"Because I've seen it—I've *felt* it before: Falthwën is the one who rescued me from beneath Kësharan," Tsharak contended.

"Then according to your prior tale, that would make him, what? at least a thousand years old?"

"It would," admitted Falthwën. He stood as though he'd never been injured: indeed, his wounds had almost healed, and his bruises, so apparent when he'd arrived, had all but disappeared. His beard, once caked with dirt and blood, now gleamed white; his penetrating eyes blazed from within; and even his torn clothes had repaired themselves, their silver threads sparkling in the torchlight.

"Falthwën?" Kalas whispered as Zhalera clutched his hand. Shosafin gripped his sword, Vàyana took an involuntary step back, but Tsharak just shook his head and chuckled.

"Yes…and no," he interjected before the cleric could respond. "I feel like I owe you an apology, *Falthwën,* for not recognizing you when you first arrived in town. True, your skin's a touch darker, your hair's moved from your head to your chin, and your bearing —your accent, too—are new, but your eyes! Unforgettable, even after all these Sevens.

"I never knew your name beneath Kësharan's ruins. Maybe it

was Falthwën; maybe it was something else entirely. Doesn't matter. Would it be safe to assume you possess other names as well?

The revitalized cleric smiled, and there was something *wholesome* in his eyes, his laughter; an impression of something lofty Kalas couldn't otherwise describe.

"It would not be beyond the realm of possibility, that's true. Tsharak, my child: it is good to see you, although I hoped we'd never meet again—not under these circumstances."

Tsharak held Falthwën's gaze a moment longer; then, with unexpected fluidity and grace, rushed upon him and wrapped his arms around the cleric and wept.

"I've waited almost nine hundred years to say thank you," he said once he'd collected himself and released his silvered robes. "Thank you...Falthwën."

In Kalas' mind, a subtle melody bubbled up from an unknown source, bobbed and weaved across his conscious thoughts like an aria, ephemeral and ineffable, and then its strains receded. He looked around out of habit and suspected both Falthwën and Tsharak heard the same tune, though both pretended they hadn't. Kalas did likewise.

"When Sharuyan set the sky on fire, we were expecting him on the other side of that door," said Vàyana. "Uh, not that we're not happy you're here now, too!"

"Like all heavenlies, *elu* and *eru* alike, Sharuyan serves the Creator's will: I can say with utmost confidence that he has his reasons for *how* he chooses to execute that will."

"Oh," said Vàyana, deflated. "I really hoped he'd be here: I've never met an *eru*..."

6.

"What do we do now?" wondered Kalas aloud, giving voice to the question gnawing at the edge of everyone's thoughts. "My mother and father are...I can't go home! I *can't!* And Zhalera...

"You, Falthwën: you know *magic,* but even that's not enough! What is there for the rest of us to do?"

For a protracted moment, no one spoke. The silvered sage had closed his eyes, his brow furrowed in apparent thought—or prayer, or some other form of communication. He twined his hands together, extended his index fingers, and pressed them against his lips.

"'What do we do now?'" he repeated. "An excellent question, Master Kalas. Excellent question...I hadn't intended to reveal so much in so short a time: now, I must travel to Ïsriba—and, I think, you should come with me. Mistress Zhalera, too."

"Ïsriba?!" Kalas and Zhalera murmured together.

"And the rest of us?" said Vàyana, her features etched with a mixture of fear and wonder.

"Vàyana, my dear, I hope you and Tsharak will be kind enough to remain here in Lohwàlar—"

"But we can help!" insisted Tsharak. "Let us come with you!"

"Tsharak, my child—and you as well, Vàyana: nothing would make me happier than to have you accompany me, but as much as I might desire your presence, this town, its people: *they* truly need you. I won't insist you remain here—I haven't the authority—but someone with your depth of knowledge and experience, someone with your unfathomable empathy, would be best suited to shepherd the survivors, to care for their present needs and, in the days and weeks ahead, to assist with rebuilding."

Tsharak's spirits seemed to sink, but Kalas read in his expression that he recognized the wisdom in Falthwën's counsel. Vàyana nodded, her relief palpable.

130

"Well you're not leaving tonight," she insisted. "Kalas, Zhalera: it's not much, but I have a spare room. You're welcome to it. Come with me and I'll get you settled; then, I'll need to triage the rest of the wounded and—"

"Leave that to me, Vàyana," interrupted Falthwën. "Tonight, your talents would be best employed in caring for this young man and woman. Would you not agree?"

"Of course, *Âu* Falthwën," she bowed. "Thank you."

Something in the way the old cleric spoke unraveled a thread of subtext Kalas didn't quite understand, nor did he try: the day had already taken its most severe toll, and the suggestion of sleep reminded him just how exhausted he was. Vàyana beckoned the young pair to follow her, and they let her lead them through the temple's quiet, musty levels toward the rising cacophony swelling within the Sanctuary. Through lesser-used passages, she guided them toward the street, away from the swell of townsfolk and their shared lamentation.

"Thank you," said Kalas, somewhat numb, as Vàyana brought them into her home: a small, unassuming structure not too far from the Sanctuary. Her spare room housed two small beds with a single table between them. A simple lamp with an undulating flame adorned the table, its light a welcome hint of warmth against the night's oppressive chill.

"It's not much," she began. Zhalera interrupted.

"It's enough. More than enough. Thank you," she repeated. Vàyana smiled.

"Well, should you need anything, don't hesitate to ask: I'm in the next room."

With a small bow, she left, pausing for a glance back at Kalas. Mixed with compassion, he thought he read *curiosity* in her expression. She seemed to feel his scrutiny: her face reddening, she smiled again and disappeared.

"Was she looking at me funny?" he asked and turned toward Zhalera. That's when he realized she'd already shed her massive sword and collapsed atop one of the beds. From the slow, rhythmic rise and fall of her shoulders, he knew she was asleep.

"I'm probably just tired," he convinced himself as he approached the remaining bed.

Too tired, too spent to do much else, he too lay down and closed his eyes.

The lamp. I should put it out before Mother—

With as little noise as he could make, Kalas cried into his pillow, hoping neither Zhalera nor Vàyana would hear him.

When he finally fell asleep, the lamp, still burning, glowed orange-yellow against the shadows.

Chapter VIII

Outside the Skin of the Artifact

"I HAD THE STRANGEST DREAM," SAID ZHALERA WHEN Kalas finally woke. Threads of suns-light shimmered through the loose weave of Vàyana's window coverings: their interplay created intricate patterns on the far wall.

Zhalera sat on her bed, her eyes closed as though she were attempting to will the departing images into focus. Kalas said nothing as he, too, sat up. For a moment, he wondered why Zhalera was here, in his room—then the unspeakable truth of the prior evening rushed upon his consciousness and hammered his mind's eye with scenes of his mother and father.

"Oh?"

He shook his head, tried to forget—for now, at least—the dispassionate fact that his parents were forever gone.

"Yeah, I don't know...I was in a smithy—not Father's, but still, there was something familiar about it. Except it was *clean* —too clean!—like it had never been used, or at least not for a long, long time. I had a hammer in one hand, tongs in the other, and I was standing over an anvil made of some material I've never seen —something even stranger than what you found in the Empty Sea. All around me, even though I couldn't see anyone, I heard voices. Not talking: *singing.* I couldn't understand the words, but there was some message underneath it all, like the voices were trying to guide me. Warn me, maybe. I don't know.

"There was a flash, like oil catching flame from a quench, but more intense, and suddenly an ingot of some…*substance* was *hovering* over the anvil. Metal glows when it reaches a certain temperature—you know that, you've seen it—but this…I don't think this was metal: it glowed, but it was a different glow, a purer glow, like something other than intense heat had made it shine. Like its *essence* was a source of light all its own. It was so bright it cast shadows across the rest of the smithy. The singing got quieter and more intense at the same time. I felt like I was supposed to *do* something, but I didn't know what, so I asked the voices: 'What do you want from me?'

"That's when some vast silence overpowered the singing: everything just *stopped,* and I couldn't shake the feeling that the voices were disappointed in me. There was another burst of light—I closed my eyes, and when I opened them, the ingot was gone! Maybe *ingot* isn't the right word, but whatever it was, it was gone, and everything was dark.

"But out of that silence, I heard a new voice—a woman's voice… singing. I couldn't make any sense of it, not at first, but it kept ringing out, and when I was *just* about to understand it, I woke up."

She looked at the floor, the lines on her face suggesting a mind hard at work. With a sigh and a hitch in her voice, she said, "I wish Father had been there. He would have known what to do…"

Kalas sat down beside her and placed an awkward hand on her shoulder. He started to say something: when he produced tears instead of words, he wasn't all that surprised. Zhalera pressed his hand against her shoulder and squeezed it as if it were her only tether to reality.

"I wish those…those *rudzhegume* had never come here!" he fumed and jumped to his feet, forgetting his sorrow for the present as raw, untapped fury surged through him. "I wish that lightning killed every last one of them! Forever!"

Zhalera nodded, not sure how to respond, though in her features, beneath her shared anger and anguish, Kalas glimpsed uncertainty; perhaps the thought (however distant) that simple, unadulterated rage wouldn't suffice. He knew she was right, but now, however impotent, rage was comfort: grief was misery.

His outburst attracted Vàyana, who soon appeared in the small room's doorway.

"Master Kalas? Is...is everything all—I mean, I—"

With a knowing exhalation, she closed the distance and wrapped her arms around Kalas, burying his head in the fold of her robes. He felt her tremble, felt her gesture for Zhalera to join them, and for one merciful, silent moment, she held the two of them in what felt like a ritualistic embrace: practiced, but wholly sincere.

Of course, thought Kalas: I wonder: *How many times has she had to comfort the ones who remain when the people they love...go away?*

"Madam Vàyana," he said, attempting to redirect his thoughts, "People keep talking about a prophecy. My...my mother: she said something just before she...before she...*died...*"

The words seemed to catch in his throat: for some reason, giving voice to the reality he'd tried to ignore felt like watching Màla perish all over again.

"I'm all right, I'm—no, I'm not. Just...just give me a minute."

The cleric sat him down on his bed. She and Zhalera sat on either side of him.

"*Shâu,* my mother, before she died, she said something about a prophecy from 'before the world was cracked.' Dzharëth said something about a prophecy, too. Tsharak knows something about it: you do, too, I'm guessing, and so does Falthwën. It seems like Zhalera and I are the only ones with no idea what's going on!

"Dzharëth, before Shosafin—what was it, *unskinned* him?—before Shosafin unskinned him, he said something about ending the prophecy, and he came after *me!* What *is* this prophecy? *What does any of this mean?!*"

"Master Kalas, it's not my place," began Vàyana as the color drained from her face. "Mister Falthwën—or even Tsharak, perhaps: it should be one of them. I'm telling you the truth when I say I don't know the particulars myself!"

"Madam Vàyana, please! I just learned I'm not my parents' natural-born son! I just watched them die! And some devil-wolf ranting about prophecy wants *me* dead, too! Is there *nothing* you can tell me?"

The cleric remained seated, her eyes far away, until at last, with a reluctant heave, she confessed, "Here's what little I do know: hundreds—maybe thousands of Sevens ago, the world was shaken. *Cracked,* perhaps, though the prophecy isn't specific. The *edhume* who inherited this changed world had much to overcome.

"Unless I miss my guess, Falthwën—Tsharak, too, I'd say— believes you have an important role to play in events that have yet to unfold. That's really as much as I can tell you."

"A pawn, then," muttered Kalas.

Vàyana opened her mouth to object. Discovered she couldn't.

"Even a pawn can shift fortunes when played by a wise hand," Zhalera suggested.

Kalas' thoughts turned to the night he'd returned home from the Sanctuary and the similar comment she'd made then.

"Like a knife," he whispered.

2.

With her guests awake, Vàyana ushered them into her cramped kitchen and prepared a light breakfast.

"Këndan and I never had children, and with him gone for all these Sevens, this room always seemed so much bigger to me," she apologized.

"No, thank you," insisted Zhalera as she enjoyed Vàyana's fresh-ly-baked *golfras* bread. "It's plenty big—right, Kalas?"

"Yes," he agreed through a mouthful of the same. "You didn't have to put us up. We're grateful."

The cleric smiled, deepening the subtle creases at the corners of her eyes. Kalas had assumed she had five, maybe six Sevens, but maybe she was closer to his mother's age...

"In the Sanctuary, before Falthwën left," he continued, tabling his painful memories, "he'd asked me to keep an eye out for any-thing unusual. Do you remember?"

Vàyana nodded.

"Well, it's nothing that happened *in* Lohwàlar, but if he's really hundreds of Sevens old, maybe he knows about that strange thing in the Empty Sea."

"I'm sorry, what strange thing?" said the cleric, confused.

"Oh, right," he began, and told her the story.

"Strange thing indeed!" she remarked after Kalas had described it to her (with Zhalera's help). "Maybe he does know something about it—I've certainly never heard of such things before! And you know, I wouldn't be surprised if Tsharak might have answers for you, too—if he's as old as he says."

"You don't believe him?" wondered Kalas.

"Oh, I believe him," she countered, "although I'll admit it's something of a shock. The oldest person I ever knew, personally, had only attained three and twenty-one Sevens—and looked like he'd lived hard through every year!

"But Falthwën will most likely be preparing for his trip to Ïsri-ba: you might catch him at the Sanctuary, you might not. Tsharak might be easier to track down. Come, I'll help you find one of them."

Bathed in the light of day, the destruction wrought by the *zhàrudzhme* was all too evident. As Vàyana led them through Lohwàlar's disheveled streets and smoldering structures, neither Kalas nor Zhalera could fully comprehend the extent of the debris that had been peoples' homes and businesses as recently as last night.

The distance between Vàyana's home and the Sanctuary wasn't great, but the streets still thronged with townsfolk in the throes of shock. She led the young pair through the same back door from which they'd escaped the previous night. The halls of the ancient temple had quieted some, but the timbre of pain and suffering persisted.

At the dais, Vàyana inquired about Falthwën's whereabouts, but the young man with whom she spoke hadn't seen him all morning.

"I'm not surprised," the cleric admitted, "but please, if you see him, let him know we were looking for him. We have…some questions for him."

Back outside, Vàyana wove a path for them through the crowd, stopping from time to time to offer what help she could. Despite his own losses, his own fears, and despite the impatience gnawing at his thoughts, Kalas smiled when she knelt before an injured child, whispered something in his ear, and handed him a translucent green lozenge: the lad's surprised gasp sounded curiously familiar.

As they gained some distance from the Sanctuary, the river of bodies thinned; soon, it seemed as though they were the only souls around.

"Father's smithy!" shouted Zhalera as the cleric's path brought them near.

Most of the ancient structure, passed down through generations of Gandhan's line, had been reduced to rubble. Its roof had collapsed—or imploded: regardless, it was gone. Its stone walls, once believed to be unmovable, had visibly shifted and crumbled. Zhalera rushed into the mess.

"Zhalera! Wait! It's not safe!" warned Vàyana. Zhalera didn't listen.

Fire had burned the immense wooden doors from their now-blackened hinges. The young smith leapt over their ashes, climbed over fallen rafters and disrupted stock, and approached the biggest forge, where Gandhan performed most of his work. Now wrecked, most of its bricks had been broken and tossed at odd, canted angles.

"Zhalera?" said Kalas, who'd followed her into the building's remains.

"It's gone. All gone," she whispered to no one in particular.

"Zhalera, I'm so sorry," he offered.

"Right here," she continued. "Right here is where Father used to stand when he was heating steel. I can't remember how many things I watched him make from just over there. Swords, spears, plowshares…things like that. This place feels empty—feels *wrong* —without him here."

"Gandhan definitely had a presence," agreed Kalas.

Vàyana waited for them at the threshold without impatience or any sense of urgency, and for that, both Kalas and Zhalera were grateful.

After a few silent minutes passed, Zhalera turned and, shaking her head, admitted, "There's nothing here for me anymore. The forge is gone, and I—hey, wait…"

She interrupted herself and walked a few steps toward a former piece of the roof. It had landed atop some other debris and formed a small cave-like space. Kneeling, she peered into it; then, belly on the floor, she snaked an arm into the dark cavity and struggled for a moment.

"Kalas, can you lift this?" she asked as she unbuckled her father's sword. It looked like it weighed a lot, but he understood why she chose to carry it.

He found a corner suitable for grasping and made his first attempt.

And failed.

"Heavy," he muttered.

Bracing himself, he squatted and tried again: this time he succeeded in lifting the mass just a few inches—and just for a few moments. Zhalera crawled into the opening he'd made.

"Zhalera!" he wheezed through gritted teeth.

"Almost..." she said. Not to him.

"Zhalera!" he wheezed again as sudden sweat slicked his hands. "I can't—"

"Got it!" she exulted as she cleared the wreckage. Just in time, too: Kalas lost his grip, and the beam he'd been holding smashed the floor where Zhalera's body had been a moment before.

"Children?" Vàyana said and appeared beside them.

"We're fine," said Zhalera. She stood, dusted herself off, and held out a rather unremarkable hammer.

Kalas, still panting, cocked his head. He said nothing, but Zhalera, noting his confused expression, laughed.

"Four-pound hammer," she explained. *"My* four-pound hammer. Father gave it to me on my second Seven. It actually weighs a few grains less than four pounds, but no matter. I have his sword, sure, but that's been passed down for generations. This hammer? He made it just for me."

Now Kalas understood. He nodded. "How'd you even see it under all that stuff?" he asked.

"I don't know—maybe the suns-light hit it just right. Maybe... maybe Father's *kelâ* gave me a nudge..."

"Maybe," agreed Kalas. Vàyana nodded, too.

"That knife I made you? Started with this," she said, hefting the hammer again. "Now, though, there's *really* nothing left for me here."

"Lohwàlar will rebuild," the cleric reminded them.

Their course carried them quite some distance from town, past its outskirts, and up into a series of small hills. Both suns shined bright against the heavens: when they met at the top of the deep blue sky, Kalas *felt* the Song again, with more force than he'd experienced in prior weeks. He stumbled as its melodies seemed to swoop and swirl within his thoughts, much like before, although today its tempo communicated urgency.

"Kalas?" said Zhalera. Vàyana stopped and turned around.

"I'm fine—uh, just…thought I heard something." He made a casual swipe at his upper lip: all he touched was sweat.

"Something…musical?" she prodded.

"Did you?! No, of course not…Uh, I mean, yes: the song."

"Song?" wondered Vàyana.

Kalas thought for a moment, unsure of his next words.

Falthwën trusts her, he reminded himself. *Tsharak, too…*

"Sometimes I hear music no one else seems to notice. Sometimes it's barely there—sometimes *I* don't really notice—but other times, it almost feels like I'm being pushed. Or pulled. I don't know how else to explain it. You don't…*you* don't hear music like that, do you?"

Vàyana smiled: "No, child, I am not so blessed. Tsharak calls it *erunoriyël*—star music: yes, he hears what you hear. Falthwën calls it *Zhi Helim.*"

"The Song?" nodded Kalas. "That's what I call it, too."

"Do you hear it when the suns rise and fall? when they touch?"

"I do!" Kalas confirmed.

"Eru*noriyël*," she repeated. "The suns are stars, too, remember."

3.

Not too much later, the party passed beneath a tall, wide arch and into an almost bowl-like depression. Smaller than Lohwàlar's Crescent, the peculiar space sported many mature trees—some of which threatened to peek above their confines—and patches of grass bedecked with varying species of wildflowers. Toward the elevated center of the basin perched a small, unremarkable structure Kalas assumed was Tsharak's home.

"How did he build those walls?" he wondered aloud.

"*Âsrutaru*—'fire mountain.' Volcano," Vàyana explained. "Dozens of Sevens ago—maybe more—the earth split apart right here. Dozens later, when everything had cooled…this was the result, more or less. That's what Tsharak says, anyway.

"I always wondered how he just *knew*. When you're one hundred twenty-something Sevens, I guess you see a lot!"

In his peripheral vision, Kalas thought he caught a glimpse of something moving from tree to tree. He stopped and Zhalera bumped into him.

"Why'd you stop, Kalas? More music?"

He didn't say anything: whatever he'd seen in the trees was gone by the time he turned for a closer look—which only made him more suspicious.

"Shosafin?" he called out.

"Should chasing prophecies prove not to be to your liking, you'd make a fine watchman," said a voice just over his shoulder. Kalas whirled and drew his knife, but by the time he raised it, Shosafin brushed his arm aside with almost no effort, as though the boy's advance was but a game.

To him, it probably is, Kalas thought.

"Shosafin! Where did you come from?" said Zhalera. Kalas returned his knife to his belt, did his best to hide his embarrassment.

"Adventure has a tendency to follow you," the soldier answered. The question had been Zhalera's, but his gaze remained on Kalas. "It seemed prudent to keep an eye on you. And I mean it: you're prone to rash decisions—pure reaction in most situations—but there's an element of something...*noble* in your choices, from what I've seen, and that attribute is sorely lacking in Ïsriba.

"But don't let me keep you! I'm interested to hear what Tsharak has to say about that object in the Empty Sea, too!"

"You've been eavesdropping!" accused Vàyana.

"*Hish,*" he affirmed without inflection.

Tsharak seemed unsurprised to see everyone—Shosafin included—when he opened the door to them.

"Come in, come in," he said as he stepped aside.

They entered, and as their eyes adjusted to the shaded interior, Kalas noted just how much *stuff* Tsharak had accumulated over his many Sevens: though arranged in neat stacks, his shelves seemed on the cusp of breaking from the weight of all the books and other objects they bore. Laid out on a small table he saw piles of city maps and architectural elevations, as well as copious blueprints. Tsharak noticed his interest and explained, "I thought the city planners could use some of these old drawings for the rebuilding effort: compare what worked in the past with what might be improved. It's providential you arrived when you did—tomorrow, I planned to deliver my findings to Lohwàlar!"

"You and Grandfather probably would have been great friends," said Kalas.

"We were, actually," corrected Tsharak. "Some of these drawings are probably his. In in fact, it's probably my fault his collection became what it did! Sevens ago, I asked him to hold on to a few things for me—including that unwieldy stone table!—and, well...

"I don't receive that many visitors—actually, Wodram might

have been the last person to step inside this place! Anyway, you'll be leaving for Ïsriba soon, yes? Surely Falthwën is better able to answer any questions you might—"

"It's not about Ïsriba," Kalas interrupted. "It's about this...I don't know, this *thing* Father and I discovered in the Empty Sea. In the *side* of the Empty Sea. Gandhan thought it must have been there *before* the Empty Sea *became* the Empty Sea. Falthwën asked me to keep an eye out for anything out of the ordinary before he left. We wouldn't have bothered you, but no one seems to know exactly where Falthwën is, and next to him, you're the most knowledgeable person we know..."

Kalas described the *artifact* and its behavior to Tsharak, who expressed keen interest in the boy's story; however, when he'd finished, the old man wasn't sure what to make of it.

"Your description sounds like nothing I've ever encountered!" said Tsharak. "Do you still have that—what did you call it? *Notpaper?* Doesn't sound like anything of mine: Wodram must have discovered that one on his own."

"I think it was in Father's pack..."

"Say no more. I'm sure it's waiting for you back in town. Whenever you're ready to retrieve it. I'd be curious to see it, of course, but I'm even more curious to see this—what did you call it? An *artifact?* Yes, I'd be most curious to examine this artifact of yours."

"That would mean a trip into the Empty Sea," said Vàyana as the color drained from her face. "I'm not...I don't think I could—And the cliffs! Oh! The stories I've heard! The injuries I've tended! And Falthwën's leaving for Ïsriba soon, and—"

"*Shâu* Vàyana," Tsharak said, his eyebrow raised, "you're under no compulsion to accompany us! Now, I know Falthwën charged you with ensuring the children's safety, but consider this: *Sharuyandas Âsru* unskinned most of the *zhàrudzhme*. The others, even if they returned to Lohwàlar—and I doubt very much they will!—would probably search for the boy among the villagers, not leagues and leagues across the desert!

"I have reason to believe Falthwën's preparations will take some time—days at least—and what Master Kalas has discovered certainly sounds 'odd' to me!

"Ilbardhën, can I impose upon you to escort Madam Vàyana to the Sanctuary and these drawings to Sàrush and the rest of the town Council? Tomorrow, of course: the suns will set before you reach Lohwàlar, and although my home is admittedly small, I have room enough for everyone. And, if you'd further indulge an old man, I'd be grateful for the company."

4.

In the morning, before both suns had risen, Tsharak prepared a simple breakfast for everyone. Over the meal, each complimented their host for his hospitality—as well as his considerable prowess as a cook. Tsharak laughed it off, mumbled something self-deprecating about how it only took him a few dozen Sevens to learn how not to burn the toast, but Kalas understood the old man appreciated their praise.

After the five had finished eating, Shosafin and Vàyana—her relief and gratitude writ large across her face—said their good-byes and returned to Lohwàlar. Tsharak disappeared from room to room, reappearing each time with packs, food and water, and tools for the long hike ahead of them. He'd pause, wiggle his fingers and close his eyes, then resume his task.

"Can we help?" asked Zhalera.

"Thank you, dear one, but we're almost ready—Ah! There you are!" he replied as he tossed another handful of items into his pack and grabbed a sturdy wooden staff. "Let's go! The suns won't last forever!"

• • •

Despite his advanced years, Tsharak seemed to *flow* across the desert: every change of pace well-considered, every movement precise.

Like my father, Kalas couldn't help thinking.

He led them down the Pump Road, pointing out various geological features and describing what they used to look like, how they'd changed over the centuries.

"Those mounds over there: if you were to dig deep, you'd find what's left of New Lohwàlar."

"*New* Lohwàlar?" said Zhalera.

"Some hardy souls attempted to build a settlement closer to the Pump, but the terrain out here, as you can see, seems to invite wind- and sandstorms. The settlement didn't last two Sevens before the desert swallowed it whole. Back then, the wind used to come up fast and hard: there are more than a few skeletons under all this sand."

"Back then?" said Kalas. "Father and I used to come out here all the time. Everything always looked pretty much the same to me —the strongest winds we ever felt were strong, sure, but nothing capable of this!" He gestured at the mounds Tsharak had pointed out. They were little more than gentle rises, easily overlooked by the casual observer.

"Hundreds of years ago—maybe thousands, but I'm not *that* old!—the world was…less stable, let's say: the 'wall' around my home is an example. Volcanoes, earthquakes, floods—yes! floods! —and windstorms were much more frequent. So was rainfire. The sky would change, take on that hot, orange color, and chew apart the ground. As a child, before Kësharan fell, I remember sneaking to the window and watching the storms. My birth mother—*o shelu fie ith nir*—she didn't appreciate my enthusiasm!

"Over time, the storms became less frequent, and when they did hit, they weren't as powerful as they'd been in days past. My adoptive father believed the earth was healing from whatever sickness had befallen it. He said it wasn't as fragile as some people thought, that the Creator had designed it better than that. In the Sevens of Sevens since, from what I've seen, I think he had the right idea."

They reached the rim of the canyon just after the second sun had passed the first. Tsharak happened to be scanning the horizon with his hand raised to shield his eyes when the suns conjoined: Kalas noticed the old man's tattoo shimmering in time to the Song they both heard. He whispered for Zhalera to look: she did, but wondered aloud what she was supposed to be looking for. Kalas told her.

"Ah, yes," explained Tsharak as he caught their stares. "In all my Sevens, Master Kalas excepted, I've only known one other who could see the fire within these marks."

"Who?" Zhalera asked.

"It was a long time ago, dear one…I shouldn't have mentioned it. Anyway, let's be careful—as I know you will be—making our way down into the Empty Sea—the *Ilmilëlas Shada,* or the *Shada pïn Milëlme,* as it used to be called.

"'The Bejeweled Sea'?"

"Just so, my boy! I still have faint memories of its sparkling waves, visible from Kësharan all those Sevens ago. You would have loved it, I'm sure!"

Descending into the canyon proved to be much easier than Kalas had anticipated. Tsharak exercised his uncanny dexterity, and Zhalera proved to be a quick study, their previous excursion still fresh in her muscles. She'd piled her hair in loose buns on either side of her head to let the sweat collecting atop her neck and shoulders evaporate, and all of them had tightened their garments about their bodies to maximize their freedom of movement. After a couple of unremarkable hours, they reached the bottom of the Sea. When they passed beneath the ancient stone archway, Tsharak paused and ran his fingers over its weathered surface, traced its fading contours. Kalas wanted to ask him about it, but something in the old man's expression—

Longing? Sorrow? Regret?

—made him hold his tongue.

As they neared the Pump, Kalas marveled at its almost inaudible rhythm, remembering how loud and asynchronous it had been not too long ago.

Father always did good work, he permitted himself to remember. *Gandhan, too.*

The canyon's cool breezes had made short work of the perspiration that had gathered during their hike: so much so that Zhalera shivered as she unpinned the buns in her hair. Both she and Kalas questioned Tsharak about various topics, amazed at some of his answers and skeptical of others. After a time, the punctuated silences on either side of their scattered conversations stretched until the it was the *silences* that were infrequently interrupted; indeed, the forest itself seemed unnaturally quiet: birds neither chirped nor sang, squirrels and chipmunks withheld their chatter, and even the melody of the River's usual music seemed subdued.

Sap and resin scents, so fragrant and invigorating when they'd first arrived, had dissolved into the background. Soon, an altogether different odor wafted through the air.

"What is that?" said Kalas as he tried to cover his mouth and nose.

"It smells like death!" agreed Zhalera as she followed Kalas' example.

"That's because it is," finished Tsharak as he stepped to the front of the line and scanned either side of the path. "Oh yes, right there."

With the tip of his staff, he poked at the swollen mass he'd discovered, almost hidden by a tangle of thick scrub. The deceased animal's head lolled back, Tsharak's prodding having dislodged its antlers from the low branches in which they'd gotten stuck.

"That looks a lot like the deer from the other day!" exclaimed Zhalera, echoing Kalas' thought. "Could it be?"

"I don't think so," said Tsharak after poking the carcass a few more times. "Putrefaction's already set in—that smell—and that takes a few days. If you saw this fellow only two days ago, even if it died right then, it would still be a few days before he reached this stage."

"But he was...*sick* or something," Kalas insisted. "Could that have made a difference?"

Before Tsharak could respond, Zhalera noticed something plastered to one of its tines: "Hey! Look!"

She unsheathed her sword and pointed to a small scrap of cloth, scratched at it until it peeled away.

"This *is* the deer that attacked Father!" she said, convinced. "This piece of cloth! Kalas, do you remember when it flipped him through the air? It ripped his shirt, and this is part of it, I'm certain!"

She reached down to retrieve it, but Tsharak stayed her hand.

"*De!* No, dear one! Don't touch it! I was wrong: if that fabric came from your father's shirt, and if this animal was sick, then you two are correct, and something...*unwholesome* must be at work. This much decay in such a short time is...abnormal."

He wiped the filth from the end of his staff. With leaves and grass, Zhalera cleaned her blade as best she could before returning it to its scabbard.

5.

"Father said something had been fouling the water," remembered Kalas as the three of them reached the artifact and began erecting their shelters, "but then we found Ëlbodh and Dzharëth and all of that. He thought something might be wrong with the Pump. I guess after I was attacked and he went back to work, he didn't find anything in the River. What if it wasn't the Pump? What if something else is responsible?"

Here, the trees were no longer thick and healthy like those at the trailhead. They'd been displaced by sick-looking trees whose remaining leaves bore splotches of purple fungus. Strips of bark hung like shredded rags from a majority of trunks, and this portion of the forest as a whole seemed generally stunted. Originally, Kalas thought these ill effects resulted from the *ilâegsal;* now, he wasn't sure.

"An idea worthy of investigation," nodded Tsharak as he tensioned his tent.

When their shelters were in place, both suns had passed beyond the narrow aperture formed by the canyon's upper reaches. Twilight filtered through the sparse branches and wrapped everything in a diffuse, warm gray. Kalas gathered firewood and built a small pyre in the ring Gandhan had built only a few days ago. Zhalera tossed him a fragment of flint, and with his birthday present, he showered his handiwork with sparks. Before he put his knife away, Kalas spent a moment admiring it in the fire's waxing light.

"This really is a great knife," he said, and even in the deepening shadows he caught the color rising in her cheeks.

Tsharak walked the perimeter of the dig site, being careful not to touch the object now protruding from the cliff. He paused every now and then, taking mental notes, Kalas assumed, of the shapes and lines etched into or painted on its skin. Satisfied for now, and with the last of the suns' rays dwindling high above, he returned to the fire. From his pack, he retrieved a well-used mess kit, assigned roles to his companions, and, together, the three of them prepared a simple meal.

When they'd finished, Kalas and Zhalera lobbed occasional questions at their guardian while the embers in the fire pit rippled with heat, fading from bright orange to dull purple. Tsharak answered with long, detailed stories—some naught but creative tall tales, he confessed; however, most, he assured them, were a matter of record.

After a while, despite Tsharak's skillful retelling, both Kalas and Zhalera realized the long day was catching up with them. Before they entered their shelters, however, the young man posed one last question.

"Tsharak, you never said what, exactly, you think this…artifact is. Or was. Now that you've seen it, what do you think?"

"I've traveled vast distances during my many Sevens, and I've seen a lot of strange and unusual things. This artifact of yours might top the list. What is it? I have no idea! There *is* something vaguely familiar about it, but I can't place it. Tomorrow, show me those lights, those noises—in the morning, when there's suns-light enough to see! And ask me again."

6.

An almost death-like stillness hung heavy in the air when Kalas awoke. No animal sounds, no wind: just an oppressive, disquieting sensation that permeated everything. Neither sun had risen, not fully, though streaks of light, reflected from long, thin clouds, had begun to stretch across the sky above him.

Father was right about this thing, he thought. His eyes had ad-

justed to the darkness, and he stared down the object, daring it to...
do something.

Tsharak joined him, rubbing his hands together in brisk fashion
as the chill in the morning crept across his skin. Zhalera joined
them moments later.

"I've changed my mind," said Kalas, his voice almost inaudible.
"We're not supposed to be here. *No one* is supposed to be here. This
place is...*wrong.* Father knew it—Zhalera, remember how he got...
weak while we were here the other day? How he got better the further we got from this thing? It was like that when we discovered
it the first time, too, I just didn't realize it then. It took me a while
—too long—but now I know. Let's just pack up and get out of
here."

Tsharak listened with polite restraint. He nodded when Kalas
had finished.

"Two things, my child. One: that apprehension you feel? I feel
it, too. This place is poison, a slow poison that seeps into you, mind
and body, supplants vigor and strength with timidity: I feel that,
too.

Two: in spite of—no, *because* of—those feelings, we *have* to
better understand what you've discovered here. Think about what
you said yesterday: there was a problem with the Pump's output
—something wrong with the water. You wondered if something
other than a Pump malfunction might have caused it. Now compare that with what you just said: something about this place, this
artifact, made Tàran ill. What if that 'something' finds its way into
the River? Into Lohwàlar? We're not that far from its course."

Kalas' mind strove in two directions. His compulsion to get
inside the thing persisted, but so did his father's admonition. After
weighing his thoughts for a moment longer, he reached his decision.

"Father was...*afraid* of this thing," Kalas admitted in a soft, low
voice. "He wasn't afraid of anything. On one hand, he'd want me to

leave it alone, to keep my distance and never return; on the other, he'd want me to do the right thing, and letting his fear become mine is *not* the right thing. C'mon, let me show you what I know."

All three of them approached the place where Gandhan had chipped away enough rock to reveal what looked like writing, and Kalas invited Tsharak to take a close look. He stared at it for a long while: squinted, made frames from his hands, tilted his head…

"I have no idea what this says," he admitted after considering the markings for some time. "Quite plainly, I'm not sure if these are words: if they are, they're like nothing anyone has used for hundreds, maybe thousands of Sevens. Still, I can't shake the feeling I've seen something like this before…Show me again what you did the other day?"

Kalas pointed at various shapes, drawing lines in the air as he tried to remember the sequence. Zhalera contradicted him from time to time until they reached an agreement.

"Something like that," he said, unconvinced. Zhalera offered a weak smile.

Tsharak nodded and eyed the symbols a moment longer. He rested a hand on the rocks, tapping in time to the clucking sounds he made with his tongue. With each tap, a small cloud of dust swirled upward toward his nose, until at last, he sneezed with enough force to lose his balance. He grabbed at the edge of the exposed rock for purchase and steadied himself.

"Mister Tsharak! Are you all right?" Zhalera shouted.

"I'm fine, dear one!" he assured her. "Powerful dust out here! Hey, wait! What's this?"

Where he'd grabbed the wall to keep from falling now displayed obvious signs of fracture. Tsharak's eyes caught flame as an idea seized him: he disappeared within the shelter—long enough for Kalas and Zhalera to exchange confused looks—and reappeared with his staff. With a few well-placed jabs at the new cracks, a hefty slab of rock sheared away from the artifact. Zhalera shoved Kalas away as it tumbled toward the spot where he'd been standing. When the dust settled, they could hear Tsharak's triumphant laughter.

"Look here, Master Kalas! Master—Oh! Sorry about that! But look! More symbols—and *this!*"

Kalas coughed, spat out a mouthful of grit, and scrambled up the fresh talus toward the old man. He followed the end of his staff as he swished from mark to mark, hovering over an unremarkable divot in the thing's side.

"What? It's just a hole in—Oh!"

"What are you two looking at?" Zhalera asked, now standing between them. "A...hole?!"

"It's more than a hole—has to be! See, look right here," instructed Kalas as he pointed first toward the small depression, then traced a vaguely circular shape tangential to it.

Zhalera stared, let her eyes dart from Kalas to the half-moon scoop a few times, but in the end, shook her head and admitted, "I don't see—wait! Yes, right there!"

When her eyes shifted focus, Kalas knew she saw it too—the almost imperceptible thread of black spreading from either end of the "cup," suggesting an ellipsoid path. He followed her eyes as she looked up, to the left; then back to the cup and down and to the left again.

"It's incomplete," Tsharak nodded. "Or, more likely, it's still inside the cliff."

"This can't be natural," insisted Kalas as he let his finger touch the artifact and traced away the thin film of dust that had already settled. The thin line shimmered and glowed a dull blue as some of the newly revealed markings caught light and cycled through various hues. An inaudible, low frequency wave they could feel in their teeth made the ground hum. Loose rocks shook and slid around, and as the three of them each fought for balance, Kalas clutched at the cup until he could regain his feet: only then did he feel the higher frequency buzz thrumming in his bones. A mark just above the cup flashed a bright green and sent out pulses just beneath the object's skin—pulses that traced myriad razor-fine paths, many of which converged at or near enough the edge of the hole.

"Again?" muttered Zhalera, her meaning clear despite her chattering jaw.

"This is great!" exclaimed Tsharak as he followed as many filaments as he could, stepping back to acquire a greater field of view.

"You think so?!" shouted Zhalera as she backed up, too.

The green mark pulsed again, yellow this time, and a low, rhythmic *beep-beep-beep* grabbed Kalas' attention. Some of the other marks—ones they'd unearthed days ago—took up the pattern.

He touched one of the symbols. Then another. And another. He let the palm of his hand linger for a moment on the last glyph.

The mark blinked one last time—a vibrant blue—then went dark, although the artifact's filaments continued to glow for a while. The beeping noise ceased. So did the hum.

The outline Tsharak had discovered faded to its original black. No one spoke. No one moved.

"Is that—?" the old man began: he was interrupted by a hiss as reeking sheets of compressed air jetted from the contours of the outline. Half an oval sank into the side of the artifact about a foot. Thick red light bloomed out of the darkness, revealing an immense network of interconnected rods and fibers within. The still-buried half tried to do the same, but quit with an ear-splitting grinding noise and a burst of multicolored sparks. When the first half ceased its backward motion, some internal mechanism pulled it sideways —in the early morning half-light, the red aura looked like fire inside the canyon wall. The semielliptical shape reached the end of its travel, but something within the artifact continued to pull. With a loud pop, it quit, surrendering in a cloud of thick, blue-white smoke that poured from invisible fissures scattered across its shell. The deep red light blinked out, too; then, the entire exterior seemed to shimmer, fluctuating between its usual rock-like appearance and something wholly alien. A moment later, aside from the gaping hole where impenetrable "rock" once stood, everything looked the same.

"It's a *door!*" coughed Zhalera. "But how did it *do* that? Was that magic?"

"It…*changed,*" noted Tsharak with peculiar coolness.

Kalas had staggered back and stumbled when its contours shifted; now, righted, he jumped up to the opening and peered inside.

Chapter IX

Inside a Darkened Home

"Just what do you think you're doing?!" Zhalera demanded as Kalas thrust a leg over the threshold. "There's no way you're going in there! No way!"

Kalas responded with a sheepish grin. He grabbed onto the door's sill and pulled himself inside.

"It's all right!" he insisted before she could object. "The floor's all tilted, so be careful, but there's another door a few feet in. Here, come take a look!"

She reached up, took his hand, and joined him while Tsharak continued to survey the exterior: with a tentative touch he played his fingers along the now-exposed curve; when nothing happened, he explored each symbol, one by one. It seemed whatever energy they once possessed had dissipated.

"This looks nothing like the outside," said Zhalera. "This isn't metal—not all of it, at least. This part right here: touch it. Feels squishy, like raw meat. I don't know, maybe it's some new kind of metal…but it can't be, because it's been here for ages, right? I'll bet Father would have known."

She coughed, stirred the air, and something vile caught in Kalas' nostrils.

"Hey, I think we should keep our faces covered while we're up here," he said as he pulled his shirt over his mouth and nose. Zhalera did the same. Tsharak, who'd plucked a brand from the fire and a torch from his pack, clambered into the small room. Opposite his light's strange shadows they saw what Zhalera had described as *squishy:* thick ropes of some glistening, iridescent construct connected here and there to various apparatuses, including some embedded in the "door." Those particular cables had ruptured when the door opened—too much pressure, perhaps?—and viscous, dark-green goo oozed from their ruined membranes. Tsharak dipped the end of his torch in a small puddle of the stuff and, with his free hand, wafted its scent.

"Oh! That is *unpleasant!*" he exclaimed, his eyes tearing up.

"Is that what the smell is from?" asked Kalas after a brief series of coughs.

"Only partially, I think: there's something…older underneath it. I don't like it—and not simply because it stinks."

I don't trust *it,* Tàran had said: *The world is* gilded, Tsharak himself had said.

"Maybe we should leave?" suggested Zhalera.

"There's still another door back here!" Kalas reminded her. "We've come this far: let's see if we can get it open."

In Tsharak's dim torchlight, the trio examined the second door, its frame, and its surrounding surfaces for some means to open it. After a few fruitless minutes, the old man passed the torch to Kalas and hopped down onto the fallen rocks outside.

"I think Zhalera has the right idea," he said. "Here, dear one: I'll help you down."

He offered his gnarled hands to her and guided her to the ground. Kalas gave everything another quick appraisal: seeing nothing new, he sighed and turned toward the exit—and slipped on a thin film of slime. Because of the floor's angle, he fell backward, dropped the torch, and, arms flailing, tumbled onto the interior door.

"I'm fine," he muttered in response to Zhalera's giggled question about his well-being.

He grabbed onto one of the shredded, dangling objects and hauled himself to his feet. Tried to, at least: with a wet snap, the thing tore away from its anchor and gushed more of that nasty-smelling green stuff. Kalas was facing the exit again, but the small chamber suddenly filled with cool, bright light. It took him a moment to realize its source was behind him. He whirled. Part of the inner door had become transparent. He took a step toward it, and as he looked through the new window into whatever lay beyond, the light vanished in a fresh shower of sparks: in the fetid dark, he screamed.

2.

"Kalas!" shouted Zhalera, sincere this time, as the young man, still slippery, bolted from the artifact's interior. "Kalas! That light? What happened? What's wrong?!"

He panted, his eyes wide. He held up a hand, signaled for a moment to collect himself.

"Dead!" he said, his voice distant. "Dead!"

"Dead?" probed Tsharak.

"On the other side of that second door! I slipped, must have activated something. I turned around when I saw light coming from behind me. I could see through the door—not a lot, but enough—and just before the light went out, I saw *bodies!*"

He paused, willed himself to revisit the moment, then shuddered and continued: "Almost skeletons with skin—"

"Mummies?" offered Tsharak.

"No, not mummies: just skin-wearing skeletons…well, maybe: they were wearing weird clothes. Wrappings? Like nothing I've ever seen! I don't know how to describe it, but their faces! The one

159

I remember, at least: it looked like it died from terror!"

He coughed, felt something in his throat, and spat blood into his hand. Zhalera raised an eyebrow.

"I—must have hid my head harder than I thought," he said.

"No, my boy, I think it's this atmosphere: just being near this place made Tàran ill, you said? Hmm. Must have been more sensitive to its humors than the rest of us. Come now, let's pack up and head back to town: perhaps Falthwën is back, and we can ask him about—"

"No need," said a familiar voice.

"Falthwën?!" all three exclaimed as one.

"But how—? Where did you—? I mean—?!" stammered Kalas.

"A friend," intoned the mysterious arrival. He made a quick survey of each of them, his gaze more than a mere visual assessment, examining what was *inside* of them as well, it seemed.

"Come on out, Ilbardhën," Falthwën said.

"I should have known," muttered Tsharak as the deft soldier materialized from the thin woods surrounding them.

"I must be getting rusty," he half-smiled as he padded into the site. Acknowledging Tsharak's unspoken accusation, he continued: "I returned to Lohwàlar with Vàyana, as you requested. She insisted on returning to work at the Sanctuary—the state of the town and all. That's where we ran into Falthwën."

"*Shâu* Vàyana told me what you'd uncovered," the cleric took over, "so I set out at once. Your friend Shosafin followed me!"

He gave the *Ïsribarin* a kind smile; shifting his attention to the object behind Kalas, Zhalera, and Tsharak, however, his features turned severe.

"This is your…artifact?" he asked Kalas without looking away from it. There was…ice? steel? something cold in his tone. The way he said *artifact* belied his distaste with the thing protruding from the canyon wall.

"You've…opened it, I see," he added. He held his staff in front of him, tapped his fingers against one another, against his unattractive ring, and closed his eyes for a moment. Although the suns were well above the horizon, not yet touching, Kalas sensed the Song welling up, just above the threshold of perception.

What's going on? he wondered.

Its melody no longer sounded hopeful: it sounded *angry,* and as that perception registered, the young boy flinched.

If Tsharak felt it as well, he gave no indication. Kalas looked skyward, double-checking the suns' positions, then back at Falthwën, who'd since opened his eyes and softened his expression.

"No, not quite," he said, his voice barely audible. "Almost, but not quite…"

No one else moved or spoke. Something in Falthwën's manner seemed to immobilize them in thought, word, and deed. When he relaxed, so did the "spell," and Kalas spoke first.

"I'm sorry, Falthwën, I—after Dzharëth attacked, I forgot about this. When I remembered, you were gone, so I told Vàyana. And Tsharak. Then you came back, but that was after…And—"

"My child, you misunderstand!" the old cleric said with a wave of his hand. "You sense anger, I know, but it's not mine—not wholly. And none of it is directed toward you.

"But I have another favor to ask of you—perhaps not so easily granted as the last. Will you *forget* about this place? this…artifact? Will you all?"

"Yes," insisted Kalas without hesitation.

"Thank you," he nodded. "Now, let's get away from here, get back to Lohwàlar. We should be ready to depart for Ïsriba two days hence."

Falthwën and Shosafin helped the others break down the tents and pack up. The cleric lingered when they started for the trail.

"Falthwën, are you coming?" Kalas asked. He turned, and from over his shoulder, he watched the ancient cleric bow his head and trace a line—a circle? a series of shapes?—in the earth, retrieve a dull, unremarkable stone from its center, and heft it a time or two. Falthwën nodded and hurled the missile high above the fresh wound in the cliff. Maybe it caught the suns-light just right, but Kalas thought it sparkled as it sailed through the air. The others turned toward the noise and looked up as it struck the larger rock face somewhere overhead. It bounced from place to place until it disappeared beneath the rubble.

"Shall we?" Falthwën gestured toward the path. Before Kalas turned away, the old man offered him a secret smile.

Watch, he whispered—no, *thought*—as he passed by the observant youth.

"Coming, Master Kalas?" he said aloud.

"What? I—Yes, sir!"

A couple of minutes later, a sound like thunder pounded the air and rocked the ground beneath their feet. Heat and pressure pushed them to the point of stumbling. Kalas reached out for something —anything—to keep from falling and grabbed at Falthwën's outstretched staff.

"What was that?!" shouted Zhalera as she stood and helped Tsharak to his feet.

After coughing away the sudden cloud of dust, Kalas turned toward the source of the explosion: it had come from behind them, from the artifact site. He retraced his steps: the others followed.

"It's gone!" he said, kicking at the blast-wrecked remains of Gandhan's fire pit.

The spot where the object rested was now buried beneath an immense wall of rock—hundreds of feet tall and half as many thick—that had separated from the larger cliff. Smaller boulders and debris filled in any gaps. No one would ever suspect anything untoward had ever existed here beside the River.

"What are the odds?" said Shosafin, his tone flat, his eyes on Falthwën.

"Astronomical, I'd say," the cleric grinned. "I suppose it's a good thing it didn't happen a moment sooner! Now then, let's make haste: we still have much to do, all of us."

3.

Nothing noteworthy happened as the party continued its trek back to Lohwàlar. When they passed the place where the deer had died, Tsharak whispered something to Falthwën, who nodded, his expression grim. Kalas saw the exchange but couldn't make out their words. Each sun had passed its zenith and begun its descent by the time everyone reached the foot of the trail leading out of the canyon. Shosafin was somewhere ahead of them—or behind, or perhaps on either side: his indifference to the path reminded Kalas of one of Rül's farm dogs. Zhalera had again stacked her hair in twin buns in preparation for the climb, and one after another, they began their ascent, the relative silence punctuated with occasional stabs of conversation.

Kalas slowed his pace and let the others get ahead of him and Falthwën. When it was just the two of them bringing up the rear, in conspiratorial tones the young man asked: "That shape you drew in the dirt: that circle…that rock you threw at the cliff: it flashed like the lightning from the other night right before it hit the rocks, then a couple minutes later…? Magic?"

"Some people call it that," said Falthwën with a bemused expression, "but I'd say it's more like…exercising a privilege, if you will."

"A privilege?" said Kalas as snatches of civics lessons flashed across his thoughts, "So someone gave you the…ability, the permission to do magic?"

"That's…more or less accurate," he said, his crows' feet crinkling.

"Who? Can they give…*others* the ability?"

"Master Kalas, let's suppose for the moment you discovered you *could*, in fact, 'do magic.' What's the first thing you'd do?"

"Mother and Father," he said right away. "I'd bring them back to life—Gandhan, too. And Fërin, Zhalera's mother—"

"I thought as much," Falthwën sighed. Kalas, caught off guard by his tone, looked up at the cleric's fading smile and sad eyes.

"Fortunately for the created order—although, I'll admit, most *un*fortunately, from your perspective—the 'privilege' does not—*cannot*—work that way."

"So you can't just do whatever you want?"

"I'm afforded a certain latitude, but no, I can't exercise my privilege solely as *I* see fit: there are expectations, limitations, restrictions…and I'm thankful for them."

"You're *thankful* for them?!"

"Consider this purely hypothetical situation: Tragedy befalls a little child, bereaving him of his mother, his father, and everything he knows and loves. Time passes, and many Sevens later, another child's father dies right in front of him: this second child is furious and, without thinking, chooses then and there to avenge his father's death. He doesn't appreciate that such a choice will result in *his* death as well, nor does he appreciate the effect his death might have on the world. However, the first child, now a man, just happens to be right there, and he prevents the second from acting out his laudable—yet foolish—decision. This second child, though his world is shattered, forever changed, *lives*."

"That's exactly what happened at the Crescent…but you weren't there! How could you know—?"

"What this second child doesn't know—nor the world, for that matter—is that he has a greater purpose ahead of him. Had the tragedy that shaped that first child never happened, the second would have been cut down, and *his* death would have portended a cataclysm of such magnitude the world has never seen…

"I, too, am a created being, my child: fallible, prone to error; neither omniscient nor omnipotent—and my recall isn't what it used to be. Were I unrestrained and able—and willing—to do *anything* my will conceived, who knows what horrors I might unintentionally wreak upon the cosmos?

"Yes, there are times when I've wanted to be able to do more, but I'm only considering things from *my* limited perspective: I am not the Creator, nor do I possess *his* perspective."

Kalas considered Falthwën's point of view, unsure if he understood—or agreed with—everything he'd said. The way he'd spoken, however, had the taint of some long- and bitterly-remembered experience the cleric seemed loath to discuss further. Kalas let it go.

Back in Lohwàlar, at the still-crowded Sanctuary, Vàyana rushed toward them when she heard they'd returned, eager to learn the details of their recent adventure. As one, all faces turned toward Falthwën for direction.

"Did you learn more about that 'strange thing' you described?" she asked Kalas.

"Uh, yeah…It's covered under a whole bunch of rocks now. A rockslide, I think."

"Oh? That's too bad," she said, her narrowed eyes now on Falthwën.

"The boy's not wrong," he defended, "but I have to ask the same of you as I asked of them—of everyone who knew about that artifact: forget anything you know or thought you knew about it. Please."

"But why? I—Of course! Forgotten! I have no idea what you're talking about! Falthwën, you're scaring me!" she whispered as she considered his stony features with greater care.

"Good," he said without malice. "Now then, Kalas, Zhalera: please remain with Tsharak for a while. When it's time, I'll return to the Sanctuary to collect you, but between now and then, perhaps the lot of you might assist the townsfolk in their endeavors?"

"Why can't we come with you?" Kalas blurted, hurt by what he assumed was Falthwën's casual disinterest in them. The ancient cleric understood his tone and, in a hushed voice, confided: "Young Kalas, the next phase of my preparation is returning to your home. I only wanted to spare your emotions, but perhaps…As I speak, I'm reevaluating that decision—fallible, remember? If you're up for it, perhaps it would be best if you did come with me. Âsrufin: I extend the invitation to you as well."

"Only Father ever called me Firebird!" she said. "Well, and Kalas, one time. Where did you hear that name?"

"Hmm? I…perhaps I overheard it somewhere?"

"Why do you—what do you want from my home?" said Kalas, confused. As soon as Falthwën mentioned it, his mind called up blood-chilling images of Gandhan, the unskinned *rudzhegu,* and his mother.

"We just left them there," he admitted, his voice hushed. Embarrassed.

"I know, my child," said Falthwën as he knelt and placed a strong, comforting hand on his shoulder. "I will ensure their remains are properly addressed before I call either of you to join me… If you prefer, you can stay with Tsharak while I—"

"No, I want to help you," interrupted Kalas. "Not *want to,* but *have to.* I know Mother isn't really there anymore—this might sound crazy, but it's like I sensed her *kelâ* leave her body. Maybe that doesn't make any sense, but all the same…"

"It makes sense enough," the cleric nodded. He stood and patted Kalas' shoulder. With another nod to the others, he said good-bye. Zhalera and the boy followed close behind him.

4.

The first sun had already set by the time the three of them reached Kalas' house. From the outside, it looked like nothing had ever been amiss, but each of them knew the inside would tell an altogether different story. In mere minutes, maybe, the second sun would follow the first and wrap the night in darkness, and the longer Kalas stared at the lightless window high above the main entry, the more it seemed to stare back: a dead eye, glassy in the deepening twilight. He shuddered, and Zhalera, observing, took his hand and tried to shoulder some of the unspoken dread both of them tried to ignore.

"Are you ready, my children?" said Falthwën.

The second sun disappeared, and somewhere beyond the shadows—perhaps from some well-lit place, Kalas thought—the Song insinuated its melodies within the fraying edges of his resolve, gave him strength and renewed purpose; indeed, even though its minor keys were most prominent, a series of subtle major chords undergirded every phrase, and in the boy's thoughts, the music painted scenes of a coming respite, an *elevation* from the sorrow all around him.

"I am," he said. Zhalera, on Kalas' cue, squeezed his hand and said the same.

Falthwën nodded, closed his eyes, and whispered something: the tip of his staff burst into emerald flames which soon settled into more familiar oranges and yellows. Zhalera gasped, and Kalas could tell she wanted to ask the cleric how he did it, but for some reason, she said nothing.

"Follow me," he said.

Once inside, Falthwën produced a pair of scented lanterns—from where, neither Kalas nor Zhalera could say—and handed one to each of them. Their fuel, he told them, contained ethereal oils from various plants and other sources to help mask the fetor of decay.

"Are you sure you want to be here for this?" Falthwën asked again before they rounded the couch and saw the shape of Gandhan's corpse. Neither child said anything, but they held their ground, unwilling to walk or look away.

"Very well."

Falthwën approached Gandhan's remains, knelt, and removed the blankets the children had used to cover them. He began a low, almost whispered prayer of sorts when the bloated figure stirred, supported its mass with its flayed hand, and attempted to rise.

"Falthwën?!" warned Kalas.

"Father?" Zhalera whispered, though she took a step back.

She knows better, Kalas hoped.

The cleric said nothing and acted like he didn't hear the creature or the boy, but as the revenant stretched its putrescent limb toward Falthwën's throat, he swept it away with a gesture and a flash of light, completed his prayer, and stood. With a sharp crack, what had once been Gandhan's corporeal remains became a heap of ash.

"Màla," he said to himself, and took a step toward the great room.

"Who—*what* was that?" Zhalera demanded.

"Something rare. Something I haven't seen in…many, many Sevens: a *shosayedhu,* a corpse 'worn' by a lesser *egu.* I suspected we might encounter such, but I didn't know for sure. That's why I'd originally intended to come here alone, but perhaps it's just as well you gain a better sense of what awaits us in the world at large."

"A ghost?" Kalas wondered.

"No," said Falthwën, his voice flat. He explained: "Without a physical body in which to 'dwell,' as it were, one's *kelâ* enters the *shosathesh,* from which it cannot return: there are no 'ghosts' as such. That doesn't mean that a wandering *egu,* on occasion, might choose to ignore an available host.

"It's rare—most *egume* choose to operate from the darker places within the *shosathesh,* or tether themselves to living persons, the physical and spiritual stresses of which become unbearable for the inhabited, as you've seen. Given the circumstances under which your parents died—and given that *Sharuyandas Âsru* unskinned the *zharudzh* who came here, it seemed likely that 'sentries' of sorts would keep watch."

"Keep watch? Why?" asked Zhalera.

"Indeed," said Falthwën as he made his way to the great room.

He knelt again when he reached Màla's side and removed her shroud. Apart from the dark red stain around her abdomen, her contented expression suggested mere repose, as though she might wake at a moment's notice. Falthwën whispered his prayer, and Kalas walked around his mother's body and knelt too. The cleric stopped as if interrupted. He opened his eyes, looked from side to side, and nodded, his expression quizzical.

"Nothing has claimed her," he said, though the way he said it suggested the observation perplexed him. "Nonetheless, let's ensure nothing can."

He repeated his prayer and reached down for Màla's arm. When they touched, another flash of light overwhelmed their eyes; another sharp crack reverberated in their ears. Kalas blinked, squeezed his eyes shut against the blinding brightness, and when he could see again, his mother's remains had turned to ash and Falthwën was across the room, splayed out like he'd been thrown.

"Falthwën?!"

The cleric said nothing as he stood, brushed away the dust, and returned to Màla's side. Something in his curious expression stayed Kalas' questions. Falthwën studied the silvery pile of dust: with his finger, he traced a series of shapes through the powdered remains.

Kalas' first instinct was anger: *How dare he!* he thought, but there was reverence in the old cleric's eyes, and the boy knew he meant no disrespect.

"What are you *doing?!*" Zhalera demanded in Kalas' stead.

"It's all right," said Kalas, and Falthwën stopped his examination and tapped away the ash from his fingertip.

"Aswanthalu, dhëmmeyahal, although I should have known."

"Known what? What just happened?" Kalas asked.

"The one who delivered you to Tàran and Màla, no doubt," Falthwën said, mostly to himself. Addressing Kalas and Zhalera, he continued: "No *egu* could have profaned your mother's remains —nor your father's, I suspect. Someone who exercises similar privilege must have done something to prevent it."

"The one who delivered me to my parents? Do you know who brought me here? Do you…do you know my birth parents? Why I was taken from them?"

"I do," said Falthwën, sighing.

Kalas waited, rapt, for the cleric to continue.

He didn't.

"Well?!" he demanded.

"I cannot tell you," Falthwën answered after a while.

"What?! Cannot or will not?!"

"Both, Master Kalas. I *will not* because I *cannot.* Perhaps that sounds like sophistry to you, but I have my reasons…For now, I'll have to ask you to abide my reticence. It's asking a lot from one so young, but I believe—I *have to* believe—you're capable of rising to the challenge.

"I'm sorry, my child, for the straits in which you find yourself: none of this is your doing, nor your fault; yet here you are…"

In Falthwën's tired eyes, still sparkling in the lanterns' aromatic light, Kalas caught a glimpse of a simple, unadorned hope. A single chime, deep and resonant, pealed within Kalas' thoughts, and

Falthwën blinked, his eyes suddenly wide. He regarded Kalas a moment longer, then smiled.

"Yet here you are," he repeated. He stood, stretched, and beckoned the two to follow him into Wodram's study.

"What are we looking for? Father and I looked all through this place," Kalas explained, "but all we found was…some kind of weird *not-paper.*"

"Perhaps you'll indulge an old man's desire to look around some more?"

5.

The study looked much the same as it had a few weeks ago, although wind from the home's open door—or perhaps the hole in the ceiling—had strewn a few loose leaves of parchment across the floor. Falthwën stooped to retrieve the nearest page, chuckled as he examined it, and handed it to Kalas. He and Zhalera also laughed at the inartful, child-like illustration.

"Wait—I think *I* drew this!" Kalas realized, and Zhalera laughed even harder.

The two of them pored over the various items contained within the study while Falthwën moved with careful steps throughout its confines, examined not just the codices and scrolls but the surfaces of every shelf, the mechanisms of every lock or drawer. On occasion, he'd tap, press, push, or pull as he conducted his search.

"I told you, sir: my father and I searched this place not that long ago…" Kalas reminded him.

"So you did, my child. So you did…"

"What are you looking for? Maybe I'd remember seeing it?"

The cleric nodded, stroked his beard, and, noncommittal, allowed, "Maybe…"

"Oh? Well, all right, then. We'll, uh, we'll let you know if we find anything," he said.

"Hey, Kalas, is this the book you were talking about?" Zhalera asked as she dropped a weighty volume atop the odd stone table. She opened its pages and flipped to one of the woodcuts featuring *zhàrudzhme* and *zhàfàrokme* engaged in battle.

"Yeah, that's the one," he agreed. He flipped a few pages further and analyzed the foreign glyphs, but he still couldn't understand them. He stopped at a page with an image depicting another battle scene: in it, a lone, sword-bearing *zhàfàrok* defended itself against a horde of *zhàrudzhme;* in the sky above the surrounded creature, seven points—stars?—cast threads of light against the dark mob.

"Hey, Falthwën: can you read this?" Kalas wondered. With the book in his hands, he knocked several works off the table when he turned toward the cleric.

"This room could use a little organizing," Falthwën winked. "Here, let me see."

He accepted the manuscript, flipped back a few pages, scanned its contents, flipped forward a few more—and laughed and shook his head when he reached the image of the solitary *zhàfàrok.*

"Long, long ago, celestial armies battled for the fate of the heavens. Most have heard that story, in one form or another, since childhood. This text relates that story from the perspective of the *erume:* here, in this image, the stars are sending *eruyâsru* against the *zhàrudzhme.* That's all I can say about it, really."

As he handed the book back to Kalas, something near the edge of the now-exposed stone table caught his eye.

"Oho! What's this?" he said as Kalas took hold of the book.

He knelt, examined the edge of the table, and ran his fingers along its border, across its surface, along its every facet. He traced its asymmetrical contours from top to bottom, closed his eyes, and repeated portions of the process.

"Tell me, young sir: did you and your father look *inside* this table?"

"Inside? It has an inside? I thought it was just a piece of solid rock!" Kalas gasped: "Is this table made from something like that artifact?!"

"No, my child: I simply meant appearances oftentimes only tell a portion of the story—or an outright lie. Here, watch!"

Falthwën stood, traced a shape in the air: luminescent green streaks trailed behind his fingers until he brought his hand down hard and fast. Kalas and Zhalera jumped at the loud smack as a surprise gout of flame spurted from beneath the cleric's palm. He withdrew his hand and examined it with a shrug. Aside from the imprint of Falthwën's blow, the table had turned black, like a sooty explosion had rimed its surface with residue. Other than that, it looked much the same.

Sensing the boy's unasked question, Falthwën nodded at the scorched stone and said, "Yes, that's it. Go ahead: touch it. It's perfectly safe!"

Kalas hesitated.

Zhalera did not.

"What did—*how* did you do that?" she asked as she gave the table a quick tap.

Falthwën laughed. Before he could elaborate, the desk disintegrated, its substance crumbling to dust in a series of expanding circles emanating from Zhalera's touch until nothing remained —nothing except a curious object that had been trapped within its structure

"Magic," Falthwën dismissed. Zhalera nodded, contented with his terse explanation.

So much has changed in so little time, Kalas mused.

"Next question," Zhalera continued: "what is *that?!*"

Kalas followed the implied line of her outstretched finger toward whatever had been inside the stone table. It was the approximate size and rough shape of a large knife—a short sword, perhaps—smooth, jet black, and fashioned from a single piece of some unknown substance. In the lanterns' dancing glow, it shimmered in coruscating waves of violet, and Kalas thought it *changed* the light rather than simply reflected it.

Its edge—it *was* a sword, a bladed weapon of some sort, Kalas decided—looked like it had been chipped and polished rather than forged and ground. Somehow, he sensed its edge was sharper than anything he'd ever encountered: he thought, though it made little sense, it somehow cleaved even the shafts of light that dared touch its gleaming surface.

"It's beautiful!" Zhalera exclaimed. She knelt to retrieve it, but, perhaps experiencing the same subtle disquiet as Kalas, looked to Falthwën for approval, which he granted with a bemused nod.

She wrapped her hands around its hilt and lifted—tried to, anyway: it remained immobile, like it was part of the floor, or maybe part of the earth itself. She tried again with identical results.

"Kalas?" she asked, and he placed his hands around hers. Operating in tandem, they tried to move it again, but it wouldn't budge.

"I don't get it," Kalas panted after repeated attempts. "Tsharak said he gave the table to Wodram, said it was heavy, but still, they were able to move it, right? So now that the table itself is gone, how is it that we can't move this thing that was inside it?! It should be lighter!"

"A reasonable deduction," Falthwën agreed. "However, what was *inside* the table was also…elsewhere—and else*when*—for a time. For millennia, actually. I've been searching for it throughout the years. Indeed, that's one of the things that originally brought me to Lohwàlar. I've since learned it's more than mere coincidence that Lohwàlar is also where *our* paths would cross."

"*One* of the things? said Kalas, his interest piqued. Falthwën ignored his question.

"Yes, it's a sword; and yes, it's heavier than anything you're ever likely to encounter. It belonged—belongs to a friend of mine, who lost it many Sevens ago. *Hàfilrifar,* she called it. I think she'll be pleased it's been recovered. I'm hopeful we'll be able to return it to her in Ïsriba."

"How are we going to get it there? We can't even move it!" Zhalera wondered.

"Maybe *you* can't…" replied Falthwën as he grabbed its hilt and hefted it like it was ordinary steel. He smiled, his eyes twinkling, as Zhalera's jaw dropped. With a flourish, he carved another series of shapes within the air before placing it in a nondescript leather sheath neither had seen him wearing before.

"That's just not fair!" Zhalera marveled. Falthwën grinned.

"No, I suppose it is not."

"You have a friend who's hundreds of Sevens," Kalas accused.

"More than one," the healer nodded. "Many of whom I hope to introduce to you. Right now, however, the suns have set and the night grows cold. Let's go."

6.

They walked in silence through the dimming streets, headed toward Zhalera's home, Kalas realized after a short while. When they arrived, it looked like no *rudzhegume* had disturbed it: closer to the Crescent at Lohwàlar's center than Kalas' place, the late Gandhan's estate was far enough removed from the most common routes that it never saw much traffic. In the lengthening shadows, its simple, rustic features seemed more weathered, more *used up* than Kalas remembered.

"Why…*here?*" Zhalera wondered, her words stained with the faintest shade of hurt.

175

"My apologies, my child: I thought, given the hour and our need, we might make use of your home for the night. If you'd prefer, we can always—"

"No, here's fine," she insisted.

She stepped ahead of Falthwën and tried the latch, which lifted without incident.

"Wait!" she hissed as her free hand flew toward Gandhan's massive sword strapped across her back. "Door's unlocked!"

Zhalera started to draw her father's ancient blade from its scabbard but stopped herself.

"What is it?" Kalas whispered, his knife already in hand.

She shook her head, let go of the sword, and said, *"I'm* the one who left the door unlocked. That night: Father told me to come get his sword. I was hurrying and, well…"

"All is well within," finished Falthwën, opening his eyes after a contemplative moment. "If you're certain here is all right with you…"

"It is. Come on in."

With torches lit and placed within their respective sconces, Zhalera raided the larder and spread out what items she could find. Kalas' stomach growled its approval, and he and the cleric joined her in preparing a meal of cured strips of meat, fruit preserves, and stale bread.

When they finished eating, Falthwën nodded toward the mammoth weapon Zhalera had been toting, now leaning up against a wall without ceremony.

"I noticed your sword earlier, in the Empty Sea. It's a beautiful piece: surely your father must have instructed you regarding its lineage?"

"He was most proud of it!" she agreed. She retrieved it, removed it from its sheath, and held it up to the dancing light, which caressed its edge with almost lurid movement.

"He said Sevens of grandfathers passed it down from generation to generation. Everything he made, he judged by this sword. So did his father, and his grandfather, and…well, you know. Before I even began apprenticing with him, he told me it was made from some kind of mysterious metal, something unbelievably strong and flexible. The way he went on about it! Probably what made him curious about the artif—oh!

"He also said no one—none of his grandfathers, even—had ever produced an alloy like the one this sword is made from, and not because they didn't try! Somewhere along the way, one of them tried to melt it down—out of frustration, probably—but no matter how hot he got his furnace, it never took color, never showed any reaction! It's all in his notes at the smithy—I mean, until it burned down…

"But here's the weirdest thing: it looks heavy, right? Like someone my age, my size, shouldn't be able to carry it around without breaking her back? The truth is it's really light! Probably weighs about a quarter what you might think…"

Zhalera grew quiet as sudden melancholy sapped her spirit: Kalas watched her features change with her thoughts. She caught his stare, blushed, and continued, "I guess now it's down to me, but there's so much I still don't know. So much I needed him to teach me…"

Kalas, speechless, raised a trembling hand to wipe away her fresh tears. She smiled, took hold of it with her free hand and pressed it against her cheek.

"My dear, would you permit me to examine your sword?"

"Of course."

She let go of Kalas' hand, turned the hilt toward Falthwën, and offered it to him. He accepted it with peculiar reverence and seemed to search for something within its lines. No one spoke while the old man ran his fingers across its surfaces, tested its weight, its balance. At last, he locked eyes with Zhalera and smiled as he held it sideways for a moment—a moment in which thousands of razor fine, honey-colored lights swirled within and across its faces in subtle ripples—before he presented her the hilt.

Awed, she took it back and stared at it as though seeing it for the first time.

"That wasn't the lights, was it? The lights? Was that the lights?" said Kalas, surprised. Falthwën cocked an eyebrow.

"No, of course not," the boy mumbled.

"Your forebears, Firebird, were men and women of remarkable skill: it's no wonder all of them aspired to the greatness contained within this blade! It's true: Gandhan, your father, had more to teach you, but it's my contention he taught you far more than you realize. One day, I suspect you will surpass him. All of them."

"Thank you," she whispered. Her cheeks flushed as she looked away from Gandhan's—from *her* sword.

"No maybe about it!" puffed Kalas. "Why, just take a look at this knife she made for me!"

He drew his birthday present from his belt and handed it to Falthwën.

"Kalas! Please!" Zhalera hissed. And blushed even more. "It's just a knife!"

"Perhaps the boy's confidence is well-placed?" the cleric suggested as he handed the blade back to Kalas.

"I don't—I mean, uh…perhaps," she allowed.

"Very good! Now, I recommend you two get some sleep: in the morning, we'll make the last of our preparations, say our good-byes, and begin the journey to Ïsriba."

Chapter X

On the Eve of Departure

"**W**e'll need horses. Enough to draw a cart. Of course, we'll need a cart, too," said Falthwën as Kalas and Zhalera, still groggy, sat up. They'd been so tired, so reluctant to entertain the darkness alone that they'd fallen asleep on the great room's floor while Falthwën, Kalas guessed, kept watch.

"I'll admit: I am concerned that people have already employed every available resource in the clean-up effort; nonetheless, without such things, our trip, long enough without complications, will take weeks—maybe months—longer."

"My friend Rül:" said Kalas. "His family runs a farm near Lohwàlar's outskirts—away from all the stuff that happened nearer the Crescent. Most of their horses are probably being worked, like you said, but maybe they could spare one or two. I'm not sure about a cart."

"Horses should be our priority. Let's visit your friend and see how his family might be able to help us."

Despite the fresh wounds inflicted on the town by the *zhà-rudzhme,* the lamentations from prior evenings had given way to the shouts of people barking orders, the blows of hammers driving pegs, and other sounds describing Lohwàlar's resilience. Horses neighed and pulled their carts from site to site. Zhalera ran ahead for a look down the cross street that led to Gandhan's smithy—what remained of it, at least. She returned with a bittersweet smile.

"Someone's cleared away most of the wreckage. That's good. I guess. I just wonder what will become of the lot: that smithy has been in Father's family for generations. Now it's gone, and I have no idea how to start over. Where do I even begin?"

They passed through the rest of the town, the animated noises growing fainter with every step, until they reached the long, gradual incline leading toward Rül's family's farm. The ground here bore sporadic patches of mixed grasses on which a handful of goats and an occasional cow were munching. As they followed the dry, rocky path toward the house—a squat, sprawling structure composed of various eclectic additions erected over the years—a farm hand Kalas didn't recognize almost bumped into him as he stepped from behind an out building, his mind on something other than his surroundings.

"Oho! Sorry, *sà!* Didn't see you there!" he apologized. The suns, still somewhat low, had begun heating the day, and the man mopped his brow with his sleeve. "Looking for Barish? Should be down at the stables. You know where that is?"

"Yes, thank you," said Kalas. "Hey, is Rül around?"

"I…yes, he's at the stables, too…"

"Oh? Is something wrong?" said Falthwën, noting the subtext in the man's frazzled tone.

"Well, ain't my place, and I probably shouldn't say anything—"

"Very well. We'll just—"

"—but lately Barish has been…in a mood, ever since that Dzharëth kid killed half the town. Thinks the rest of 'em might think he was part of it, since he sold Ëlbodh a bunch of goats just before his boy, well, y'know…"

"No one thinks that!" insisted Kalas. The man shrugged and

held up his hands.

"That's what Rül's been tellin' him—what we've all been tellin' him, but Barish won't listen."

"That's…unfortunate," Falthwën frowned.

"Sure is! Well, stables is that way."

The farm hand tipped his broad straw hat and dabbed at his brow again before returning to work.

"The good news is this," said the cleric, his expression wry: "from that man's description, Barish's paranoia probably means most—if not all—of his horses are still here. *Technically* still available. The bad news, of course, is that he's unlikely to part with them. But we're here: there's no harm in asking."

The three figures walked in the direction they'd been given. The few people with whom they crossed paths regarded them with a mixture of curiosity and pity, as though they somehow knew no matter why they'd come to the farm, they'd wasted their time.

After a few minutes, Kalas pointed out the stables, which he'd seen a time or two before. Drawing nearer, two loud, animated voices intermingled with the sound of their footsteps.

"Rül's really getting into it with his father!" Kalas noted with a frown.

Without intending to eavesdrop, they heard Rül say: "How do you think hiding at the farm makes you look?! If you just took a few days—a week, maybe—and sent a team of men and horses and supplies into town, people would realize you didn't know what Ëlbodh was up to! What Dzharëth was up to!"

"No! They'll think I'm tryin' to put a good face on things! That I'm tryin' to throw off suspicion by makin' a big show of it! They'll say, 'Hey, it's Barish! Tryin' to make us think he weren't in on it!'"

"Then send a smaller team! Maybe two or three hands—and yourself! *You're* worried about what people might *think: they're* worried about how they're gonna go on without their fathers, their mothers, their children! Father, I mean no disrespect, but it's been years since you've left the farm: when you send me into town, if anyone says *anything* about you, it's 'How's Barish? How's the farm?' They're concerned for your well-being. I'm telling you: go into town! Offer the farm's services—donate a cart full of staples to the Sanctuary or something! Just—"

"No! I can't! They won't—"

"Forgive the intrusion," Falthwën interrupted, "We've come to—"

"You there!" gasped Barish. "I've never seen you before! What do you want? Did Sàrush send you? You here for my hide?! And *you,* lad! Rül says you said Dzharëth was dead! Maybe the townsfolk should take a closer look at *you!*"

Kalas had no response. Rül, however, disgusted, retorted: "Tàran—Kalas' father—died that night, too! And the townsfolk aren't taking a closer look at anyone! You have no idea what you're talking about anymore! Y'know, it's a *good* thing that a cleric has come to us! Now Mother and I won't have to trick you into an examination!"

"*Âu* Barish, we're here on our own behalf," said Falthwën. "We'd like to borrow a few horses. Perhaps a cart? We have a long journey ahead of us."

"Where you headed?" Rül inquired, forgetting his father's tantrum.

"To Ïsriba," he answered.

"Oh? Yes! Of course we'll lend you some horses! And a cart! If Father won't send them into town, we might as well send them with you!"

"You can't do that!" spluttered Barish as his eyes widened and his cheeks reddened.

"Father! Enough!" shouted Rül. He allowed himself a moment and a deep breath; then, in more measured tones, added, "Never mind. I have…I should get back to work."

With a nod, he stormed from the stables. When he was out of sight, Barish, addressing Falthwën again, continued, "No, friend: I can't spare any horses today. Busy, busy, busy. Perhaps another time. Now, you must go: we're running a farm here!"

Falthwën held the man's gaze. Barish was nearly as tall as Gandhan had been, less girthsome but wiry. A shaft of light snaked through the stable's walls and fell across his face, giving his eyes a manic gleam. The cleric looked past him at the seven or eight horse noses protruding from their respective stalls and tasting the air with their velvety nostrils.

"Very well," Falthwën said with a slight bow. He turned and exited the stables. Kalas and Zhalera, unsure, followed him.

"What now?" Zhalera wondered. "With no horses, no cart, how are we going to make it to Ïsriba?"

"The same way we made it here," he shrugged. "We'll walk."

"Walk?!" said Kalas in disbelief. "Why, that'll take us forever to make it to Ïsriba!"

"Not quite, but come, let's return to your home, Zhalera, and reconsider our options. At this time of year, we may have to postpone our travel: it would be winter before we got there. Perhaps it's not altogether a bad thing: if we're in town, at least we can help with reconstruction."

They reached the bottom of the long hill when the sudden sound of frenzied hoofbeats shook the ground.

"What's that?" Kalas asked, turning. "I got the impression Barish's horses weren't going anywhere."

A swelling cloud of dust obscured the source of the sound and pounded ever nearer.

"Hey! That looks like Rül!" Zhalera shouted.

"Kalas! Zhalera! Mister cleric! Get in!" the farm boy instructed as he reined in his team. Two large, well-muscled draft horses drawing a cart trotted to a halt, snorting and pawing the earth: they looked to Kalas like they'd been anxious for a chance to stretch their powerful legs.

"Rül! What are you doing?!" Kalas exclaimed.

"Getting you to Ïsriba!"

"Master Rül, I appreciate your, ah, initiative, but as much as I disagree with your father's position, I can't condone the theft of his—"

"They're not *his* horses! They belong to Mother as well! The farm belonged to *her* family back in the day. And you saw how unreasonable he was: it's been like that for years! I don't know what happened, not exactly, but I knew he wasn't going to help you. I talked to Mother, explained your situation, and *she* helped me pack the cart!

"Now come on! Climb in! Let's go before Father figures out what's going on!"

"What about your mother?" said Zhalera.

Rül laughed.

"Mother will be fine! She knows how to handle herself—*and* Father! She's the only person I've ever seen talk him down, put the fear in him. When she needs to!"

"Very well!" said Falthwën, his smile genuine this time as he helped the others into the cart.

With a snap of his reins, Rül drove the horses from his family farm in a writhing cloak of dust.

2.

"Where we headed?" Rül asked as they approached town. The horses seemed grateful for the reprieve as he reined them in.

"Gandhan's—that is, Zhalera's residence, if you please: I—we have some things to retrieve," said Falthwën. With a nod, Rül steered his team toward their destination.

With the thunder of hoofbeats abated, the sounds of rebuilding echoed in the distance. Rül passed a few people here and there, each with a surprised (and jealous) expression on his or her face.

"Head up to the farm!" he suggested: "Tell Thara Rül sent you! Mother has a few more horses available!"

The passersby thanked him as the cart trucked away: *"Àd ëthu dàbirafíme nir!* And on Thara, too!"

Rül laughed. "Father won't like it, but Mother will make him understand. And it'll be good for the farm to act like part of the community. It'll be good for the town, too: our horses have been bred for strength and endurance, and it shows! Sometimes I think Father forgets that everything he earns comes from Lohwàlar!"

Both suns had exceeded their apex by the time Rül delivered Falthwën, Kalas, and Zhalera to her home. Before the three of them entered, she told their driver where to find shade and water for the horses.

"I packed most of what we'll need during the early morning hours," Falthwën said. "Zhalera: pack a few changes of clothes and anything else you'll need for the next few weeks—or months. And...pack your sword, but keep it sheathed. Hidden. Here in Lohwàlar, it doesn't matter who knows about it: beyond its borders...who can say?"

Somewhat puzzled, Zhalera obeyed, returning in moments with an old stuffed leather bag slung across one shoulder and a peculiar cloth-wrapped shape across the other.

"It's the best I could do!" she insisted when Kalas fought (and failed) to hide his smile.

"It will suffice," said Falthwën. "That others know you bear a sword isn't the concern: that you bear *that* sword...that's what needs to remain a secret. Keep those cloths in place and none will be the wiser."

Outside, Rül returned with his horses looking fresher. He jumped from the cart and helped Falthwën with his bales, heaving each as though it weighed next to nothing.

Glad he's on our side! thought Kalas.

Zhalera let her bag slip from her shoulder while she adjusted something else. When Kalas reached for it, she started to protest: "You don't have to do that, Kalas! I can carry my own luggage!"

"I know I don't—and I know you can! Probably better than I could! But Mother and Father raised a gentleman, and…well, I just want to."

She grinned, silent except for the subtle clink of her bag's contents as she handed it to Kalas.

When everything had been loaded, Falthwën, seated beside Rül, instructed him to head toward Kalas' home.

"You'll need to pack your clothes and essentials as well, my child. I'd intended for you to collect your things the other day, but I got excited when we discovered Hàfilrifar and, I'm embarrassed to admit, I forgot."

"I'll only be a minute," said Kalas when Rül stopped outside his house. "You can wait in the cart."

"Kalas?" said Zhalera.

"I'll be fine. I'll be fine. I'll be—"

"—coming with you," Zhalera finished, her voice cutting in from outside his darkening thoughts. She'd already started for the door when Kalas caught up to her.

Thank you, he thought.

"You're welcome," she whispered, as though she'd heard his unspoken gratitude.

Inside, Gandhan's ashes had been swept away: in their place, commingled suns-light, descending from the hole in the roof, stood guard like a luminal sentry. Zhalera walked into its warmth, closed her eyes, and waited for a moment. Kalas followed.

"I wouldn't have been able to come back here without you, Kalas," she confessed. "This light, though, shining on the spot where Father died, having done everything he could to fight against the darkness…I thought I never wanted to set foot in this place again, but now, I think I could stand here forever, surrounded by this."

With a reluctant sigh, she stepped into the relative gloom, shivered, and looked to Kalas, who nodded, turned, and took a step toward his room. He realized at some point he'd taken hold of Zhalera's hand—or maybe she'd taken his?

"I, uh, it's this way," he stammered." She giggled, and the suggestion of cold sloughed away.

After cramming a few changes of clothes into a pack, Kalas ducked into Wodram's study and scanned it for the ancient book with its elaborate woodcuts and indecipherable text. He stuffed it into his pack, too.

"I don't know, it's just, well, Father and I ended up spending a lot of time studying this thing, and…" he began, but Zhalera understood.

"Is that everything?" she asked.

Kalas didn't answer right away. After a long moment, he shook his head.

"You stood in the light. Now I have to stand in the shadow. One last time. Will you—will you come with me?"

You know I will, he read in her expression as she followed him into the great room where Màla had breathed her last.

No heavenly fire had punched a hole in the roof above her, and with the suns still hours from descending beneath the horizon, the shadows here were deep, tempered only by trace amounts of daylight. Someone had swept away her ashes as well, and a few weak sunbeams highlighted the indelible stains of Màla's blood. Kalas knelt and traced the undulating scarlet outline with his finger.

"I'm not sure what I expected," he admitted, standing after a moment of silence, "but if nothing else, the…the *emptiness* of this place makes it clear that Mother is altogether gone. I didn't *think* I doubted that, but now I *know* I don't. Let's go."

3.

"There are a few items I must discuss with Vàyana—and Tsharak—before we leave for Ïsriba, which, it seems, will be tomorrow. Master Rül, if you and your horses would be so kind?" said Falthwën as Kalas tossed his things into the cart and he and Zhalera took their seats. With a curt nod, Rül flicked his reins. His horses snorted and headed out.

The drive through town revealed more progress with reconstruction than Kalas would have thought possible in the intervening days. People had cleared away vast piles of rubble and started repairs on the damaged structures. Sweat-soaked citizens offered brief waves here and there: most seemed too engrossed in their labors to notice the team's presence.

Kalas had been so rapt with the panoramic spectacle that he didn't realize Rül was taking them through the Crescent until they were already there. He sucked air through his teeth with a sharp hiss, and even though he didn't want to see the place where Dzharëth had killed his father, he couldn't keep his eyes from wandering, scanning the earth until he—there! Just ahead of them, where a small gathering had congregated and blocked the road. Rül stopped.

"What's going on?" said Kalas as he stepped forward.

"Not sure," Rül answered. One of his horses—the darker bay

—pawed the ground in his impatience.

Kalas' question—and the impatient horse—grabbed a member of the crowd's attention.

"Master Kalas!" he said with surprise, and Kalas realized it was Azhëk, the man who'd been on shift with his father. "It's gonna go right here—*right* here! And it's gonna be beautiful! And Tàran's name is going to be at the top!"

"What? I'm sorry, what are you talking about?"

Another, somewhat more somber figure Kalas knew by face but not by name joined Azhëk and explained: "The Council has decided to erect a monument celebrating the *kelâme* the *zhàrudzhme* took from us. You'll have to forgive Azhëk his exuberance: we haven't finalized such details. But Tàran was a good man. A great man. Did much for Lohwàlar. He understood the Pump better than anyone I've ever known—"

"That's the truth!" Azhëk interrupted, nodding his hearty agreement.

"When it's time to decide such matters, I'll do my part to ensure his name is writ large. Màla's, too," the unknown man finished.

Kalas didn't know how to respond. He thought of all the people slain—the ones he knew, at least, even Commander Valderïk—and had to fight back tears.

"Uh, thank you. Thank you, Mister…?"

"Hebul."

"Thank you."

Their conversation over, Hebul gestured for the others with him to move aside. Rül reminded them his farm had a few additional horses that could be of service: "Talk to Thara—*not* Barish!" he said as he guided his cart along the street.

Activity at the Sanctuary had subsided, although a steady stream of people still flowed in both directions through its doors.

Falthwën, having instructed Kalas, Zhalera, and Rül to remain with the cart, stepped down with a grace his age belied and made his way through the human river. In minutes he returned with Vàyana and Tsharak. Even though the former had made it clear she was most content to remain in Lohwàlar, Kalas thought he saw the tincture of regret mingled with apprehension cloud her expression. Tsharak's face spoke the opposite: as much as he wanted to travel to Ïsriba, to be part of an adventure unlike anything he'd experienced in well over one hundred Sevens, he understood and accepted Falthwën's rationale that he remain in town and assist with its rebirth.

"How long will you be away?" Vàyana asked as she glided toward the horses, stroked their manes and scratched their cheeks.

"Are you asking because you're concerned about our welfare… or because you'll miss these horses?" Falthwën laughed.

"Maybe both," she teased. "Long before you came to Lohwàlar —long before Thara ever married that clown Barish—I spent Sevens tending her father's stables. In fact, if I'm not mistaken, this buckskin's sire was a grullo named *Wir-zhi-bethru*."

"You've got a good eye, lady!" said Rül. "This here's *Palev-ho-thalme*—Dancer for short. Racer's grandson."

"Oh? You're familiar with Hirom's stable? Well, *Thara's* stable now!"

"I should hope so!" he laughed.

"Vàyana, this is my friend Rül," said Kalas.

"Rül? Where have I heard that name before?"

"Thara's son."

The typical warmth in the cleric's features drained away as she froze mid-stroke. Dancer snorted his displeasure, canted his head into her motionless fingers.

"Oh…" she said, her voice small. "I'm sorry! I—"

Rül laughed again, louder this time.

"No offense taken, lady! Lately, Father *has* been acting like a clown. Can't blame you for calling it like you see it! Oh—the bay's name is Runner. Strider's offspring."

"'Racer,' 'Dancer,' 'Runner,' 'Strider'?" said Kalas, his eyebrow raised. "Seems like there's a theme here!"

Rül shrugged. "Runner's easier to say than *Reshir-dïl-âsru!*"

"Strider must have been after my time, but Dancer and Runner are beautiful creatures, Master Rül," said Vàyana, succumbing to Dancer's insistence and massaging his cheek again.

"I can't say with any certainty just how long we'll be away. A month, I suspect, is an aggressive estimate," Falthwën stated. "Probably a month and a half at least. There are just so many variables, and I can't account for all of them. Not yet, anyway."

"You'll take the King's Highway?" asked Tsharak as he peered at the cart's contents. "You're prepared for more than a few nights under the stars, I assume? I'm sure you know better than I do that towns are sparse between here and Ïsriba. The kindness of strangers even more so."

"I'm well-aware, old friend," Falthwën concurred. He glanced at Kalas and Zhalera, at Rül, and added, "I suspect we'll manage."

Something shifted at the fringe of Kalas' perception. He looked around; seeing nothing, he almost dismissed the sensation when he thought to look *up* as well.

"We'll have Shosafin with us, too," he smiled.

4.

With a series of effortless leaps, bounds, and somersaults, the soldier descended from his almost-unnoticed perch among the friezes of the ancient Sanctuary.

"At your service, Master Kalas," he said with a nod as he planted his feet on the ground.

"Very good!" exclaimed Falthwën. "Perhaps your membership

within our company will grease the wheels of the court once we've entered Ïsriba."

"Perhaps," allowed Shosafin. "Perhaps not."

"Oh?" said Falthwën, though his tone implied he suspected as much.

"It's no secret among the queen-regent's courtiers that I'm… something of a misfit. One of the reasons I volunteered to come to Lohwàlar."

"Nonetheless, you know the ins and outs of *Poyïsriba* society, its customs and mores, and whether you fit in or not, such knowledge should help us avoid excessive attention."

The soldier nodded his agreement.

"Uh, mister cleric, sir? I'm not sure there's room in the cart for anyone else—or his stuff," said Rül: he'd been trying, without success, to rearrange things while Shosafin and Falthwën had been speaking.

"Oh, I won't be traveling *with* you—not in the cart, that is," said the soldier. "I've, ah, made other arrangements!"

"Did your horse from Ïsriba survive the *rudzhegume* attack?" Kalas wondered.

"Sadly, no: they destroyed the entire garrison and all the horses in its stable."

Shosafin glanced at Rül, offered him a sly half-smile, and added: "Here, let me show you."

He tucked his tongue behind his teeth and gave a shrill whistle; soon, hoofbeats thundered ever nearer until his mount—an immense, raven black stallion with a silver blaze—galloped into view. The imposing creature came to a stop and pawed the ground, and even in the rising dust, he shimmered.

"Breaker!" shouted Rül, his amazement bare. "He's Mother's most prized horse! One I would have taken—if I'd dared! (No disrespect Runner, Dancer!) How did you ever convince her to let

him go?!"

"I heard you were volunteering Thara's horses," he explained with uncharacteristic detail as he ran a hand over Breaker's withers. "When I got to your farm, I spoke with your mother and learned all of her other horses had been borrowed. I was about to leave, but she saw my scabbard with its *Poÿisriba* crest: she grabbed my arm and insisted I keep you safe—to that end, she confessed she had one more horse...

"Though I doubt you need to hear it from me, your mother's most proud of you. Concerned, but not overly so.

"And I can see why *Kursh-pïni-nimhàfil* is her favorite! Catches onto things quickly: by the time we reach Ïsriba, we'll be old friends."

"Master Kalas, a word, please?" said Tsharak. Shosafin had checked and double-checked Breaker's tack and the rest of his gear; Rül secured his cart while reassuring Runner and Dancer that they were good horses, too; and Zhalera, having glanced in the old man's direction, made a show of listening to Falthwën and Vàyana discuss something.

Probably Sanctuary stuff.

Tsharak beckoned Kalas to follow him a short distance, just out of earshot of a quiet whisper. With his back to everyone else, he reached beneath his outer garment and produced a small package wrapped in a fragment of treated skin.

"At the bottom of the Empty Sea: do you remember me saying there was something familiar about that...that artifact that we're not supposed to talk about?"

"Yeah, that's right! You told me to ask you about it again in the morning, but I never did. But should we be talking about it now? Falthwën told us to *forget,* right?"

"That he did, my boy, that he did—and maybe he has the right idea about that thing, but when I returned home, I couldn't ignore that familiarity, so I did some digging around in my collection and stumbled across *this*—"

With haste, Tsharak unwrapped his prize. Cupping it within his shaking hands, he showed it to Kalas.

"I think it's made from the same material as that thing! And look: if you're careful, you can see similar markings all around its faces!"

Stunned, Kalas reached for it, then pulled away.

What if it reacts?

What Tsharak held bore an unmistakable resemblance to the skin of Kalas' artifact, but it was darker in places, like it had been through fire, perhaps. As he turned it, exposing its different angles to the suns-light, Kalas noted the glyphs carved or etched into its surface. Overall, it had an ovoid shape, interrupted in spots with flat planes. He nodded, and Tsharak quickly rewrapped it.

"I wish I could remember where I found this—or maybe who gave it to me? Eight-hundred years does a number on one's memory! I've had this for Sevens of Sevens—at least—and I've never known what it was nor where it came from. In fact, if you'd never shown me your artifact, I probably never would have remembered it at all!"

Maybe that would have been best?

Tsharak must have gleaned Kalas' thought from his expression.

"Maybe I shouldn't have shown you…I'm sorry, Master Kalas! I know what Falthwën said—and when I know more, I'll bring it to his attention, but for now, I thought you, of all people, would want to know…"

"No, it's okay, Mister Tsharak. Really." Warming to the subject, his tone less strained, he added: "What do you think it's for? Do you think it has anything to do with the…thing, or is it just made from something like it? Where do you think it all came from?"

"*Âu* Tsharak! A moment?" called Falthwën.

"I'll keep digging," Tsharak whispered as he slipped the object back into his pocket. "Maybe I'll learn—or remember—something by the time you return from Ïsriba!"

He offered Kalas a clipped nod, then smiled broadly as the pair joined their peers.

5.

"Oh, that's right," said Vàyana, and she disappeared within the Sanctuary. After a minute or two, she reappeared with Tàran's belongings. She offered them wordlessly to Kalas, who hesitated just a moment before accepting his father's pack.

"Uh, thank you, *shâu,*" he said, somewhat numb.

He allowed himself a moment; then, remembering the translucent object within, rifled through tanned skins and stale rations until he found it. Kalas held it up to the suns, let their light filter through it, and studied the symbols scribed upon its surface. Here, under the open sky, the item *consumed* rather than reflected the suns' rays just as it had back in his grandfather's study: this time, however, as its internal filaments absorbed and pulsed with solar energy, the symbols shifted to reveal a separate arrangement of markings *in between* either side of the leaf.

"Did you see that!" he shouted as he turned the sheet over and examined its other side.

"See what?" said Zhalera.

"Look! *Look!*"

He held it out for everyone to examine. Zhalera studied it, squinted, and tried to discern the source of Kalas' excitement. She couldn't.

"It looks like it did before. I think. Mostly. Doesn't it?"

"It changed! These pictures—markings, glyphs, whatever— they changed!"

195

"Did they? I guess I don't remember what it looked like."

No one else present had seen Kalas' *not-paper* before, but he'd piqued Falthwën's interest. Tsharak glanced at his breast pocket then looked away.

"That's what you and Tàran discovered in Wodram's study? I believe you mentioned it. May I see it?"

Kalas handed the object to the cleric, who ran his eyes across its surfaces, held it up to the light, and tilted it much like Kalas had. He poked and prodded and furrowed his brow. His lips moved, but he made no sound.

"Interesting," he said at last. He handed the item back to Kalas.

"Do you know what it is? what it says?" he asked.

For a moment, Falthwën said nothing. Even though his eyes stayed opened, flashed a brilliant green in the waning suns-light, Kalas sensed he was somewhere else—maybe some*when* else.

"The writing—I'm pretty sure it's writing—is familiar, some-how, but I can't read it. Not now, at least. Maybe I could have, once upon a time..."

"Doesn't it look like those symbols on...uh...yeah, never mind..." Kalas blurted before catching himself. He felt his cheeks burn. Falthwën only chuckled.

"Yes, it does. I had the same sense then, too. In a way, it's maddening, feeling like something's right on the cusp of conscious perception, only to have it slip away without resolution. I spoke to you of *privilege*. Of restrictions. My inability to understand these words—if they *are* words—is, I believe, one such restriction, and, maddening as it is, I trust there's a reason for it. A good reason. But come, let's discuss what happens here while the rest of us are away."

On their way to the chamber deep beneath the Sanctuary—the *Temple,* Kalas remembered—most everyone said nothing, although

Rül couldn't refrain from expressing his surprise:

"What is this place? It's always been here? What's this *Randa pïni Sharumilël?*"

Kalas and the others did what they could to bring him up to speed.

"That's…that's a lot to take in! Sounds like a story my grandfather might've told! Who else knows about this place? This…*Order?* How come no one talks about this stuff anymore? I mean, if this Sharuyan character can really help with crops, I bet even my father would make the trip! I know I would!"

"Just because the *Lohwàlarrinme* have forgotten him doesn't necessarily mean he's forgotten them," suggested Falthwën as they reached the last of the spiraling steps.

Invisible lights, tinted with subtle green coronae, whooshed into existence along the cavernous room's perimeter as the old cleric ushered them inside.

"What was that?!" shouted Rül, his voice echoing throughout the abandoned space.

"Long story," Zhalera grinned.

Shosafin disappeared into the flickering shadows, but he kept within earshot as Falthwën outlined his intentions.

"Tomorrow, before the second sun breaches the horizon, the five of us will begin the journey to Ïsriba.

"Ilbardhën, while you're free to move as you will, it's my hope that you and Breaker will range the land around us and keep us informed of anything untoward you might discover. It will take us weeks should nothing unexpected happen; still, we should reach Ïsriba just as the leaves begin to fall.

"Vàyana, you'll resume your administrative duties. Be mindful of anything out of the ordinary: I know you will be. It appears the starfire managed to spare Lohwàlar the worst parts of Kësharan's fate, and for that, I'm grateful! Your people possess astounding resilience."

"Tsharak, my son: Sàrush knows about your bravery when the wolves fell: he knows you summoned Sharuyan's fire. He's been made aware of your command of *Polohwàlar* history as well. Become a mentor to him: you'll find he's put away his former arrogance.

"Listen to The Song: let it guide you where it will. Learn from its rhythms, divine the signs and portents from its prosodies and counterpoints, and bear witness. Though I'm loath to admit it, there's dread woven within its melodies: subtle, but present.

"That's enough, I think. Children, return to Zhalera's place: eat, *sleep*, and expect me in the morning, when Nalënahwu sunders the darkness.

PART II.

CHAPTER XI.

Away from Lohwàlar

OHWÀLAR DISAPPEARED IN A ROSE-COLORED CLOUD OF dust, the shape of its ancient temple glinting in the slant rays of the first sun's rising light. South of Lohwàlar, the earth descended many feet toward the rim of the Empty Sea. Returning to town had always been an uphill climb—a minor one, but a climb nonetheless—and home had always seemed so big, so present. The road to Ïsriba took them farther north than Kalas had ever ventured from his hometown, and seeing it shrink into the distance behind and beneath the road's gentle slope punctuated his acute and over-whelming sensation of insignificance.

My world has been so small, he noted.

True to his word, Falthwën arrived at Zhalera's home within moments of Nalënahwu creeping into view. In silence, the four of them wolfed down a quick breakfast, found their places in the cart, and—*finally!* Kalas grumbled—started for Ïsriba. Shosafin kept himself hidden most of the time, but on occasion he steered Breaker across the cart's path, let the party ken his presence, then dissolved into the surrounding dunes and scrub. He and Falthwën shared a whispered conversation just before departing, but Kalas hadn't been able to make out its substance.

"He wasn't wrong," Rül remarked with a shake of his head. "Breaker is *Mother's* best horse, meaning so long as *she's* the one behind the reins, he's the strongest, fastest creature on the farm. Sometimes—on good days!—I can get him to obey, but not like Mother. I'll be honest: I'm more than a little jealous he's taken so quickly to Shosafin!

"It's all right, though: Runner and Dancer make a great pair. Don't you, fellas? You'll get us to Ïsriba, won't you?"

Runner and Dancer snorted, and Kalas laughed to hear the begrudging acknowledgment in their reply.

The skies were clear, the suns vibrant, but the accumulation of hills and valleys eventually obscured Lohwàlar from view. As the leagues piled up behind them, the desert sands gave way to firmer, rockier ground: squat trees dotted the landscape and displaced some of the boundless scrub. After a few more hours, the trees grew thicker. Taller. More like the forest at the bottom of the Empty Sea, thought Kalas, who said as much.

"This is so different from home!" Zhalera agreed.

"Even out there, I always knew I'd be home in a day or two," Kalas continued. "Part of what makes this so different is not knowing when we'll be home. I guess now there's not much of a home to return to…"

The woods through which they traveled became denser still as undergrowth thinned out beneath the spreading limbs of ancient, twisted oaks and maples, sprinkled here and there with pines and firs. Kalas looked up at the last rays of the first sun piercing the lofty canopy with faint, silvery light. A breath of cold air slithered across his skin. He shivered.

"Mister Falthwën?" said Rül as he reined in his horses. In front of them stood an immense ash, perhaps seven feet in diameter. The road split at its base. Long ago, perhaps, the faded sign tacked to it would have been legible; now, it seemed as though the tree had grown around the sign, swallowing portions of it within its ever-expanding trunk.

"To the left, Master Rül," Falthwën said without hesitation.

"Couple days to the right will take you to Serular," added Shosafin as he and Breaker appeared without warning. "Nasty place. Nowadays, anyway."

"Serular? What's so nasty about it?" wondered Kalas, but Shosafin had already disappeared.

"That guy," he muttered. Zhalera laughed.

"He's not wrong," noted Falthwën. "Anyway, what little light remains is fading fast. Perhaps an hour more—maybe less—and we'll camp for the night. I don't anticipate much company. Probably no more than we've had all day."

"We haven't seen anyone—oh!" said Kalas as he realized the old cleric's joke. Falthwën smiled and continued: "Still, I'd prefer to be *prepared*, should the need arise. Some distance off the main road." He cast a glance in Shosafin's approximate direction.

"It sounds like you're expecting trouble. Are we safe out here?" said Zhalera, her eyebrow raised.

"I'm not *expecting* trouble, Firebird, but one never knows. And are we safe? No, my child, we are not."

2.

At Falthwën's direction, Rül drove his team down an almost invisible trail, forgotten over long years by all appearances. Roughly a mile from the main thoroughfare, he and Kalas set up camp. When they'd finished with the tent, the cleric told Rül about a nearby stream. The farm boy nodded, grabbed a bucket, and disappeared into the woods.

Kalas' eyes adjusted to the weak light, but the *weight* in the air still unnerved him. In the desert, every variation in temperature conjured some suggestion of wind, whether breeze or bluster; here, however, between these massive trunks and beneath this almost impenetrable shroud, the air seemed to hang, immobile, suffocating any noise and pressing against his ears. The forest at the bottom of the Empty Sea—the only forest he'd ever known until today—felt *nothing* like this.

"It's weird, isn't it?" said Zhalera. Kalas jumped: he hadn't heard her approach through the blanket of pine needles and leaves piled high atop the forest floor.

"The air," she continued, divining, it seemed, his own unspoken thoughts. "It's weird. Heavy, almost. Makes me miss the desert.

"Falthwën, have you been here before? I mean, how did you know where to turn? where to find water?"

"Not too long ago, in fact," he nodded. "And you'll get used to the atmosphere. Eventually."

Kalas dug a shallow pit for a small fire. With every turn of his spade, he remembered the joy in Gandhan's face when he handed it to him. Sharp as a knife, its blade made short work of the thinner roots just beneath the ground. He tossed a few more sticks on the pyre when Rül stepped into the circle of light, his full bucket at his side.

"I thought I heard voices!" he hissed at Falthwën. "Somewhere down the stream, maybe. I don't know—sound is weird in here."

"Voices, you say?" The cleric arched an eyebrow.

"Yeah! Well, maybe. I don't know, really. Could've been the stream, I guess. Like I said: sound is weird in here."

"That it is, my child. That it is. Still, it never hurts to keep alert. I suspect Shosafin is evaluating our perimeter, but Kalas: let's keep the fire low tonight, yes? Now, the three of you: Eat. Get some sleep. I'll keep an eye on things."

"Wake me when it's my turn," said Kalas as he spread the smoldering elements of his fire. Falthwën nodded, his eyes twinkling —from within or from the fire, the young man couldn't say.

After a quick meal, Rül, Zhalera, and Kalas retreated beneath the shelter of their tent.

It's amazing how tired I am when all I did was sit *all day!* the young man acknowledged as unexpected fatigue swept over him. He blinked and looked over at Zhalera, who had already fallen asleep; at Rül, whose shoulders heaved with slow rhythm in time to his subtle snoring; and, through the flap that served as a door, at Falthwën's back. The old cleric sat a few yards from their tent, his staff across his lap.

A rising prickle against his senses gave him pause just moments before Shosafin, sword drawn, stepped into the dying fire's feeble glow. As he turned to address Falthwën, Kalas thought he caught a glimpse of something red (or maybe black) along the length of the warrior's blade. He turned again and obscured Kalas' view.

"Rül's 'voices'?" Falthwën whispered with a nod toward Shosafin, who said nothing, only wiped his sword with a handful of pine needles before returning it to its sheath.

"It seems, then, that you were right. At least now we know."

3.

"Kalas!" Zhalera whispered as she gave him a gentle shake. "Kalas! Wake up!"

"What? Where—Oh! Right! I'm awake, I'm awake!" he insisted as he sat up and rubbed the sleep from his eyes.

"Here, eat while Rül and I pack up. Falthwën says we need to get back on the road soon."

She thrust a handful of *golfras* bread toward him and disappeared. Kalas chewed with mechanical indifference as he recollected his thoughts from the night before. When he finished his breakfast, he exited the tent and looked around, wondering if—there! He locked eyes with Shosafin, wholly unsurprised that the grizzled warrior seemed to be waiting for him.

"I'll be right back," he said to no one as he approached the man.

"Master Kalas," he nodded.

Kalas said nothing, just held Shosafin's inscrutable gaze.

"No questions, then?" the soldier said at last.

"Maybe one," confessed Kalas as his eyes flicked toward Shosafin's sheathed sword. The first sun had almost crested the horizon: precious few of its rays pierced the depths of the forest; some, however, glinted red from the steel peeking from Shosafin's scabbard.

"That's more like it!" he smiled.

"Did you...? Whose voices did Rül hear?"

"The other day I told you all I was something of a misfit in queen-regent Ësfàyami's court. *Misfit* might have been an understatement. In simpler terms, I don't belong there. Not anymore."

"What?! Why not? From what I've seen, you're the best—"

"Oh, I belong in *King Rufàran's* court. *Not* Ësfàyami's."

Kalas said nothing. After a while, Shosafin laughed and continued: "You have other questions, yes? Let me give you a brief history of Ïsriba, see if that answers at least some of them.

"Sevens ago, before Queen Helëstal died in childbirth I joined King Rufàran's service as a soldier, as was...*expected* of me. I was young and inexperienced, but I quickly learned the ins and outs of service, and within a few years, I distinguished myself as someone who followed through, someone who got things done. Most officers didn't like the sight of a lowborn cur rising so swiftly through the ranks, and I knew it. Yet every task they assigned, every trial they put me through only strengthened my resolve to demonstrate my worth.

"It must have worked, because King Rufàran himself took notice of me when I wasn't much older than you. I think it was *because* the other commanders were so put out with how well things were going for me. Hence the nickname. The king assigned me to his personal security detachment: within two Sevens, he appointed me his chief bodyguard. Helëstal, his bride, had died three years prior, and her unexpected death broke something inside of him. In his grief, he gradually ceded more and more authority to his counselors. I realized too late that not all of them had the kingdom's best interests at heart.

"One of their shrewder machinations was to replace the child princess' caregivers and instructors with assets who shared their aspirations. It was a long game, to be sure, but they played it so well, so flawlessly…

"In time, the king sought to shrug off his grief and requested I and a handful of others join him on a hunt. One of his lords repeated tales of *huge wolves* in the nearby forests, and perhaps now you've guessed what drew me to Lohwàlar. Still, there's more to tell.

"Ësfàyami attained her first Seven. Her handlers had already hooked her with their claws, but again, I didn't realize it at the time. Still young, she was already a favorite of the court by her own merits, and her people loved her. I can still remember her expression as we departed the courtyard that day: I thought her eyes were cold because her father was going somewhere without her. Maybe that was part of it, but now, I'm convinced it was more than that.

"We'd been away from the capital for about a week when the dogs discovered something unfamiliar. Something they didn't like at all. Instead of guiding us toward the trail's source, they whined to get away from it. This piqued the king's interest. I tried to follow him as he ran off, but my skills weren't adequate: I lost sight of him.

"Hours later, I finally managed to retrace my steps to where I'd left the rest of the party. All but the dogs had been torn apart:

indeed, the dogs were devouring their remains. I drove them off, then tried to make sense of the massacre in front of me. Only one man had managed to draw his sword—*Kindu* Marugan—and something had broken it into pieces and torn his face to shreds. Your '*rudzhegume*,' no doubt. It's ironic: it was Marugan who told the king about the wolves in the first place…

"I searched for the king for a week—our provisions hadn't been touched, and since it was just me, I had plenty. I found no sign of him, so I returned to Ïsriba with a strange tale and sad news.

"Ësfàyami stripped me of my rank, and I thought she'd have me executed for letting harm befall her father. Now *passion* while she grieved—even apathy, I suppose, would have made sense, but the way she carried herself: there was *cold* in her voice, but the *wrong kind* of cold. I'm sure I'm not describing it right.

"I'm not sure why she didn't have me put to death. Perhaps *Ilbardhën* is more accurate a name than I understand. No matter. The shorter story is that I returned to the barracks to serve under the command of those officers I'd spited in the past. They made sure I understood just how little they esteemed me.

"Yes, I was mad. At first. But something inside seemed to… not *snap*, but *shift*, perhaps, and I turned my attention inward. Back in the field, I became a student of the natural world: how to understand it, to manipulate it to some degree. I studied *people*, their words and deeds and how they aligned—or didn't. Most other soldiers learned to keep their distance from me, lest their commanders punish them. That isolation enabled me to hone my skills: I hadn't lost the determination that had carried me so far and so fast. I just…*redirected* it.

"I was *forgotten*, I guess you could say, for quite some time, but anonymity afforded me luxuries I'd otherwise be denied: because no one paid much attention to me, I discovered ways to come and go without detection. I learned to blend in.

"What's any of that have to do with this?" he said with another glance toward his stained scabbard. "I wasn't supposed to be part of Valderïk's company, but when I heard about the *rudzhún* plaguing your town, I wanted to see it for myself. When Valderïk set out, I followed.

"I've been elusive. Partly because that's become my nature, but also because I suspected certain elements within the queen-regent's court hoped to catch me unawares far away from the capital…"

"Why out here," said Kalas, having allowed himself a moment to consider Shosafin's tale. "Sounds like the people of Ïsriba would've been happy to see you dead—if you'll forgive my bluntness."

"That, lad, I can't answer. Most *Ïsribarinme* believed the queen-regent when she accused me of murdering the king. At first. Over time, the child princess' cupidity increased, and her people's affections cooled. Ësfàyami saw what was happening, but that only strengthened her thirst for power. Truth be told, she would have done well to put me to death when I first returned without her father.

"One thing that comes to mind, however: all your towns-folk' talk of wolf demons resurrected old suspicions about King Rufàran's…*disappearance*. Perhaps there's a connection there, and the powers-that-be have realized their mistake."

"You sound like you think he's still alive," noted Kalas.

"A number of Sevens has come and gone since then," he said without inflection.

"Wolf demons," repeated Kalas, latching on to Shosafin's phrase. "Tsharak told us how you handled Dzharëth. That must have been a sight! I know it wouldn't have made any difference at the time, but still, I keep thinking that if I knew how to handle a sword, maybe I could have done *some*thing. You *definitely* know your way around one! Would you teach me?"

After a moment's staid consideration, Shosafin said: "You've piqued my curiosity, lad. Like I've said: there's a quality about you that I can't quite put my finger on. Let's see what happens in the days ahead."

4.

"What were you two talking about?" Zhalera asked Kalas when he returned and helped pack up their campsite. He scattered the last embers of the fire, then filled the pit with dirt and covered it with leaves and pine needles. Almost as an afterthought, he sprinkled a few extra needles to better camouflage the area.

"Wow, it looks like we were never here!" said Zhalera. "Did you learn that from Shosafin? Is that what you were talking about?"

"Thanks," Kalas blushed. "No, we were talking about…he said he might teach me how to use a sword—at least, I *think* that's what he said! I, uh, I was thinking how you said someday you might make me a sword, and, well, I'd want to be able to use it the right way. If you did make me a sword, that is. Y'know, once you get the smithy up and running again…"

"You think that'll really happen? That I'll be able to start a business? That I'll be any good?" she asked, and it pained Kalas to hear the uncertainty in her tone.

"Zhalera, I *know* it will happen! And you'll have more business than you know what to do with! It'll be great!"

"Of course *you'd* say that," she protested—although a sly smile curled the corners of her mouth.

"I'm serious: all right, I'm not the most objective person to ask, but your father did great work, and all of Lohwàlar knows it. They know you were his apprentice, and even if it was only for a year or so, they know you pretty much grew up at the smithy. More than anyone in Lohwàlar, you know metal! Here, look:"

Kalas pulled his knife from his waistband and held it up. Zhalera blushed and looked away.

"I mean it, Zhalera! *Look!* I don't know why you doubt yourself. I could tell the moment I picked this up that it was *perfect.* In every way—and I'm pretty sure I said as much to you! But even if you thought I was just being polite…I know you hit your head and didn't see it, but this knife—this knife *you* made—felt like a part of my arm when I used it to drive away the *rudzhegu.* You know what you're doing. I believe it, the town believes it, and someday, I hope you'll believe it, too."

"That's everything," said Rül as he tightened the last straps on his cart. Zhalera grabbed its edge and hauled herself into the back. Kalas followed suit, and Falthwën climbed into the front next to Rül. Shosafin had already disappeared into that unnatural silence by the time Dancer and Runner resumed the journey.

It seemed to Kalas like they drove past the same trees time and again as the suns ascended. No one said much of anything, and the rhythm of travel across the well-worn road massaged his wearied bones. Soon, he nodded off to sleep.

When he woke, the suns were almost touching. Hours had elapsed, and soon, they'd need to stop to eat—an observation his stomach seconded with a low rumble. Beside him, Zhalera had also fallen asleep. With her giant sword, still wrapped in cloths and strapped to her body, she seemed smaller than life, more fragile than he knew her to be, and an overwhelming compulsion to *protect* her seized him.

If I'm honest, it's probably me *who needs* her *protection!* he laughed to himself.

Falthwën looked back at him, at the girl, then nodded and turned toward Rül, to whom he whispered something unintelligible while he pointed straight ahead.

"What time is it?" said Zhalera as she sat up and adjusted her sword. She yawned, stretched her arms, and looked up.

"Just before noon, I think, if I'm reading the suns right. I just woke up, too. Hey, Falthwën, what time is—"

Kalas hadn't noticed that the forest had thinned out somewhat, nor that Rül had followed the road into a small clearing. What he *did* notice, as the suns came together, was the Song. Contrasted with the unsettling silence of the woods, its notes fell like hammer blows against his thoughts: not unpleasant, just unexpected.

And *loud!*

"Falthwën!" he shouted when he recovered. Strains of music still played against the boundaries of his mind, but he discovered that with effort, he could attenuate the Song's mental impact and still perceive every chord, every note. "What was—I mean: why is it so loud?"

"What do you mean, Kalas?" interrupted Rül. "I don't hear anything."

Falthwën ignored their driver and, amused, said, "Heard that, did you?"

"Like on my birthday!" Kalas reached for his upper lip. No nosebleed.

"Certain times and places—and people, when combined, become a sort of amplifier for The Song, a spacetime nexus through which its movements gather and impart power from the immaterial."

I had no idea how much power *you hide behind that unassuming guise!*

"Power?"

"Tell me, my child: have you remembered any more details about the night the *zhàrudzh* attacked you? Have you wondered why it spared your lives?"

"What? No, I—What's this have to do with The Song's power?"

"The Song is, in many ways, an abstraction of the Creator's *Nalën Miral*—his First Act, yet it's so much more than a simple representation of a completed work…

"Consider your favorite piece of music: what *makes* it your favorite? The simple arrangement of notes? The technical ability of its performer? No! Those elements contribute to its overall gestalt, but it's how it makes you *feel,* how it makes you *think:* how it *moves* you as it moves *through* you. In those respects, *Zhi Helim* is no different from any other song.

"For certain souls, however, that…let's call it *motion:* that *motion* manifests itself in the material world as well as the immaterial. I'm not talking about the physical vibrations that our ears perceive as sound—I'm talking about…call them *spiritual* vibrations that reverberate within our hearts and minds, that resonate with *and within* our *kelâme.* That's grossly oversimplifying, of course, but it paints the picture. What I want you to realize is this: when properly understood, one who perceives The Song can harness its energies. Redirect them. I believe that on the night the wolf attacked you, with Zhalera's life at stake, you called upon The Song, and it responded with a display of power even a fallen *elu* had no choice but to respect."

"I still don't know what this 'Song' is you're talking about, but it sounds like you're talking about magic," noted Rül as he steered his cart toward a shaded spot with the clearing.

"You're not entirely incorrect," agreed Falthwën as everyone got out of the cart. Rül tended the horses while the others stretched, massaged their kinked muscles, and prepared a simple lunch.

"It's not 'magic' in the sense most people consider, but it is a form of *privilege,* as I've described it before. Because The Song is, in a very real sense, the spiritual thread that binds the Creator's handiwork together, that privilege is best exercised according to his will. Of course, people can—and have—abused that privilege over the years. While it might seem like a good idea in the short term, in the long term…"

"You're thinking of something specific, aren't you?" accused Kalas as he studied the cleric's face, watched as his eyes lost focus on the present and traveled backward through time.

"I am, my child. I am. It's a long story—a sad story—and now's neither the time nor the place…"

"All right then, well, how could I call upon The Song if I didn't even know such a thing existed?" Kalas wondered, choosing to ignore Falthwën's untold story. "I mean, how do you know that stabbing the *rudzhegu* in the chest wasn't enough to drive it away?"

"The Song isn't purely reactive. It's the music of creation, the cord of Ilun's intent: his sovereignty remains unaffected by the whims of those he's blessed with opportunity. And, more to your point: all of us—whether we perceive The Song or not, we're all bound by that common thread. Speaking plainly, I—and others —*heard* you: or, more accurately, we heard The Song *through you* on that night."

Kalas swallowed the mouthful of cured meat he'd been chewing, gulped his water, and, in a subdued tone, asked, "My parents. Zhalera's father…Could The Song help someone…y'know…"

"It's not the same for you—nor for Tsharak—as it is for the —for certain others. There are myriad aspects to The Song. But Master Kalas, we've talked about this. I thought you understood! I've already told you it *cannot* work that way. Not unless—"

"I know, Falthwën! I know! It's just…Well, what do you expect?!" he exploded. "Two Sevens! Two Sevens and suddenly I'm all alone! You *really* wouldn't change things if you could? If you were in my place?"

"I would *want* to—I've admitted that already," began the wearied cleric. "However, with clarity earned through experience, I choose not to. You're right: two Sevens is a terribly young age, even if it is the threshold of adulthood. You're also wrong: look around you! You are not alone! I'm not pretending that anyone could ever replace Màla and Tàran. Never. And I won't pretend to understand the complexity of the Creator's ultimate design. I'm not that arrogant. Likewise, I won't pretend that my heart doesn't ache for you —for you as well, Zhalera, and for all Lohwàlar, for the tragic loss you've suffered.

"What's more, to answer your question: it *cannot* work that way *unless* such a miracle accomplishes the Creator's purpose. It's less someone simply exercising The Song's energies, more someone's and the Creator's wills intersecting. That sounds unfair to you? We are not the arbiters of fairness! You've got a lot of growing up to do, Kalas, and no time in which to do it. You have my sympathy."

5.

After the horses had been fed and watered, the party resumed its trek. Shosafin had joined them for a brief moment while they ate, but he remained invisible for the remainder of the afternoon. Kalas kept to himself, and after a few attempts to engage him in conversation, Zhalera left him to his thoughts.

"I miss my dad," she'd said with a nonchalance that surprised him, "but even if I could use magic or 'The Song' or whatever, I wouldn't bring him back."

"What? How can you say that?! You really wouldn't? You said there's so much more you wish he could teach you! What about that?"

"It's been more than a Seven since Mother died: Father's been without her ever since. I choose to believe they're together again. How selfish would I have to be to take that away from them?

"So bring back your mother, too!"

"Oh yeah? Just like that? How about everyone else in Lohwàlar who died in the attack? Or for that matter, why not Vàyana's husband? Tsharak's parents? How about all of Kësharan?" Zhalera retorted.

"That's not what I meant—just one or two…maybe three or four…"

Even as he attempted to defend himself, he allowed that perhaps Zhalera—and Falthwën—were in the right.

"I…I don't want to talk about it any more," he sulked.

The rest of the afternoon passed without incident. Within a few hours, the immense and ancient forest thinned out with younger deciduous trees supplanting the ancient pines. Suns light dappled the King's Highway—

More like the King's Rutted Track, thought Kalas,

—and the interplay of alternating bursts of light and shadow as they passed beneath spreading branches created interesting patterns all around. Kalas spared a glance toward Zhalera, who stared into the distance with impassive. He shifted position and placed a hand on her shoulder. She didn't seem to notice.

"Zhalera, I'm sorry," he said. "You're right. You and Falthwën. Admitting that means admitting my parents—*our* parents—are truly gone for good. Forever. And I'm not…I *thought* I had, but I wasn't ready to do that. I am now. I don't like it—I *hate* it—but I accept it. I'm *trying* to accept it—I hold on to that last moment with her. I see that…that *peace* in her eyes, and I can almost…I'm not as selfless as you are. Maybe…maybe someday…"

Her rigid posture softened as she reached up and took his hand, squeezed it, and relaxed. She turned, offered him a smile, then continued looking at the twine of road as it unwound behind them.

As they exited the forest, the road ascended a gentle slope with alpine meadows on either side. The immense and ancient pines gave way to scattered copses of lesser trees. The first sun had set; now, the soft, warm light of the second cast a ruddy glow across the land, seemed to impart a vibrant glow to the abundance of small white flowers that blanketed the fields all around them. Rül stopped his team with greater frequency, allowing Runner and Dancer the opportunity to feast upon the succulent grasses undulating in the subtle breezes.

"Might as well stretch our legs a bit," he suggested as he leapt from the cart and unhitched his horses.

Shosafin cantered into view, making no effort to camouflage his approach. With his signature fluidity, he slid from his saddle as Breaker slowed his gait and approached his stablemates. The inscrutable figure unsheathed his sword and swung it through the air with quick motions, violent and serene at the same time. Kalas jumped down and approached him, his interest bare. The old soldier's eyes and focus never strayed: still, Kalas knew he was aware of his audience. Neither spoke, but Kalas sensed Shosafin's careful, considered movements were for his instruction.

I need to understand this, he told himself.

"What's he doing?" whispered Zhalera, who joined him. Together, they watched as he moved—danced, really—across the meadow, his weapon his partner: a harmonious spectacle synthesized from grace and danger.

"Teaching," Kalas answered.

6.

Back in the cart, Kalas struggled to balance two new ideas: Shosafin's almost hypnotic swordplay and the pains he'd taken to present his "lesson," and, of course, Falthwën's revelation about the Song. He closed his eyes and tried to exercise the *privilege* the old cleric claimed he possessed.

Nothing happened.

Laughing at himself, he half-wondered if Falthwën had been

less than forthright. He dismissed the suggestion: even when silvered sage had been rather opaque with his words, he'd never been untruthful.

That privilege is best exercised according to his will, he'd said. *You've got a lot of growing up to do,* he'd added, and Kalas felt his cheeks flush as he remembered Falthwen's sympathetic admonition.

After a couple more hours, Falthwën instructed Rül to look for another clearing coming up. To Kalas' surprise, Shosafin traveled with them for the last fistful of leagues: he lagged behind, vaulted ahead, and wove his sylvan circles through the encroaching forest, but overall, he remained within sight. Kalas thought he seemed somewhat distracted.

That's not like him…

Deepening shadows cast from resurgent woods displaced the memory of the meadows' serenity as Rül steered his team toward the clearing. Although nowhere near as dense as the forest in which they'd spent the previous night, Kalas found himself eyeing every wavering shaft of waning sunlight in search of…something. He had no concrete idea *what,* but Shosafin's uncharacteristic disinterest worried him.

"There's a small stream that *should* be flowing this time of year," began Falthwën as everyone prepared camp. "Maybe half a mile into these woods and—"

"—and down a steep bank," interrupted Shosafin. "I'll be right back."

He grabbed the buckets Rül fished from the cart and disappeared into the trees.

"He's not wrong," the cleric shrugged with a twisted grin. "It's really the same stream from last night—well, a tributary, at least. We're gaining elevation through these first few days; soon, we'll reach the steppes. Out there, water might be scarce, but there are wells—deep wells—that should suffice: the rains have been good the last few years. Still, when Ilbardhën returns, we'd do well to conserve as much as we can."

While Rül tended to his horses, Kalas dug a shallow fire pit and lined it with stones. Zhalera helped Falthwën gather fallen twigs and limbs from the surrounding area. Soon, with a few strikes from his knife against a block of flint, Kalas coaxed a subtle fire from feeble embers. The four of them huddled around its weak glow and hints of warmth as it grew stronger. Both suns were gone, leaving a chill in the dry air as their light dwindled. Rubbing his hands together, Kalas realized Shosafin still hadn't returned. He tried to see beyond the immediate confines of their campsite in the light of the rising moon, but nothing seemed amiss.

Not much later, Zhalera said, "Where's Shosafin? It's been an hour! Shouldn't he be back by now?"

"Indeed," said Falthwën. He stood to get another log and added, Something—"

With a faint thunk, an arrow embedded itself in his staff.

"What—?" said Rül: that was all he managed before rough hands reached out of the darkness, splayed him on the ground, and pressed a blade against his neck. Kalas and Zhalera suffered similar fates as figures dissolved from the dancing shadows and crowded into the light. Falthwën remained motionless until one of the figures—a bowman, string drawn, arrow nocked and aimed at the old man's heart—stepped forward.

"Then Ilbardhën *is* here, somewhere?" he said, his voice a curious mix of wind and gravel.

Falthwën said nothing. No one did.

The bowman gestured for Falthwën to sit, his broadhead's razor-like tines glinting in the firelight. The cleric obeyed.

"Yes, he's here," he continued, answering his own question. "Very well. We'll wait."

Chapter XII

On the Last Stair of the Well upon the Steppes

"Where is he?!" Kalas hissed at Falthwën. Long minutes had come and gone with no sign of Shosafin. None of their captors—other than their spokesman—had uttered a word; indeed, none of their breathing belied their recent bursts of exertion. Kalas wasn't convinced they *were* breathing.

"Watching us, no doubt," laughed the bowman, his weapon still trained on Falthwën. "Biding his time. Waiting for us to err. Waiting for an opening."

Even as he spoke, his eyes seemed to dart in multiple directions at once without moving or losing focus on the cleric. Kalas tried to parse the impossibility. Couldn't. The man's clothes, cinched at the waist, billowed with subtle ripples in the wind. Colorless against the dark grays and rich blacks of the encroaching night, he seemed to oscillate in and out of view with every breeze. He kept his face wrapped in some kind of bandage made from the same fabrics as his other garments, exposing naught but his flat gray eyes. From what Kalas could observe, his minions wore similar—maybe identical—costumes.

"What do you want with him?" demanded Kalas.

"Be quiet!" Zhalera hissed. The bowman laughed.

Without warning, one of their silent assailants flew backward without so much as a gasp. Their leader swung his bow toward the empty space and let his arrow fly. Kalas watched as he fired his missile: the stranger had already nocked another by the time he looked back at him.

"*There* he is!"

He aimed at Falthwën and loosed another arrow: before it reached the cleric, it collided with something metallic and veered into the trees with a reverberant ring. At almost the same instant, the figure guarding Rül collapsed on top of the farm boy as blood sprayed from an impossible gash across the man's neck.

"*Get off of me!*" shouted Rül, who gave the fresh corpse a rough shove. He stood, then ducked when he realized the madman was still launching broadheads with astonishing fluidity.

"Sharp as ever," the man muttered as he unleashed another volley.

Kalas closed his eyes and willed the Song to…*do* something: *what*, he had no idea.

C'mon! he insisted without result.

The figure standing over Zhalera split in two, his torso tumbling to the side as his innards, steaming in the night air, spilled onto the ground.

The remaining figures formed up on their leader, each having found an opportunity to raise his own weapon. Kalas leapt to his feet and would have charged their attacker had something not grabbed his ankle and tripped him.

Tree root? he wondered before attempting to right himself. Whatever latched onto his leg hadn't let go. He turned to look and screamed: the halved figure guarding Zhalera had dragged its upper body toward him and wrapped its fingers around his heel.

"*Alu fan hwer!*" he demanded, his heart in his throat, and with the briefest shimmer, the thing's fingers ruptured in a cloud of fine black dust. Tendrils of faint light spread along the length of its arm and didn't stop until the creature's entire substance had been reduced to powder, which the breeze soon carried away.

"What's this?!" exclaimed the bowman, his eyes wide and fastened on Kalas as the boy finally reached his feet. He let his weapon droop—and in that moment, Shosafin was upon him.

2.

"Shosa...shosayedhume?" Kalas wondered with a glance toward Falthwën. The cleric nodded, his gaze lingering over the gritty remnants the wind had left behind.

Rül stood. Zhalera, too, and raced toward the cart to retrieve her—

"Not now, child!" said Falthwën with an intense whisper.

She paused, regarded their adversaries, and, with a nod, retrieved her hammer instead.

With an enraged snarl, Rül kicked at the detached pair of flailing legs, splitting it in two. Disgusted, he wiped his booted foot with fallen leaves.

"I...I don't even want to know," he spat.

"I thought you were dead, *Kindu* Marugan," said Shosafin from behind the man. He held his sword across Marugan's neck.

"Dead enough, Ilbardhën," he laughed. With a wry smile, he tossed his bow to the ground.

"And these...these...Your friends: that's new."

Marugan said nothing.

"Where's Rufàran? Where's the king?"

Again, nothing.

"Fine," Shosafin growled, his voice tainted with the slightest hint of emotion. In one quick move, he pressed Marugan's head against his blade and drew it across the man's throat. He choked on gurgled laughter as blood frothed and bubbled from his neck.

Marugan collapsed when Shosafin released his grip: at the same moment, the bodiless legs ceased kicking, and the remaining *shosa-yedhume* crumpled like empty sacks of meal.

For an uncomfortable moment, no one said a word. No one stirred. Even the wind seemed to hold its breath.

"I...the water's by the cart," he said as he wiped the blood from his sword and returned it to its sheath.

"Who *was* that? Why'd he have *shosayedhume* with him? Was he...was he *controlling* them?!" Kalas, Zhalera, and Rül assaulted Shosafin with questions, and even though Falthwën busied himself about the camp, he couldn't hide his own curiosity.

"*Kindu* Marugan," he said. "One of King Rufàran's counselors. One of his friends, I thought. Like I told you, lad, the wolves tore him to pieces, too..."

"The wolves?" interrupted Rül.

"Ah, right..."

After recounting an abridged version of the tale he'd previously shared with Kalas, Shosafin continued: "All the men were dead," he insisted. "Including Marugan. If his face looks the way it did the last time I saw him, it's no wonder he keeps it covered. I imagine what's left of it would scare even those...what did you call them? 'Spirit-men'?"

He paused, nodded at Kalas, and added, "That was a neat trick, by the way."

"Trick?" said Zhalera. "Is that what you were shouting about?"

Did she see it? Maybe not—maybe Shosafin's the only one...

"I...uh...Trick?"

"Right," he nodded and dismissed Kalas' deflection. "I'm curious, though: I've never seen, never heard of these *shosayedhume* creatures. *You* know something about them, that much is clear."

"We met one at Kalas' house," supplied Zhalera. "It...it had taken over my father—what was left of him, that is. That was the first time I'd heard about them, too! I thought it was going to…I don't know, it looked like it was going to hurt Falthwën, but he said something, and it was gone."

"'Spirit-men.'" he scoffed after a moment's reflection. "Perhaps."

"Are you serious?" said Kalas, insulted. "You just watched half a man crawl across the ground and grab my leg! You…you watched him turn to *dust,* and all you'll allow is 'perhaps'?!"

"I know of draughts that can free a man from every pain imaginable. I've seen heads severed from their bodies mouth the shape of loved ones' names. Did Marugan command undead *shagabme* —warrior assassins? Doubtful. Did he have access to such powders and potions as I've described? Quite likely. If he's been keeping to the shadows all these Sevens, there's no telling what he might have acquired."

"And the 'trick' you saw?" Kalas whispered through gritted teeth.

"Do it again," suggested Shosafin.

"I—what?"

"Just a glimpse of magic. That's all I'm asking."

"Magic? I don't—I can't—It doesn't work that way!" Kalas stammered.

"Doesn't it?" mused the skeptical soldier, his eyebrow arched.

"Perhaps," interjected Falthwën, "you could ask Marugan for *his* opinion."

Shosafin started to laugh until he caught the cleric's gaze and followed it to the edge of the fire's inconstant light. There, at the edge of shadow, stood the *kindu.*

"Maybe your sword needs sharpening?" he cackled as purple-black tracery wove itself around the dark red chasm carved across his neck. Kalas thought the substance leaching from the figure seemed to *absorb* light, to drink it up as his gritty laughter corrupted the night.

"*Impossible!*" shouted Shosafin. In a single move, he vaulted from his seat and sliced the empty air: Marugan had already dissolved into the expanding darkness.

3.

Falthwën whispered his incantations over the discarded *shosa-yedhume* while Shosafin searched the surrounding forest for Marugan. Rül, somewhat numb and wearing a thousand-yard-stare, went through the motions of watering the horses. Kalas watched while the cleric transmuted the fallen corpses to dust. Zhalera watched Kalas.

"I missed something didn't I?" she accused.

"What?—Oh! The 'trick' Shosafin was talking about? I…yes, I guess so."

"So tell me about it!"

"I'm not sure what there is to tell! I don't remember *doing* anything. Not really. When I saw what had grabbed my leg, I just wanted it to *let go*. There was a pop and then…I don't know, tiny rivers of light that…made it go away."

Zhalera nodded.

"I tried to…I tried to make The Song do something earlier today, too, but nothing happened."

"What?"

"What?"

"I mean *what* did you try to make The Song do?" she laughed.

"I…hmm," Kalas realized he hadn't had a specific purpose in mind.

"Something to think about, maybe?" she mused. "C'mon, let's put a meal together. Maybe a full stomach will help Rül get over the shock of everything."

• • •

"So those things are real?" mumbled Rül through a mouthful of dried meat. "First skydogs, then magic, and now undead warriors…"

"Not 'undead,'" Falthwën corrected. "'Inhabited' would be a better term."

"Whatever: all this stuff scares the life out of me, and I'm not ashamed to admit it!"

"Fear isn't the answer," countered the old man. "Respect is. Appreciate the danger such things are capable of and interact accordingly."

"If you say so," Rül shrugged and reached for another strip of meat.

"He's gone," said Shosafin as he materialized from out of the shadows, sword in hand.

Falthwën said nothing, though his indifference indicated that he'd expected no less.

"You weren't acting like yourself today," Kalas noted. "Did you know he was out there?"

"I suspected. Not Marugan personally—I *know* he was dead —but yes, those two men from the other night: I suspected they had companions. I thought I might give them what they were looking for, draw them out with a sloppy, distracted target."

"Your strategy seems to have worked," Falthwën observed. "Tell me, Ilbardhën: are you familiar with *ekume?*"

"I've heard stories," he scoffed.

"Of course."

"What's an *eku?*" asked Rül.

"It's probably simplest to think of *ekume* as 'dark stars.' Once, they dwelt among the *erume* as kindred lights, but that was a long, long time ago. Now, most serve the twisted will of Ilnëshras. Which makes me curious regarding Marugan's place—his plans—within the *Poyïsriba* court."

"I thought you said *ekume* were the least of Ilnëshras' servants: yet *shosayedhume* are still *egume,* right? It looked like Marugan was commanding *them*," Kalas noted.

"It did," admitted Falthwën, his brow furrowed.

For a while, no one, it seemed, had much to say. Shosafin soon disappeared—again—muttering something about vigilance as the shadows swallowed him whole. In his absence, the four huddled around the fire and spoke in low voices.

"Exciting night, wouldn't you say, Rül?" Kalas prodded. He'd been surprised by the farm boy's acceptance of the evening's grim revelation.

"That's one way to put it," he agreed, his eyes following the twists and turns of the flames as they snaked along the firewood's incandescent surfaces. "My grandfather—Mother's father—used to tell me stories. Bits and pieces about the *erume,* I guess—though he didn't use that word. About something called *Zhi Sâash. Zhi Kathin Sâash.* Something like that. I got the idea that most of what he shared with me was stuff he'd heard from *his* grandfather. They were colorful stories, for sure, but I thought that's all they were. Father certainly didn't care for Grandfather's 'fairy tales.'"

Falthwën dropped his spoon while Rül was speaking. When everyone turned to look at him, he offered a self-deprecating smile and gestured for the farm boy to continue.

"I pretty much forgot about those stories until all of you showed me that room under the Sanctuary," he went on. "After that, I tried to remember anything—everything he told me. Came up with nothing, but after seeing Marugan, that...*dark* pouring from his neck...

"Grandfather blamed the *ilnàfëlme* for blight, for poor yields and the like. I think his 'dark ones' might have been *ekume*. Or not. I don't know, really…"

"Falthwën, why didn't you use The Song when those *shagabme* attacked?" Kalas thought aloud. "I mean, Zhalera and I saw you… do whatever it was to the *shosayedhu* that took Gandhan. Surely you could have done the same here?"

"None of us was in immediate danger, and, as perhaps you've noticed, I find it's preferable to understand as much as possible about a situation—about an adversary—before doing something I can't undo. For example: whatever his original intent, Marugan now knows you're…he knows you hear The Song."

"He had his bow pointed right at you!" Zhalera disagreed. "If you hadn't reached for that firewood…"

The cleric smiled. The creases around his eyes pooled with shadow as he said, "Perhaps. However, none of *you* was in immediate danger."

4.

When morning came and everyone and everything had been packed into Rül's cart, the party masked all signs of their presence and ascended the rising incline toward the wide, flat grasslands above. Conversation seemed unnecessary until the next day when they reached the first well. Rül would have missed it had Falthwën not pointed out an almost indiscernible side trail.

Beneath a slight dip in elevation, a column of ancient stones peppered with lichens wreathed the well's mouth. Kalas leapt from the back of the cart—thankful for the opportunity to stretch his legs—and peered into the black hole staring out of the ground. It looked empty at first, but Falthwën tied a rope around one of their buckets and lowered it into the shaft. When it hit the water's surface with a faint splash, the perturbation caused suns-light to ripple along the well's cylindrical walls.

After watering the horses and replenishing their supply, and after Rül let Runner and Dancer satisfy their hunger on the surrounding grasses, they resumed their places and their journey. Kalas looked around as they returned to the "Highway," hoping for a glimpse of Shosafin: he'd disappeared without a trace, gone before anyone had risen yesterday morning. No one knew when—if —they'd see him next. His encounter with Marugan—or, perhaps more succinctly, with an *eku* he didn't believe in—didn't *want* to believe in—seemed to have cracked his otherwise impervious veneer.

"He'll be back," said Zhalera.

Kalas gave up his vigil, regarded her with a half-smile.

"He's probably watching us even now and just doesn't want or care for us to know," she added.

"I hope he's out there," Kalas admitted. He risked a glance at the misshapen package Zhalera guarded beneath her seat and thought about Shosafin and his unconventional lesson.

"In all our years together, Kalas, I've never known you to be so interested in swordsmanship," she observed, having followed his gaze. "Where's this all coming from?"

"I've been naïve, Zhalera. Unaware of what's really out there —out *here*. If the *zhàrudzhme* had never come to Lohwàlar…But they *did* come, and all I could do was *watch*. I will *not* be helpless anymore! I watched Valderïk fight Dzharëth: he was good—*very* good—but not good enough. I watched Shosafin fight him, too: he cut Dzharëth's hand off before he even knew he was there. So yes, I'm keeping my eyes open for Shosafin. He has a lot to teach me, and I have a lot to learn."

Zhalera's expression wavered between surprise and apprehension, and Kalas realized the extent of his intensity.

"And remember," he added, hoping to demonstrate his composure, "I'll need to know how to use that sword you're going to make for me someday!"

"That's all well and good," Zhalera said, "but Kalas...The Song...Maybe your strength will come from other than the edge of a sword."

Kalas' reply must have surprised her even more than his impassioned outburst: "Maybe you're right," he allowed in mellowed tones. "Still, you heard Falthwën: The Song isn't *magic* the way the fairy tales describe it. It's *privilege*. With rules. And I still have no idea how it works. *Swords,* however..."

Traveling the semi-arid grasslands allowed the party to chew through the leagues with unanticipated speed. Having attained significant elevation earlier in the day, the slope of the crumbling, flagstone-paved road, brought them out onto a plateau with a subtle decline. Falthwën suggested Rül relax his team's pace: by week's end, the Highway would bring them to another rise, the most aggressive along their course, and his horses would need all their strength. Beyond *that* was a desert canyon, similar in many respects to Lohwàlar but colder because of the altitude and shade afforded by the canyon walls.

Shosafin had yet to make his presence known when the second sun dissolved into the haze beyond the horizon. The wind had gained strength overnight and had been more or less constant throughout the day; now, it acquired an almost malevolent bent and chilled the party members to their cores.

"This wind is so cold!" Zhalera shivered as she huddled next to Kalas, who nodded his agreement.

"It comes down from the *Taruúnme Ilkâshkit*—the Standing Mountains—after losing most of its moisture on the other side," said Falthwën as he turned up his cloak. "There's really no place to get out of it. We'll have to get creative with our camp tonight! In fact, we've made great time today: we should come to a well within the hour. Let's stop there while we'll still have daylight."

With their shelter constructed from tent skins arrayed around the cart and the walls of the well Falthwën had predicted, the winds' brutish pounding proved to be little more than an annoyance once everyone was inside and huddled around the fire. Occasional gusts would find a way in through a loose seam and stir the air, but each puff blew itself out before sapping any real warmth.

In the morning, the winds abated somewhat, but Falthwën warned them: when the suns heated the air, they'd be back, no weaker than before. Soon, after making sure they had all the water they could carry, they packed up and returned to the Highway.

Kalas wondered why they hadn't seen any other travelers (Marugan and his assassins excepted). Falthwën laughed and explained that as charming as Lohwàlar was, few people had reason to visit or do business within its borders; that, and Serular, with its reputation, being one of the nearest towns, only the bravest—or the most foolish—traveled the Highway west of Ïsriba.

"Brave or foolish. Which are we?" Rül wondered aloud.

The suns rose—and with them, the winds. As twilight approached, Falthwën informed everyone that the next well was too far away, that they'd have to conserve what they had until tomorrow. Runner snorted. Dancer didn't seem to care.

Nightfall came and went; daybreak followed. For the second day in a row, Shosafin remained absent—or, Kalas hoped, perhaps just well-hidden. Late that morning, just before they reached the next well, Kalas thought the ground looked like something had chewed through it. As they passed, he glimpsed something red spattered on the ground. Suns-light glinted from something in the distance.

I wonder if he had anything to do with that?

• • •

"What's this?" said Rül as he reined in Runner and Dancer, each wearied and in need of water. "I thought you said there was a well here?"

Kalas understood the farm boy's confusion. Unlike the other wells, this structure boasted high, faceted walls arranged in a heptagonal pattern, each with a narrow gate. Each gate had a high stone archway—or used to, Kalas guessed: wind and time had eroded the northernmost arches and caused two of them to collapse. Something in their features struck a chord, but the spectacle *inside* interested him most. Open to the sky, the walls surrounded a narrow spiral staircase carved into the earth and leading down into some kind of underground cavern.

"What kind of cistern—it's a cistern, right? What is this place?" asked Kalas as he admired the friezes carved into the stone, the craftsmanship that had withstood untold centuries of suns and wind.

"It is indeed," Falthwën confirmed. "Many kings—many *kingdoms* ago—these steppes were a place of trade between various realms. The wind was much less of a concern back then. Today, all of those kingdoms have disappeared. I guess Ïsriba could be considered a 'descendant' of some of them. Still, this cistern persists —how fortunate for us! Come, let's get the water we need and be on our way."

Hundreds of thousands of footsteps over hundreds of Sevens had left distinct wear patterns in each limestone stair. On their way down, Kalas almost slipped: he grabbed the wall for balance, but when he let go, his hand felt sticky. When he looked, it was covered with blood.

"Uh, Falthwën?" said Kalas.

"Be wary!" he nodded.

As everyone approached the lower recesses of the well, their footsteps echoed through the subterranean vault. The few shafts of suns-light that penetrated the entryway shimmered in coruscating waves along the walls. On the last accessible step (the rest continued into bottomless water), a seated figure waited for them, his back turned. Kalas recognized him right away.

"Shosafin!"

"*Lushà vam, sà,*" he said without standing.

5.

"Are you hurt? I saw blood not too far from here—" Kalas started.

"Marugan!" Zhalera interrupted. "Did you…did you find him? Is he—?"

"Where's Breaker?" demanded Rül.

Shosafin stood and almost stumbled into the water before he reached out a hand and braced himself against the wall. He kept his other, bloodied hand pressed against his side as he turned toward them.

"Yes. Yes. Around here somewhere," he answered. Elaborating, he went on: "You neglected to mention, cleric, these *ekume* can warp time. Yesterday, I found Marugan's trail. Followed it across the plains until I caught up to him. I was…focused on the wrong things, so intent on finishing the job I…failed to do the other night.

"I should have realized he was baiting me—like I baited his *shagabme.* I'm usually more in tune with my environment, but I've never seen anyone—any*thing*—move that fast!"

"Like an almost physical wave of darkness: one moment, far enough away; the next, too close?" suggested Falthwën as he and the others helped the old soldier to the ground. The cleric reached beneath his cloak for his materials, prepared some kind of ointment as Shosafin nodded."

"Exactly."

"They can warp time?!" exclaimed Rül.

"In a manner of speaking, yes: depending on their mass, their relativistic speed—"

"Their…what?"

Falthwën laughed at himself.

"Ekume—and *erume*—can travel hundreds of thousands of miles between human heartbeats. When they want to. Tell me, Ilbardhën: did Marugan say anything to you?"

"Not a word. He just…he was there, then he wasn't, and suddenly I felt something cold and hot beneath my ribs. I passed out. When I woke, I managed to get Breaker to carry me to this place. I told him to hide until I called for him—I take it you didn't see him? Good! I stumbled down these stairs—almost ended up in that water—and waited."

The cleric, having finished mixing his paste with his thin, silver instrument, cut away a portion of Shosafin's shirt to reveal the source of his blood loss. The left side of his abdomen sported a wide, fresh gash that began near his stomach and traversed his side until it ended somewhere on his back. He cried out—just a little—when Zhalera wiped away the dried blood; next, Falthwën smeared a healthy portion of his greasy compound over the wound and hummed a part of the Song.

Though light continued to twist and ripple over the cistern's wall, Kalas knew the subtle green luminescence rising from Shosafin's wound wasn't from the suns. The soldier gasped, his eyes wide. Kalas chuckled: he remembered how the cleric's cures worked. He also hummed a few remembered phrases in harmony with Falthwën: the faint glow swelled with intensity, became a multihued ball of energy. Shosafin cried out again—this time from genuine pain.

Kalas stopped, aghast, and the brightness subsided.

"What did you do?!" demanded Zhalera, not unkindly.

"I don't know! I—Shosafin! Are you all right? I'm sorry! I—"

"I'm fine, lad. Fine!"

The soldier's rapid breathing slowed as he wiped away fresh beads of sweat that had sprung from his forehead. He took a few shallow breaths, tested his lungs. Kalas thought he looked confused as he took a few deeper breaths. Shosafin looked down at his wound, where he noticed Falthwën's paste had already dried and begun to flake. He wiped away the powdery residue and gasped again.

Underneath the unguent's greasy was nothing but a thin pink line.

"*Gili ahwume á erume!*" Rül exclaimed.

"That...is not possible," muttered Shosafin as he prodded his belly, his side, his back.

"Nonetheless, it appears your wound is healed," Falthwën disagreed. He addressed the soldier with his words, but Kalas, feeling the weight of the cleric's gaze, looked away.

6.

Rül and Zhalera hauled skins and buckets filled with icy water from the well. Shosafin tried to help, but none would let him. Kalas lagged behind, stared into the endless depths of the vast pool while Falthwën, he sensed, stood just a few steps above him.

"How deep is it?" he asked.

"Deeper than you know, my child."

"Those kingdoms you mentioned: did they build this place?"

"They did not, which, judging by your tone, you've already guessed. No, this place predates them by millennia. Those aren't your real questions though."

For a protracted moment, Kalas didn't respond. He continued to peer into the water as it lapped against the chamber's walls. Falthwën didn't move, gave no indication that he had anywhere else to be.

"What…what *happened?*" he dared to ask at last. "What happened to Shosafin?"

"You healed him," Falthwën said with a subtle chuckle, as though the answer should have been obvious.

"I healed him?!" Kalas blurted, incredulous. "I—no, that can't be…can it? How?"

"As paradoxical as it sounds, you *almost* healed him to death! If you hadn't ceased your portion of The Song when you did, Ilbardhën's body might not have survived the shock. Next time, warn me before you 'assist,' all right?"

Kalas turned toward the cleric at last, saw the good-natured glint in his emerald-like eyes and confessed, "I don't understand. What did I *do?* What do you mean, 'almost healed him to death'?"

"When you woke from the *zhàrudzh* attack, four days had gone by, yes? Why do you think that was? The human body can only bear so many stressors at a time—physical, mental, spiritual…Had I or any other *ilhadzhalas*—privileged one—attempted to put you back together in a matter of moments, you would have died: The Song's demands against your flesh would have been too much.

"Ilbardhën's hewn from sturdy stuff, however. I imagine he could have borne a little more, had it been necessary."

"But *how?* I was just humming part of The Song!"

"You were thinking—*willing*—Ilbardhën to recover."

"How did—?"

"Remember: *Zhi Helim* is more than a simple collection of notes, chords, and movements."

"What about that goop you smeared all over his wound? On Ëlbodh's wounds, come to think of it: does it really do anything?

Is it real? I mean, why bother with it when you can use The Song?"

"My medicines are most definitely real!" Falthwën laughed. "Creation—the world we inhabit—is a collection of melodies within The Song. Think of the compounds I use as motifs within those melodies. Because they're part of the same composition, their intersections harmonize quite well, if you will. When *ilhadzhalasme* integrate external themes, sometimes the intersections can be quite jarring.

"You're discovering your place within The Song, my child. Continue to listen. Continue to learn. Consider which path you'll travel as many of them open up before you."

"I want to learn how to use a sword," Kalas admitted, "but Zhalera says maybe The Song is where I'll find my strength. I saved Zhalera with a knife…and I guess I helped save Shosafin with The Song, but…What do you think, *Âu* Falthwën?"

"Uh, we're all ready to go. If you are," said Rül, who'd descended into the cistern. "I mean—I'm sorry!—Didn't mean to interrupt!"

"Not at all, young man. We're on our way up."

Before they reached the surface, Falthwën answered, "Maybe she's right. Maybe she's *half*-right. Maybe she's wrong. Zhalera loves you, wants what's best for you: that much is plain to see. What might require a second look, however, is acknowledging that as tempting as it sounds, we can't let others make our decisions for us. Consider their input, weigh their counsel, yes, but ultimately, we must be responsible for our own choices.

"I suspect you've enlisted Ilbardhën's help for your education? I've known many who can wield a sword—and wield it well, and Ilbardhën…His instruction should serve you well. Just as yours will serve him."

"What? *Mine?!* What are you talking about?"

Falthwën just smiled. "Come, the others are waiting for us."

• • •

Above ground, Kalas saw Shosafin had wandered some distance away. The soldier stooped to retrieve something shining in the dirt. He whistled, and Breaker thundered into view.

"My sword," he said as he cantered toward the well. "Dropped it when I, well…"

After they'd refreshed the horses and had something to eat, the four returned to the cart and continued their trek across the plains. Shosafin and Breaker led the way.

"You're learning more about The Song, aren't you?" Zhalera asked Kalas once they were underway. She smiled.

We must be responsible for our own choices.

"I guess I am," he allowed.

"What's it like? Hearing the Song? You said it sounded like hope, once. What you were humming? Are there words? The harmonies were beautiful!"

"If there are words, I've never heard them!"

"I wonder what the whole thing would sound like," Zhalera mused, suddenly far away, it seemed.

Kalas thought about Falthwën's incomplete descriptions of the Song, the implication that creation was only a fragment of the whole.

"I don't think anyone—anything—could survive The Song in its entirety! Creation is only part of it—Falthwën called it 'a collection of melodies.' It does make me curious to know what its other parts might look like—I mean *sound* like!"

"Not trying to eavesdrop," said Rül, "but it seems to me like *all* of us see and hear part of this Song every day. All this talk about creation and I can't help thinking about the way the suns paint the sky with all those colors when they rise and when they set—and everything they rise above and set behind. There's a kind of music in the way each of us lives his life, right? I don't know…that's just the way it seems to me."

Neither Kalas nor Zhalera quite knew how to respond. Falthwën, judging from his sudden laughter, found Kalas' and Zhalera's introspection amusing.

"Well said, my boy!" he roared with a clap on Rül's shoulder. "Well said indeed!"

The winds abated with the changing terrain as grasses gave way to trees, as flat and unadorned prairie gave way to hills and valleys studded with columns of stratified rock. Nights and mornings, Shosafin practiced his maneuvers while Kalas watched. Having no sword of his own—and not daring to borrow Zhalera's—he searched among the trees for a suitable branch; finding one, he carved away enough material to fashion a crude "blade" and tried to mimic his instructor's motions.

"Stone and water," said the soldier one morning as he traded swords with the boy. "As you shift your weight, let the whole of your being fluctuate between immovable stone and flowing water."

"How do I know when to be one or the other?" Kalas hacked at the air with his borrowed sword.

It's lighter than it looks, he noted.

"Every motion is an opportunity. Consider your every movement. In time, not only will you learn when to be one or the other, but when to be both and neither."

"What? That doesn't make any sense!"

"Doesn't it?"

"How can stone move like water? How can water be like stone?"

"Tell me, lad: have you ever been swimming?"

"I'm from the desert," Kalas reminded him with a smirk.

"Of course. All right, consider this, then: that…*thing* we're not supposed to talk about. When Falthwën and I found you there, much of it was exposed—visible, right? You'd actually been inside part of it? We left, heard an explosion, and returned: what did we see then?"

"Uh, some rocks fell away from the cliff and covered it?"

"That's right! Immovable rock had to *flow* around its shape, and so it did. In a complementary manner, if one were to jump into a pool of water—that well, for example—and land on his belly, he'd understand just how inflexible water can be!

"We'll have opportunity to discuss these things later. Tomorrow, maybe the next day, we'll come to the mouth of a canyon that's as tall as your Empty Sea is wide and twice as narrow."

"Falthwën said something about that," Kalas confirmed.

"That canyon is the gateway to the *Ilvurkanzhime.*"

"The 'Wastes-that-Devour'? That doesn't sound good…"

"There's a reason for that," Shosafin remarked as he traded swords again.

Chapter XIII

Above the Gateway to the Ilvurkanzhime

THE OLD SOLDIER'S DESCRIPTION OF THE CANYON, while accurate, failed to convey the sheer magnitude of its presence. Kalas craned his neck trying to glimpse its upper reaches, but most of its rim was shrouded in swirling mists. Its vast walls seemed to stretch across the plains for endless miles. Maybe they did. A few hundred feet ahead of them loomed a razor-fine column of black: at least, that's what it looked like from their present perspective. The winds had lost most of their ferocity over the last couple of days, but here, where they collided with the cliffs, they rallied, rippling through everyone's clothes with a damp chill. Zhalera shivered and tied her hair back to prevent it from whipping her in the face.

"And I thought the Empty Sea was big!" she marveled.

"This canyon only *seems* bigger," Falthwën noted. "Come, we're almost there. Once inside, we'll be sheltered from the worst of the suns until midday. We'll rest until the first sun catches up with the second. If all goes well, we should reach the plateau late tomorrow morning."

"And if all doesn't go well?" Kalas wondered.

"We'll adapt as best we can."

• • •

At the base of the crevice, Rül stopped the cart, jumped down, and unharnessed Dancer and Runner. He strapped feed bags to their heads, then applied a pungent elixir to a towel and began rubbing their coats and the muscles beneath with gentle circles, whispering to them all the while. Kalas asked if he could help and grabbed another towel. Shosafin had also removed Breaker's tack for his rub down. All three horses neighed their appreciation.

"Looks like we've got a long, hard stretch of road ahead of us," Rül stated. "These boys haven't had a proper massage in a long time. Gotta keep 'em healthy—and happy!"

Dancer grunted his agreement. Runner just kept eating.

Hours later, after brushing the horses and giving them some time to relax, they entered the canyon's gaping maw. Maybe Falthwën was right about the Empty Sea—maybe it was bigger than the canyon, but hemmed in by its narrower, overhanging sides and its steep slope, the comparison seemed academic. Gigantic crystalline formations high above them—quartz, mostly—studded the unvarnished walls, protected from the wind and sheltered from the infrequent rains. Refracted suns-light glinted from their facets, cascaded over every surface with varicolored light that shifted with the suns.

"This is beautiful in its own way," Zhalera observed. Kalas agreed. "Makes me wonder why they call it the gateway to the Ilvurkanzhime."

The wind that had plagued them on the steppes had lessened to no more than an occasional gust; however, the acoustic properties of the canyon seemed to amplify the noises it made: though nowhere near as boisterous, now it raced along the twisting passage in streams of unsettling cries and whistles.

"The Highway only runs along the southernmost region of the Wastes," said Falthwën. "We won't have to worry about the worst of it. There's a *taruúnâsru* leagues and leagues to the north—the *Ildurgul Taruún*—that constantly belches smoke and fire. For millennia, its eruptions have poisoned the land, making it unsuitable for almost all forms of life, hence the name. If the wind is right—or *wrong*, I should say—we may find ourselves enduring the taint of its noxious exhalations."

"Sounds…unpleasant," Zhalera said while wrinkling her nose.

As the horses' hooves echoed throughout the canyon, a shower of small stones rained down from somewhere high above and behind them, glancing off the cliffs and quartz. A chunk of rock collided with one of the larger hexagonal protrusions with an almost metallic ringing sound: the suns-light split again, their rays redirected as a hairline fracture spread along the crystal's faces and altered its geometry.

"I think getting crushed by giant crystals sounds pretty unpleasant, too," added Kalas. "Let's hope everything up there *stays* up there!"

2.

Warm air supplanted the chill weather of the plains. When the suns had reached their zenith, Rül steered his horses toward what looked like a shallow cave flanked with rock crystal within one of the chasm's walls. Scattered rays filtered into the space, illuminating their surroundings with cool, diffuse light.

"This'll be a great place for a rest," Rül said with a nod. "It's cooler than the road, out of the direct suns-light. You weren't kidding, mister cleric! It was getting *hot* out there!"

"It'll take the better part of the day's remains for that heat to dissipate," Falthwën confirmed.

While the others rested, Kalas followed Zhalera toward the back of the cave. He'd watched her trace her hand along its surfaces, following and inspecting various mineral threads embedded within the strata.

"What are you looking for?" he asked.

"Nothing, really. I'm thinking of Father, wondering what he might have thought about all these crystals, all this rock."

"He'd be pretty excited," Kalas said. "Tell me, what do *you* think about all of it?"

It took a few more prodding questions, but soon, Zhalera elaborated on the various processes (as best she understood them) involved in smelting base metals from various ores. She pointed to a band of reddish material flecked with hazy black inclusions and followed it across the cave.

"This looks like hematite—a lot of it, too! If we could get this back to town, rebuild the smelting furnace…Not today! Not this trip! I mean, maybe someday, after all this…wolf-business is over with."

"Hey, what's this?" said Kalas as he spied something protruding from the ground. With his knife, he pried it free from the dirt and held it up as he wiped away the dust still clinging to its surface.

"It looks like ceramic, maybe? A piece of pottery?" Zhalera suggested as Kalas passed it to her. Perhaps a cylindrical vessel at one time, now it was just a sharp fragment etched with intricate patterns and inlaid with decorative bits of stone and crystal. They scanned the surrounding floor and discovered handfuls of additional shards

"Looks like it's been here for a long time," she said as she handed it back to Kalas. "But who knows?"

"Well, it's broken, whatever it is," he dismissed as he tossed it to the ground.

Hours after the second sun had passed well beyond the rim thousands of feet above them, the party packed up and set out again. *Almost* everyone, it seemed, had managed a few hours of sleep while the suns burned away the day's heat—Kalas doubted Falthwën *ever* slept: he thought he was the first one awake when he realized the ancient cleric had been resting—not actually sleeping —near the cave's mouth.

After another few hours, a low, repeating sound syncopated the steady meter of the horses' hoofbeats.

"Where's that coming from?" Zhalera asked, excited. "That's… that's not The Song, is it?"

"*Úrukilmukritme*," corrected Shosafin. "Cave-dwellers. Valderïk and his men…*interacted* with one of their tribes on the way to Lohwàlar."

"Interacted?" said Falthwën, and even though his back was to him, Kalas knew the old cleric had arched an eyebrow.

"Let's hope this is a different tribe," the soldier deadpanned.

"*Úrukilmukritme* are a peaceable sort. They're wary of outsiders, but they usually keep to themselves," the cleric insisted. "I can't imagine what Valderïk sought to gain from assaulting them."

"How could anyone live out here?" Zhalera wondered. "There's no water, no trees…"

"That's what Valderïk's men said about Lohwàlar," Shosafin chuckled.

The noise—drumbeats, Kalas thought—got louder as they made their way up the incline. Underneath the heavier drums ran a thread of other, faster percussive instruments.

"Sounds like they're having a party," Kalas noted.

A chunk of rock sailed through the strange twilight and knocked Falthwën unconscious.

"Falthwën! Rül screamed and gave the old man a shake. A thin streak of blood seeped from his head and ran into his beard.

No response.

"Shosafin?!" Kalas said with a waver in his voice.

The soldier had disappeared despite the unaccommodating

terrain.

"What happened? Did something fall from the cliffs?" Zhalera suggested as she looked up.

More rocks banged against their cart.

"No!" Kalas hissed, "We're being attacked!"

3.

"Rül, get us out of here!"

"How? There's only one way to go!"

"Then *go!* Go as fast as you can!"

"The cart—!"

"What good's a cart if we're all dead?! I don't know what these people want—I don't care! Runner! Dancer!" Kalas said, as if a direct appeal would help: *"Go!"*

Whether because of his pleas or Rül's reins, the horses, already wearied from the uphill climb, struggled as best they could. Kalas jumped from the slow-moving vehicle, his knife ready, and ran ahead of the cart. Zhalera did likewise, her sword in hand, though she kept it bound and sheathed for the moment.

"Kalas, what are we doing?!" she panted.

"I don't know! I can't—*there!*" he cried, spotting a subtle movement just above them. "Looks like they're above us! On a ridge or something!"

"How do we get up there?!"

"I don't...all right, there has to be—*Nëshritme!* It's too slippery to climb," he cursed, unable to find any suitable cracks or ledges. "Of all the times for Shosafin to disappear!"

Kalas heard a faint ringing sound, and a figure seemed to fly through the night, lit by the fractured rays of the setting sun before it collided with the far wall. A second followed the first.

Shosafin dàbiras nir! Kalas thought: he'd heard that subtle ringing sound before.

The drumbeats ceased; now, alien voices shouted obscure words as wiry figures buzzed like rumors within the encroaching black. Out of breath, Kalas stopped on a slight plateau and saw yawning caves dotted with distant lights on either side of the road. Even in the semidarkness he noticed thin paths on either side of the Highway, carved by these *úrukilmukritme,* he assumed.

That's *how they got above us!* he realized.

Above, an immense accumulation of quartz spanned the entirety of the chasm, collected the last of Tàfayan's light and spread it along the canyon's walls. At first, Kalas thought it was a natural formation, but as the light shifted, he decided it was man-made.

That's impressive, he admitted.

Breaker thundered into view. Shosafin reined him in and said, "I don't think this is the same tribe, but they must be friends with them. Or maybe none of them likes outsiders, like the cleric said. I disabled most of them—*not* permanently!—but more will come."

Zhalera reached the plateau as well. Though her sword remained hidden, its pommel boasted fresh blood stains.

"I only hit a few of them—in the head," she explained when she saw Kalas' shocked expression. "I don't even really know how to use it: I've never...I mean, I didn't want to—"

"You did the right thing, lass," Shosafin interrupted. "These people aren't our enemies: they're just defending their home."

Rül caught up with everyone. Falthwën remained unresponsive.

"I don't think so," he said when he recognized the horror in Zhalera's face. "Just knocked out. But the horses: they're almost spent...I don't think we're gonna make it outta here!"

The farm boy's words might as well have been prophecy. Mere seconds after he'd uttered his prediction, the scintillating lights flanking them winked out. Whispers, faint but rising, corrupted the sudden stillness. Soon, the great crystal agglomeration above them cast its fading radiance over twenty, maybe thirty quartz-tipped spears. The mob's whispers coalesced into words—recognizable words: *"Gul ihi ilnëshrasme! Gul ihi ilnëshrasme!"*

"Kalas, how do we get out of here?!" Zhalera panicked. She held his gaze for a moment—he winced at the fear he read in her eyes. When he didn't answer right away, she wilted and started to unwrap her sword.

"I don't know what I'm doing," she wept.

He stayed her hand with his own.

"Not like this," he breathed.

"Kalas—?" she began: when she turned to look at him, she stopped.

Voluminous new light collected in the construct overhead as Kalas' flesh seemed to split apart in shreds of tangible luminescence. Many-fingered ropes of iridescent energy rippled across his body in lambent waves. As one, the voices closing on them ceased; then, their singular chant unraveled into a tumultuous clamor. For an eternal, ephemeral moment, time seemed immobile, unable to move in any direction: when it *did* move again, a concussive blast flung the spears—and their wielders—to the ground. The shock rattled the gorge walls and cracked the moorings of the reflector above them. Shards rained down, spitting rainbows in all directions as they hurtled through space.

What few cave-dwellers managed to stand stared at the spectacle in front of them, arms up to shield their eyes from the violent radiance. They approached without their weapons and adopted a wholly different tone: with the backs of their fingers pressed against their foreheads, the mob uttered something else—a sobriquet whispered in reverence.

Kalas, still aflame, paid them little attention. His thoughts were elsewhere when everything around him erupted in a tantrum of ineffable light.

4.

Kalas' senses ceased to function. Indeed, for a moment he thought he'd died; however, the incessant pounding inside his head suggested otherwise. He opened his eyes. Wished he hadn't as daylight stabbed at his retinae.

Wait—daylight?

"What…what happened?" he asked the cleric who was kneeling over him. "Falthwën! You're all right!"

"Just a little bump," he deflected. "Nothing a little…*rest* couldn't fix. No, I'm more interested in your adventures! Seems you've been busy, my child!"

The cliffs on either side of them were gone; now, hilly spaces, stippled here and there with suns-bleached scrub, surrounded them. Situated at the side of the road, a smattering of tall, thin trees provided a modicum of shelter.

"Where are we?" With Zhalera's help he sat up. She let her arms remain around his shoulders.

"We're a few miles from Deridzhas, perhaps the only remaining town within the Ilvurkanzhime."

"How did we get here?" Kalas closed his eyes and rubbed his temples. "Last thing I remember was…rainbows. Why is that? I can't…The horses were spent, the *úrukilmukritme* had us surrounded…Rainbows. It was nightfall, too, but…I don't understand!"

"Rear axle's broken. Probably from the fall," said Rül from the other side of the overturned cart. "You think we can get it repaired in…Deridzhas, you said?"

"The fall?" mumbled Kalas, still confused.

"From what I'm told," began Falthwën as he held out one of his green lozenges, which the youth accepted without question, "after one of the cave-dwellers brained me with a rock, the lot of you tried to escape, but, as you said, the horses had given their all, and the

253

dwellers had you surrounded. They called you 'accursèd ones'—why, I don't know. Miss Zhalera was about to reveal her sword—"

"No! You said not to!" Kalas interrupted. Zhalera held him where he was as he tried to rise.

She's strong! he observed.

"—but she didn't! That's when you—*you*—brought us here."

Kalas said nothing, allowed himself some time to consider the cleric's story.

"It's getting harder and harder to discount the immaterial around you people," grunted Shosafin.

"You were *on fire,* Kalas!" said Zhalera as she released his shoulders and repositioned herself in front of him. "Is that what happened when the wolf—no, you don't remember, do you?—anyway, fire was all over you, but you weren't burning up! Nothing was! Some kind of energy surrounded you—all of us!—then BOOM! you knocked the *úrukilmukritme* on their backs, and seconds later, we were here! And—you won't believe it!—one of the cave-dwellers somehow ended up in our cart!"

"Did he hurt you? Is everyone all right? Where—"

"Not a *he!* A girl! Maybe five, maybe six and a Seven! She must have taken a hit, too: probably got knocked around by all that energy. She's unconscious, but Falthwën thinks she'll be all right in a few days. She had *this* with her..."

Zhalera showed Kalas a stout pole weapon tipped with a wicked-looking crystal. She helped him stand and walked with him to the cart.

"You dropped us a few feet from the ground," said Rül, attempting to repair things as best he could. He stood and rested against the handle of a huge wrench-like tool. "That's when the axle broke, I'm guessing."

"Oh! I'm sorry..."

"I'm not blaming you, *sà!* Just thought you'd wanna know!"

"The horses?"

"A little banged up, but they're safe. They'll need a few days to rest. Longer, really, but if we take things slow—a lot slower than we have been—we should be okay. They're bred for toughness. I just hope we can find what we need in town."

"Maybe," said Falthwën as he joined them, but his tone belied his doubt. "It's been many, many Sevens since I've visited these parts of the world."

Just beyond Rül, under the strongest shadow, a fragile-looking figure clothed in close-fitting garments rested on a bed fashioned from some of their baggage. Silver-colored hair streaked with black framed her heart-shaped face. Her fair, almost cream-colored skin had a few fresh scrapes and cuts in places, but the cleric had already tended to them.

She looks so peaceful. So helpless. Harmless, Kalas thought. *What happened to her—to* all *of them?*

"Made her a couch," said Rül, quite pleased with his design.

"I still don't understand," Kalas insisted as he turned the conversation toward his original question. "You told me *what* happened: not *how* it happened! The Song, right? But...but how?!"

"Your friends have told you what they know as best they can," Falthwën defended. "It's unkind to demand from them what they cannot possibly provide. To the heart of your question: '*How did I direct The Song to bring us here?*' Perhaps an illustration will help: Music has structure. Rules. Staffs, clefs, time signatures and the like. It has directions like sforzando and pianissimo. In the hands of one conductor, an arrangement might sound one way: in the hands of another, surprisingly different. Think of exercising this privilege like conducting the music according to your own interpretation.

"That's my none-too-terse way of saying: only *you* know how we got here—even if that knowledge remains locked away from your conscious thoughts...for now."

"The way we were there, then we were here: Marugan moved like that when he tried to cut me in half," Shosafin, who'd been listening, remarked.

"*Ekume* hear The Song the same as *erume*. They're party to its privilege as well. *Seranà* is *seranà* regardless of who exercises it: it's the wielder's *intent* that determines its character. Kalas' intent was to preserve his friends from harm."

"Falthwën! She's waking up!" Zhalera hissed.

The ancient cleric approached the strange girl. He knelt, took hold of one of her hands, and massaged its tendons with his fingertips. Some of the suns-light caught in the facets of his ring.

"*Dzhâra afilo nir, dhëmínahal*," he soothed. "Time to wake up, my little child."

The girl's long-lashed eyelids fluttered, opened—then opened wider still when she realized where she *wasn't*.

"This isn't—! Where—? What happened? What's—?!"

"Easy now, little one! You're safe—we mean you no harm!"

On the verge of panic, the girl's violet-colored eyes darted in every direction, searching for some means of escape or—

"*Ilosar!*" she whispered with a reverent hush when her eyes found Kalas. With rough speed, she pushed Falthwën's hands away and almost glided across the dirt toward the young man, around whom she wrapped her trembling arms and would not let go.

"Come again?" said Kalas, puzzled, as he cocked his head.

With care, he convinced the girl—young woman, really—to let go of him, to sit back down and share her story.

"Tell me, Miss…?"

"Pava. Please, call me Pava."

"Pava, my name's Kalas. This is Zhalera, that's Falthwën, that's Rül, and—where'd he go? Never mind. Pava, we're sorry for hurting any of your people. When you attacked us, we didn't know—"

"No! No, it's *us* who should be sorry! We never should have attacked, and I—Oh! Your head!" she exclaimed when she noticed the reddish brown streak in Falthwën's beard, the mottled bump on the side of his head.

"Oh, that?" the old man chuckled as he ran his hand over the wound. "I've weathered worse!" His ring sparkled in the suns-light, and the girl took a breath. Myriad questions wrote themselves on her face, but she never asked them: instead, she remained silent.

Kalas signaled for Zhalera to hand him the young woman's weapon. He offered her the shaft and coaxed, "Pava, why don't you tell us what happened. From your perspective?"

5.

The cave-dweller girl said nothing for a while, but Kalas could tell she was trying to organize her thoughts the way her eyes moved to and fro as she sorted her memories.

"Years ago," she began, "before my first Seven, something happened to our villages. The *iltithme-kal*—light collectors—that harnessed the glory of the suns for generations began to fail. We made all the adjustments we knew how, but nothing helped. It was like the suns themselves just stopped working! It made no sense! We had to abandon some of the smaller outposts, which meant more crowding in the larger districts, which led to lots of other problems, too.

"Things continued to get worse until an *eru* appeared—someone *claiming* to be an *eru,* at least. He made the collectors work again, and so we trusted him. Our elders came to rely on him more and more, and soon, in every way that mattered, he held all the power. Everyone thought his presence was fulfillment of prophecy—someone who would return the light to the world—so we did whatever he asked. We had to! When we didn't, the collectors darkened. He said it was because of our lack of faith in him, but really, I think he just wanted to punish us for our disobedience. Some of us—not enough—suspected he wasn't who he pretended to be, but what could we do?

"He always seemed to know when the *ilrâigme-edhume* were on the prowl. He was always warning us about their movements: probably to keep us under his thumb. But a few days ago, he told us a band of them would be coming up through the canyon, that you'd carve us into pieces, destroy the last of our great collectors, and plunge the heart of our civilization into darkness. Then he disappeared—I mean he *literally* disappeared, leaving nothing but black smoke. By this time many more of us were skeptical, but then our scouts saw you coming, and suddenly we weren't so sure. He *did* make the collectors work. When he wanted to…

"*Ilrâigme* haven't raided us since before I was born—something the *eru* took credit for—but he told us the one who'd be at the front of the approaching *ilrâigme* and riding the biggest horse, was the hungriest, most dangerous one of all. Told us he'd seen him eat the legs of still-screaming babies while their mothers wept. Those who've had to defend our villages against *ilrâigme* before—who've seen what they're capable of—panicked, and so did the rest of us.

"But when you started fighting back—no, when you started *defending* yourselves, it looked like you did everything you could to avoid actually killing anyone. I didn't understand. Mother and Father had ordered me to stay inside, out of sight, but there was no way I was just going to stand by while monsters ate our people! I watched you…Zhalera, yes? I watched you use the handle of your sword, not the blade. And I watched someone else…I don't see him here…use the flat of his to push some of us away. He looked like he knew his way around his sword: it would have been so easy for him—for any of you—to do whatever you wanted. We're…not fighters. Not…not really.

"And then there was so much light! Powerful light that none

of us had seen in years! I was above you, above your cart, near the Great Collector. I…I'd climbed up there hoping I'd be able to drop a rock on your heads. When the *Kathin Iltith* filled with all that light, I had to shield my eyes, it was so bright! Its crystals have never glowed like that before! Then the ground shook and I lost my balance. I don't even remember falling, but that must have been what happened…

"Whatever the rest of my village thinks, I know now the man pretending to be an *eru* was something else entirely. He wasn't the *Ilosar* we've been waiting for. We—*I* am sorry."

"This *eru*," Shosafin said. Pava jumped when she heard his voice coming from somewhere behind her.

"The 'hungriest, most dangerous' one of us," Rül nodded with a grin, and Pava relaxed. A little. "He does that a lot."

"This *eru*…You said he left black smoke behind? Hmm. Can you describe him? What he looked like?"

"He looked…well, he looked a little like…Falthwën, was it? Old, that is—I mean no disrespect! Horrible scars all across his face. Even when he smiled, there was something *cold* about him, about his eyes—flat gray, like they'd never known happiness. Or maybe they had, once, but never expected to again."

"Marugan?" Kalas asked. Shosafin said nothing. "He's really got it in for you, doesn't he?"

"I suspect Ilbardhën is no longer his primary concern," said Falthwën with a knowing look. "Miss Pava," he continued, changing subjects, "I'm afraid we have no way to return you to your home right now. Our cart is broken and our horses are in dire need of rest. Deridzhas is not too far from here: it's our hope to make repairs there while our horses recuperate. You're free to do as you please, of course, but—"

"You can stay with us," insisted Rül. "I mean, we can make some room. You're small: you could probably fit up front with me! Uh, I mean me *and* Falthwën.

Pava looked at Falthwën, then at Rül. She looked to the west and the canyon that had been her whole life, then shook her head. Rül's shoulders sagged.

"No, I can't go back. Not yet. Maybe—I don't know how, but maybe I can help you. I have to try, at least: I have to right the wrong my people have done you."

"Oh? I mean—of course!" beamed Rül, and Kalas chuckled at the farm boy's elevated demeanor. Zhalera gave him a playful punch.

"Be nice," she teased.

6.

"I'll stay with P—the horses," Rül offered while the others prepared for the hike into Deridzhas. Dancer and Runner seemed grateful for the shade and the rest as they drank from the party's dwindling reserves.

"Deridzhas," Pava said. "We know to be wary of that place…"

"Indeed? Hmm. If anyone—any*thing*—comes near: *hide*," suggested Falthwën. "Keep Pava safe: she needs rest as well. Let Ilbardhën handle any unexpected guests."

"*Hish, âu* cleric," he agreed.

Although scattered and, for the most part, inconsequential, the trees lining the road provided at least some protection from the suns as Falthwën, Kalas, and Zhalera trekked across the desert toward the town. Aside from a few variables, the so-called Ilvurkanzhime reminded Kalas of Lohwàlar. Granted, there were trees here: not as robust as the forest at the bottom of the Empty Sea, but trees nonetheless; the air, while hot by all measures, still felt cooler than most days back home—probably because of the elevation. Here, he figured they were thousands—maybe *Sevens* of thousands—of feet closer to the sky than when in Lohwàlar. It felt that way, at least.

"Let's keep a low profile," the cleric suggested as they hiked. "I'd prefer not to be surprised by Marugan again. Or anything else, for that matter."

Just under a league from their "crash site," Falthwën stopped. He surveyed their surroundings for a while before inclining the top of his staff toward a crumbling stone wall nestled within the trees a few hundred feet in front of them. Wide, irregular gaps—some large enough for a team of horses—suggested it had been some years since anyone had maintained things here. Some portions retained their weathered capstones, and Kalas guessed the wall was about seven or eight feet tall when new. Now, most of what remained was four, maybe five feet above the ground. Masses of pallid yellow tree roots had knocked down several large sections, wrapped around them and reduced them to gravel.

"Do you think those trees look all right?" Kalas whispered as he shaded his eyes for a better look. Both of his companions shook their heads in silent unison.

A tarnished metal archway, pitted by wind and rain and blasted by sand and gravel, framed what looked like the main entrance into town. No gate barred their entry: either Deridzhas was a welcoming place or, like the walls, the gate had succumbed to years—Sevens —of neglect.

"When were you here last?" Zhalera whispered as the three of them sought cover beneath one of the larger trees and stared at the town for any signs of movement.

"The Wastes? Many Sevens ago. Deridzhas? I don't remember. Probably within that same time frame. And no: it did not look like this! Now, there's a malevolence in the air. Be wary, my children..."

•••

"Anyone else feel...queasy?" Zhalera wondered as she put a hand over her stomach."

"Queasy?" repeated Kalas. Falthwën said nothing.

"I just feel like...I don't know. This place is...*weird.*"

For a few minutes, they watched and waited in the heat, but nothing in the town moved. Satisfied, Falthwën led the others through the gate and into an open square. Some of the strange, yellow-rooted trees had taken over the place, with more than a few of them nearing five feet in height. Several curious-looking metallic objects—most on wheels—lie rusting here and there along their path. Kalas tried each one, but they'd been abandoned for so long their hubs had seized. Closer inspection indicated none of their components would be of any use—even if the three of them could have moved the peculiar items.

The remains of the road deposited them in front of the largest visible building: perhaps ten or twelve feet tall, it still dwarfed most other structures. Constructed primarily from stones and mud, most buildings showed the same signs of dilapidation as the wall around the town. The "town hall," as Kalas considered it, seemed mostly whole from where they stood, although it had no door. With a shrug, he and Zhalera followed Falthwën across the square; down a few steps into a shallow, walled depression that ringed the cylindrical edifice; and through the naked portal into shadow.

Inside the domed room, shafts of suns-light poked through a few holes in the building's roof and illuminated a tangle of debris scattered across its rough-hewn wooden floor. Years of dust covered almost everything with a light rime.

"It's nice and cool in here!" Zhalera couldn't help whispering. "But that *smell!*"

"Doesn't look like anyone's been here since...well, since you, Falthwën. Whenever that was!" Kalas observed as he walked across the open chamber, his footsteps coaxing creaks and groans from the floorboards. Near the room's center, he stopped and cocked his head.

"What—?" Zhalera began when he signaled for silence.

Her eyes widened when she heard it, too: a faint scraping coming from somewhere beneath them. Both of them looked to Falthwën for instruction.

"Àya? Àya, Deridzhasrinme?" he called out in a low voice. *"Soram dusidzhu nir?"*

From under the floor came a muffled thud. More scraping.

"Wait, over there," said Zhalera as her eyes adjusted to the gloom. *"Someone's* been here!"

She followed a dirty path toward a series of thin, dark lines carved into the grit. She knelt and tried working her fingers into the cracks. Kalas joined her and pried at the floorboards with his knife. Less than a minute later, the pair uncovered a panel hidden within the floor. Neither was able to raise it.

"Locked?" Zhalera suggested.

"Stand aside, my children."

They obeyed, and Falthwën rapped the heel of his staff against the door. After a flash of greenish light (somehow familiar, Kalas thought), the latch securing the panel gave way with a metallic pop. Kalas reapplied his knife: this time, he managed to lift the lid just enough for Falthwën to pry it open with the heel of his staff.

The smell Zhalera had noted earlier felt like a punch in the face as the cleric tipped the panel out of the way. She gagged and scrambled away from the dark hole.

"That smells like—" she choked on the bile rising in her gorge. Her olive complexion seemed almost as yellow-green as the diseased-looking trees they'd passed outside.

"It is," agreed Falthwën as he leaned over the black source of the foul odor. "It's something *worse,* too, I think, but our noses will adapt—trust me on that!"

The thud from before repeated itself. So did the scraping noise. Closer each time. Falthwën muttered something under his breath and the head of his staff glowed with subtle phosphorescence. He held it above the hole as the sound came nearer.

Something covered in filth crawled into the weak green light, stared up at them with its eyeless face. Zhalera clutched Kalas' arm and stifled a scream: Kalas failed to stifle his own.

"What is *that?!*" he cried despite his efforts. "What *happened* to him?"

The man had gaping wounds where his eyes should have been. His jaw moved but his voice was gone. The arm he held up toward the sound of their voices ended just below the shoulder. Falthwën swished his staff: the light shifted, revealing ragged stumps where the man's legs used to be. With his remaining arm, he dragged himself as best he could, landing with that nauseating thud with no other limb to brace him. Behind him came similar noises, some followed with feeble groans.

There are more *of them?!*

"Falthwën?" Zhalera hissed, still clinging to Kalas' arm.

"We'll find no help in Deridzhas!" he growled. With a heavy sigh and an angry prayer, he took his staff and drew a hurried shape in the air above the dungeon. Roiling energy crackled in thin lines that trailed behind his movements.

"Master Kalas! The lid!" he instructed.

Kalas freed his arm from Zhalera's grip and grabbed the panel. He slammed it into place atop the cleric's arcane symbols, still shimmering in the dust.

Hey, those shapes look familiar...

He grabbed Zhalera's arm and pulled her toward the door. With a word, Falthwën slammed his staff against the panel, and hot light erupted from the depths where the maimed had lain, coruscated between the planks of the floor as it burned away the dust and stung their eyes.

"Those people! What *happened* to them?" she keened, repeating Kalas' question.

"It seems the lie Marugan told the cave-dwellers about us had some basis in truth: Deridzhas is now haunted by the *ilrâigme-edhume*—the eaters-of-men!"

CHAPTER XIV

Toward the Fringe of Civilization

OUTSIDE AGAIN, THE SUNS SEEMED TWICE AS HOT AS they had before. With his free hand, Kalas swiped at the sweat beading on his brow and rolling down his face. Nothing seemed out of sorts nor any different from when they'd entered the eaters' abattoir, though even that brief exposure to the fetor that accompanied its underground horrors had seeped into the fabric of their clothes. Zhalera clutched at Kalas' arm and turned aside as she lost her battle with nausea. As the stink of vomit mingled with the reek of human filth, he felt his own stomach flip once or twice. An unexpected wave of debility seemed to lap against his feet, soak into his legs, and weigh him down. He stumbled, but he caught himself against the side of the building.

"Kalas!" Zhalera begged. "Can't you get us out of here? Like you did in the canyon?"

"I can't!" he lamented after a moment's concentration. "I don't know why—I don't know *how!* Falthwën! You know The Song! Can you get us out of here?!"

Falthwën had already stepped in front of them as they ascended the steps toward the road. He held his staff in both hands and looked from side to side, closed his eyes for a moment, and…Kalas had no idea what he was doing.

"Uh, Falthwën?!"

"I can't. Not like that. Doesn't work that way. We're all right, though. For the moment. It seems we're the only ones in town. Still, we need to hurry back to Rül and the others."

"What do you mean you *can't?*" Kalas argued as they quickened their pace.

"Not the time, my child! Now, come!"

Kalas and Zhalera followed Falthwën through a gap in the wall, past several of those unhealthy-looking trees, and back onto the neglected road. From there, they sped toward the rest of their party, pausing only to catch their breaths. Despite Falthwën's insistence that he couldn't spirit them away from Deridzhas, Kalas had a sneaking suspicion that the enigmatic cleric was…*augmenting* their pace somehow. He thought about the night Falthwën and his father had returned to town with Ëlbodh, about the impossible speed they'd achieved; now, things made more sense.

As they got farther from the abandoned town, Zhalera quickened her pace, and Falthwën commented on how much her color had improved. A short distance beyond the wall's irregular border, the air seemed cleaner, less tainted, and Kalas wondered if it was just his imagination.

"Falthwën, the *ilrâigme-edhume:* Why? Why do they, well… y'know?" he asked.

"I don't know," he confessed. "Could be desperation: living in this suns-blasted place for who knows how long would test anyone's spirit. Or it could be…something else."

"Why would they…it looked like they went limb-by-limb?" added Zhalera. "Like they were *farming people!*"

"No wonder Pava and her people attacked us: if I thought eaters were coming for *me*…" Kalas said. "But the town! It looked like no one's lived there for ages. Sevens even. Would the *ilrâigme* have been responsible for that?"

"Perhaps indirectly. Especially if some of the *Deridzhasrinme* succumbed to…something that suggested cannibalism was their best alternative. That is, I wonder if these eaters-of-men were the original inhabitants of Deridzhas."

"What were they like the last time you were here? I mean, they probably weren't eating people, right?" said Kalas.

"Deridzhas was a mining town, renowned for its abundant mineral deposits. Those piles of rust we passed were probably the remains of mining equipment. If memory serves, the last time I was here the *Deridzhasrinme* were planning a new shaft, one intended to reach deeper into the earth than anything they'd ever attempted in all their history. My business took me elsewhere before they'd made much progress."

"What if those people underground were *also ilrâigme?*" Kalas continued. "What if they just…Maybe Zhalera's right: maybe they *are* farming people. *Each other.*"

"Let's keep walking," Zhalera suggested as she stepped ahead of the others. Looking over her shoulder she added, "And please! Let's talk about something—*anything*—else!"

2.

Even before they reached the cart, Kalas sensed something had gone wrong. When it came into view, its scattered contents confirmed his suspicion. Neither Rül, Pava, Shosafin, nor any of the horses were anywhere in sight. Suspending caution, Kalas took a few hurried steps towards the overturned vehicle—he would have taken more, but he tripped over something. He picked himself up, dusted himself off, and turned to see the wrench-like tool Rül had been using earlier. It was covered in blood and what looked like chunks of skin and hair.

"Rül?! Shosafin?!" he cried out as he picked up the implement.

"Kalas? Is that you?" said Rül's voice from the other side of the cart.

When he stood, fists wrapped around the handle of an axe, Kalas saw the farm boy's clothing was streaked with blood, his eyes laced with an unsettling mania. Upon recognizing his friends, however, Rül lowered his axe, and the unstable light in his eyes disappeared.

"You're back! *Zhi Ilun dàbiras nir!* We were attacked! Some—"

"Rül, you're bleeding!" Zhalera interrupted.

"What? I—oh, no: it's not *my* blood!"

"Eaters!" spat Pava as she stood as well, clinging to Rül's arm like the act required all of her strength and a healthy portion of his.

"Eaters!" Falthwën repeated as he raised his staff and scanned the area.

"They came for us about an hour after you left! Shosafin lured them away—*most* of them!" Rül said. "He took the horses, too. Said the *ilrâigme* weren't picky, and given Runner and Dancer's condition..."

"Some of them caught our scent," added Pava. "We tried to hide, but we could hear them...sniffing, slavering, getting closer and closer. One of them came around the cart, grabbed my ankle —tried to drag me away! I tried poking it with my *tëvët*—my crystal-tipped pike—but that fall took more out of me than I thought!

"But before it could get a second hand around me, Rül smashed its head with a wrench! He kicked it away—what was left of it! —when *another* came at us from the other side of the cart! He grabbed my *tëvët* and ran it right through the eater's throat! Others must have heard the fighting: they started coming for us, too, so Rül handed me my pike, took his wrench, and..."

"I don't know what came over me," said Rül, somewhat sheepish beneath Pava's grateful gaze. "I just...No way was I going to let them get Pava! I think there were five, maybe six that didn't chase after Shosafin. I, uh…I sort of lost count after the first few. One ran off with my wrench stuck in his head, but I got to my axe, so…"

Kalas, Zhalera, and Falthwën circled toward the back of the cart as Pava and Rül told their stories. From their altered perspective, each stopped and took in the spectacle their friends had created. The crystal tip of Pava's *tëvët* lie half-buried in someone's abdomen. It looked like he'd died trying to throw himself on top of her: his momentum, coupled with her weapon, had ripped a jagged hole through his belly that started near the bottom of his stomach and disappeared high within his chest. The one whose skull Rül collapsed rested in an uncomfortable heap just behind them, a wash of gore splayed out where his brains had been. A few other bodies in similar straits accented the macabre scene. Again, Zhalera fought against the rising bile in her gut.

"You're 'not fighters'? 'Not really'?" Zhalera repeated, incredulous—and impressed. Pava looked away.

"Uh, yeah, sorry," apologized Rül, assessing their shocked expressions. "Guess we should have covered this up or something. We didn't know when they'd stop coming, though, and, well…"

"Did you find what you needed in Deridzhas?" Pava piped up. "Will someone there be able to help us?"

"There is no Deridzhas," Falthwën said with a sad shake of his head. "Not anymore. Not for Sevens of years, it seems."

"Oh?! We thought they were just stories! I mean, we *suspected*, but—You could have been—I'm so sorry!" cried the *úrukilmukrit* girl.

"It's all right," Rül promised. "You're not alone: turns out a lot of things I thought were just stories are real, too!"

"What will you do now?"

"Well," he said with the faintest hint of pride, "before those eaters showed up, I was looking at these trees. A few look straight enough: I think I can make a new axle from one of 'em. It'll take some time, and it won't be perfect, but since the horses need rest —and since it's our only real option, I think it's worth a try."

The gentle *trip-trop* of hoofbeats on the packed sand and rock signaled Shosafin's return. Dancer and Runner looked just as exhausted as before, but Breaker seemed flush with excitement as he pawed the air with his flashing hooves. The soldier held reins in one hand and his sword, black with blood and bits of flesh, in the other. His garments and Breaker's flanks bore the same stains as Rül's and Pava's. He, too, seemed more energized than enervated.

"That was the last of them," he said, addressing Rül. "For now. Might be days—might be a week or more—before others come looking. If anyone comes at all. Still…"

He caught Falthwën's eye and continued: "What did you find in Deridzhas?"

"Deridzhas has been gone for Sevens," he said. Shosafin nodded.

"There's something…*wrong* with it," Zhalera insisted. "I can't be the only one who felt sick—*weak*—just being there, can I? Something's not right with…I don't know, the *air* in that place."

Things the world over, under, and above aren't always what they seem.

"It wasn't just you," Kalas admitted, remembering his own sensations of frailty while attempting to flee. "Zhalera, do you remember how Father acted when we were, uh, down in the Empty Sea? The way we felt in Deridzhas: I wonder if that's how *he* felt. I wonder *why* he felt that way. Falthwën, you said the *Deridzhas-rinme* were planning their deepest shaft ever: what if they…found something? Maybe that's why *we* felt that way…"

"It's possible," the cleric allowed. "Probable, even."

"So where does that leave us?" Shosafin asked.

Rül outlined his plan, adding, "We'll need the straightest tree we can find. I don't have the right tools to plane it down properly, but I think we'll manage."

"So long as it gets us through the Ilvurkanzhime," the soldier grunted. "We're too exposed out here."

"Al mekâyëthu, âu tanag," Rül nodded. He retrieved his axe, ran a fingertip along its edge, and walked from tree to tree. Pava's eyes, Kalas noted, followed his every step.

3.

"Won't your family wonder what happened to you?" Rül asked Pava on the second day after the *ilrâigme-edhume* attack. He felled what he believed to be the choicest tree available, stripped its limbs and branches, and started scraping away some of its unevenness. Pava had almost wholly recovered from her fall—and from defending herself against the eaters. She assisted Rül as best she could.

"They will," she ceded, "but there's nothing to be done about that now. And that's all right—they probably saw what your friend did, and even if they didn't, someone will tell them about it! They'll assume that I followed the *Ilosar* as penance. Which turns out to be the truth, even if it's not what I set out to do!"

"Shining One?" said Kalas, who happened upon their conversation. He and Zhalera had been helping Shosafin patrol the area. The day before, the three of them had piled up the eaters' bodies and burned them to keep scavengers away. This morning, he practiced swordsmanship with the soldier. Zhalera, too, all but the hilt of her weapon still wrapped. They stopped as the suns—and the temperature—continued to rise: their exertions cost them precious water. To supplement their shrinking supply, they built moisture traps. Pava helped: her people made use of similar contraptions.

"We cave-dwellers have a legend," she explained. "We've always believed we were waiting for an *elu,* maybe an *eru:* someone who would *bring the light.* And that's exactly what you did! Sure, sure: there are probably hundreds of interpretations, but…Anyway…

273

"Our villages are beneath the *Áthradho*—the Gateway. Underground, but that doesn't mean they're musty, lightless places! The *iltithme-kal* channel the suns' glory through mirrored passages carved into the rock. By bouncing suns-light from mirror to mirror, everything's as bright as we want—*most* of the time! We use that light to illuminate our homes, grow our gardens—"

"Gardens?" Rül interrupted. "Underground?"

"The *Áthradholarme* are beautiful places! You should…you should visit sometime! Now, where was I? Oh! Right! When that *ilímbâ*—Marugan, you called him? Our villages *had* been getting darker, it's true, so when he was able to lift some of that darkness, lots of people interpreted that as *bringing light*—but after seeing what *you* did, it'll be a long time before anyone believes another weak interpretation like that! Whether you're *the Ilosar* from our legend or not, we've done you a great wrong…"

"Pava," said Kalas, pensive, "do your people have any legends or stories about a time 'before the world was cracked'?"

"'Before the world was cracked'? Hmm…None that I remember," she said after a moment's reflection. "Why do you ask?"

"Just curious." Kalas smiled, but even he could tell his smile reached nowhere near his eyes.

"I'm sorry," she apologized as she read his expression. "I'll ask some of our elders when I get home—maybe one of them knows what that means?"

"No, it's all right. It's just…something I heard not too long ago. Really, it's fine." He smiled again, meant it this time, and Pava relaxed and smiled in return.

"You said your collectors had been getting darker? For generations?" said Zhalera. "How is that possible?"

Pava laughed. "If you figure it out, let me know! Let my people know, all right?! We're used to adjusting the collectors' angles from season to season—the suns don't always hit them in the same place throughout the year—but it seems no matter how many adjustments we make, it's not enough. We polished the crystals, replaced the mirrors, did everything we could think of, but nothing worked!"

"Tell me, child:" said Falthwën, who'd been listening from a short distance. "has the earth been well-behaved of late?"

Well-behaved?! Kalas wondered.

"No!" Pava exclaimed as though she knew exactly what Falthwën meant. "For years now—maybe Sevens, maybe longer, I'm not sure—there have been rumblings. Not too bad underground, really, but some are worse than others. We've actually had to readjust some of the collectors after the stronger quakes! Do you know what might be causing them?"

"You're familiar with the Ildurgul Taruún?"

She nodded and waited for the cleric to go on.

Falthwën nodded, too. He scratched his beard and looked toward the north. The suns-light caught in his ring again. Its sparkles prodded Pava's interest.

"Your ring—!" she began.

"The mountain is waking up. Even now its smoke is tainting the atmosphere across the Wastes; soon, its murk will clog the air, scattering the suns-light before your collectors can make the most of it," he said, deflecting her curiosity about his jewelry.

"The mountain?" she said, puzzled. "But it hasn't been awake for hundreds of Sevens! What could have woken it? Why now?"

"Fair questions, my child. Fair questions…"

About mid-morning the next day, Rül finished his work on the replacement axle. He fitted it onto the cart and, with help, got it upright. Hoisting the pole onto his own shoulders, he struggled, but managed a few steps. He smiled as he brought it to a halt.

"This'll do. You can feel a slight wobble, but it's nothing Runner and Dancer can't handle. I'll need to have it replaced at the first opportunity, but at least we can get moving again!"

After loading what remained of their supplies, Rül harnessed his team, whispered something to his horses that Kalas couldn't make out, and gave each a loving rub behind the cheek. Shosafin and Breaker had been patrolling the area; now, they maneuvered closer to the cart, still scanning for any signs of trouble.

"These horses," Pava said. "They're…they're really big, aren't they?" She maintained a polite distance from them as Rül helped her into the makeshift seat between him and Falthwën.

"You don't have horses?" he asked.

"No, we don't! Donkeys, yes…I mean, I've seen horses before, of course—a few months ago, a bunch of them came down through the Áthradho. This is the closest I've ever been to one!"

"Well, you have to respect them, for sure," said Rül, noting her uneasy gaze, "and so long as you do, you shouldn't have anything to worry about from Runner—the dark one—or Dancer. C'mon, let's get you situated."

As Rül flicked his reins and the horses started for the road, Pava almost lost her balance and clutched his arm for support. Rül tensed and puffed out his chest. This time, Zhalera gave Kalas a knowing look.

"Be nice," he grinned.

4.

Faint hints of sulfur tainted the air as the party crossed the southern portion of the Ilvurkanzhime. Small, sick-looking trees and splotches of thorny scrub made an attempt to grow on either side of the Highway without much success. For the most part, it wasn't too bad, and their senses adjusted. Tuned it out. On occasion, however, the winds shifted, bringing greater quantities of the malodorous scent. When asked, Rül admitted he'd prefer to move with greater speed, but reminded everyone that the horses were still recovering, that swallowing more of this air than necessary might be worse for them over time.

After a while, Zhalera tugged on Kalas' sleeve and pointed toward something moving near the road just up ahead. As Rül approached the scene, several huge, black birds with glistening, naked heads flexed their wings and took to the sky with angry cackles and hisses. Their gathering place had been the weathered carcass of a horse—and its rider. Though both had been picked almost clean, their skeletons still boasted a few scraps of flesh and sinew.

"One of yours," said Shosafin, who'd drawn up beside the cart. "That's what the other *Lohwàlarrinme* said on their way back from Ïsriba. Didn't catch his name."

"Dzhamïs," Zhalera supplied as she pointed to the shreds of cloth and leather still clinging to the bones. "You can kind of still see the *Poyïsriba* falcon sewn into his shirt. I remember him because he was wearing it when he came by the smithy to pick up tack for the trip. His wife had stitched it special for the occasion. He was so proud of it...Did anyone say how he died?"

"He took ill on his way through the Wastes. Horse got injured somehow. Neither recovered."

"Those birds are a bad omen," warned Pava as she looked up at the lazy circle of winged specks orbiting above them.

The others agreed. Zhalera whispered a brief prayer for Dzhamïs; when she finished, Rül gave the reins a light snap. Dancer and Runner snorted, thankful not to have to wait around any longer than necessary, it seemed.

Just before nightfall, they reached Wastes' boundary, and Rül had to rein in his team: despite their fatigue, the first few breaths of cleaner air provided an unexpected burst of energy which the two were loath to squander.

"Easy, *átemme!* Easy!"

Maybe it was because of the inescapable nastiness through which they'd had to come during the daylight hours, but Kalas thought the sunsets had never looked more beautiful. Vast swaths of vermilion, layered atop far-reaching splashes of rose, hung beneath a topaz sky crowned with subtle hints of deepening violet. Far away, occasional streaks of lightning saturated the display with momentary brightness.

"Look at all those colors in the clouds!" agreed Zhalera.

"We sometimes see the sky like that," Pava volunteered. "Not very often, but more and more over the last few years."

"If it weren't for the Wastes, just imagine what it would be like to see this every night," Kalas mused.

"It's *because* of the Wastes—the Ildurgul, I mean—that the sky looks that way," Falthwën informed them. "As its rumblings become more frequent, as it belches increasing amounts of ash and smoke, its ejecta will scatter the suns-light more and more."

"That means our collectors will be less and less effective, doesn't it?" posed Pava after thinking about it.

"It does indeed, I'm afraid," the cleric nodded.

"Can anything be done about it?" she asked with open concern for her home.

"That...I can't say."

'Can't say,' not 'don't know,' Kalas thought.

"Let's turn aside here," Falthwën instructed in the last rays of the remaining sun. The Wastes and their poisonous fumes were about an hour behind them, and beyond the reaches of the Ildurgul's miasma, the landscape began to thrive. On the other side of the plateau, the road acquired a gradual decline as it lost elevation. Here, a small stream bubbled alongside the Highway. Rül reined in his horses, grabbed a bucket—and his axe—and headed for the water. Everyone else helped make camp.

Strong, healthy trees replaced the withered, blasted scrub that had been the only flora for leagues and leagues. Though neither as vast nor as tall as some of the others through which they'd come, the woods provided better shelter—better cover—than they'd had in days. Within a small glen, they pitched their tents and prepared a light supper.

"Do you think anyone…the *ilrâigme*…will bother us tonight?" Pava asked between spoonfuls of soup. "It's so *open* out here! I guess I'm still not used to it."

"We should be all right," said Rül. The others agreed.

"Ilbardhën has an uncanny sense about his surroundings— which also happen to be *our* surroundings, and an *ilrâig-edhume* would have to be desperately hungry to travel so far across the Wastes," Falthwën added.

When the others—Shosafin excluded—had disappeared into their tents for the night, Kalas sat up with the ancient cleric. Neither spoke. Neither needed to. Somehow, as the Song wrapped around their thoughts, wove itself within their consciousnesses, it seemed to carry portions of those mental elements from one mind to another: nothing as overt as coherent thought, but a nuanced intimation of mood.

This is creepy, Kalas thought.

Falthwën chuckled, mostly to himself.

As he looked away, the young man glimpsed a faint red streak arcing through the heavens.

Why does that remind me of something?

5.

Nothing untoward interrupted them during the night, but in the morning, Pava seemed more exhausted than the others. When asked, she admitted that she hadn't slept too well, that she'd half-expected something malign to happen at any moment. The injuries sustained from her fall had made sleep not only necessary but inescapable; now that she'd recovered, she found time to entertain her darker thoughts about things that might be lurking within the boundless shadows.

"It just seems so *unnatural*," she laughed as her cheeks reddened. Indeed, a few days in the suns had already begun to tan—and burn—portions of her alabastrine skin. Falthwën mixed a cream to ameliorate her discomfort: Kalas wondered where he kept all his ingredients.

"I guess if you're used to sleeping in caves your whole life, I can see how it might," Rül agreed with a vigorous nod. "I'm sure you'll get used to it!"

They packed up their campsite, brushed away any trace of their presence, and, after watering the horses and topping off their stores, headed for the road. It ran through a forest featuring brilliant white birches, their stems gleaming in the first sun's silver light. Some leaves remained a rich, vibrant green; most, however, had taken on a muted yellow color. Low grasses in shades of green and brown lined either side of the Highway. Kalas took a deep breath—then another—of the pleasant, unfamiliar fragrance of fresh air mingled with the subtle, earthy smell of prior years' fallen leaves returning to the soil.

"Don't hurt yourself," Zhalera laughed as he relished yet another lungsful, held it for a moment before he exhaled. She, too, however, tasted the air more than once.

"I could get used to this," he smiled.

"It'll be winter soon," said Falthwën as he considered the gold-hued foliage. "Up here, winter is different from what you're used to in Lohwàlar. Colder. *Much* colder. We should reach Ïsriba long before the worst of it, however."

"Winter nights in Lohwàlar get pretty cold," Kalas insisted. Even Shosafin chuckled from somewhere nearby.

"I wonder if we'll see snow while we're there," Zhalera wondered aloud. "Father said he'd seen snow—once—when he was a boy. None of us ever have."

Kalas and Rül nodded their agreement.

"Sometimes we'll see snow from the Áthradho," said Pava as she turned toward the back of the cart. "I've had to help brush it away from the collectors a few times."

"Depending on how long we're there, how the weather behaves, it's possible we *might* see snow," Falthwën allowed. "We'll only know for sure when we see it—or when we don't."

"I hope we do see snow," Zhalera continued. "Water you can hold in your hands without a bucket? *That* would be something to tell our friends back home!"

"Because nothing else we've been through on this trip would make a good story?!" said Rül. Kalas laughed.

A few days later, the party came to an old stone bridge that spanned a deep, narrow ravine. From somewhere far below came the muffled churn of running water. The suns had just separated in the sky—it was just after midday—and Kalas hopped down and peered into the fissure.

"I hear water, but I don't see anything," he remarked.

"And now you know how the *Óronas Lohwà* earned its name," said Falthwën. "There's a hidden trail, too, just beyond those rocks, that leads to the water itself. It's steep, usually slick, but this late in the year it's probably not too bad. On the other side of the bridge, the road widens: we're perhaps three or four days out from Ïsriba. We'll reach the town of Thosha before day's end: it's just at the bottom of the valley, and that's where we'll resupply. Two or three days from Thosha, we'll come to the city of Âivambar, not quite a day's journey from Ïsriba."

Kalas offered to fill the water buckets and followed Falthwën's directions past a collection of mossy boulders toward the trailhead of the hard-to-find path. It took him a while to reach the bottom: loose leaves and fraying mats of desiccated algae made some rocks deceptively slippery. Beyond a small cove strewn with smooth stones, he saw a waterfall with a drop of maybe fifteen, twenty feet. Dark lines of mud cemented to the cliffs suggested the water should have been about two feet higher. As wide and powerful as the waterfall appeared even now, Kalas wondered how much more impressive it might have been in the spring.

The first sun, just past its apogee, still reached into the gorge, creating rainbows in the cascading spray. Despite Tàfayan's tepid presence, Kalas felt the skin on his arms turn to gooseflesh in the chilling mists. As he gave himself a moment to observe the shifting colors in the air, to breathe in the peculiar scent that reminded him of the lesser falls along the Ilswàr, he thought he glimpsed something dark just behind the waterfall. A cave, perhaps. Kalas considered fording the river—it was only ten or twelve feet wide —but soon thought better of that idea: large, rectangular blocks of granite banked the fast-moving river, and its bottom was just as hidden from his sight as the river itself was hidden from those waiting for him high above.

If it's deeper than I am tall, I could drown before anyone knew anything had happened...

"Lad," Shosafin muttered from over his shoulder. Kalas spun, surprised. The soldier had been invisible for most of the last few days.

"Shosafin?! Where'd you come from? You know what? Never mind…"

"Listen, Kalas," he continued. "Be wary when you get to Thosha: you should be all right, but it's a little too close to Ïsriba, not that far from Âivambar…

"I haven't told you everything—I didn't think I'd need to. Just know this: Ësfàyami's spies are all around. In Thosha? Maybe, but I'm certain she's got some in Âivambar. She'd love to see my head on a pike, but I have reason to believe she has other goals as well.

"I won't be with you—not even in the shadows. Not for a while. I need to find out what Marugan is up to, how he fits into Ësfàyami's accession. I need to know his endgame. You, your cleric: you should be just the distraction I need. Yes, it sounds callous. And it is. Still, don't mistake pragmatism for indifference…

"Here's what you need to know: be careful, be vigilant, and abandon your naïveté—you trust too readily, believe too easily. Those qualities might serve you well elsewhere, but in and around Ïsriba, they'll get you killed—or worse.

"Take this. Hold on to it for me until we meet again. It will be a bane to me—perhaps it'll be a boon to you."

Shosafin tossed something to Kalas, who knew what it was even before he caught it.

"Your sword?" he whispered with unvarnished awe.

He offered no explanation. By the time Kalas looked up from the weapon, its *Poyïsriba* crest glaring at him with its singular emerald eye, the soldier had already disappeared.

6.

"You look like you've seen a ghost!" remarked Zhalera when Kalas reappeared with his buckets full of water—and Shosafin's sword.

He laughed, remembering his first impressions of the man, his early attempts to learn more about the enigmatic figure.

"Maybe I have," he admitted.

She noted the scabbard slung across his shoulder with a quizzical look.

"A 'ghost' asked me to hold onto it for a while. He'll want it back. Someday. I'll still need a sword of my own…" he winked.

"You're persistent, I'll give you that," she sighed and helped him with the water.

On the opposite side of the bridge, the Highway had been paved with immense flagstones—long ago, judging by their cracked faces and canted angles. Within a few miles, the forest thinned out as the road traced its path along the ridge of a series of fallen rocks. It turned and descended through the valley, a dangerous decline tempered through numerous switchbacks. Despite the pavement's condition, it still felt smoother than most other portions of the Highway—even with Rül's hand-carved axle.

Vast meadows clothed in golden grasses and late-blooming flowers swayed with the gentle breezes rolling down from higher elevations. The air's bouquet held weak floral notes underscored with an almost powdery scent. On the road's flatter parts, Runner and Dancer quickened their pace: the improved roads and pleasant smells worked wonders.

"Now *this* is something *I* could get used to!" said Zhalera after a deep breath. "And just look at all these flowers! I don't think I've ever seen so many in one place!"

The others agreed. Falthwën suggested with a wink that she return to the valley in the spring or early summer for an even more impressive spectacle. Kalas looked around, hoping for some sign of Shosafin, for that irritating prickle along the periphery of his senses, but he wasn't surprised when he neither saw nor sensed a thing. From the front of the cart, Rül and Pava laughed at some shared story as the road unwound behind them.

Within a league or so, the valley's slope decreased, the switchbacks disappeared, and the road flattened out. As they entered the lowlands, they witnessed signs of recent harvests in the fields on either side of the Highway. Soon, they noticed sickle-wielding figures cutting wheat or performing other, similar tasks. Rül waved at each person they drove past: some returned cautious approximations of the gesture, but most simply stared, jaws slack, unsure of what to make of this curious collection of travelers.

"What's with the looks? Rül wondered, somewhat frustrated. "You'd think we salted their fields or something!"

"We've reached the outskirts of Thosha, which isn't much larger than Lohwàlar. It's a place where everyone knows everyone. How do you think *Lohwàlarrinme* would react if a stranger showed up in town?"

He smiled, and Kalas blushed. It seemed like such a long time ago when the unknown cleric first arrived in Lohwàlar...

"Not only are we strangers," he continued, "but we're coming down from the West—a realm of sand and waste by their reckoning. You must understand: *nothing* comes down from the West —nothing good, at least!

"Still, *Thosharinme* tend to be friendlier than most. So long as we present ourselves with the appropriate decorum, we should be welcome...Master Rül, follow the road for another two leagues or so, if you please."

Each field they passed seemed smaller than the last, and before long, what had been a random assortment of farm houses assumed a denser, more ordered configuration. Within a league, they reached a crossroads. One corner displayed an empty steel cage, about the

size of a man. Though filthy and speckled with rust, it looked otherwise sound. It hung from a wooden boom and swayed—just a little
—with the wind. Rül stopped the cart at the intersection: before he
signaled his horses to continue, a mob of people—commoners like
themselves, from their looks—thronged into the streets, cursing at
an older man, smirking and bound in irons, and pelting him with
reeking rotten vegetables.

With wide eyes, one of the mob noticed the cart and stormed
toward the company. Kalas bristled and wrapped his fingers around
his borrowed sword. Zhalera must have felt him tense: she gripped
his arm and held him where they sat.

"Lushà vam, sàyahal," said Falthwën with a cheerful voice. Nodding at the spectacle, he continued: "But not such a good day for
him, no? What was his crime?"

Something in the cleric's tone, perhaps, gave the woman coming
toward them pause. She cocked her head and squinted, like she was
ransacking her memory for an answer. After a moment, she nodded and, with a jerk in the direction of the commotion, screeched,
"Theft! That's what it is! Nïmrïk, the old *thragad!* Up to his old
tricks! But none of you is from around here! No, there's something
off about the lot of you, there is! No matter: keep the peace, and
you won't end up gibbeted like ol' Nïmrïk!"

"I assure you, *shâu,* we harbor no mischievous intent toward
Thosha's people! You're right: we're not from around here…If I
might trouble you further, perhaps you could recommend a lodging
place in town?"

The woman, aged perhaps five or six Sevens, with pale green
eyes and light brown hair tied back in thick braids, regarded them
with suspicion for another moment or two. Kalas shifted his position, causing the setting suns' light to flash from the gilded hilt of
Shosafin's sword.

Her eyes darted toward the source of the gleam and widened

again: her tone turned almost deferential as she said, "Go straight. Past the wall, look for *Mbirin's Place*. She'll take good care of you. Tell her Rashab sent you!"

"Mbirin's Place?" said Falthwën with mild surprise, as if the name conjured up some long-forgotten memory. Kalas thought he glimpsed a faint smile bend the corners of the cleric's mouth.

With a toothy grin and an odd curtsy, Rashab let herself get swallowed by the glut incensed villagers as they caged "ol' Nimrïk" in his gibbet. Rül gave his reins an urgent flick. Dancer and Runner seemed only too happy to comply.

"What was that about? I thought you said *Thosharinme* were friendly!" Kalas asked once they'd gained enough distance from the crossroads.

"*Friendlier*—not necessarily *friendly*," Falthwën clarified. "It seems we've come to this part of the world in uncertain times…"

Kalas spared a cautious glance at the crested pommel of his borrowed weapon. "Sh—uh, our friend, I mean—said to *be wary* in Thosha…"

"Something to keep in mind," conceded the cleric with a look over his shoulder. "Most definitely something to keep in mind."

Chapter XV

Within Sight of the Capital

FALTHWËN CLAIMED THOSHA WAS SIMILAR TO LOHWÀLAR in size, but from Kalas' perspective, size was the sole similarity shared between the two towns: Lohwàlar had no wall —none that had survived into the present age, at least—whereas roughly twelve feet of wood and stone encircled Thosha's oldest structures. A pair of disinterested guards (whose uniforms bore Thosha's crest—not Ïsriba's) leaned against the wall on either side of a large, opened gate. As Rül drew up and slowed the cart to a stop, one of the guards gave him a curious glance. He mumbled something to his partner—who laughed and shook his head—then waved them through.

"Thosha is a *Poyïsriba* protectorate—same as Lohwàlar, really —but in most respects, it considers itself a sovereign state. In truth, because it's reasonably close to the capital, and because its resources are unremarkable, no greater entity has given it a second thought," said the cleric when Kalas asked about the emblem on the guards' uniforms. "Centuries ago, in simpler times, Ïsriba maintained a garrison in Lohwàlar, too."

"That's where Valderïk and his men stayed," Kalas confirmed. "Before that, I don't think anyone had really used the place in Sevens."

The homes and buildings outside of Thosha's wall had maintained some measure of distance between one another; inside, however, everything seemed cramped: the streets narrowed, and Rül wondered if he'd be able to squeeze through some of them.

"When you said it was about the same size as Lohwàlar, this isn't what I had in mind!" Zhalera said as she looked around.

"This isn't what your town looks like?" Pava asked. "In a way, this place reminds me of home: everything's right next to everything."

"And you don't feel like it's all packed too close together?"

"I guess it's what I know," the *úrukilmukrit* girl shrugged. "Never seemed all that 'packed' to me."

"No, I suppose it wouldn't," Zhalera allowed after thinking about it. "Like you said, it's what you know. I'd probably be just as uncomfortable under the Áthradho as you were sleeping outside!"

"So, uh, we're past the wall…do you think we keep going straight?" said Rül as he steered his team along the road. A few children pointed grubby fingers and shouted for their parents as he passed: "*Ildozhatme*, Mother! *Bar*, Father! *Ildozhatme!*" Much to such parents' displeasure, Falthwën smiled and waved, which sent most of them scurrying for their mothers' skirts.

"Nice kids," Pava smirked. Zhalera chuckled.

"Follow the road, my child," the cleric suggested with a sweeping gesture and a grin. "Thosha's not so big we'll remain lost for any length of time!"

After they passed a few more side streets—all of which looked the same to Kalas—Rül reined in the horses. With a sideways nod, he indicated a large sign hung above a well-worn door. Despite their apparent age, both the sign and the door seemed sturdy, a testament to their construction and upkeep. Carved into a bright, pale yellow field, faded dark red letters and flaked gilding spelled out the establishment's name:

"*Mbirindas Diru.* That has to be it, right?" said Rül.

"How many places do you think this Mbirin has?" Kalas smirked as he jumped onto the street. Its flagstone pavement felt strange to his legs, like it was *too hard,* somehow. "I'll go in and check—"

"Permit me, young sir," Falthwën insisted as he alighted from his seat. Though his tone was amiable enough, Kalas had learned to interpret its subtleties with more aplomb. He stopped, looked around, and suddenly felt the invisible pressure of unnumbered eyes upon him. At that moment, the walls of the surrounding buildings seemed to lean in, to press him down and remind him just how *small* he truly was. He shivered in the late autumn air, wrapped his arms around himself and felt the press of his sword's hilt against his ribs.

It…will be a bane to me…

"I mean, all right, that sounds good," he finished. He made a show of stretching his arms and legs—taking pains to keep the old soldier's weapon concealed—before climbing back into the cart.

Perhaps it'll be a boon to you.

The ancient cleric held Kalas' gaze for a weighty moment, then nodded and tried the door. Hung on well-oiled hinges, it opened without effort, spilling candle light onto the road. The laughter and conversation transpiring within Mbirin's Place wilted when exposed to the dark edge of twilight.

"*Lushà rist, sàmeyahal!*" Falthwën boomed as the heavy wooden door swung shut.

2.

"What do you think's going on?" Pava wondered with a nervous undertone in her voice. Kalas felt like the few minutes that had passed since the cleric entered Mbirin's Place had been much longer. He climbed into Falthwën's place in the front and kept a hand on his sword.

Just in case.

"I'm sure he's fine," the young man insisted. He looked back at Zhalera, who nodded with just a touch too much emphasis.

"I'll bet he's just making arrangements," Rül smiled, attempting to convince himself as much as the others. "Y'know, maybe asking where to find things in this town? Like a cartwright, maybe?"

None of them had ever been away from home before: not like this, far removed from Lohwàlar's well-known confines and its relative safety. Before the wolves, Kalas couldn't remember a time when anything *bad* had happened there: now that they were leagues and leagues distant from everything familiar, the world at large seemed suspect. With nothing else to do, they waited.

A minute or so later, Falthwën exited Mbirin's Place, the sounds of revelry restored inside. With him was a thick, middle-aged woman, her arm draped around his waist. Clothed in a taut, dark red gown overlaid with a drink-stained apron, her gold-colored eyes danced in the scattered torchlight as she examined the cleric's companions. From her movements and the way her muscles shifted beneath the sheath of her glittering dress, Kalas thought she looked like someone who knew how to handle herself. Catching his stare, she smiled, released her grip on Falthwën, and approached the cart. Something in Kalas' harried expression must have amused her. When she reached him, she pressed her considerable bust against the cart's frame and held Kalas' stare for a moment. Then she laughed and introduced herself, spilling kinked, pumpkin-colored curls from the pile pinned atop her head.

"Master Kalas, yes? Call me Yëlisha! Welcome to Thosha!"

"Uh, hi, *Shâu* Yëlisha," he stammered. Helpless, he risked a glance at Falthwën. "Uh, I…*sushoyëthu al nir pirathas…*"

"And I you!" she returned. Despite her build and bearing, her voice had an almost childlike quality about it, and even though she spoke at a conversational volume, it had *presence,* too.

"Let's see: Rül, Pava, and Zhalera, *hish?* Come, come! I'll have rooms prepared for you by the time you've tended to your horses! Falthwën: the stable's where it's always been!"

Before she turned to re-enter the tavern, she spared another glance at Kalas—at all of them, winked, and whispered something to the cleric as she squeezed his shoulder. With a swish of her hips, she disappeared into the raucous din.

"I'll just say it: who was *that?!*" said Rül, just as bewildered as the rest.

"I thought we were looking for someone named *Mbirin?*" Pava added as she looked to the others.

"Mbirin was Yëlisha's great-great-grandmother. It's been Sevens since I've heard that name. To my shame, I'd almost forgotten!" Falthwën informed them as he chuckled to himself: some private memory, perhaps, that he opted not to share. "In those days, this place was…less than safe: that's why I didn't want a child—forgive the term—to be the first to go inside. Mbirin *acquired* the establishment from her father, foul creature that he was, with a little help. W—I had to leave Thosha before I had a chance to see what she'd done with the place."

"'With a little help,' you say?" Zhalera said, intrigued. The others shared her interest.

"It's late *urínme,* and the horses need care…"

"No! Tell the story!" insisted Kalas. "I mean: please?"

Falthwën laughed, shook his head, and said, "I'll say this:

Mbirin was a spirited young woman, a hard worker with a big heart. She…made a request—something small, really—and it was within my power to help. This place had a different name back then, and under Mbirin's father's control, its infamy was well-known. I played a part in putting such things to an end…

"Yëlisha's the spitting image of her great-great-grandmother —even more so in her character, her attitude, than in her form. I'll bet it's been Sevens since Mbirin's last customers walked the earth, but her portrait still hangs on the wall, and the resemblance is astounding. It's easy to see why Yëlisha's customers have taken to calling her by Mbirin's name.

"Again: it's late! Come, children! I can't speak for all of you, but I'm looking forward to something other than stale bread and strips of cured meat! After we've tended to Dancer and Runner, we'll see if Yëlisha's kitchen is anything like her great-great-grandmother's!"

3·

Although he hadn't known just what to expect, once inside Mbirin's Place, Kalas realized everything seemed exactly the way it should. Intricate woven-metal constructs bearing oil lamps hung above a number of stout wooden tables laden with plates and tankards belonging to a healthy number of patrons. The walls, mostly stone, looked like they'd been whitewashed, once: now they were covered with a warm yellow patina. Dark-stained beams spanned the ceiling. On one side of the main room, an immense fireplace, filled with crackling logs, spat an occasional ember into the air and spilled its warmth into the comfortable environment; on the other, a broad staircase led to a second level and a balconied hallway lined with doors. An eclectic array of figures enjoyed their hostess' hospitality while a string trio played a jaunty tune from a small stage. At the back, on the far side of a maze of chairs, Yëlisha filled someone's cup from behind the bar. Above her, Mbirin's portrait surveyed her legacy. Yëlisha's resemblance to her great-great-grandmother was irrefutable; indeed, Kalas found it hard to believe Yëlisha herself hadn't been the artist's subject.

Once finished, she beckoned for them as she stepped through a small gate. On the floor with the rest of them, she looked almost a foot shorter than Rül, a few inches taller than Pava. Maybe Zhalera's height. She wiped her hands on her apron, barked an order to a barmaid, and led the party to an empty table insulated from most of the tavern's restless energy. When everyone was seated, she motioned for a tray loaded with steaming meats and vegetables and set it in front of them.

"Eat! Enjoy!" she ordered as she poured each person a mug of warm, sweet-smelling liquid. "Your rooms are at the top of the stairs, down the hall, and to the left. When you're finished, just come find me!"

Before they came inside, Zhalera asked Falthwën what to do with her sword. He suggested she keep it close, so she slung it across her back. The cleric said so long as it remained wrapped, no one would think twice about it. Kalas kept Shosafin's scabbard hidden beneath his tunic. The woman at the crossroads—Rashad? Rashab?—had expressed a curious interest in it, but he still wasn't comfortable advertising his possession of someone else's *Poyïsriba* weaponry. They left the rest of their things with the cart. Rül kept an eye on Yëlisha's stable hands until he was satisfied his horses would be well cared for.

When they finished eating and drinking as much as their stomachs could handle, the cleric waved for their hostess, whom they followed up the stairs and toward their rooms.

"Uh, Falthwën," Kalas hissed: "how are we going to *pay* for all of this?"

Before he could answer, Yëlisha turned and gave the boy a stern look.

"I'll thank you not to mention such nonsense in my house again, young man! Understood?"

"What? I just...uh, I mean...Yes! *Al mekâëthu, Shâu* Yëlisha!"

She held his panicked gaze for just a moment, then gave him a conspiratorial wink as her lips widened into a grin and displaced her severe expression. Kalas finally realized she'd only been teasing him.

"I don't know what...Falthwën's told you, but this place wouldn't be what it is today had not he and his—"

The cleric cleared his throat. Kalas and the others turned their heads to ensure he was all right. He was. He gave them all a smile and nodded at their hostess.

"My family owes him a great debt."

Addressing the cleric, she continued: "My grandmothers would be jealous to learn that you've returned to Thosha on my watch!"

She offered Falthwën another wink, pointed out where they'd be staying, and returned to her duties behind her bar.

Yëlisha provided the cleric with three keys, but he suggested they all share the largest room: Falthwën trusted their hostess—not her other guests. With a self-deprecating laugh, he confessed he hadn't quite abandoned the late-remembered lessons learned from his prior experiences in Thosha. Inside the best of the three rooms, Falthwën closed his eyes for a moment and hummed something almost inaudible before he relaxed.

"Very good," he said with a curt nod. Pava gasped when he blew subtle breaths of pale green fire from the tip of his staff into each lantern. She reached for Rül, who stifled a laugh as he reassured her with a squeeze of her shoulder.

"Oh, right!" he said. "I'm sure I had that same expression the first time I saw him do that, too!"

"Do all of you have…powers? gifts? abilities as well?" she wondered.

"Afraid I'm just a farm boy," he smiled. "No 'powers' to speak of."

"Same," added Zhalera.

Kalas drew his knife, tested its balance, and tossed it at the floor between Pava's dusty leather boots where it stuck fast without so much as a wobble.

"She's too modest," he insisted, gesturing for the cave-dweller girl to pull the blade from the boards. "She's gonna be Lohwàlar's best blacksmith! Made that for my birthday. Go on, pick it up, tell me—no, tell *her* what you think!"

"Kalas!" Zhalera began, but Pava was already holding it in her hands and examining it in the lanterns' idle light.

"You *made* this? It's *beautiful!*" she exclaimed as she traced its lines, felt its edge with a fingertip. "Kalas is right: you *definitely* have a gift!"

"It's…it's just a knife," Zhalera demurred.

Pava handed the knife back to Kalas, who aimed a smile at Zhalera as he sheathed it. The lanterns, though dim, cast light enough to reveal fresh pink circles blooming in her cheeks—and her own attenuated smile.

Despite the room's utilitarian air, its minimalistic furnishings gleamed with fresh polish, and the bed linens smelled like the outdoors. Four beds, two to a wall, formed a path toward a large, low chest of drawers against the back. On the chest stood a ceramic pitcher filled with water, a wash basin, and a collection of towels.

"Hey, Falthwën, there are only four beds," said Zhalera as she dabbed her face and the back of her neck.

"Those are for each of you," he insisted. "Don't worry about me: I have a few things to discuss with Yëlisha anyway."

Before she could protest, he flashed a quick, reassuring grin and stepped into the hallway. Kalas heard him mutter something; somehow, he sensed the movement of the old cleric's staff as he scribed his symbols in the air. Faint green radiance pooled at the edges of the door as Falthwën's steps faded into the evening.

The room's stone walls must have seemed more familiar to Pava: she fell asleep within minutes. Rül, too, climbed into a bed—fell on top of one, at least: faint snores accented his breathing, deep and slow.

"Driving that cart for weeks on end must take a lot out of him," Kalas remarked as he sat on one of the remaining beds. Zhalera nodded, sat down beside him, and leaned her head against his shoulder. Neither said a word, and they rested in wearied silence for a while.

Soon, she fell asleep as well. Taking pains not to wake her, Kalas eased her into her bed's warmth. As he covered her with bedclothes, something in her features held his gaze: fatigue, yes; sadness and frustration, too. He whispered a remembered phrase from the Song and kissed her forehead. Straightening, he watched some of the tension in her eyebrows dissolve, the downward bend in her lips flatten out before curving into a smile.

"*Theshahal ëth shir nitsar, Âsrufin,*" he breathed. "*Al mazhëthu, ëth seyit, hish? Sarad al shir al sofer, á sarad al nirest...*"

4.

When morning came, Pava, Zhalera, and Kalas left Rül, still sleeping, and headed downstairs. Falthwën was already at the bar, listening to some story of Yëlisha's. Kalas couldn't make out the words, but her expression shifted through myriad emotions as she and the cleric shared their tales.

"Good morning!" she beamed with a wink when she noticed

them. She gave Falthwën a look, a light touch atop his forearm, and turned toward the newcomers. "Lose someone?"

"Still asleep," Pava volunteered.

"From what Falthwën's told me, he has every reason to be tired! As do the rest of you! Come now, let's get some breakfast in your bellies!"

As she addressed them, her gaze seemed to linger a moment longer on Kalas than on the others. He thought about saying something, but she disappeared into the kitchen before he could open his mouth. At the same time, someone entered through the heavy door at the front, shuffled toward a table, and collapsed into a chair. His head hit the table with an echoing thud; soon, his snores shook the fixtures overhead.

"Rough night?" whispered Pava. Kalas thought there was something familiar about the man, but he dismissed the idea when Yëlisha returned with trays filled with bowls of spiced oatmeal and plates of sizzling sausages. As she arrayed them around her guests, she looked up at the new arrival. She looked again when she realized who he was.

"Nïmrïk!" she muttered with a bemused grin. "Haven't seen him in…what? a week or two? Which is odd, because he's in here all the time! And I thought they tossed him in the gibbet yesterday?"

"*That's* why he looked familiar!" Kalas exclaimed. Nïmrïk stirred, smacked his lips, then resumed his snoring.

"When he's not in here, he's usually up there," Yëlisha chuckled. "Always escapes somehow."

"A woman—Rashab, I think?—said he was a thief?" Zhalera coaxed.

"Thief? Hmm…no, he's really more of a trickster," she allowed. "I think most folks just get tired of his never-ending mischief: *that's* probably what gets him tossed in the gibbet. Also, that's probably why no one's too upset when he turns up again a day or two later."

Yëlisha thought for a moment, laughed to herself, and added: "It's a shame, really: I've watched him long enough to know he doesn't have a mean bone in his body! Most of his misadventures are just harmless larks."

"I guess when Rül wakes up we'll have to find some place to get the cart fixed?" Zhalera wondered as she sawed through a sausage link.

"No need!" Yëlisha interrupted with a dismissive wave. "Falthwën told me about…your trip. Seems you, ah, ran into some trouble, *hish?* As it turns out, I happen to own a few coaches. I'd like to have a discussion with your friend Rül."

"With me?" said Rül, still groggy, as he shambled down the stairs and toward the bar. "What's—Oh! *Aswanthalu!*"

He banged his leg on Nïmrïk's table as he passed by, but the codger only raised his head and looked around for a moment; then, with an airy flick of his hand, he resumed his nap.

"There he is!" laughed Yëlisha as she set a plate next to Pava's.

She pays attention, Kalas noted.

"I was telling your friends…Your cart: how attached to it are you?"

"What? Not very. I mean, it's a cart. Needs a new axle, which I was hoping—"

"Rül, my dear! You're not much of a salesman, are you?" she said with a gleam in her eye. "I'll tell you what I'd started telling them: I have…a coach or two. I'd be willing to trade one of them for your cart—and I think I know just the one! Its suspension might not be the greatest—rides a little too soft sometimes, but its bones are solid."

"You'd…trade a coach…for a farm cart?" puzzled Rül, still not quite awake. "Why would you—?"

"Make the trade!" Kalas hissed.

"I—yeah? Okay, sure," said Rül, still unsure of what was

happening.

"Excellent!" Yëlisha exclaimed as she took his hand and gave it two enthusiastic pumps. "Now, have a seat! Eat! Afterward, I'll take you to your acquisition!"

"This is way nicer than the old cart!" Rül whispered to Falthwën as Yëlisha showed them around the small carriage house attached to her tavern. The coach she'd elected to exchange sat higher than the cart from Lohwàlar, but its pole was positioned in about the same place. Rül examined its undercarriage and discovered axles suspended from sturdy straps of oiled leather. The cabin boasted dark red upholstery the color of Yëlisha's dress from the night before. The boot was big enough to hold most of their gear; the imperial was sturdy enough to hold the rest. The box seat boasted plush cushions fringed with gold: Rül climbed into position and seemed to sink into them, grinning from ear to ear.

"Lady, are you sure—?" he began before Yëlisha cut him off.

"We had a deal, young man! There's no backing out! We shook on it!" she winked. "I trust this coach will satisfy your needs?"

Rül nodded.

When they returned to Mbirin's Place, Nïmrïk was gone. Several other customers occupied tables in his stead. One of her barmaids caught her eye and called for her attention. Before Yëlisha went to check on things, she invited Falthwën and his company to stay as long as they liked and informed him that their horses had been massaged, brushed, and fed and would be ready to go when they were. She'd also taken the liberty of laundering their clothes and replenishing their foodstuffs.

"Yëlisha, this is too much," Falthwën began, but their hostess would hear none of it.

"Don't you start in, too! You and—you might have left before my grandmothers undid all the wrong my great-great-grandfather wrought, but they never would have been able to accomplish so much had you not been here at just the right time. No, you and anyone you deem worthy companions are always welcome here! Consider it a down-payment on a debt neither I nor my grandmothers could ever hope to repay."

"Mbirin owes me nothing. I thought I'd made as much clear when I'd left. Perhaps she didn't understand?"

"Oh, she passed down what you said. That doesn't mean I can't express our gratitude in some small way!

"Yëlisha," Falthwën acquiesced with a sigh, "you sound *just* like her, you know?"

"A compliment!" she grinned. Her expression turned dour as she continued: "But I must tell you: things at the capital aren't…well, you probably know better than I do: rumors of war, the queen's lust for power…You've come at a curious time, *âu* cleric!

"Now, if I'm not available to send you on your way, promise me you'll stop in again on your way back to…Lohwàlar, was it?"

Falthwën inclined his head, and, with her signature wink, she resumed her responsibilities.

"All right, *urínme*," he said when Yëlisha vanished into her kitchen, "You heard the woman! The cart—the *coach* is packed and ready to go! Let's collect our things from the room and get back on the road: we're still a few days out from Âivambar—and the next leg of our journey!"

5.

Runner and Dancer weren't quite sure what to make of the new coach, but after a few easy miles, they seemed to enjoy its smoother ride. Yëlisha's stable hands had worked wonders on the horses' wearied muscles and tender hooves. While most everyone had been sleeping, she'd also had someone reshoe both horses: judging by the team's almost playful gait despite their load, it seemed her farrier plied his trade with admirable skill.

"Almost as good as Gandhan's work," said Rül over his shoulder, his tone plaintive. "Almost."

A small sliding window, now open, separated the coach's interior from the box where Rül and Pava sat. Zhalera smiled as her eyes moistened. Kalas took her hand and gave it a gentle squeeze. Falthwën, who'd joined them in the cabin, said nothing. They'd invited Pava to ride with them as well, suggested the enclosed space might be more like her caves, but for some reason, she'd opted to ride up front with Rül.

"It's not like I *never* went outside!" she insisted. "We only have a few more days before we reach Ïsriba, and there's so much more to see from up here!"

Kalas and Zhalera shared a smirk when she rationalized her choice, but both confessed that the scenery through these more settled realms was breathtaking. Well-dressed flagstones topped the surface of the roads that cut through rock-walled meadows, traveled over sturdy stone bridges, and curved through towering forests thinning with the chill of autumn. The Highway inclined as they distanced themselves from Thosha: its increasing elevation provided gorgeous views from their ever-changing perspective.

They passed a few carts, coaches, and other travelers over the next few days, and Kalas found himself surprised at the unadulterated normalcy of it all: being on the road for nearly a month had become *familiar* to him. He kept hoping for some sign of Shosafin, but the old soldier remained elsewhere.

"What do you think Yëlisha meant?" he asked one night over a crackling fire. "Rumors of war?" He stabbed the coals with a pine branch: it snapped and popped as the fire consumed its tip in seconds.

"Yëlisha assumes I'm better informed than I really am," Falthwën admitted. "If I had to guess—and I *am* guessing here—I'd assume she meant the kingdom of Ralothova, in the distant East. Or perhaps Tsobarut, toward the North. I suppose it could be any number of realms: those are the two closest. Kësharan would have been a distant third, but, as you know, it hasn't been a kingdom for hundreds of Sevens."

"Kësharan?" said Pava, her interest piqued. "I've heard that name before!"

"That's no surprise," said the cleric: "Thousands of years ago, Kësharan was the capital of a powerful kingdom—Lohwàlar would have been well within its borders. Anyway, if memory serves, I believe Kësharan traded with the *úrukilmukritme* for mineral crystals—"

"Father and I saw pieces of crystal there," Kalas interjected. "Part of a huge, broken window, I think."

Falthwën nodded, "Those pieces could have very well come from the Áthradho. Probably did, in fact. I know the window you're describing: even the Night of Falling Skies hadn't wrecked it wholly, although I suppose almost nine hundred years of wind and rain and *ilâegsal* have exacted a heavy toll…"

"Why would Ësfàyami want to go to war?" said Kalas as he steered the conversation back to his original question.

"I'm guessing Yëlisha answered that for us: her 'lust for power,' she said. Without a better understanding of the geopolitical landscape, that's the best I can come up with for now. If we're observant, if we're careful, we'll probably learn more in Âivambar—and more, of course, Ïsriba."

Three days out from Thosha—Dancer and Runner had made great time—they reached the gate to Âivambar. High and imposing, separated from the surrounding terrain by a deep gorge and protected with a sturdy-looking portcullis, even the walls of the city suggested nobility. As Kalas unstrapped his sword and hid it beneath his seat, he suggested Zhalera do the same with hers. Shosafin's admonition pealed in his thoughts—

A bane to me...a boon to you...

—and still, he wasn't quite ready to test the old soldier's theory.

Rül drove them over a wide stone bridge and stopped just shy of the pointed iron teeth dangling in the air above them. A pair of guards approached from opposite directions, and Kalas sensed rather than saw others waiting on the ramparts. One of them knocked on the coach's door and tried to open it before anyone inside had a chance to respond. Falthwën raised an eyebrow, undid the latch, and suggested the guard try again.

"Good day, friend!" said the cleric as the soldier opened the door. He said nothing as he poked his head inside and looked around. When he finished examining the interior, he left the door open. Falthwën kept his smile in place the whole time: Kalas and Zhalera, taking his cue, adopted deferential expressions as well.

"Point of origin? Destination? Intent?" growled the other guard as he kept an eye on Rül and Pava. Whether appreciating her exotic paleness or her striking form—or both—even from within the cabin Kalas noticed Rül bristle as the guard's unsubtle leer.

"Lohwàlar, good sir! We've come from Lohwàlar," Falthwën informed him. "We're headed to the capital—to Ïsriba—to speak with the queen."

The guard erupted with laughter. Cruel, belittling laughter intended to communicate his superiority over such lowborn folk.

"Is that so?" he dripped. "Lohwàlar, you say? Seems I've heard of such a place. Recently, too. And you're on your way to see the queen, you say?"

He glanced toward the bow slits in the tower above the gate, then at his fellow sentry, who nodded after looking toward the Highway, as though he'd seen or heard something behind them. With a dismissive huff, the soldier waved them through.

"Welcome to Âivambar," he said, making sure they understood that they were *not*, in fact, welcome.

6.

"I don't like this place," Zhalera whispered as they rode through well-maintained avenues, past manicured landscapes and bright, cheerful-looking shops. As in Thosha, only more so, residences were piled on top of one another. Most windows, tall and elaborate, were open to the afternoon suns; others remained closed or bore shades to blunt the intensity of their rays.

"Sure, it *looks* nice enough—beautiful, really…I just don't like it."

Kalas agreed. After wrapping its scabbard in cloths, he returned Shosafin's sword to his leg, though he still did his best to keep it hidden. "Shosafin said Ësfàyami had spies everywhere. Maybe it's just me, maybe it's just because of his warning, but I can't shake the feeling we're being watched, even now."

"We'll keep our visit brief," Falthwën nodded. "Âivambar is a big place—aptly named, too: soon, we should be able to see the battlements of *Âiva pïni Ilrâidh Fin*—Castle of the Hunter Bird."

"Yëlisha told me about a place we might stay the night. Someplace…not *safe*, but less dangerous than most others. Young lady, your intuition serves you well: I, too, sense an unwholesomeness about us.

"Rül," he said through the small window, "Look for the inn with a red door and three windows: you'll know what I mean when you see it. *The Black Falcon*, it's called."

"Red door, black falcon. Got it!" said Rül as he flicked the reins.

After another mile (and reluctant directions from some of Âivambar's less surly citizens), they reached The Black Falcon. Falthwën instructed them to remain with the coach as he entered the establishment.

Like most other façades they'd observed, the Falcon's exterior sparkled in the waning suns, especially its polished steel hardware. Painted a deep red the color of fresh arterial blood, the door seemed to drink in the light. The cobblestones leading to its hitching posts (recently oiled) had been swept not too long ago, too.

Falthwën emerged from the Falcon about half an hour later and showed them where to park the coach and where to board the horses. After that, he led them through a side door, away from the inn's main hall, and toward a dim staircase. At the top of the stairs, he produced a key from within the folds of his robe and let them all inside. He waited a few minutes for each of them to find a place within the small room—smaller than the room at Yëlisha's—before he explained what he'd learned from Firïg, the innkeeper:

"Something portentous hovers just beyond the horizon," he began in low tones as he eased himself into an unremarkable chair. "Ësfàyami's grip on the kingdom has been slipping for the last few years. According to Firïg, she's been issuing decrees that, on the surface, seem to benefit her subjects; on closer examination, ultimately, they serve to consolidate her power. What's infuriating, he says, is that until recently, most people—particularly the ones most injured by her edicts—have been unwilling to take an objective look at things: they've remained convinced her hurtful policies are somehow helping them.

"'She's proven herself adept at statecraft,' Firïg said, 'but it seems she's overplayed her hand. People are waking up to the true costs of her schemes, and they're not happy!' She's attempted to placate as many subjects as she can, but her reach has at last exceeded her grasp. Firïg thinks *she's* the one hinting at the possibility of war, trying to gauge the people's reaction.

"His points may be valid, but there's an underlying…call it *energy,* I guess: there's an underlying *energy* running through the world of late. Ësfàyami will be held accountable for her choices—some day—but I suspect there are other players we've yet to encounter.

"Kalas, the day you woke from the *rudzhegu* attack, I told you I had some errands to attend to: until recently, *zhàrudzhme* had remained content to prowl the shadows. That's changed. I can't help thinking about your friend Dzharëth. I can't help thinking about Ilbardhën's tale, about King Rufàran's disappearance. I can't help thinking it was more than coincidence at work that day. Conferring with my colleagues would have been one of my 'errands.' I say *would have been* because, as you know, I never reached my destination. Ïsriba."

"You looked like you were in bad shape when you showed up under the Temple," Kalas prodded. "Like you'd lost a fight or something. You never did give Shosafin a real answer about *how* you got there…"

"You're not wrong, *dhëmahal:* I *had* 'lost a fight,' as you put it," the cleric said with a self-deprecating air. "Time, I believed, was of the essence, and so I chose to *kalswàr*—'light-travel'—not unlike what you did when you moved us away from the Áthradho. I realized too late that certain other powers had been watching me: as soon as I merged with the *kalthesh*—the 'light realm'—these powers captured me within the event horizon of a singularity. Think of it as a cage that's all but impossible to escape. Loradan—a dear *friend,* shaken by my absence, searched high and low for me for weeks. She found me and managed to collapse the singularity. This freed me, yes, but the stresses nearly unmade me, which is why I had to wait before returning to Lohwàlar. In Deridzhas, you asked why I couldn't *kalswàr* away from there (though not with those words): *that's* why. Our adversaries have writ their mark upon me, preventing me from merging with the *kalthesh* lest they capture me again.

"It's that *energy* that's undergirding the upheaval the world is facing. An *absence* of light that seeks to subsume the entirety of creation within its utter darkness. It's my hope that we'll be able to put an end to this encroaching night before it's too late."

"I have *so* many questions and *no idea* where to begin," Kalas reeled.

The cleric smiled and offered the boy an understanding nod.

"That's fair," he confessed. "Right now, though, even though it's a little early, let's get cleaned up and head downstairs, get something to eat. No doubt we'll attract attention: if we're in and out before the regulars stumble in for the night, we might be all right."

More spacious and better appointed than Mbirin's Place, Kalas noted The Black Falcon's common room lacked the same warmth, the same charm. A handful of townsfolk occupied tables over here, a bar stool over there, all of whom regarded the newcomers with abject suspicion: even the drunks, it seemed, believed themselves to be of higher station than this out-of-place band of travelers.

Firïg, for his part, saw them enter and offered a familiar nod as Falthwën led the others toward a secluded table. At the cleric's curious suggestion, Kalas wore Shosafin's sword across his back: as he moved, its falconine crest flashed in the inn's hazy light. Once seated, Falthwën began a superficial conversation: his companions understood and responded in kind. The innkeeper brought them a round of drinks, promised someone would be with them soon, and pretended not to notice Kalas' sword.

More people filtered into the Falcon as the suns sank ever lower. They'd almost finished with their meal when a rough figure with a tankard in each hand bumped into a chair and sloshed mead or beer all over their table. Kalas recognized him as someone who'd been at the bar even before they arrived: judging from his faltering

steps, reddened cheeks, and apparent inability to navigate his surroundings, the beverages in his hands weren't his first.

"Hey! Watch where you're going!" he slurred as he rounded on
Zhalera, who happened to be closest to the brute.

"I'm sorry," she said, head down after risking a glance at
Falthwën.

"You made me spill my drink, *nimdzhastur ádhemín!* What are
you gonna do to fix it?"

Although the man was a mountain, perhaps seven feet tall
and half as wide with scarred hands the size of Kalas' head, Kalas
couldn't—no, *wouldn't*—tolerate such belligerence. Raw courage
—or foolishness—welled up from some hot place within him as
he grit his teeth.

"Sir! *You* bumped into *her*. You owe *her* an apology."

"Child!" cautioned Falthwën even as he realized his warning
came too late.

"Oho! The doxy has a friend!" he snarled. He downed the contents of one of his cups and tossed it over his shoulder: it clattered
to the ground somewhere behind him. Though it seemed a struggle,
he brought both of his watery, bloodshot eyes to bear on Kalas. He
raised his empty fist and waggled it just in front of the boy's face.
Rül, large in his own right, stood—tried to, at least: Falthwën
sensed his movement and stayed him with a touch.

"Tell me, *rudzhín:* what are you gonna d—"

Kalas was on his feet before the lout finished his threat. In one
fluid motion—*stone and water,* he remembered—he unsheathed
his sword and swatted the man's arm away with the flat; next, he
pointed its gleaming tip at the man's throat. He noticed the rest of
the blade still bore traces of *nimilrâigme* blood: so did the ruffian,
despite his compromised faculties. His bloodshot eyes remained
fixed along its length.

No one moved. No one made a sound as the inn's patrons held

their collective breaths. Light from a pair of fireplaces flickered along the lines of the sword's crossguard and crested pommel, catching in the emerald eye of its *Poyïsriba* falcon.

CHAPTER XVI

In the Custody of the Crown

THE HOT ANGER THAT HAD RISEN IN KALAS' BLOOD subsided—and with it, his bravado. He maintained the façade as best he could, however: praying his voice didn't crack from the stress of the situation, he demanded, "You were saying?"

The drunkard backed away, knocking over a table in the process. Someone complained; others chuckled. The boy held his sword high and took a step forward.

When did this thing get so heavy?! he wondered.

"You tell him!" someone shouted. Others grunted their agreement. "Irudh should've known better than to pick a fight with a *Poyïsriba* soldier—even if he is a little short!"

"Irudh, is it?" said Kalas. "Well, Irudh? Don't you have something to say?"

"I—I'm sorry! I should have watched where I was going! I'm sorry!" he blubbered. His watery eyes glistened as he dropped his other mug and held up his empty hands.

Kalas raised his sword and, after giving Irudh an opportunity to anticipate the worst, brought it down with a snap, flipping it sideways and absorbing its momentum at the last second so the once-belligerent figure received no more than a slight tap on the forehead. The combination of fear and alcohol must have overwhelmed his system: his eyes, struggling to keep track of the blade, rolled toward the back of his head and stayed there while he collapsed onto the Falcon's floor.

Most of the Falcon's patrons erupted in cheers and laughter as Irudh fell. Several came up to Kalas, patted him on the back, and congratulated him for his restraint.

"Irudh's in here most every night, making a scene whenever he thinks no one'll mess with him!" someone said.

"I can't believe he didn't recognize the color of your scabbard! Serves him right, the ne'er-do-well!" said another.

"I told him to knock it off! Just a matter of time before he picked the wrong fight!"

"Lemme buy you a drink!"

His adrenaline nearly spent, Kalas glanced at his friends for help. Rül stood and made his way to Kalas' side.

"Uh, K—I mean, mister…soldier! It's time we, uh…"

"We have…a mission—The mission! In the morning!" added Pava, who joined them. "We really should get some rest. Long day tomorrow, right?"

"I, uh, yeah—yes! Right!" said Kalas as he put away Shosafin's sword.

Despite his best efforts, Falthwën tried to hide a smile behind his prodigious beard; Zhalera, however, remained impassive as she and the cleric stood and followed the others toward the exit.

When they were free of the revelry on the other side of the door, Falthwën led Rül and Pava toward the room while Kalas, exhausted, and Zhalera remained in the hallway. Someone almost ran into them as he pushed the door open. Surprised to see the pair still standing there, his eyes darted toward the green leather scabbard, toward Kalas' face, before he apologized and made a show of stepping back into the main hall.

"Shosafin's instruction sure paid off!" Kalas began. "I just hope

I didn't overdo it! I just—"

She slapped his face with her open palm.

Caught off guard, he fell silent, his mouth open in mid-sentence as he gave the sting in his cheek a moment to subside.

"What—?" he began: she interrupted him with a kiss.

He smiled as she pulled away. Cocked his head when she slapped him again.

"All right, what's going on?" he demanded as he rubbed his jaw.

"That man could have killed you," she said with a glare.

"But he didn't!" insisted Kalas, still puzzled. "And he's the one who was in the wrong! There's no way I was going to—"

"You still don't understand, do you? You're my—you're the only family I have left! The only family that matters to me! What if...?"

He softened, took her hands and held them tight.

"Don't forget: you're *my* only family, too, Zhalera. And...you're right. As usual, it seems! I know you're more than capable of fighting your own battles. You're better at picking them, too, I'd say. Still..."

"I will admit," she conceded, "you handled your sword quite well! Enough to convince a tavern full of people that you're a *Po-yïsriba* soldier!"

"*Shosafin's* sword," he smiled. "I'm just glad we got out of there when we did: that thing gets heavy, and I was running out of things to say! C'mon, let's head back upstairs with the others."

They started for the room when Zhalera paused and looked over her shoulder at the door to the main hall where they'd had their somewhat heated discussion.

"Did the door just move?" she whispered.

Kalas stopped and looked over his shoulder as well. He remembered how Falthwën always closed his eyes whenever they entered someplace new. He did the same and concentrated, not sure what to expect. Other than a sense of foreboding associated with the door, nothing happened. He placed a finger against his lips and gestured for Zhalera to continue toward the room. He drew his sword without a sound and tiptoed toward the door. As Zhalera's footsteps receded, the door opened and the same figure from before crept into the hallway.

"Can I help you?" demanded Kalas.

"Ah! I…uh…I'm sorry! I'm just…uh…"

The man turned toward the main hall one more time, but before he could escape, Kalas brought the pommel of his sword down —hard—against the nape of the wiry, weaselly man's neck. He collapsed without ceremony.

Nëshritme! he swore. *Now what?!*

2.

"What are we gonna do with him?" huffed Rül as he slung the unconscious figure onto one of the beds: when he heard Kalas and Zhalera trying to haul him up the stairs, he offered his assistance.

"He was eavesdropping: I'm pretty sure he knows I'm not a real soldier," Kalas panted as he tied a length of cord around the stunned man's hands and feet. "I don't know what that means for us, but I can't imagine it's a good thing. Shosafin told me Âivambar was full of Ësfàyami's spies: I wonder if this guy's one of them…"

"He went into the other room before he came back and you smacked him," Zhalera added. "What if he told others what he was up to?"

"The horses!" Rül exclaimed. "What if this guy's friends do something to Runner and Dancer? What if they take our coach?"

"Right now, any 'friends' he may or may not have don't know that we've detained their companion. And we don't know for sure if he's one of the queen-regent's assets—that said, it's probably safest to assume that yes, he is.

316

"Rül, go to the horses. Be discreet. Keep watch. Just in case. One of us—or, depending on how things go, all of us!—will come for you once we've learned more."

"Let me come with you!" insisted Pava as she grabbed her *tëvët* and followed him into the hallway.

"He's waking up!" Zhalera noted with a tug on Kalas' arm. Rül and Pava had only been gone a few minutes: the three of them had been discussing what their next steps should be when their captive started struggling against his bonds. When he realized he was being watched, he stopped. A sinister smile twisted his lips as he regarded his captors.

"You have Ilbardhën's sword," he observed. "At first, I'd hoped you'd…relieved him of it. Permanently. But after I saw how you handled Irudh, I knew I'd hoped for too much: it's clear you learned swordplay from him! I don't suppose you'd tell me where he is, would you?"

None of them said a word. The figure struggled to sit up, prompting Kalas to place a hand on his hilt.

"Easy! Easy! These knots are tight! I'm just trying to get comfortable!"

When he continued to fidget, Zhalera balled up a fist and punched him in the jaw: his head spun around with a satisfying crack, and he lost consciousness once again.

"Zhalera?" said Kalas, his sword now in hand.

She reached behind the man, ran her fingers along the hem of his trousers, and removed a small knife.

"He'd almost cut through these ropes!" she said as she discovered two additional weapons concealed on his person. "There was something too rhythmic about his movements: I figured he was up to something!"

"Well done, my child!" congratulated Falthwën. Kalas noticed he held his staff with a different grip than usual: he, too, must have anticipated trickery from the queen's spy.

"As you suspected," he continued with a nod toward Kalas. "It's a shame we weren't able to ask him any questions, but given our straits, I suppose there's not much we could've done differently. A few things we've learned, however: the queen does, in fact, want Ilbardhën dead; those she's enlisted have studied Ilbardhën, it would seem; and lastly, she's unaware of his current status. Perhaps such information will prove to be to our advantage."

"Another thing," added Kalas: "we know her spies recognize Shosafin's sword. His scabbard, at least. Shosafin told me it might be helpful, but it marks us, too. Maybe he didn't realize how recognizable it is?"

"Or maybe he knew *exactly* who would recognize it," countered Zhalera after brief consideration. "Maybe that was his goal in giving it to you—one of his goals, at least: get the queen's spies to follow *you*, leaving *him* a little extra breathing room."

"'Pragmatism,' indeed," said Kalas, mostly to himself. "Well, it seems his strategy is working—I mean, I *hope* it is: maybe *one* of us will figure something out!"

"At least one of us will, I believe. That said, we should be leaving now," said Falthwën as he bundled what few items they'd brought up to the room. "Kalas, tie our guest to one of the beds—nice and tight!—and let's go. Rül and Pava will be waiting for us. I hoped to avoid traveling at night, but we've little choice."

When they reached the coach, it looked like no one had touched it. Yet. Neither Rül nor Pava were anywhere in sight, and Kalas feared the worst until he heard the farm boy's coarse whisper.

"Hey, guys! Over here!" he hissed as he and Pava emerged from the shadows. "I don't think anyone followed us or saw us leave, but I don't know for sure. I could be wrong."

Pava nodded, maintained a firm grip on her weapon's shaft.

"Very good," said Falthwën. "It won't be long before our visitor is discovered or escapes. When that happens, he'll undoubtedly come straight for the coach house. Probably with friends.

"Runner and Dancer are still in the stables. Doesn't look like anyone messed with 'em. I'll get 'em harnessed," said Rül, and he dashed toward the horses. Pava followed, looking from side to—

"Rül!" she shouted and hurled her *tëvët* toward a man who'd separated from the shadows. He'd raised a club and had been about to strike when the girl's weapon struck his side just beneath the armpit. The assailant cried out—a weak, thready sound—as his last breath escaped his punctured lungs. Pava rushed forward, pulled her pike from the body, and prepared for more attackers.

"Hurry!" demanded Kalas as he drew Shosafin's sword.

"I am! I am!" the farm boy insisted as he and Pava raced from the building.

Moments later, they returned with the horses: Runner and Dancer seemed to recognize Rül's sense of urgency. He tacked them up in short order while the others climbed into the coach. Falthwën leapt onto the footman's rumble as the party tore through the carriage house, knocking a couple of men to the ground as they burst through its doors and into the torchlit gloaming. In the distance, someone shrilled a few blasts from a horn—an alarm, probably. Despite the racket and the skull-jarring vibrations from rushing over the cobblestone avenue, Kalas thought he heard fast-approaching horses as Âivambar's shops and side streets whipped past in a blur of gray.

3.

"What do they want?!" Kalas asked no one in particular as he and Zhalera bounced around inside the coach. "Why is Shosafin

319

so important to them?"

Rül raced across the city as Falthwën shouted directions: "Left! Right! Right! Left!" It felt like every sudden change in direction threatened to tear the coach apart. The last bump launched Kalas from his seat and dropped him on the floor. He risked opening the door for a peek outside—ducked just in time to avoid clipping his head on a low-hanging shingle, then looked again.

Aside from an occasional pedestrian, the streets ahead of them seemed clear: behind them, however, two—no, three riders bore down on the coach. Two looked like common townsfolk, clothed in nondescript garments and driving unremarkable horses. The third, however, bringing up the rear and closing fast, wore *Poyïsriba* livery and rode a sturdier-looking horse. Although hard to discern in between shadows, every street light illuminated his angry-looking features. He appeared to be shouting something at them: something unpleasant, judging from his expression.

"Another mile!" the cleric shouted. When he noticed Kalas, he flashed the boy an unexpected grin. He whispered something the wind whipped away from his mouth and aimed his staff like a lance: soft green light blossomed along its length and collected in a ball at the tip; from there, it rushed toward the earth, collided with the ground just in front of their pursuers, and spit rocks, dirt, and tongues of fire into the air.

The two men reared their horses, spun around and ran away: the *Poyïsriba* soldier vaulted over the still-smoking crater, drew his sword, and smacked the flanks of his horse with its flat as he whipped his reins.

That fire! It looks just like the fire that stopped the wolves! But—
"Kalas! Ahead!"

The young man tore his eyes from the frothing beast at their tail and looked at the road in front of them. All seemed clear until, at the cleric's command, Rül turned hard to the right: a few hundred feet up the road another band of adversaries blocked their escape.

"More of them!" he shouted over his shoulder.

"I can't avoid them!" warned Rül.

The Song! Falthwën shouted inside Kalas' mind: *The Song, my child! Call upon its power!*

I don't know what to do!

Kalas focused on the fast-approaching guards now just tens of feet in front of them. He turned all his attention toward his surroundings, and struggled to bend reality to his will. He closed his eyes and conjured what fragments of the Song he could remember and held them in his mind...

He felt the outside world fade away as the Song swelled and wrapped around his thoughts. The coach stopped.

"Did it—?" he began. He stopped when he realized it was just Rül tightening his reins. Soldiers with drawn swords stood mere inches from the coach: the one who'd been behind them drew up and barked orders to the others.

"Why—?" he wondered until rough men pulled him from the cabin.

"Careful! The queen wants them alive and unharmed!" insisted the soldier who appeared to be in charge.

"And untouched!" he added with disgust when he noticed the lascivious grins on his subordinates' faces as they groped with greedy hands at Pava and Zhalera.

Kalas looked to Falthwën, but the cleric didn't notice: he'd already stepped down from the rumble and placed his staff on the ground. He held his empty hands in front of him in a gesture of peaceable surrender.

There is no reason to be afraid, my child, Kalas sensed from the old man. With a self-recriminating sigh, he stepped onto the street, and held up his hands too.

4.

"The queen's been looking for you," said their captor with an odd, bemused quality to his voice. Rougher- and older-looking than his prior exertions indicated, he regarded them with a mix of annoyance and curiosity. "Not *you*, per se, but that sword—its owner, that is. She's obtained new information from an unexpected source and—well, never mind! The fact remains: you're all coming with me to Ïsriba!"

Above them, several *Âivambarrinme* peeked through their windows at the spectacle unfolding in the street.

"Very good!" said Falthwën with an exuberant smile. His handlers, caught off guard, flinched and loosened their grip on his arms. The cleric never moved. "I should thank you, friend! We were on our way to the capital: your escort should speed things along!"

The soldier, still a formidable-looking man despite his apparent years, allowed himself a moment to process Falthwën's request before he burst into genuine laughter.

"You've got moxie, I'll give you that," he admitted. "I'll be honest: I'm not sure why the queen is so interested in Ilbardhën, but she is, and it's my honor to obey. Call me Nashmur. Commander Nashmur.

"Do—did you know him?" asked Kalas. "Did you know Shosafin?"

"I did," the commander admitted without elaborating. He raised an arm, and Kalas thought he was going to instruct his men to bind them all, but he seemed to change his mind before he gave the order.

"Tell you what, friends—there's no reason we can't be friends, right? You're on your way to Ïsriba where, as I imagine you've guessed, you'll spend some time in the queen's dungeons. I'm here to make sure you get there…I have no particular instructions regarding *how* you get there, and you've been cooperative—more so than I anticipated. Give me your word that you'll cooperate, and I and my soldiers will escort you to the capital—per your request. You're free to drive your own horses, ride in your own coach—that's a nice coach, by the way! Just surrender your weapons and—"

"No," interrupted Kalas. Nashmur looked stunned. "I'm sorry, Commander: I mean no disrespect, but Shosafin—Ilbardhën asked me to look after his sword. I can't…I can't give it to you."

Gasps from the dusky figures overhead resounded through the shadows and the feeble street lights.

"Oh?" said Nashmur, gesturing for his men to stand down as they tensed at the boy's impertinence. He reached for the hilt of his own sword—similar to Shosafin's, Kalas noted, but distinct. "What if I…*insist?*"

Kalas sighed, looked at the ground, and shook his head before returning the commander's gaze with as much severity as he could muster. He hoped it was enough.

"Then…I'll fight you."

More gasps.

"Kalas!" someone shouted. Zhalera, probably.

"You'll win," he admitted, "but he asked me to keep it safe…"

Nashmur released his grip on his own sword and approached the boy.

"I think I've got an idea about what Ilbardhën saw in you," said the commander as he knelt and studied the boy's features. "I can see why he entrusted you with his sword."

After assessing him for a moment longer, he stood, placed a heavy hand on Kalas' shoulder, and said, "Hold on to your friend's sword then. For as long as you can."

The commander's men looked at each other with confused expressions. One raised a hand and made a sound, like he had something to say, but opted to keep quiet instead.

"They'll take it from you before you're permitted to enter the queen's presence, of course," he continued. "There's nothing to be done about that: if she gave the word, her personal guardsmen would kill you without question. Instantly. Still, we've got at least a day between then and now. So what do you say? Do I have your word that you'll…maintain your bearing while under our… *protection?*"

Answering for all of them, Kalas said, "You have it." No one contradicted him. He thought he *felt* rather than saw Falthwën's smile, hidden as it must have been beneath his beard.

"Excellent!" said Nashmur as he dismissed his men with a wave. "There are more than a few hours before the suns rise. I suggest you return to your room at the Falcon until morning. We'll be waiting for you."

As the onlookers disappeared into their apartments, the commander helped Rül get his coach turned around, then galloped into the darkness. Alone in the shadows, no one spoke for a long time; at last, his voice uncertain, Rül asked, "What…what do we do?"

"We go back to the Falcon," said Kalas before Falthwën could say anything. "We gave our word."

Rül glanced at the cleric. Runner and Dancer gave light snorts as they flicked their tails but made no other movements: they, too, appeared to be waiting.

"Well?" said Falthwën with some slight roguish quality in his voice. "You heard the young man! To the Falcon! Today's been an adventure, to be sure, and I think all of us could use those few hours of rest!"

5.

Before the suns had risen, Falthwën gave Kalas' shoulder a gentle nudge, waking him from fitful sleep. The boy sat up, remembered and reflected on the prior night's events, then stood and splashed his face with water from the wash basin.

They collected their things, and when they were ready, the cleric pulled Zhalera aside and whispered something to her. She nodded, and the two of them turned away from the others. Kalas remained focused on the unpleasant truth: despite the chilly kindness Nashmur afforded them, they were prisoners of the queen. With a sigh, he shifted Shosafin's sword, now strapped across his back.

If I just understood The Song better! Kalas chided himself. *If I really knew how it worked, maybe I could have kept us from these soldiers…*

"And maybe there's purpose—however inscrutable—in our present circumstances," said Falthwën, as though he were aware of Kalas' thoughts.

To no one's surprise, two of Commander Nashmur's men waited in the hallway. Neither said a word as the cleric led everyone through the isolated stairwell toward the street. Outside in the damp air, Rül's coach waited for them. Nashmur himself sat atop the box seat.

"Good morning, friends!" he beamed with too much enthusiasm. "Master…Rül, was it? Your horses are remarkable! Just as good as any from Ïsriba, I'm not ashamed to say!"

Rül's expression must have triggered something within the commander. His smile—toothy and *genuine*, Kalas thought—broadened as he explained himself.

"Oh, there's nothing to worry about! For the…short while your property is in my keep, I figured I'd give these two an opportunity to stretch their legs without all that weight behind them! Forgive my saying so, but I think they rather enjoyed the exercise! Especially this darker fellow!"

"That's Runner," said Rül, not quite sure how to respond. "Takes

Dancer a while to get into the swing of things when he's on his own. Uh, please, sir: I know it's not my place to ask, but *please* take good care of my horses—my *mother's* horses!"

"You have my word, young man," the commander nodded. "Now, please: load your things—ah, there it is! Good to see you still have your—that is, Ilbardhën's sword with you! I'll confess: I stationed a few men around the Falcon last night—just in case your word wasn't what I believed it to be. You have no idea how rare it is to meet someone who keeps his word—especially when the cost is so high. There's a nobility about you, Master Kalas!"

That's what Shosafin said, Kalas remembered. He gave Nashmur a look, but the commander had already stepped down from the coach and turned to address his men.

"It'll take us most of the day to get to Ïsriba, but we should reach her gates before the first sun sets," he continued as he turned back toward Kalas and the others. "For what it's worth, I do hope the queen is…lenient with you."

Rül took his seat atop the coach box and Pava followed. She clung to his arm as her eyes darted from side to side.

"I'm sorry," Kalas muttered to her as he and Zhalera entered the coach. The *úrukilmukrit* girl spared him a glance and a weak smile. "I'm sorry," he repeated as he unslung his sword and took his seat. Zhalera, seated next to him, said nothing; instead, she took his hand, squeezed it, and rested her head on his shoulder.

"I know neither of you slept particularly well last night," noted Falthwën as he sat across from them. "Sleep now. I'll wake you should anything untoward come to pass."

"Falthwën, why couldn't I—"

"It's my fault, really," interrupted the cleric. "I've asked more from you than I had any right to ask. You're still learning about The Song, about your place within its strains. You have yet to fathom its depths, to understand the complexities and boundaries of the privilege you wield…

"You offered an apology. Allow me to counter with an apology of my own: *I* am sorry for asking you to shoulder a burden that never should have been yours. *Su pirathëzhu—Aswanthalu.*

"With all that out of the way, however, I suspect we're in the midst of an act of providence the scope of which we haven't yet begun to appreciate. Commander Nashmur, for one: unless I miss my guess, he's *everything* he appears to be…and more. It's no coincidence we're in *his* custody."

"It sounds like you're saying it's a *good thing* we were captured," said Zhalera with a raised eyebrow.

"'Good'? Hmm…that's a stronger word than I'd use. 'Necessary,' maybe."

Kalas considered Falthwën's supposition before permitting himself an inward chuckle. Zhalera raised her head and gave him a sidelong glance. Sensing her unasked question, he said, "Shosafin said his sword would be a bane to him and perhaps a boon to us. I was just wondering if he thought it could be both at the same time. Zhalera, you thought maybe he gave it to me because it would put his pursuers on our path. You're probably right—no surprise there! —but I was thinking about what Falthwën just said, about how maybe…*this*…is *necessary:* Shosafin knew our goal was an audience with the queen. If he's chasing after Marugan, why would he go without his sword? Even if mere steel isn't enough to kill him, he's sure to encounter perfectly killable resistance along the way, right? Wouldn't he want his sword with him?

"I think Falthwën's right, too. I think Shosafin knew we'd be discovered in Âivambar. I think he knew someone would recognize his sword, at least. And he knows Nashmur: the commander admitted as much. Falthwën thinks he means well: I'll bet Shosafin did, too…Maybe I'm just desperately hoping these 'coincidences' keep adding up for our benefit. Maybe I'm assuming too much, but even though Shosafin calls himself an outsider to the queen's court, he does know how it works. Maybe I'm just trying to convince myself it's not my fault I couldn't…get us out of here, but at this point, I don't think it's unreasonable to believe that we're moving in the right direction."

"I guess we'll find out before the day's over," she said with a faltering smile betrayed by the uncertainty in her eyes.

Falthwën, for his part, said nothing.

Outside, trees and fields whipped past them (distant mountains moved a little slower) as Rül followed their escort up and across the countryside. The warm suns-light on an otherwise cool day and the rhythm of the horses' gait soon lulled Kalas to sleep.

Later, Nashmur brought everyone to a halt. Lunch time, he said, and afterward, they resumed their trek.

"It gets even steeper about a quarter mile from Ïsriba's walls. Gives the capital a distinct advantage against a direct assault: gives us a nasty climb! Rül, my lad! How are Runner and Dancer?"

"They're well, Commander!" beamed the farm boy. "They've, uh, been through a lot recently, but this pace seems just about right."

"Excellent!" he nodded as he guided his destrier toward his place at the front of the line.

While they were stopped, Pava stepped down from the box seat and asked the cleric, "Mind if I ride with you?"

"Of course!" said Falthwën as he pushed the door open and helped her into the seat next to himself.

"Rül said it would probably be a good idea for me to get some rest," she explained through a yawn, "I'd rather be up next—up there, outside, but I have to admit, he's probably right."

After Nashmur engaged in a few moments' consultation with his men, things started moving again. A few hours later, the terrain's slope increased just like he said it would.

"We must be almost there," noted Zhalera as she craned her neck for a better view through the coach's windows. Pava, awake now, looked out as well.

"I'll admit: you two seem like you're all right with what's happening," she continued. "Me? I'm not so sure. Nashmur said *dungeons*. We could be down there for a long time. And how does that help Lohwàlar? I know, I know: a lot has changed while we've been on the road, but there are wolves other than the ones who murdered our parents and wrecked our home! Who says they won't come back? What if they've *already* come back?! What if that lightning —*Sharuyandas Âsru*, Tsharak called it? What if this Sharuyan takes even longer to send it than last time? What if he doesn't send it at all?"

Pava looked from face to face, her eyes wide, suddenly regretting leaving her seat next to Rül. Kalas said nothing. He rifled through his thoughts, but he couldn't come up with a satisfying response. Falthwën, too, remained silent. As the cleric looked away, the boy thought the old man's eyes shimmered.

"'What if?'" Kalas said at last. When she looked at him, he continued: "Everything you said, I get it. I do. And a lot *has* changed, but the people back home have already started rebuilding. Falthwën said Tsharak should talk to Sàrush, and I choose to believe your grandfather will listen to the people this time.

"'What if?' indeed. Whatever happens in Ïsriba—wherever we end up—we'll figure it out. Together. The four—the *five* of us: Pava, you're part of our family now, too! The *six* of us if Shosafin ever returns. And I believe he will."

Pava smiled—a real smile this time, and relaxed. Falthwën massaged the bridge of his nose. Wearied, he offered a nod of agreement.

• • •

"Feels like we've hit the switchbacks," Pava observed as their coach slowed and changed direction every few minutes. A quick peek through the window confirmed her supposition. After about an hour of jarring back-and-forth travel, the slope lessened and the road—the *Highway,* Kalas reminded himself—straightened. With a mischievous grin and a conspiratorial wink, the cave-dweller girl opened the door, whirled herself around as it closed, and said, "I'll see you soon!" as she laced her arms around part of the imperial and somehow curled her body against the pull of gravity.

"What—how did—?!" Zhalera murmured as Pava's footsteps made the slightest sounds against the roof. After a light pressure —and a surprised yelp from Rül—they realized she'd returned to her seat up front.

"I'd say she's feeling better," said Kalas. "Nap must have done her some good!"

"I had no idea she could move like that!" Zhalera marveled with a touch of envy.

"Life among the sheer cliffs of the Áthradho provides un-counted opportunities for practice, I'm sure," said Falthwën. He still had a faraway look in his eyes.

A few minutes later, Rül brought their coach to a stop. Al-though the first sun hadn't quite set, something blocked it from view, even through the coach's windows. Kalas stood. He was about to step into the spreading twilight when the sounds of an argument changed his mind. He sat and tried to see what was going on from within the cabin.

"Zhalera, might I see your sword for a moment?" said Falthwën. She nodded and handed it to him, and he continued: "Regarding our prior discussion: may I...keep it safe?"

Zhalera understood and glanced at the folds of his silvery robe. The cleric risked a look outside and uncovered the weapon, and

Kalas remembered the weapon he freed from within his grandfather's stone table. Falthwën had held it up to the light for a moment before making it *disappear.*

"Of course," she almost whispered. With reverence, the cleric ran an unhurried hand across the length of its blade: as he did so, Zhalera's sword vanished beneath his callused fingers; when he reached its hilt, he waved his hand with a subtle flourish and it was gone.

"Can you do that with this?" breathed Kalas as he tapped at Shosafin's sword.

"My child, if it were possible, I would, but it's not: Loradan's and Âsrufin's weapons are…of a different nature than Ilbardhën's. You'll have to trust Nashmur with it, and, as I've said, I believe we'll find him worthy of our trust."

Kalas wanted to press Falthwën for more details; before he could, however, Nashmur knocked on the door.

"We're here, my friends!" he boomed as he helped them exit the coach.

Kalas shivered. Zhalera, too. He took a few steps to loosen his stiff muscles: when he looked up, stopped.

Before him loomed a vast, polished gate carved out of the living rock, at least as high as four grown men standing on one another's shoulders. Ramparts had been cut from the same. Between their battlements soldiers kept watch on the horizon, paying little to no attention, it seemed, to the scene beneath them. Behind and high above *them,* the capital's towers stood stark against the deep pink streaks in the sky, the lights in their windows glinting like precious stones as the suns' rays caught and danced within their faceted panes.

He looked at the wall again and realized portions of it disappeared within the mountain: Kalas assumed tunnels connected the exposed sections to one another and wrapped around the whole city.

He found it difficult to comprehend just how much time and effort and skill must have been required to raise up the capital's walls, to circumscribe its perimeter with such a monumental barrier.

"Shâume á âume!" Commander Nashmur laughed as he allowed them a moment's wonder. "Welcome to Ïsriba!"

CHAPTER XVII

In the Dark of Ïsriba's Dungeons

COMMANDER NASHMUR MOTIONED FOR A PAIR OF SOLdiers to move the coach to an unspecified destination. Before he led everyone through the gate, he pulled Kalas aside and asked him one more time if he might hold on to Shosafin's sword: "I'll do everything within my power to return it to you when the time is right," he promised. Other than the few soldiers who'd traveled with him, the commander hadn't called for additional support. Maybe, Kalas allowed, Falthwën's impression of him was on point.

"That's just it, isn't it?" he said. "*Within your power.* You're not as powerful as the queen, are you?"

"A fair point," Nashmur conceded. "Maybe I won't be able to guarantee what happens with your friend's sword, but what I *can* guarantee is this: right now, it's safer with me than it is with you. I've explained as best I can what you're about to face: if you'd prefer to let one of the queen's…less accommodating guardsmen relieve you of it, that's your choice. I won't mention it again."

"You're *really* interested in Shosafin's sword," noted Kalas. "Why?"

The commander shrugged but said nothing else as he rode beneath the vast iron teeth of the portcullis suspended above the entrance. Kalas looked up at their gleaming points. Shuddered at the thought of their chains giving way.

"What was that about?" Zhalera whispered as Kalas joined her.

"Sword," he said, and she nodded.

As they walked through the gate, Kalas learned it was much wider than he'd expected. Although portions remained uncut mountain, others had been built up from dressed and mortared stones into small houses or quarters. Torchlight glittered through bow slits, interrupted now and then as someone inside changed position.

This place is impenetrable, Kalas assumed.

On the other side of the wall, within the limits of Ïsriba proper, instead of residences or commercial structures stood additional defensive constructs. The well-worn road—a *genuine* highway since Âivambar—cut between vast pillars of polished basalt as it snaked toward the capital's center. Within those canyon-like pillars, pin-pricks of light revealed they, too, were occupied.

"I'm not sure how much you know about Ïsriba's history, but she got off to a rough start," said Nashmur as he noticed Kalas and the others gawking at their surroundings. "Something of a mash-up of two, maybe three kingdoms—there's still debate about that—from millennia ago. Not everyone liked the idea: lots of animosity and mistrust between those original kingdoms, but her first king— Ulobir the Steadfast—held her together somehow. These defenses were his idea: a subtle reminder of the threats the new nation faced from opportunistic countries, *and* a means to force these different cultures to come together as a new, united entity. It worked, and for hundreds of Sevens, Ïsriba has been the embodiment of her first king's iron will."

"Almost sounds like you think that's a bad thing," observed Zhalera as they followed the commander. Kalas looked at her with mild surprise: he'd wondered if anyone else had sensed that almost morose quality in Nashmur's speech. Even Rül nodded. Pava, too.

"Oh?" he said with surprise of his own, as if he realized he'd communicated something he hadn't intended. He grunted, snapped his reins, and said nothing else until they reached a series of other, lesser gates. The commander spoke with the guards on duty: after a short exchange, the one in charge motioned toward one of the heavy wood-and-iron doors.

"With these smaller gates, we're able to keep the West Gate closed until we've marshaled our forces in this staging area. Should the West Gate ever fall, invading forces would have a much harder time attacking en masse."

Outside the door, Nashmur continued: "We'll wait here. It'll only be a few minutes." He shot a reproving glance at the guard, who disappeared between the moon- and torchlit battlements.

Maybe fifteen minutes later—it was hard to tell in the dark— the gateway's doors opened inward. Beyond their ironwood planks and tempered steel bands, everything he could see within the city looked…ordinary. The streets seemed rather empty, but maybe that was because it was almost nightfall. In the distance, however, sounds of merriment intruded upon the shadowed stillness.

They're getting closer, Kalas thought to himself. *Almost sounds like…children?*

Peering through the gate, he saw a few boys, none older than two, maybe three and a Seven, appear at the end of the street, giggling and clapping each other on the back like they'd accomplished some great feat.

"I think that was the last of the guards!" said one. The others nodded.

"Wonder what they're guarding?" posed the next.

"I can't believe we slipped by all of 'em! These streets are normally—" began a third: he was interrupted with a sharp blow to the head.

"What—?!" gasped the others as a soldier stepped into the light.

He said nothing as he held the remaining children with his indifferent gaze and wiped blood spatter from the shaft of his spear. The youth he'd jabbed didn't move. *None* of them moved. The soldier inclined his head toward the injured lad, and, with vigorous nods, his accomplices grabbed his arms and dragged him away as fast as they could. When the children were gone, the guard turned and noticed Nashmur. He nodded, offered him a prim salute, and merged with the shadows again.

"All right," the commander sighed and shook his head. "Let's go."

"Commander Nashmur," said Kalas with a tug on the soldier's leg. Nashmur reined in his horse and waited.

"You're right," the boy admitted as he unslung Shosafin's sword and handed it to the commander. "Falthwën thinks we can trust you. I'm still not sure, but I trust Falthwën. *Please* don't prove yourself a liar!"

"You'll find my word is good," he promised. "And, maybe, that my 'power' is greater than you assume."

2.

Nashmur led everyone through deserted streets toward an undisclosed destination: given the hour, Kalas assumed they were headed nowhere pleasant. Even in the dark, he felt a *tainted magnificence,* springing up from the city's roots and twining around its structures, spreading throughout the simple fact of its existence.

This is wrong, he thought as he strained his eyes against the night. Once or twice, he sensed the presence of something just within the shadows—

Shagabme?

—but nothing interrupted their reluctant procession.

"Commander, why is the queen so interested in Shosafin? His

336

sword?" Kalas wondered. "Is it because of King Rufàran—"

"I…wouldn't mention that name, friend. That title. Not outside the right circles, at least. That's part of it—*most* of it, probably: she's always been suspicious that he was the only one to survive the… incident."

"He told me what happened. What do you think?"

"Most of that was before my time…"

"*Most?*" Kalas prodded. Nashmur sighed and shook his head. He didn't say anything right away. Kalas thought the commander abandoned the conversation when, in whispered tones, he warned: "Best not to speak of such things. Anywhere."

He walked them past vast structures, illuminated by the moon and nothing else. Whether residential, commercial, or public, Kalas couldn't tell. Decided it really didn't matter. Not now, anyway. In the soft pink moonlight, he sensed, on occasion, the presence of more *shagabme.* As they walked past a dark lamppost, Kalas said aloud, "Ah, I see…"

"See what?" wondered Rül. "I can't see anything!"

"Why we had to wait when we got to the main gate. No one will know we're here—no one's supposed to. Except maybe a few soldiers: can't you feel them waiting in the shadows?"

"I can," Pava nodded. "I thought everyone could. I guess my eyesight's more adapted to the dark than most. But what do you mean? Why are they out there?"

"They don't want anyone to see—to know about—the people Commander Nashmur's about to toss in the dungeon," insisted Zhalera with more than a hint of steel in her voice, daring him to contradict her.

"You're quite right," he admitted without reserve.

"I told you," Zhalera chided.

"As anxious as the queen might be to receive her…guests, it can wait until morning," he continued. "The dungeon is not the height of sophistication, true, but it's still much nicer than a hole in the ground."

"What do you mean by *that?*" Pava bristled. Rül stifled a nervous chuckle and whispered something in her ear. The commander observed the exchange and spared a closer look at the *úrukilmukrit* girl. And laughed at himself. "My apologies, *urín*. I meant no disrespect. If it means anything to you, I think the labyrinths underneath the Áthradho rival some of Ïsriba's most stunning structures."

"You've been there?" she asked with skeptic tones, though softer than her prior outburst."

"Many times. It's been a while, but I can still picture the…what's it called: that huge, crystal thing suspended above the chasm?—the *Kathin Iltith*, right? It's a marvel, to be sure!"

"Oh…Yes. Yes, it is," she agreed.

For almost an hour, Kalas guessed, Nashmur escorted them toward the base of an immense and forbidding construct flecked with regular squares of light. When they reached what looked like nothing more than a solid wall, blank and unremarkable, the commander stopped, looked from side to side and cleared his throat. At his signal, portions of the wall slid inside the mountain with reluctant shrieks as grinding gears dragged them across tracks bolted to the floor. Dim torches bobbed into view, carried by soldiers emerging from the secret doorway. Nashmur dismounted as they approached.

"Gentlemen: ensure the queen's guests are…protected until morning, *hish?*"

"By your word, Commander Nashmur," they replied in unison.

Turning toward the party, he added: "When the queen's captain of the guard learns about your presence, he's sure to send *his* men to guard you. Until then, I've placed my own men outside your… quarters."

"*Cells*, you mean," Zhalera corrected him.

"You say *your* soldiers are trustworthy: what about the others? It sounds like you don't tr—"

"Master Kalas," interrupted Falthwën, his thoughts again in the present. His tone had a cautionary quality to it as he glanced at the boy. Smiling at Nashmur, he continued, "I'm sure the commander has work to do: processing *guests*, as he likes to call us, and all. Am I wrong, Commander?"

"No, you're quite right. Quite right…This way, friends."

Why does Falthwën seem so…disinterested in these things?

Rather than ask the cleric aloud, he held on to his frustration as the party made its way along the packed dirt floors bordered by rough brick walls. Something unpleasant hung in the air: a fetor suggesting mildew and rot. They passed numerous cells—most empty—before reaching theirs, and Kalas had the distinct impression they'd traveled in circles once or twice. Separated from other blocks by a series of twists and turns, the stench was much less noticeable here, and the floor looked like someone had covered it with fresh straw.

Nashmur pointed toward a row of cells. "Each of you pick one. Cots and commodes, and I instructed my men to provide blankets and basins as well. I'll send someone with a meal as soon as I can."

Falthwën nodded at their jailer and chose the farthest cell. He stepped inside, and door closed of its own accord: the lock's tumblers slid into place without a key. The commander shook his head and rubbed his eyes before testing the door.

"Been a long day," he muttered as the cleric began whistling bits of the Song.

Still not sure what Falthwën was up to, Kalas took the cell next to his—but not before Nashmur relieved him of his knife as well.

"This knife…it's more important to me than that sword. I *need* it back!"

"You'll have it. On my word."

He heard the others choose their respective chambers, followed by Nashmur closing and locking their doors.

"I'll return for you in the morning," he told them when everyone's door was locked. No one spoke as he turned and walked away, his footsteps growing ever fainter until the only sound echoing across the dungeon was Falthwën's haphazard whistling.

"Why do you sound so…so *cheerful?*" Zhalera demanded.

3.

Supper, while not the worst meal any of them had endured, wasn't much: especially when compared with the feast Yëlisha had prepared for them not so long ago. Although the bread was almost warm, the water clear, and the meat—whatever it was—edible, the uncertainty waiting for them in the morning weighed heavily on them all.

"It's the *not knowing* that's the worst," insisted Zhalera between perfunctory mouthfuls. "Thrown in jail because of what? Some sword? Kalas, can't you…y'know…?"

"I don't know," he admitted. "Didn't work in Âivambar…"

"These cells aren't so bad," suggested Pava, trying to lighten the conversation. "I mean, they're nowhere near as nice as the caverns back home, but at least we're away from that smell! What do you think that was? Smelled like something died!"

"Or some*one*," added Rül. "No, I mean: it's a dungeon, right? I've heard stories—from Grandfather: not sure where *he* heard them from! Anyway, he said sometimes they just leave people to *die* in dungeons!"

"Far be it from me to malign your grandfather, Master Rül, but whatever the source of that odor, I'm confident Commander Nashmur won't allow us to end up like the poor *kelâme* in your grandfather's tales."

"I really hope you're right," said Rül, still not convinced.

Kalas wished he could see everyone's faces, read their body language, but the small, barred opening set into his cell door only faced an indifferent wall of brick and stone.

"*Why,* though, are you so confident in this guy? Do you know him from somewhere? Or did you know *his* great-great—whatever—grandparents?" Rül continued. From her cell, Zhalera grunted her approval.

"I'm asking a lot, I know, but Master Rül, if you'll allow events to play out over the next…day or two—at most—you'll see. And if you *don't* see, then I'll confess my poor judgment and beg for your forgiveness all the way to the gallows."

"The *what?!*"

"Please: trust me. For a few days," the cleric laughed, much to Zhalera's consternation and Rül's confusion.

"What was that song you were whistling?" Pava said, again trying to steer the conversation toward lighter themes. "It reminds me of something I've heard before."

"Oh?" said Kalas, his interest piqued.

"Yeah! The crystals—the collectors: sometimes, when the suns are right, they make a sound. *I* hear them, anyway, but maybe it's nothing. Most cave-dwellers look at me like I'm crazy, but Falthwën's whistling reminded me of it. Do you know it, too?"

"I…yeah, in a way, I guess," Kalas admitted. He went on: "Do your people know about *Zhi Helim?*"

"*The* Song? We have *songs,* sure, but *The* Song? I don't know. Doesn't sound familiar. Is that what you were whistling, Falthwën?"

"In part, my child," he confirmed as he ceased his subtle warbling. "And it comes as no surprise that its strains would resonate through the crystals in your collectors…"

"Well, it's beautiful," she concluded.

"That it is," said Zhalera without the prior hostility in her voice. "I'd love to hear more of it. Someday. Somehow."

"Same here!" Pava agreed.

Kalas thought Falthwën was about to say something else when the clamor of annoyed soldiers dragging someone through the dungeon interrupted him.

"Where'd he even come from?" one soldier asked another.

"No idea. The other guys say one minute, no one's there: the next, this drunkard's stumbling through the restricted area," replied a second.

"What was that all about, anyway? Has there ever been a time when whole sections of the city were just *blocked off* like that?"

"Not that I—*Knock it off!*" began the second: he raised his voice and backhanded their prisoner for some unknown infraction. (That's what Kalas thought it sounded like.) The soldier continued: "I've never heard of it before. I got the impression no one had—not even the old-timers."

"Weird."

"No argument here. C'mon, let's get this guy locked up and get out of here: this place stinks!"

Once they left, Kalas asked: "Hey! Pava! You're closest to the corridor: did you see anything? What'd he look like?"

"Couldn't tell. Smells like a beer, though."

Moments later, their fellow prisoner's snores threatened to rattle the bars from their doors.

"Maybe more than *a* beer," Pava corrected herself.

"Why's his snoring sound…familiar?" Rül wondered aloud.

4.

"Falthwën, I have a question," said Zhalera when the new arrival's snoring subsided. "Why is it that only some people can hear

The Song? If it's—I think you called it the cord of the Creator's intent? If that's what it is, wouldn't he want everyone to hear it?"

"You're assuming I know the mind of the Creator!" the cleric laughed. "And maybe, once, I could have answered you with authority, but now…My memory's not what it used to be, as I've shared with Master Kalas. Still, what I do know is this: the Creator bestows his gifts on whom he chooses for purposes only he can fathom. Sometimes, he permits us a glimpse of his intentions; other times, he provides us opportunities to prove our faith—not to him: he already knows the extent of our conviction—but to *ourselves*."

She remained silent for a minute or two, considering Falthwën's words, Kalas assumed, when Rül spoke up.

"Mister cleric, have you ever known of someone who didn't hear this Song when they're a child…maybe hearing it when they're older?"

"I have not, although your question reminds me of a different event that took place long, long ago: before any child of man ever experienced its melodies."

"Seriously?" said Kalas when Falthwën didn't elaborate right away. "You're going to say *that* and nothing more?"

"It's an unpleasant story. *Unpleasant,* really, is too kind a word. I will tell you this: at a time when the ears of *edhunàm* heard nothing but their own discordance, a woman, having suffered incalculable tragedy, took her place among the stars. She not only *heard* The Song: she *became a part of it*."

"What?!" Kalas exclaimed. "You're telling us someone—a *human*—became an *eru*? How could that even happen?!"

"Again, you assume I know the mind of the Creator!"

"You've told us a lot of weird, crazy-sounding stuff over the last month or so, but *this*? It's almost too much!"

"It's true, though," said a voice from the cell next to Pava's.

"Oh? Who's that? How would you know?" insisted Rül.

"I don't mean to eavesdrop, but I've, uh, I've heard the same story the old guy's telling. It's true. *Pretty sure* it's true, anyway!"

"How would you know? You're drunk!" accused Pava.

"Am I? Maybe…Still, your cleric's got his story straight, as far as I remember. Don't believe me? Ask me again in the morning. I'll be sober by then. Maybe…"

"Then maybe you can tell us the rest of the story?" Kalas proposed, but the voice's invisible owner resumed his snoring.

5.

Kalas woke with a start, sat up on his cot, and waited for his eyes to adjust to the darkness. They never did. Every torch had burned itself out, and the dungeon was so far removed from suns and stars that nothing penetrated its environs. He had no idea how long he'd been asleep, but he figured it must've been the middle of the night. Earlier, Rül's snores had overwhelmed those of their unseen acquaintance, but now, other than the relaxed rhythm of his breathing, there were no other—

There it was again! Kalas hadn't realized until now he wasn't hearing with his ears—he was hearing with his mind: an unadorned melody that conjured thoughts of contrition, someone seeking a means of giving voice to unimaginable regret. Its phrases swelled with a sense of penitence. It sounded like a flawed variation of the Song, *almost*—but not quite—harmonizing with the whole. Perhaps with a few tweaks, here and there…

Falthwën? he *thought* as quietly as he knew how. *Falthwën?* he sent again when the cleric offered no reply.

"Oh, you're awake?" said the stranger.

How did—?!

"I—yeah, I guess I am," he allowed in hushed tones. "Thought I heard something. Music."

"Music? Down here? Now wouldn't that be something?" the voice suggested.

"Yeah, I guess it would be."

For a minute or two, his companion said nothing, but Kalas sensed he hadn't gone back to sleep. He was about to ask him a question when the prisoner asked him first: "So, child—no, not a child. Not anymore. Anyway, what brings you to these finer parts of Ïsriba?"

"I'm sorry?"

"What's the charge?"

"Oh, right! I…Actually, I don't know! Nashmur never—"

"Innocent, are you?" he laughed for a moment before his tone turned somber. "Not me. Not for a long time now. Maybe too long…"

"Oh? What did you do?"

A lengthy silence, then: "I'm a traitor. Simple as that."

Kalas wasn't sure how to respond, though he heard himself say something about Ïsriba. His counterpart laughed. Not a mirthful sound: a despondent, helpless bark, perhaps.

"Were I merely a traitor to the queen-pretender up there, it wouldn't—ah, but no, friend, my treason is against another, better kingdom."

"Uh…Ralothova?" Kalas guessed.

"Better! Better than *all* the kingdoms! But no, none of that's why I'm here…Anyway, you never did tell me why they tossed you and your friends into this hole."

"I guess it's because I tried to keep a promise to a friend," Kalas mused.

"A man who keeps his word! Astounding! Yes, that'll often get you in trouble! No, I'm not mocking you! It's the truth. However regrettable it might be!"

The boy nodded and let the silence lengthen. Almost as an

afterthought, he asked: "Earlier: that wasn't you, was it? *Singing*, I mean?"

The stranger said nothing, and Kalas supposed he went back to sleep.

That's what I should do, he observed as he lay back down and stared into the blackness overhead. As he closed his eyes, he thought he heard that same heart-rending tune as before, just as plaintive and just as beautiful.

It seemed like only minutes since his shared conversation with the unknown figure, but Kalas new morning had arrived as he sat up and massaged his temples. Someone had placed fresh torches throughout the block: their light, as well as the heavy, almost medicinal fragrance of their burning fuel permeated their surroundings. Near the door to his cell, someone—perhaps the same someone who'd brought the torches—had slid a tray of watery oatmeal beneath a small flap at its lower edge. He stumbled from his cot, took a few steps to loosen the kinks in his limbs, and retrieved the meal. When Kalas tasted it, he wondered if there were any way to prepare a blander breakfast, but neither he nor his gurgling stomach entertained the thought for more than a few seconds as he gulped it all down.

"Zhalera?" he called between mouthfuls. "Falthwën? Rül? Pava?"

"Still here," said Zhalera in between bites of her own breakfast. The others followed suit.

"What time is it?"

"No idea," Zhalera answered.

"The first sun rose maybe an hour ago," said Rül.

"How can you tell?"

"I don't know, I just…well, it *feels* like the first sun rose not too long ago. On the farm, I'd just be finishing mucking out the stalls about now. Makes me wonder how Mother's doing. I hope the town's getting put back together."

"*Lohwàlarrinme* are a hardy breed," said Falthwën. "I'm sure they've made wise use of the last several weeks."

"Where do you think Nashmur—" Pava began when the clank of booted footsteps echoed through the corridor.

"You're awake. I'm not surprised," said the commander without inflection as he rounded the corner. Kalas almost didn't recognize him without his armor; instead, he wore a pale gray doublet beneath a jerkin cut from green leather. His dark-gray breeches disappeared within high, black riding boots. Two swords hung at his side: one his, the other Shosafin's. Two serious-looking soldiers sporting light, maneuverable armor flanked him and blotted out most of the torchlight.

The queen's men, Kalas assumed.

"Come, let's get you cleaned up before your…audience with the queen."

He undid the locks, starting from the rear with Falthwën's cell and finishing with Pava's. With a nod, he beckoned everyone to follow him. No one said a word as they queued up and started moving. As they exited the block, Kalas craned his neck, hoping for a look at the stranger: when he saw him, he gasped. Seated atop his cot with his back against the wall, the haggard-looking man offered Kalas an unsurprised smile.

"*Nimrïk?!*"

CHAPTER XVIII

Before the Queen of the Kingdom's Throne

NONE OF THE OTHERS SEEMED TO HAVE NOTICED Nïm-rïk, and Kalas wondered if he'd only imagined the stranger was the *Thosharin* from the crossroads and Mbirin's Place. He tried to get a closer look, but one of the larger guards slapped his hinder parts with the shaft of his spear and growled for him to keep moving.

What would Nïmrïk be doing here? he wondered, his memory colored with doubt.

"Rül, you said his snoring sounded familiar. What if that's because it was? Back at Yëlisha's, you bumped into him while he was snoring at a table, right? You really didn't get a look at the guy back there?"

Rül shook his head. "Sorry, *sà*, can't say that I did. But Thosha's days away from here: why would someone like him make the trip all the way to Ïsriba?"

"I don't know," confessed Kalas. "More taverns?"

"Nice!" Pava laughed as Nashmur and the queen-regent's muscle led them through a new series of corridors and stairs. The torches seemed brighter the higher they ascended, the air less dank: but they were still prisoners, and the modest environmental improvements failed to erase that fact.

When they reached the lowest level of the castle proper,

Nashmur led them to a room billowing with floral-scented steam.

"What's that smell?" marveled Zhalera, drinking in deep gulps of the much improved fragrance.

"Shadow lily, mostly," said Falthwën with an absent-minded manner.

"He's right," said Nashmur. "It's—"

"—it's used to induce a mildly compliant state in anyone who breathes its vapors for any significant amount of time," Falthwën interrupted. Zhalera held her breath.

"Well, yes, that's true, but I was going to say it's pretty effective at erasing the…less flowery odors from the dungeon. Can't have such an…*earthy* aroma in the presence of the queen.

"Anyway, there's a change of clothes for each of you on the bench inside. You can leave your old clothes on the floor. The queen's guards will be outside the door should you need anything. There's something I have to take care of right now, but I'll return in about an hour."

"We should be nice and 'compliant' by then, right?" scoffed Zhalera, who'd since placed a hand over her mouth and nose.

"Ladies, gentlemen," the commander nodded as he disappeared around a corner. The two guards who'd been trailing him remained. Despite their seeming indifference, Kalas suspected neither would hesitate to strike should anyone get any clever ideas.

"Zhalera? Pava?" offered Falthwën with a light pat on the shoulder and a sweeping gesture toward the chamber's interior. The girls descended into the room's warm moisture with tentative steps. As Rül and Kalas followed after them, the latter sensed an instruction to *focus* race across his thoughts.

Focus? he wondered. *How? On what?*

Once across the threshold, he retrieved a robe and a towel from a low bench before selecting one of several stalls that lined the back walls of the steamy space. He chose the alcove next to Zhalera (who'd wrapped herself in a towel), shed his filthy clothes, and wrapped his own towel around his waist before he plopped down on the hewn stone seat. With a heavy, exasperated sigh, his nakedness a reified expression of his present state of mind, he closed his eyes, breathed in the hypnotic mist, and tried to ignore the anxious thoughts reeling inside his head.

Focus, he remembered.

Had Falthwën made that suggestion? Who else could it have been? He opened his eyes and stared straight ahead.

On what? he repeated to himself. He glanced at Falthwën: a few stalls down, he'd taken his seat, filled his lungs with the sweet-smelling air, and closed his eyes. Sputtering torches lined the walls, and in their inconsistent light Kalas saw occasional twists of something gleaming from the old man's direction.

Like what he did beneath the Sanctuary, he noted.

He turned toward Zhalera, who startled him with her intense tawny gaze. She'd been watching him for a while, he supposed, her forearm draped across the shoulder-height partition and her chin nestled atop her forearm. She'd piled her hair in loose, twin buns; now, she regarded him with a curious look.

"Is this where you'd thought we'd be?" she said without much emotion.

"What do you mean?"

"I'm not sure," she admitted. After a while, she continued, "I mean, we should be back in Lohwàlar, living out our lives, right? In a few years, we'd...I'd take over for Father at the smithy, you would...? I just never thought we'd be...*here.*"

"Yeah, me neither," Kalas agreed with a yawn.

Focus!

"What was that?"

"I didn't say anything," said Zhalera as she raised her head and looked around.

"No, not you: I...I'm trying not to fall asleep. I thought—"
Focus!

"'Focus'?" mumbled Pava as she opened her eyes. "What?"

"So you're hearing that, too?" said Kalas. "Falthwën?"

The cleric's eyes remained closed, but with a subtle smile he breathed, "Not me, my child, but it does seem like a sensible course of action, yes?"

"On *what* though?" Kalas wondered aloud.

"Our thoughts are on the queen-regent. On her designs for us. So long as they remain there, these vapors accomplish their intended purpose. If you—all of you—could be *anywhere*, could be doing *anything*, where—*what*—would it be?"

No one answered the cleric's question, but Kalas' thoughts turned toward home. In his mind's eye, he could see himself standing before the *zhàrudzh* that had killed his father; in his hand he held Shosafin's sword, and with a fearsome cry that echoed across the heavens, he charged and—

No—what's already happened...has already happened...

He shook his head and let the vision dissolve in a floral haze before he thought about the artifact buried in the Empty Sea.

Why that *thing?!*

The rocks hiding the object from view were gone. Maybe they'd never fallen. He ran a hand across the symbols, and in his new thought he understood their purpose. The exterior door slid inward without incident: the outline of the interior door glowed, split apart, and gushed uncolored light that obscured anything beyond its threshold.

No, that's not where I want to be! he insisted. *I want...*

Kalas closed his eyes this time and saw Zhalera, some years older—not quite a couple of Sevens, maybe—with a vibrant shock of champagne-tinted sterling sprouting from the deep black that framed the rest of her forehead. She looked up from her task, set down her four-pound (less a few grains) hammer, and approached him with an impish smile. He thought he heard laughter. A child's laughter, maybe: the kind that arises from untainted joy. Zhalera wrapped her arms around his neck, pulled him toward the curve of her mouth, and—

"C'mon, Kalas! Time to get dressed!" Zhalera prodded him.

"What? I—is Nashmur back?" he stammered as he stood and toweled dry.

"Sorry that took…a little longer than I thought," said the commander as Kalas covered himself with the ill-fitting robe. "I see you're all changed. Well, most of you."

"I, uh, must have dozed off," the boy muttered as he thrust an arm through a sleeve that was too long.

"It happens," Nashmur said. "Come, this way. The queen is waiting."

2.

"Where do you think that steam comes from?" said Rül as they ascended through the castle's various levels, each more elegant than the last.

"It's piped in from hot springs far beneath the ground. Volcanic activity, I'm told."

"A volcano? Like the Ildurgul Taruún?" Pava wondered.

"The what?"

"The Death-bringing Mountain at the far north of the Ilvurkanzhime," supplied Falthwën. You haven't felt its rumblings of late?"

"No, I can't say that I have. I divide most of my time between here and Âivambar. Nowadays I don't have much reason to travel any farther west."

"Probably different plates," the cleric said to himself.

"Different what?"

Falthwën smiled. "No matter. I suspect the Ildurgul will erupt in the not-too-distant future. If—*when* it does, not even Ïsriba will escape unscathed."

"Unscathed? How do you mean?"

"It gets cold here in the winter, yes? It'll get colder. And the summers won't be as warm, nor as long. It wouldn't be a bad idea to anticipate the necessary adjustments to Ïsriba's economy—its society at large, really. Get ready for when the time comes."

"How do you know all this? What makes you so sure?" said Nashmur as he stopped and turned, narrowed his eyes as he regarded the curious old man.

Falthwën smiled. "I didn't mean to cause you any undue alarm: the not-too-distant future could be tens, maybe hundreds of Sevens from now. Anyway, you said the queen is waiting, yes?"

The commander nodded, suspicious, as he appraised the cleric. "You're not wrong. Just a few more levels and we'll—"

As he resumed walking, he turned a corner and collided with someone wrapped in loose, ragged clothes. The figure stopped: when Nashmur offered an apology, he said nothing; instead, he peered at everyone through his tattered black hood, fixed his jaundiced gaze on Kalas, and seemed to vanish around another corner.

"What was that?" the boy asked as cold sweat beaded on his skin. Some half-remembered thought ran its fingers along the cusp of conscious recall, then retreated toward less accessible places in his mind. He shivered.

"One of the queen's new servants," Nashmur allowed, bristling, and Kalas discerned the commander also sensed something unwholesome about the man.

After three more flights of marbled stairs, accented with pale yellow metal sporting a greenish tinge, the commander brought them to one end of a long hallway lined with dangerous-looking soldiers. Entire walls had been overlaid with *Poyïsriba* green gold, and flakes of the stuff glittered like miniature stars as suns-light cascaded through skylights of smoked quartz high above. Toward the center of the passage, in the middle of a vast rotunda stood a golden statue with an indomitable expression. Perhaps twelve feet tall, the daunting figure held an enormous sword in one armored fist; a giant bird-of-prey, wings spread, grasped the other.

"Ulobir's tomb," said Nashmur. "Commissioned by his son and successor, Ulobir the Second."

"Looks like someone you wouldn't want to mess with," Rül acknowledged as they circled the monument to Ïsriba's first king.

"It's not solid…gold—whatever that metal is, is it? Why is it green?" Zhalera wondered.

"Not solid, no: it's chiseled stone overlaid with an alloy of gold and…nickel? silver? Some other metal, anyway."

"It's really…pretty."

"'Pretty'?" the commander laughed. "I think Ulobir was going for something other than 'pretty,' but I have to agree!"

At the end of the corridor, Nashmur stopped everyone in front of twin doors, roughly fifteen feet tall and covered with the same gold as the statue, each resting on tremendous hinges. Fourteen guards lined either side of seven broad, basalt stairs polished to a deep, mirror-like finish. Kalas couldn't help succumbing to the sense of *smallness* the architecture impressed upon him.

The commander ascended the stairs and nodded toward the guards. He held up a finger before he turned and addressed the party: "No one of your…standing gets an audience with the queen. Not a pleasant one, at least. Say nothing until she makes a specific request; at such a time, answer her directly. Succinctly. Tell the truth.

"Master Kalas: since Ilbardhën entrusted you, specifically, with his sword, the queen will assume he's entrusted you with information, too. Keeping your secrets from me is one thing: keeping them from *her*, however, is entirely another."

Nashmur knelt, placed a hand on the boy's shoulder and whispered, "You trusted me with his sword. Perhaps we can avoid what's sure to be an inquisition if you'll also trust me with his intentions?"

Kalas replied, "I really don't know where he is or what he's up to. Not specifically..."

"Specifically?"

"I just know he's looking for someone. Someone named Marugan."

The commander stood, his eyes wide. All the color drained from his face as he wheeled around and gestured for the guards to open the imperious gilded doors.

He knows that name! Kalas observed. *And he's* afraid *of it...*

3.

With stiff steps, Nashmur preceded everyone into the throne room: a cavernous space half as long as the hall through which they'd come and twice as high. Its polished walls had a subtle inward slope and terminated in a vault-like configuration overhead. Like the hall, the room's apex boasted similar stretches of tinted mineral quartz. Curtains actuated by a complex-looking assortment of cords and pulleys obscured most of the suns-light; indeed, only a thin ribbon reached the sparkling floor, creating a narrow pathway toward a lofty block of stone atop a terraced pedestal—the room's sole furnishing—at the far end of the chamber.

Not just a block of stone: a throne.

Posted at each step, armored soldiers stared straight ahead, seemingly indifferent to their surroundings. Like the other guards, Kalas figured they probably saw or sensed everything taking place within every corner and crevice of the vast space. Each held a gleaming halberd, heel planted on the floor and sharp-looking blade facing the entrance. At each man's hip hung an ornamental scabbard cut from green leather and adorned with emeralds and diamonds fixed within settings of that ever-present *Poyïsriba* gold; each scabbard held an ornately-hilted sword.

Some distance from the bottommost step, the commander stopped and knelt. The others followed his example.

Silence.

Nothing—no one—made a sound.

"Rise."

Commander Nashmur stood. So did everyone else. The soldiers held their positions until the same voice—mature, rich, and unmistakably feminine—bade them depart. It echoed across the throne room's walls, each half-repetition underscoring the severity of the queen-regent's commands. Without a word, each guard disappeared within the shadows, performing his part of a well-practiced routine.

"Commander Nashmur. You've recovered intelligence regarding that traitor to the crown, Shosafin?"

It wasn't a question. Even Kalas caught the queen-regent's uncomfortable subtext. The *Poyïsriba* throne sat beneath a column of filtered light: a broad finial at the tip of the thin ray that bisected the darkness.

"*Hish*, my queen," said the commander as he held out Shosafin's sword: one hand on its hilt, the other supporting its scabbard. "These travelers were his companions. For a time, at least. Here: I present Ilbar—that is, Shosafin's sword."

The queen-regent stood, the train of her robe billowing in her wake. Unnumbered beads of crystal sparkled along the sleeves and bodice of her ice-white gown. Around her slender neck she wore a stole of contrasting black fur, rough and stringy. As she descended, each faceted work caught fire as it passed through that singular unobstructed beam.

She approached Nashmur, who knelt again, and made a cursory examination of the sword he held aloft. Her cream-colored skin appeared flawless in the room's curious light. Her hair, the same color as her gown, had been plaited and tied back in perfect symmetry beneath a crown of ornate golden wings decked with diamonds and emeralds. She ran her delicate-looking fingers along the length of the weapon's sheath: her dark eyes, framed by high, chiseled cheekbones, flowed over its surfaces without betraying any hint of emotion.

She's breathtaking, Kalas admitted to himself, *but Shosafin was right: there's something* cold *about her.*

"It's his," she nodded, satisfied at last with its provenance, and something flickered in her eyes. "You retrieved it from these people?"

"From the boy, my queen," said the commander, still kneeling with his head bowed.

"From the boy. Tell me, child: your name?"

"Kalas. Uh, Queen Ësfàyami," he stammered. A cruel smile touched the corners of her mouth.

"Tell me, young Kalas: who are these with you?"

He provided everyone's name as the queen-regent glided from person to person. When he finished, she took the sword from Nashmur, drew it, and instructed the commander to stand. With a few adept flicks, she played its edge within the light: with uncanny speed, brought its tip to bear against Kalas' throat.

"Shosafin. Where is he?"

Too surprised to move, to think, to do anything other than stand where he was, he didn't even flinch: dumb beneath her withering gaze, her dark irises naught but a faint halo around her fathomless pupils, he returned her stare.

"I don't know," he heard himself whisper.

"You don't know?" she spat in her disbelief.

"I don't! I—we—none of us has seen him in weeks!"

Ësfàyami held him a moment longer, then returned Shosafin's sword to its sheath.

"Very well," she said, apparently satisfied for the moment. "What do you know of his plans? His goals?"

"All I know is he's looking for, uh, someone."

Nashmur flinched just before Kalas said *Marugan*. The queen-regent discerned his hesitation.

"Who?"

"He calls himself Marugan," Kalas wilted.

In a flash, the sword was at his throat again, closer, this time, and he winced as he felt it prick his skin.

"What did you say?!" she demanded, her tone a mix of disbelief and rage.

"M—Marugan."

"I see…" she said, slowly removing the sword from his neck. "You will tell me everything Shosafin told you about Marugan."

Kalas relayed as much of the old soldier's story as he could remember: "We ran into Marugan in the woods, on our way here from Lohwàlar, in the West. He and his warriors tried to kill us! Shosafin saved our lives. He left after that, but we found him some time later with his—Marugan attacked him! Almost killed him! Not long after that, he gave me that sword, then disappeared. That's the truth."

"Marugan. He was one of my father's most trusted lords. When Shosafin returned from that ill-fated hunting trip alone, I *knew* he was responsible for my father's death. For *all* of their deaths! For long years I've regretted my decision to let him live: he was *Ilfadan-pini-Elïgar!* Neglecter-of-the-King! His life was *supposed* to be a portrait of abject shame; his days were *supposed* to be filled with exquisite humiliation until, at the end, he would finally summon his last shreds of dignity and fall upon his sword!

"Your story rings true, young Kalas. True in the sense that I believe that's what Shosafin-Ilfadan told you."

Kalas wanted to rebut her smug certainty, but some strange compulsion—like whispers within his thoughts—convinced him not to speak.

"Here's what *I* know: Shosafin, son of a lowly *rasak* weaver, tricked my father into promoting him well above his station. Such insolence might have been forgiven, but my father, still grieving the loss of his bride—my mother—deigned to invite him along on a hunt with his most trusted *kindume*—lords and nobles. Having attained so prime an opportunity, he slaughtered every last one of them!

"I've since learned that he sought to prove his worth to the empire of Tsobarut, to bring Emperor Kematu my father's head as the price of his *Potsobarut* nobility! However, with his dying breath, my father escaped Shosafin's plot, and the murderer never recovered his body. Without his prize, Kematu—*zhi âsru—ib imu sathrin fie id màr*—would have nothing to do with him, and so he returned to Ïsriba with his impossible tale about monster wolves."

Stunned, Kalas wasn't sure what to say. While the queen-regent's story held an air of plausibility, he couldn't—he *wouldn't*—believe it.

"Why would he return to Ïsriba if he'd just killed King Rufàran?" Kalas blurted. In his peripheral vision, he saw Nashmur's head droop. "Surely word of the king's death would've reached Tsobarut after a time: why not just wait a while, then make his case before the Emperor? And how could you know all this? His plan? What happened to your father? I can't imagine he'd be stupid enough to brag about his failures—if your version of things is correct. And with all due respect, your majesty—"

"Kalas, don't!" Zhalera hissed.

"—I don't believe it is."

Queen-regent Ësfàyami stared at him with her hard, cold eyes. Kalas' heart pounded against his chest: he thought it might burst from his ribcage as its furious rhythm echoed back and forth.

She laughed. A mellifluous, musical sound. Devoid of context, Kalas would have thought her laughter most beautiful; instead, it registered as wholly mirthless, almost maniacal.

"You're bold, young Kalas. Unrefined. Uncultured. *Simple*, perhaps, but bold, nonetheless. I *almost* like that, and so I'll answer some of your questions.

"Shosafin may have believed he'd killed everyone in my father's hunting party, but one member survived—"

"Marugan."

"Do *NOT* interrupt me!" she boomed, her voice and authority echoing across the throne room.

"Marugan," she continued, as though Kalas had never interrupted her. "His wounds were grievous. It's no wonder a substandard soldier like Shosafin thought he was dead. His attempt, however, left more than its physical mark on Marugan: his mental injuries were most cruel, too. Years passed. Sevens, even, before his memory returned—before *he* could return to Ïsriba:

"He'd been wandering the forests, the lesser villages to the north. Relying on the alms of kind-hearted *kelâme* willing to guide him back to health. A little more than a month ago, he approached Ïsriba's gates, again in full control of his faculties.

"At first, he was loath to speak ill of his would-be-murderer —such a kind, generous, and *noble* man! At last, after realizing the ills the kingdom had endured through Shosafin's treachery, he revealed to me the depth his malevolent schemes."

"What makes Marugan's story more believable than Shosafin's?" Kalas prodded. "All you've presented is hearsay: one man's word against another's!"

"*Simple,*" Ësfàyami repeated and shook her head, apparently embarrassed for the boy.

"Years ago, Marugan showed up under the Áthradho, claiming he was our prophesied *Ilosar,*" Pava began. "He called himself something else, but even as recently as a few weeks ago, he was there. And you say he's been *here* for more than a month?"

"You forget your place, child!" Nashmur whispered, but the queen-regent simply laughed that beautiful, disconcerting laugh.

"You are mistaken, cave-child," she scoffed.

"He's not human," Rül added, having found the same store of confidence from which the others drew. "He's *eku. Ilnàfël.* Shosafin slit his throat in front of us: just a few minutes later, the wound closed up and he disappeared! He was leading a pack of spirit-men —former *shagabme,* we think!"

"With your own tongues you condemn your friend!" exclaimed the queen-regent. "Shosafin *believed* this unfortunate person to be Marugan—an impossibility!—so he attempted to kill him a second time?! Oh! The lot of you have crafted a most *marvelous* fiction!"

The faintest twinge of fire flickered within her eyes as she continued: "Shosafin murdered my father and all his *kindume.* And even if he *didn't,* he had the *gall* to survive when my father did not!"

"Your majesty, we've lost our parents too, me and Zhalera," said Kalas. "Slain by *zhàrudzhme* that attacked our village! That's what we came all this way to talk to you about. I even wondered if there might be some way to bring them back, but—"

"—there isn't," Ësfàyami finished, her belligerence muted for the moment, and the young man wondered if she once entertained the same thoughts.

"My queen," said a voice from deep within the shadows. Kalas felt the hairs at the back of his neck stand straight as a figure emerged from the darkness. He knew who the voice belonged to before its owner's scarred face pierced the veil of light.

"With your permission, perhaps I can help free these people from Ilbardhën's enchantment?" offered Marugan.

4.

"*Ímbâ ilosar!*" Pava rasped. "Pretender!"

"Come now! Name-calling isn't necessary! It seems Ilbardhën's done quite a number on your minds!"

Beneath the skylights, despite the harsh shadows cast by the waxing suns, Marugan's neck bore the faintest trace of purple scar tissue, almost hidden beneath a scraggly salt-and-pepper beard. His face, however, was a mask of wrecked flesh. Ragged, parallel lines—from *rudzhegu* claws, no doubt—stretched from above his forehead almost to his chin, each with yellowed edges that looked like they'd never properly healed. His close-cropped hair seemed to make his scars more pronounced, and his eyes—gray and indifferent—surveyed the vast chamber from beneath thin, arched eyebrows. Although clothed in court dress, he jingled as he walked, and Kalas noticed he still carried his bow from the forest.

"Rather, it's you who've 'done a number' on the queen's mind," said Falthwën with just the slightest touch of steel in his voice. "Even if *she* remains unaware of your true, traitorous nature, *we* are not so ill-informed."

"Cleric! Kalas! The rest of you! Please!" begged Nashmur.

"No, Commander," countered Marugan. "Let these enemies of the crown state their treachery plainly! It's clear to me—as it should be to you—that Ilbardhën's lies have corrupted their judgment!"

"You're *afraid* of him," said Zhalera. "You're afraid of *us!*"

"Nonsense! Why would I be afraid of people I've never met? Never heard of?!" Marugan insisted.

"That man we bumped into on our way up here: he was one of your *shosayedhume,* wasn't he?!" accused Kalas. "Watching us?

Reporting back to you?"

"'Spirit-men'? I have no idea what you're talking about!" he deflected.

"*Kalswàr!*" said Rül as he smacked his forehead. "*That's* how you moved between the Áthradho and Ïsriba! And the forest!"

"Of course! *Ekume* can—how did Shosafin put it? 'Warp time'?" agreed Kalas. "Your majesty, Shosafin—"

"Enough!" roared the queen-regent, her hand outstretched, a single shaking finger mere inches from Kalas' face. "Shosafin is a liar and a traitor! Soon, however, it won't matter! He sought Ïsriba's destruction for the glory of Tsobarut; however, it is *Tsobarut* that will fall to the glory of Ïsriba!"

"Well said, my queen!" exulted Marugan.

Falthwën shook his head. "Then the rumors are true…"

"I've waited too long. *Too long!*" Ësfàyami elaborated. "I had to ascertain my enemy's weaknesses, discover how to best exploit them! I hoped to extract such details from Shosafin-Ilfadan before sending *his* severed head to Emperor Kematu; now, it doesn't matter! My armies stand at peak strength! When the first snows of the season fall, it will be upon the smoking ruins of Tsobarut!

"Ralothova won't abide such rapacious expansionism," Falthwën warned. "Nor the neighboring kingdoms…"

"Of course not!" crowed the queen-regent. "That's why I've marshaled *additional* armies dedicated to the destruction of Ralothova, Gambarad, and beyond! I will break the teeth of all who stand in my way: within a Seven, this entire hemisphere will be united —*crushed* beneath the unyielding talons of Ïsriba!"

He kept quiet, but Kalas noticed Commander Nashmur wince with the queen-regent's every manic pronouncement.

"My queen, you've lost perspective," soothed the cleric. "King Rufàran would have never wanted this!"

"King Rufàran is *dead! Ilfadan-pïni-Elïgar* saw to that!"

"Shosafin believes King—he believes your father is still alive!" insisted Kalas.

Stunned, Ësfàyami's eyes widened, and in their depths he glimpsed what looked like *hope*. Feeble, but hope nonetheless.

"*Lies!*" raged Marugan as he raised his bow, nocked an arrow, and fired.

Kalas thought time had stopped: a moment stretched into minutes, or so it seemed, and in that expanded, timelike event—

Time has done this to me before...or did I *do this to* time?

—he raised his hand, and the missile disintegrated into a cascade of harmless, unhurried sparks as it collided with his blazing, upturned palm.

"*Nalëndas!*" Marugan cried, unable to disguise his fear.

"*Ilbarshme!*" shouted the queen-regent, summoning the shadowed guards. With a rough shove, she returned Shosafin's sword to Nashmur. "Commander: return these prisoners to their cells! I want—"

"Please, your majesty! Kill them here! Now! I beg you!" Marugan implored.

"You forget your place, *kindu!*"

"I only mean—you said yourself you wished you'd executed Ilbardhën when you had the chance!"

"Shosafin, yes, but this one? This one has *power*. I will understand it. I will *own* it!"

At the commander's instruction, hulking, menacing-looking soldiers grabbed Kalas and the others and dragged them from the throne room.

5.

No one spoke as Nashmur and the queen-regent's guards strong-armed the party down through the castle's many levels.

Along the way, a few of Marugan's *shosayedhume* revealed their presence, their cold, dead eyes watching the procession with methodical indifference.

"What are they looking at?" said Pava, unnerved.

"Marugan's afraid of Shosafin—and us," Zhalera insisted again. "Kalas, at least. He called you *Nalëndas.* Falthwën, what's that mean?"

"It's part of a legend that hearkens back to a time before the world was cracked, when everything was an island in the midst of an endless sea. *Nalën* means 'first,' as you know. It's also the 'name' for *Zhi Milël pini Ilundas Ilunas*—The Jewel of Ilun's Creation. She sought to protect *edhunàm* from Ilnëshras' cancerous corruption. She failed. Her sacrifice, however, precipitated the advent of the prophecy that concerns you."

"Why are you just *now* telling me this?!" Kalas demanded.

"I…didn't remember until now—until *just* now," the cleric apologized. "As I've told you: my memory's not what it used to be! By design, I think. Certain events, certain conversations sometimes pull back the shroud a little…"

"Dzharëth said I was one of *hers,* Kalas said, recalling the words of the wolfish remnant of his friend. "Is that what he meant? Is that what Marugan meant by *Nalëndas?*"

"I don't know, my child. I'm sorry. Perhaps."

"This prophecy," said Nashmur after a silence. "What's it all about?"

"This world is not what it was intended to be," Falthwën began. "Nor will it remain ever thus. For good or ill remains to be seen."

For our good? or for our doom? Tsharak wondered, Kalas remembered.

"And Kalas has something to do with this prophecy, you said?"

Falthwën said nothing, but Kalas felt a peculiar tension rise up all around them. With a sigh, the commander muttered, "I hope you're right…" before drawing Shosafin's sword: with a quick twist and a flash of torchlight, he separated the nearest guard's head from his shoulders, then tossed the sword to Kalas. With another lightning-like move, he produced his own sword and ran it through the next guard.

Kalas caught the sword by the hilt, adjusted his stance, and raised it just in time to block one of the remaining two guards from bringing his halberd down upon his neck. He hadn't quite found his footing, and the blow sent him reeling. Another guard raised his weapon against Rül, but the farm boy turned and shoved him against the wall.

"Commander, what are you doing?! *Why* are you doing this?!" Kalas wheezed as he stood. He parried another blow, maintaining his balance this time.

"The queen's lost her way. Maybe her mind," he grunted between his strikes. "Nothing good will come of war for war's sake. With Tsobarut, or Ralothova, or Gambarad, or any other nation. I hope you're right, cleric: the world could use a change."

With a subtle shimmer, Falthwën's ill-fitting garment from the steam room became his regular robes. He reached within its folds and retrieved the black sword Hàfilrifar. One of the fallen guards regained his feet, raised his polearm, and lunged for Pava: Zhalera intercepted him with a barefoot kick to his nethers and sent him tumbling onto Nashmur's waiting blade. A few fast hacks ended him. The surviving soldier—the one Rül pushed—assessed his altered circumstances: after hesitating, he turned and fled. Kalas, his blood hot, took a few hasty steps in the man's direction when the commander called him back.

"Let him go! Even if you stopped him, it won't be long before the queen figures out what's going on. We need to find a way out of here!"

Focus!

"'Focus'? What?" he added, his head cocked.

"You all heard that, right?" said Kalas as the others nodded.

"All right, let me think," said the commander, his eyes closed as he contemplated various scenarios. "These dungeons are like mazes: intended to keep people lost should anyone ever escape his cell. No single guard knows its entire layout: probably for reasons just like this. Still, I know *these* parts. I *think*. I was stationed here—once. It's…it's been a while. C'mon! This way!"

For the next few minutes, Nashmur led everyone through the dungeon's numerous corridors and pungent reek, doubling back now and again as he tried to remember (or stumble upon) some means of escape. The tromp of armored boots and the shouts of angry soldiers flitted through the passages: one moment it sounded like they were right around the corner; the next, some distance away.

"All right, over here! I think we'll come to—" the commander began: as he rounded what turned out to be a dead-end corner, Marugan, bow raised, stood waiting.

"How did—?!" Nashmur stammered.

"Kalswàr," said Rül. "He's an *eku*. An *ilnàfël*—a dark one. We were telling the truth."

"It's true," sneered Marugan, his gray eyes alive with fear and hatred. "Doesn't matter though! None of you is leaving this place! I don't care *what* the queen says!"

He fired his arrow, but Falthwën flicked it away with the flat of his black sword. Before the *eku* could ready another, Nashmur was upon him, his sword pressed against the flat line of violet scar tissue stretching across his neck from ear to ear. Marugan laughed: the gravel in its tone sent shivers down Kalas' spine.

"Your cousin tried something like this not too long ago," he teased. "Ask your friends how well that worked out for him!"

"Wait—your *cousin?!*" said Kalas.

"What's your endgame, fiend?" the commander demanded. "I know the stories…"

"Oh? And how do those usually end?!"

A band of shambling *shosayedhume* separated from the shadows. They surrounded everyone and hauled Nashmur away from Marugan's throat.

"Yes, this seems about right!" he jeered. *"Shagabme! Tzhafodhu!"*

As the inhabited corpses pressed in all around them and tightened their collective grip, their polluted fetor clung to Kalas' nostrils: *Is this what death smells like?* he wondered.

For a moment.

A huge black paw reached out of the darkness and ripped one of the *shosayedhu* into pieces: each shred evaporated in a stinging cloud of rancid smoke. A *rudzhegu,* larger than any Kalas remembered from the attack on Lohwàlar, bounded into the light. He caught the boy's gaze, then turned against another assailant and, with slashes, barks, and growls, spilled its viscera onto the ground. He went after another, then others, until he dispatched the last of them.

"No! Not—What are—*Who do you think you are?!*" shouted Marugan, his whispery voice cracking with fear. He glanced at Kalas, raised his bow, and launched another arrow: the wolf lunged, and the projectile struck him through the ruff of his neck. He collapsed with a yelp. Within an undulating splash of *void,* Marugan blinked out of sight.

The noise attracted the queen-regent's soldiers: they were no more than a few corridors away.

"I'm sorry, friends," Nashmur sighed, his sword hanging limp at his side.

"Why did you *help* us?" Kalas wondered as he pointed his sword at the collapsed *zhàrudzh.*

The wounded beast held him with his yellow stare, his breaths fast and shallow. Before he could respond, however, guards poured into the opposite end of the long and narrow hall.

"Over here! You there! By executive order of Queen Ësfàyami! *Stop!*" one of them shouted.

Behind Kalas' shoulders, faint purple luminescence started glowing, growing ever brighter and rising from a thready flicker to a blinding violet wash. The approaching soldiers held their positions and raised their arms to block its glare. Kalas turned: Falthwën raked Hàfilrifar through empty space in a pattern of repeating shapes. Every stroke left a strand of scintillating brilliance that hovered like tangible phenomena, each building upon the last.

"It *was* her! *She* is *here!*" the cleric exulted.

The symbol-lights expanded, swelled with energy from some other spacetime, and mingled together until they enveloped Falthwën and the others in a burgeoning wave of amethyst radiance. What Kalas could only describe as a *wedge* of music welled up from within the glare. One moment they were in Ïsriba's dungeons; the next, a place unlike anything they had ever seen.

Chapter XIX

Beyond the Reach of a Lightless Star

"**K**ALAS! WHAT'S GOING ON?! DID...DID YOU DO that?!" Zhalera whispered, her voice almost inaudible and laced with fear.

"No! I—Where are we? Falthwën, who's *she?* Where is *here?* Falthwën? Falthwën?!"

The unbearable fire from the cleric's sword burned itself out, and Kalas' voice echoed through a cold, lightless environment. Aside from the physicality of the floor onto which they'd been dropped, *nothingness* surrounded them. Subtle wind swirled within the black space and amplified the rising apprehension poisoning the atmosphere.

"Here, my child," coughed the cleric at last. "Is everyone here? Everyone all right?"

Other than their shared, sudden confusion, everyone was fine.

"Zhalera: your hand, please?" he said. Kalas felt the cleric's fingers flex against the darkness as Falthwën reached for the young blacksmith.

"I'm here!" she said, taking a few steps toward his voice.

"This belongs to you—for a time, at least. Here's your family's sword. There's no longer any need to keep it secret. Not here!"

Kalas imagined the cleric reaching into his remarkable robes and retrieving Zhalera's blade from whatever impossible dimension in which he'd hidden it. As he raised the object, waves of soft, yellow light rippled across its surfaces.

"Thank you," she said as she received the heirloom from his gnarled hand.

The weapon's subtle radiance caught in the facets of Falthwën's ring and frolicked from stone to stone.

"Where did you get that ring!" queried Pava, seizing the latest opportunity to press him about it. "I've been meaning to ask you that ever since I woke up in the back of your cart!"

"Ironic—or providential, perhaps—that you'd choose this moment, *this place,* to raise that question!

"Where *is* 'this place'?!" Rül wondered on everyone's behalf.

Kalas took a few steps toward the cleric, anticipating his answer, when his shins brushed against something coarse and wiry.

"Falthwën, the *rudzhegu* from the dungeon!" Kalas exclaimed. "He's here! In this place with us!"

"Is that so?" said the cleric with an odd quality to his voice. Something between disbelief and curiosity. "That is…unusual," he admitted.

"He's hurt—Marugan's arrow got him!—but he's breathing…" Falthwën knelt and examined the creature.

"He's unconscious, and his *music* is…strange. Hmm. For now, all we can do is keep an eye on him…

"To answer your question, Master Rül: 'Where is this pace?' We're within the *Wànuk pïn Erume*—the Vault of Stars. This place, my children, is where I intended to come so many months ago: this place is where I hoped to confer with my colleagues about that prophecy into which you've all—yes, *all*—been thrust. We're well beneath what is now considered Ïsriba."

"The 'Vault of Stars'? Nashmur mumbled. *"Beneath* Ïsriba? But none of Ulobir's records mention a place like this!"

"Nor would they," nodded Falthwën. "The Vault predates Ïsriba by many hundreds of Sevens! It even predates the three kingdoms whose ashes Ulobir's golden falcon first ascended from!"

"*Three* kingdoms!" the commander muttered. "I *knew* it!"

"No one knows about this place? this Vault?" Zhalera shivered. The absence of light and the ever-present breezes robbed the warmth from their bones. "Wouldn't someone have found after all those Sevens?"

"It's not *exactly* beneath Ïsriba," he conceded.

"*Loshar shusa*, Sharuyan!" intoned a voice that shook the room. A woman's voice, sweet and pure and coming from somewhere above—no! all around—no! right beside them! Kalas whirled, and next to Falthwën, a spark no larger than a pinprick popped into view from some separate existence. It hovered in space for a moment before a familiar crack of violet light blinded everyone again.

"Well met indeed, Loradan, *Ilmazhasahal!*"

"*Sharuyan?!*" gasped Zhalera.

"Of *course!*" Kalas laughed. "Oh, so many things make sense now! Tsharak had you figured out, didn't he?"

"Well, he *did* get a nine-hundred-year head start!" the cleric winked.

"What do—wait! You mean Falthwën is—?!" blurted Rül.

Pava dropped to her knees and bowed her head in reverence. "*Ilbarsh pïn alasdra: di nimsulum-paramahal aswanthalu!*"

"Please, my child! None of that! *I'm* the one who should be seeking forgiveness. From all of you! So much is changing! So much has changed—*and* so quickly! Oh! My manners! Friends and fellow-travelers, allow me to introduce Loradan, my—"

"*Beloved*," interjected Kalas. "That's what you called her, right?"

Falthwën—*Sharuyan*—offered him a knowing smile, and with a gesture, he willed light to fill the room.

"Loradan, I have a gift for you," he said and offered her Hàfilrifar.

The *eru* accepted her old weapon with awe and ran her finger along its light-cleaving edges.

"So *that's* how you made all that racket! I heard my name, like someone shouting from a great distance—through an even greater fog. When I saw the light, I knew—I just *knew* it had to be you!" she exclaimed, "but where—*when*—did you ever find this?!"

"Lohwàlar, of all places! Trapped within a fragment of The Arch! Some might consider it a coincidence: you and I know better! I'm glad I'm finally able to return it to you," he said as she held him tight.

"Falthwën, I'm—should we call you Falthwën? Sharuyan?" stammered Zhalera. "I said some things on the way here that I'd like to take back. I didn't know...I didn't understand..."

Sharuyan cupped her downturned chin and raised it up. He held her gaze for a moment, then swept her into his embrace and said, "All is forgiven, my child."

"Oho! What's this?!" said a new voice as another spark—tinted blue—winked into view before assuming human form. "An *egu* inside the Vault?"

Other lights split the darkness, their respective hues brightening the room. Now Kalas saw that it had seven faceted sides, similar to the Temple beneath Lohwàlar's Sanctuary yet immeasurably greater. Each wall looked like it had been cut from some kind of otherworldly stone and polished to mirrored perfection. Looking up, he could see neither ceiling nor stars: just *black* where the light waned. Seven arcane symbols, each constructed of inlaid gemstones, radiated from an eighth, unadorned symbol at the Vault's center. Between these seven walls, Falthwën introduced the arrivals:

"Loradan you've met. This is Sifuran, Peradan, Yayan, Heshradan...Where's Valaran?"

Silence.

"You don't know..." someone soothed.

"An *ekume* singularity," Loradan explained. "She and Peradan were observing the signs and portents when it happened…"

"Both of us might have been undone had she not expended all her strength to save me," said a morose-looking figure. The spessartine *eru*. Peradan.

Sharuyan nodded. "I knew a day like this would come," he sighed, having permitted himself a moment. "Still…I'd hoped to reacquaint her with—Zhalera, would you show these *erume* your sword?"

Puzzled, she held the weapon aloft. The assembled stars murmured and nodded. Some smiled.

"Beautiful work, as always!" someone said. Yayan? The "red" one?

"I was taught that my ancestors forged this sword," she frowned, confused.

"Oh, one of them most assuredly did, young lass!" Sifuran was quick to affirm. "Valaran—*o shelu fie ith nir*—made something of a name for herself assisting skilled artisans and makers, helping them improve their art and science. Sometimes, she'd suffuse a piece with a portion of her essence: what *edhume* might perceive as patterns of light coming from within."

"Oh!" she said, now smiling. "But I've only ever seen those lights when Falthwën held it…"

"You've a number of Sevens ahead of you: I wouldn't let it bother you just yet," the *eru* said with a wink.

During the demonstration, Heshradan kept a close eye on Kalas. When Zhalera lowered her sword, he approached the boy.

"Two Sevens," he said, his eyes far away. "Tell me child: Màla? Tàran? Are they well?"

"They're dead, sir" said Kalas. *Rudzhegume.*

Heshradan reacted as though struck.

"Kalas! I'm so sorry!" he wept.

"You knew my parents?"

Through his tears, the *eru* offered him a subtle nod and a sad smile. Kalas' eyes opened wide: "You're the one who left me with them!"

"I am," he nodded again.

"Do you know where I'm from? Who my birth parents are?"

"I do…" said Heshradan with a guarded tone.

"Oh, right," Kalas remembered. "Falthwën—Sharuyan, sorry! —says he couldn't tell me, either."

"Rül," said Sharuyan as he approached the farm boy. "These represent the *Kel Erume*—the *Kathin Sâash* your grandfather told you about! I thought you'd be pleased to know his stories had their roots in truth!"

Rül smiled and nodded as his grin threatened to split his ruddy cheeks. "I wish I could tell him about meeting you all, that's for sure," he said. "The Great Swath! I wonder what other stories of his were true?"

The *zhàrudzh* stirred at last, Marguan's arrow still protruding from his matted fur. A thin trickle of that black, oily substance dripped onto the polished floor.

"He's waking up," Falthwën noted.

"In the dungeon, he *helped* us," Kalas repeated, addressing the assembled *erume*. He poked it with the tip of his sword. "No idea why."

Falthwën knelt, the creature's eyes following his every move. Gingerly, he placed a hand over the exposed portion of the shaft so that his index and middle fingers straddled either side. He closed his eyes for a brief moment, frowning when he opened them.

"It's your music: I can't…*see*," he said to the wolf. "You understand?"

The beast nodded. Yelped as the movement triggered new pain.

"Do what you must, cleric," it growled.

Falthwën traced familiar shapes in the air while Loradan whispered phrases from the Song.

"I'm sorry," he said. The wolf nodded again, closed its eyes, and *howled* as Falthwën ripped the arrow from its chest. Its eyes flew open as viscous filth and black fumes spurted from the wound. The cleric held up a hand for Kalas to keep his distance—and his silence—as he harmonized with Loradan. After a few moments, its howls became sobs, and its massive shape seemed to shrink. Its furred hide split and shriveled as the haunting yellow light in its watery eyes dimmed and clouded like dirty glass.

2.

"Is he—?" Kalas wondered, asking the question on everyone's mind.

"I think he'll be all right, but honestly, I don't know, said Sharuyan. "His music is *changed*…I've never done this before!"

"Nor should you have," said Sifuran as he jabbed a toe at the smoking, crumpled heap. It shivered from the contact, but the *egu* remained where it lay, covered with the macabre blankets that had recently been its skin. "*Egume* have always lorded their position over us. Would have been better to let the *ekudas* arrow unskin it, I say."

"Perhaps," allowed Falthwën, "but, like the boy said, he *did* help us. I'd understand his reasons before returning him to the *shosathesh*."

"Hmmph! I'm not convinced," Sifuran dismissed as he stepped away from the spectacle.

"He's coming to!" said Yayan, who'd been keeping an eye on the fallen figure. The others stopped their conversations and surrounded him as he righted himself and let the last vestiges of his former skin fall away. There, arms and legs wrapped around his shivering, naked

377

frame, sat Nïmrïk.

"*Again?!*" Kalas exclaimed.

"You…you *know* this *rudzhegu?*" said Peradan, his eyebrow arched.

"No, not really—not as such, anyway! Nïmrïk! What are you doing here? How did you—no, never mind! How long—*why* have you been following us?!"

"Looks like you were right about the man in the next cell," said Pava, her hand on Rül's forearm.

As Nïmrïk continued to shiver, Falthwën whispered something to Loradan. She nodded and seemed to shimmer for no more than a fraction of a second: when she *resolved,* she held a simple robe, which she draped around Nïmrïk's shoulders.

"It was right where you thought it would be," she told Falthwën. "I…moved it to a safer place. I'll show you later."

"It *was* you, wasn't it?" Kalas said, addressing the *egu.* "Singing the other night?"

"Aye, lad, that it was…Maybe someday, I'll get it right. That's my hope, at least, unlikely as it seems."

"What do you mean?"

"You asked why I was following you. For how long. I heard the emerald thunder—its music—when it fell, just over a month ago: that had to mean that others of…my kind had stepped out of the shadows enough to rouse the ire of Sharuyan. I tried to find you then, but…I failed.

"Now, I've been searching for *elume* for millennia: my estranged brothers and sisters would have nothing to do with me, and really, I don't blame them at all. With nowhere to go, with nothing left to lose, I approached the *erume.* Most suspected I was up to something, which came as no surprise. I knew I'd need an opportunity to prove my worth.

"Sevens came and went with little progress. Perhaps a handful of *erume* came to view me with a touch less suspicion than at first, but it wasn't enough: my *music* still clashed with *Zhi Helim*, sounding like fingernails on slate in my mind. I lost hope. Assumed the best I could attain was a life among *edhume* attired as one of them. I forswore my *otherform* and tried to blend in as best I could.

"For Sevens, I wandered from kingdom to kingdom, watched some fall and others rise as I tried to unmake my ancient sin. In Këcharan, on the Night of Falling Skies, I hoped I'd find the opportunity I sought, but I arrived too late. That's where I first saw you, Sharuyan, walking through its rubble. I kept my distance, watched you rescue that child. I followed you for a while after that, kept an eye on the boy: I thought maybe I could protect him somehow when you left. I forget the name of the town where you left him. Doesn't matter: other *erume* chased me away, assuming, no doubt, that I intended to visit evil upon him. None was interested in an explanation, and so I walked away.

"I wandered the earth for dozens of Sevens until I ended up in Thosha. It seemed a nice enough place. Until Liro, proprietor of that…ill-reputed place of his, started pursuing darker things. I'd become something of a regular there—no, not for that!—as unsavory as its reputation was, its customers provided a wealth of information.

"Anyway, I knew where Liro was headed—even if he didn't. I'd traveled a similar road myself, and I felt compelled to do *something*. I pictured notes in my mind. Notes I remembered from under Këcharan all those Sevens ago, and willed them into music. I didn't know if it would work, but not long after, Sharuyan and Loradan showed up in town. Maybe they'd had business in Thosha all along, but inside, I felt a spark of something I hadn't known for a long, long time.

"After you left, Mbirin crafted something new from the wreckage her father had wrought, and I offered her my services as a hired hand. One day, Liro returned: I was there when he tried to…

"I killed him. There's no other way to say it. Maybe it wasn't my place, but I couldn't just stand by. After that, I fled. I stayed away, wandered the countryside until I heard about Mbirin's passing.

"When I finally did return, I couldn't escape a sense of responsibility for her daughters and her daughter's daughters. I kept a low profile—well, sort of: I guess you could say I developed a knack for skylarking. It passed the time, kept most townsfolk entertained —kept me close to Mbirin's children—while I waited. For what, I wasn't sure: not until I saw the lot of you from the gibbet at the crossroads.

"You weren't the same, Sharuyan. Not entirely, but somehow, I recognized you. Strange as this'll sound, I recognized the boy, too. With all the change taking place across the world, I wasn't about to lose sight of you again. I watched as Nashmur's men tried to ambush you in Âivambar. Followed as they chased you down along the Highway. When I saw those blasts of *eruseranà*…

"Even from the dungeon, I sensed Marugan's *shosayedhume*. Rampant *wrongness*, at least. I didn't know they were his at the time —I didn't realize Marugan was an *eku* until he *kalswàra* through those passageways where I found you."

"That's quite a tale, *egu*," said Yayan, intrigued but guarded.

"Your song…it *almost* fit within *The* Song," Kalas commented.

Nïmrïk's weary eyes filled with tears. He ignored them as they swelled atop his lids before spilling onto his borrowed *rasak* garment.

"That, lad, is how it's been ever since I realized—too late—the magnitude of my transgression. I catch bits and pieces of it from time to time—parts performed by others—but I don't know if my music will ever harmonize with The Song again…"

"You want to become an *elu* again, don't you?" deduced Sifuran. "You hope to regain your first estate!"

Nïmrïk said nothing as he bowed his head.

"Is such a thing possible?" posed Heshradan. None was sure.

"Even if it is, would the *elume* accept him?" Peradan added.

"Probably not. Don't know that I would," scoffed Sifuran. "Assuming anything he's told us is true in the first place!"

Falthwën listened, his eyes darting back and forth as he followed the flow of the discussion.

"You took an arrow intended for one of us. Why?" he said, extending a hand and helping the injured figure to his feet. "How's the wound, by the way?"

"It hurts, but not like it did. Thank you. I guess I thought if Marugan's arrow hit *me,* the worst thing that could happen was I'd lose my skin for a time. Moments? Months? Millennia? Small penance. For one of your mortal friends, however…I wasn't willing to let that happen."

"Convincing," allowed Yayan as she gave the man a closer look.

"You might have helped us, but you're an *egu!*" Zhalera began. "You—one of your kind killed my father! Kalas' parents! You act like you want to help us, but what makes you think we'll trust you?"

"You've no reason to, although I'll say this: when those ruffians in Âivambar accosted you in The Black Falcon, did you come to mistrust the entirety of humankind?"

"I—no! That's different!" she insisted, her bronze cheeks reddening in the Vault's soft light.

"If you say so," nodded Nïmrïk. "I won't argue with you."

"The girl raises a fair point," conceded Peradan as he walked in a slow circle around the pitiable figure. "Perhaps it's unfair, but consider this: not a single *egu* has sought reconciliation with the *elume* from time immemorial. Why you? Why now? Perhaps there's some unseen trickery underlying your motives? You said yourself you'd taken to…what was it? *Skylarking?*"

"I won't try to excuse the choices of those in whose sin I've partaken! If the lot of you would prefer I leave, I'll leave. Before I go, however, I'll tell you this: my travels over the Sevens have carried me through numerous places. Numerous kingdoms. Ïsriba is not the only one with a 'Marugan' twisting the ears of power. *Egunàm* and *ekunàm* alike have conspired to thrust the entire world into a singular war until *edhunàm*—humanity—destroys itself.

3.

At Nïmrïk's revelation, the assembled stars shared anxious murmurs. The humans watched. Listened. Tried to understand as best they could.

"Wait, *egu*—Nïmrïk," said Sifuran as he placed a hand on the man's shoulder. "We know this. We've suspected, at least, but your story supports our worst suspicions."

"I can't say that I'm convinced," chided Peradan as he clucked his tongue. "It seems a little convenient, don't you think? He thinks we're about to cast him out, so he conjures up this gem of intelligence?"

"Be that as it may, he didn't *know* we knew," nodded Loradan. "His bond with The Song is broken—there's no way for him to share our thoughts. That he uncovered this conspiracy and chose to share it with us is worth something, in my estimation."

"He *claims* it's broken," noted Heshradan.

"It's true," insisted Kalas as he locked eyes with the unappreciated *egu*. "In the dungeon, something woke me. A song. *Nïmrïk's* song. It sounded—it was *so close* to becoming part of *The* Song! Nïmrïk! Maybe if you…sing? That's not the right word, is it? Maybe if you…*sing* to them, they'll understand!"

Fresh tears—a peculiar mixture of sorrow and relief—formed anew in the wearied man's pale blue eyes.

"Master Kalas, I have tried! For thousands of Sevens, I've tried!

Those attuned to *Zhi Helim* don't perceive the fruit of my imperfect labors. You have no idea how surprised I am that you can hear it!"

The boy looked to Falthwën, who offered him an apologetic shrug: *Sorry, my child. He's right…*

"How can that be?!" said Kalas, amazed and skeptical. "*I* can hear it, but none of you can? Falthwën, I thought you said *others* —I thought you meant *egume* and *ekume*—heard The Song, too?"

"It's true," interrupted Sifuran. "They still hear parts of it, at least. Perhaps there is more to Nïmrïk than we've allowed…"

"Look, I'm not trying to buy your confidence," he insisted. "I've had a long time to learn that people either believe me…or they don't. Maybe I'll never attain to *elunàm* again. My curse is just, and I will suffer it throughout eternity if it pleases the Creator. That said, I remain a part of his handiwork, and I'm unwilling to do *nothing* while Ilnëshras' servants attempt to *unmake* it again!"

As Nïmrïk spoke, his eyes acquired the faintest glow of yellow from within. Most—not all—took a step back at the sight.

"There's fire in your soul, there's no denying that!" marveled Heshradan as he turned toward the others. "And…I believe him. I do. *Âu* Nïmrïk, I don't know whether such a thing is possible, but should your curse ever come undone, I look forward to hearing your voice returned to The Song!"

Stunned, Nïmrïk said nothing. He held Heshradan's gaze for a moment, then collapsed onto the remaining fragments of his old skin in a paroxysm of wracking sobs. Heshradan knelt and placed a hand atop his heaving shoulder.

"You've no idea—*no idea!*—how I've longed to hear such words!" Nïmrïk managed between his tears. "Thank you, fr—No! I won't assume too much! Just…*thank you!*"

Heshradan helped Nïmrïk to his feet again. Peradan ceased his pacing and said, "Yes, very good, but we're still no closer to a plan for disrupting the Accursèd One's presumed intent. Unless, of course, any of you have devised new stratagems since our last gathering?"

None of the other *erume* said anything as all eyes turned toward Kalas. Aware of their weighted gazes, he looked around and tried to understand why they were staring at him.

Prophecy!

"Me?!" he gasped, perplexed and more than a little uncertain. "I'm just a boy! Barely attained two Sevens! I…I'm a nobody! From nowhere! Zhalera, you heard Valderïk: he said the queen-regent wouldn't even take our claims seriously! How…what do all of you expect from *me?!*"

"You know the prophecy," said Yayan, arms folded across her sturdy chest.

"I don't!" Kalas insisted. "No one's told me what it is! All I've heard are vague suggestions—the first of those from the *rudzhegu* who killed my father!"

"The prophecy is a vast work—a book in its own right, really," said Falthwën, "but the part that I—that others, too—believe relates to you, my child, is this:

Isre zhi alasdrame dâeth nira,
Isre zhi erume nath nira,

Kathin kelësh al para
Tsheth zhi theshedhume vâl:

Zhi kal duro
Hir aóroyimu;
Zhi vam duro
Hir zhi nàfël veluro:

Dhëm rò pïn dzhâra,
Tsa tabîit firitha;
Pïn hwag Kelme ádhem
Ohi valom pïn bàrifu:

I virnàfël nombàyaru
Hir yev vam tànadharu?
Ib sulum zhi thesh gâfut
Hir tsa revehwa sàvesharu?

Kathin kelësh al para
Dëni theshedhume ádhan

Isre zhi alasdrame dâeth nira,
Isre zhi erume nath nira.

While the heavens were silent,
While the stars were black,

I saw a great power
Fall upon the realm of men:

To bring the light
Or to banish it;
To bring the day
Or embrace the dark:

A child out of time,
Confronted with a choice;
A youth of two Sevens
At the crux of consequence:

Surrender us to darkness
Or hasten us toward day?
Bind the world in shadow
Or cover us with glory?

I saw a great power
Ascend from the realm of men

While the heavens were silent,
While the stars were black.

"I've heard that before!" said Pava with a tug on Rül's sleeve. "Part of it, at least! That's— '*Zhi kal duro*'—that's where the *úruk-ilmukritmedas* legend of the *Ilosar* comes from! Kalas, it *is* you!"

"No! I...that prophecy doesn't even make sense!" he insisted. "The heavens aren't silent! We—all right, some of us hear the Song every day! Falthwën, Heshradan: you don't really think—?! Is this why Dzharëth killed my father? Over something as—over *nonsense* like this?!"

"None of us knows the future, my child. And as I said, these couplets and quatrains only represent a fragment of the whole," said the cleric.

"I would not have...placed you with Màla and Tàran were I not convinced that the time had come," added Heshradan, the diamond *eru*.

"'A child out of time.' What's that even mean?!" Kalas wondered. Heshradan said nothing. "And what's this 'great power' that's supposed to 'fall upon the realm of men'?"

4.

Seated with his back wedged in a corner between two facets, Kalas watched and waited while the *erume* discussed their present circumstances. He thought he heard his name a time or two, but he wasn't sure. It didn't really matter anyway, he thought:

They think I'm something I'm not.

Nashmur leaned against the wall beside him, eased himself onto the cold stone floor, and sighed. He nodded toward the luminescent figures congregated near the center of the Vault and said, "So... *Erume?* I'm trying to imagine the look on my cousin's face if he were here right now!"

"Why didn't you tell us Shosafin was your cousin?" Zhalera demanded from Kalas' other side.

"Ah, that," he nodded again. With a wry smile, he explained: "His mother was nobility, but she married for love. A common *rasak* weaver. Infuriated her parents when she ignored their designs.

They fled the capital for a time; when they returned, they'd had a son. Her parents, naturally, refused to acknowledge the child. Refused to acknowledge their rebellious daughter.

"His mother's *sister*, however, had no qualms about following her parents' instructions. So I'm told: she died before I'd attained a single year. My father—I really don't remember him. Is that sad?—was crushed when she passed away: they'd struggled for almost two Sevens to conceive, and they'd come to love each other after all they'd been through, but I think he was relieved when the king sent him away on a mission or something. I don't know. He deposited me with his estranged in-laws, and I never saw him again. For all I know he never returned to Ïsriba—if he did, he never looked for me.

"He did do one thing for me before he left. He made sure my records were in order: with my name in the registrars' books, his station would elevate my own when the day came.

"All I know about my parents I learned from Shosafin's: despite the ill treatment they'd received from his mother's family, they cared for me like I was their own son. Shosafin was more like an older brother than a cousin. Enlisting was his only real option: under other circumstances, perhaps, he might have joined a guild, but his grandparents manipulated all the necessary societal levers to make sure he never sullied their good name in public. I learned a lot from him growing up...

"There's no reason to pretend anymore: I never believed he killed King Rufàran! I...lacked the clarity of purpose he possessed: he truly is his mother's son! And I am mine...

"So yes: Shosafin is my cousin. Maybe now you understand why I was so interested in his sword? After Ësfàyami assumed the throne, he changed. Turned hard. Indifferent. I hoped to hear that he'd regained at least a measure of his former character, but it doesn't sound like he did."

"I think we'll see him again," encouraged Kalas. "I don't think he would have asked me to hold on to his sword if he didn't intend to retrieve it. It didn't sound like that, at least."

"Oh, that reminds me!" Nashmur said as he dug within a hidden pocket. "Here you go! As promised!"

He held out Kalas' birthday present, hilt first. With a thankful nod, the boy took it and traced its familiar contours with his fingers. He tried to tuck it within his belt before he realized he was still wearing his borrowed robe.

"Bad as they smelled, I kinda want my old clothes back!" he confessed. "At least they had pockets!"

"Yeah, these robes are terrible!" Zhalera giggled. Turning serious, she added: "The horses! The coach!"

Kalas ran a quick mental inventory of their possessions. While Runner and Dancer were two of the finest horses he'd ever known, there were others. Other carts or coaches as well. Replacing them wouldn't be easy—nor pleasant—but it would be possible. While he didn't know the contents of either Zhalera's or Rül's packs, he drew a sharp breath when he remembered what had been inside his own:

"The book!" he gasped. "The...*not-paper!*"

"The what?" said Nashmur, his eyebrow raised.

"Uh, just some things we left in the coach. The book was from my father's collection. My grandfather's, really. The other thing was something I...another piece from the same collection."

The commander nodded, "Irreplaceable, I'm sure. I think all of your things will be all right: I assigned my most trusted lieutenants to guard them...to go through them, really, just in case my cousin left something with you." He offered them an embarrassed half-smile.

"Shosafin kept mostly to himself. Had his own horse: another one of Rül's."

"How long do you think they'll be?" said Rül, having heard his name. He jerked his head toward the *erume* and added, "I don't know about the rest of you, but that slop we had for breakfast has pretty much run its course. I'm starving!"

"*Erume* can talk and talk," offered Nïmrïk, who'd plopped himself down not too far away from the others. He raised himself up, winced a little, and massaged the place where Marugan's arrow had pierced him.

"Are you all right?" Pava wondered.

"I'll be fine. I think. That *eku* must've done something to his arrowheads. *Nimnàfël seranà*, probably. In time, your cleric's magic should undo the worst of it. I hope. Guess I'll find out.

"Anyway, from our perspective, that lot has probably been conversing for days. Weeks maybe. Time—and space—are more fluid for them."

"What about for *egume?*" Kalas asked, curious.

"*Elume*—and *egume*—are spirit-beings. Our relationship with the temporal and the spatial is…arbitrary; that is, we're exempted from its physical laws, though most of us, when we take physical form, find it simplest to obey them all the same. Most of the time. Our power—our privilege is, perhaps, greater than that permitted the *erume*, but I don't consider it relevant. I used to, once, but that was thousands of Sevens ago."

"'Privilege'? You sound like Falthwën," noted Kalas.

Nïmrïk returned a wry smile. "That privilege—its scope and exercise—has long been a point of contention between the *elume* and the *erume*, but it doesn't have to be—"

"I kinda got that idea from one of the Swath," said Rül as he attempted to ignore his rumbling stomach.

"Ilun fashioned each of us according to his will, according to his purpose. When people—*elu, eru,* or *edhu*—forget—or, perhaps more accurately, *ignore* that truth, things tend to fall apart. I know. I've seen it. *Lived* it. My point is when we exercise our privilege in accordance with the Creator's will, his purpose for us, things…hold together, if I might extend the metaphor."

His purpose for us, Kalas thought with a wry smile of his own. *Wouldn't it be great to know what that was?*

5.

"I think they're done!" shushed Zhalera. The others ceased conversing as the loose circle of *erume* broke apart. Falthwën and Loradan approached while the other four shimmered, then disappeared.

"It pleases me to learn you received my message," she said.

"Your message?"

Focus!

"That was you?! But how—? I mean, I thought you didn't know—"

"Sharuyan told me about you after I freed him from the *ekumedas* snare. He described your *frequency* as something wholly new, wholly unique. We've been waiting, after a manner, I suppose: when they brought you near the dungeons, I sensed a presence unlike anything I've ever known. I couldn't be sure it was *you,* but The Song told me to pay attention."

"It…*told* you?"

"Not in words. More like a strong suggestion woven within its notes. A compulsion, perhaps. You've a strong constitution, from what I'm told. You very well might have endured the shadow lily's powers on your own."

"Well, thank you!" said Kalas with a slight bow.

"Of course! Now, Sharuyan tells me you discovered something

in the canyon near your home?" the amethyst star continued. Her dark-bronze skin, the color of coffee with just a touch too much cream, seemed to glow in the chamber's peculiar light. Unlike Falthwën's, hers bore almost no lines or wrinkles, the exceptions emanating from the corners of her dark blue eyes. Lavender-tinted tresses, kinked and twisted blonde ropes, fell just above her waist. She smiled as she spoke, reached inside her simple gown, and withdrew a leaf of something and held it out to Kalas.

"The *not-paper!*" he shouted. "Where did you get this?!"

"From your coach, of course!"

"The horses!" Rül interjected. "Did you see them? Are they all right?"

"They're fine, I promise!" Falthwën assured him.

Kalas turned the item over in his hands. It looked the same as it had on the day they left Lohwàlar. Struck with a thought, he held it up, hoping to view it through stronger light before he realized the room's illumination had no apparent source.

"Falthwën, does that mean it's all right to talk about...that thing?"

"Here, none can uncover our discussions. Within these walls, anything we say remains with us."

Kalas' mind replayed a brief scene as the cleric spoke. In it, Tsharak, his back turned away from the others, held up a small item bearing all the hallmarks of the artifact at the bottom of the Empty Sea.

"About that," he began, searching for a way to explain himself. With a shrug and a sigh, he kept going: "before we left Lohwàlar, Tsharak showed me something. I don't know what it was. He didn't, either, but it looked like it might have been from the object under the cliff. I think it was made from the same material, and it had similar symbols—others, too. About the size of a small brick, but almost egg-shaped: a mix of curves and flat parts. Said he'd had it in his collection for a really long time. Maybe we—maybe I should have said something then, but I wasn't sure…Tsharak said he'd keep it safe, and I thought that was enough."

He recoiled as something flickered within the old man's eyes, something that reminded him of Falthwën's anger when he'd first arrived at the artifact. The cleric turned toward Loradan as Kalas said, "I'm sorry."

Falthwën whispered something, turned toward Kalas again, and, with a rueful smile, said, "That object buried beneath thousands of Sevens of rock is…not unique, my child, though it is the most complete instance I've ever seen."

Kalas, stunned, allowed himself a long moment to parse what he'd just heard.

Things the world over…aren't always as they seem.

"There…there are *more* of those things?! How many more?! What *are* they?! Where do they come from?!"

Loradan answered: "In our *humanness,* we *erume* have imperfect access to our vast stores of celestial memory; from time to time, however, something will…*connect* one memory to another, perhaps *another,* and…you understand? Sharuyan has told you some of this, *hish?*

"We know we roam the detritus of a broken world. Most remnants have been washed away, erased by flood and fire, or, as in this case, buried beneath the earth's surface. We know, on occasion, that sometimes those remnants 'bubble up' into the present. It's rare. Even rarer for someone to encounter such *vàsume*—artifacts —before we do. Most are harmless: nothing more than peculiarities even to us. Those we come across, we *unmake* when we can, conceal when we must. Usually. Not always.

"Some, however, are dangerous. Deadly. Things that helped crack the world in the first place. From Sharuyan's description, your *vàsu* is one of the *most* dangerous, the *most* deadly."

"It made my father sick," Kalas said, his thoughts at the bottom of the canyon. "Made us sick, too. Tsharak, Zhalera, and me, when we went back for a closer look."

"That's why I buried it," admitted Falthwën. "I would have preferred to *unmake* it, but without knowing the extent of what the *ekume* had done to me, I couldn't risk such a flagrant display of privilege: I had to hope all those tons of rock would suffice.

"If Tsharak's object is indeed of the same origin as that craft, for now we'll have to hope it's less potent. You said he's had it for some time, yes? Then it's probably nothing to worry about: still, I'll ask to see it when we return to Lohwàlar."

"Wait—'craft'? Like a boat or something?" said Kalas, catching Falthwën's word.

The cleric smiled. "Like a boat…or something."

"Right. It *was* at the bottom of what used to be an ocean," Kalas convinced himself.

The *erume* who shimmered out of the Vault—out of time and space as well, for all Kalas knew—returned, *resolved* like Loradan had when she procured a robe for Nïmrïk. Yayan, hefting a double-bladed bearded axe made from some ruby-like material, arrived first, followed by Heshradan, Sifuran, and, perhaps a minute later, Peradan.

"I encountered an *eku*," Yayan affirmed as she secured her weapon. "Fought him for two days before I managed to *unmake* his physical presence."

"*Two days?*" said Rül, somewhat bewildered; then, remembering what the *egu* told them, added, "Oh, right! I get it!"

Neither Heshradan nor Sifuran encountered any resistance: Peradan needed a moment to catch his breath before he admitted, "Another singularity trap! I recognized this one, though, before it was too late. Three, maybe four *ekume*. I'm not sure. Lost my sword while making my escape. I don't think any of them figured out where I was headed, but at this point I can't be sure. Maybe now is *not* the time to get started."

"Get...started?" Zhalera ventured. The other shared similar expressions of uncertainty.

"I thought you'd be finishing up...whatever it is you've been doing for the last few hours!" lamented Rül. His stomach growled again, emphasizing his dismay.

"Oh! My apologies!" laughed Heshradan as he disappeared: moments later, he reappeared with a tray of smoking sausages, a wheel of cheese, and a couple of waterskins. "It's easy to forget *edhume* need to eat!"

"Get started," repeated Sifuran with a grim nod. "I disagree with Peradan: I think we *must* get started! There's never been a moment like this in all of history—including from before the cracking of the world. It's true: we're rushing into unknown realms with our hands bound, our eyes blinded, but what better choice is there? Why, today could be the day when prophecy is fulfilled in our presence!"

"*Or*...it could be the day when everything comes undone and our every hope is lost!" Peradan countered.

Sifuran took a deep breath and held it for a weighty moment.

"One way or another, we'll find out soon enough."

Chapter XX

At the Center of
the Seven-Sided Room

"**P**eradan's not wrong: what we're about to attempt could—no, *will*—have dire consequences," the sapphire *eru* elaborated as he beheld Zhalera's still-perplexed gaze. "But there's *another* prophecy, a precursor to the other, maybe, handed down to *elunàm* before creation came undone… We've discussed this from time to time across innumerable Sevens, but the…call it a *balance* of components: it's never been…I'll say *stable*. Once, we thought all the pieces were in place, but we were too…*scared*—there's no other word for it—to follow through. That's when Ilun cracked the world in his wrath and sorrow."

"Who gave these prophecies?" Kalas muttered.

None of the *erume* answered him; indeed, all seemed to have some place else to look until Peradan admitted, "No one knows."

"*No one* knows?!" scoffed Pava. "I can't—I *won't*—believe that!"

"Most think it was one of the chief *elume*, not long after Ilnëshras pit his will against the Creator's," said Yayan as she ran a length of diamond-gritted stone along the heads of her axe. "He had a different name then, Ilnëshras. No one remembers what it was. By all accounts, the *elu* who gave the prophecy met his end at the hands of Ilnëshras' chief lieutenant, a former *elu* named *Tsathrâuda*. It's ironic that the prophet's name would disappear within the spool of time while his murderer's would not.

"No matter: Sifuran is right. We missed our opportunity millennia ago. None but the Creator can say what might have been had we been more bold: today, I, for one, will not be undone by fear!"

Yayan returned her glittering weapon to its sheath, offered the other erume a curt, solemn bow, and walked toward the ruby-encrusted emblem carved into the Vault's polished granite floor.

"I don't understand why Ilun doesn't just *unmake* Ilnëshras and be done with it," grumbled Rül. "I mean: *millennia?* Why let the world fall apart? Why crack it in the first place? He could hold it together if he wanted to, couldn't he?"

"He could," insisted Heshradan, "and if he considered his creation naught but a motley collection of programmable automatons, that's just what he might have done. However, we're more—so much more!—than mere puppets to him! *Elume, erume, edhume* —even our fallen brothers and sisters—retain the gift of choice. Choice requires, at a minimum, *bifurcation,* however subtle, along the paths of our existence: each split brings us closer to or drives us further from his purpose for us. It's well within the Creator's *power* to treat us as his playthings, but he chooses otherwise, and while it's true we make our own choices, it's also—necessarily—true we must endure their consequences."

"You sound like Falthwën," said Rül, his eyes glassy.

Heshradan smiled. "High praise, indeed!" With a nod, the slightest bow of his own, he followed Yayan toward the markings on the floor and stood above the diamond-studded symbol. Loradan offered Sharuyan a kiss before she, too, took her respective place within the Vault.

"C'mon, Peradan! Let's make history!" insisted Sifuran. He clapped a hand on the reluctant spessartine *erudas* shoulder and steered him toward his emblem.

Before Falthwën joined the others, he removed his ring and held it up to the curious light. In its sourceless glow, each gem sparkled as he turned it over a time or two. With a smile, he reached for one of Pava's hands. She held it out to him, and the *eru* placed his ugly jewelry on her right index finger.

"The *úrukilmukritme* have stories about this ring. No doubt that's why it seems familiar to you. Each stone represents a member of the Great Swath: indeed, each stone has been imbued with a measure of…call it *magic* from each of us. I return it to the cave-dwellers with the hope that its power might preserve the blessing of the suns' light against the rising shadows."

Pava stared at the ring, unsure of what to say, what to do. After a dazed moment, she said, "This belonged to the *eru* who made our *iltithme-kal!* The *nalën Ilosar* who taught us how to use them!"

"It did, once," said Falthwën, his expression somber. "Now, it belongs to you. To your people.

"What happened to him?" wondered Pava as she examined every facet of every shining jewel. When Falthwën didn't answer, she looked up, saw pained sadness in his features, and said, "No, never mind, I—Thank you! On behalf of all of us who dwell beneath the Áthradho, thank you!"

The cleric offered her a bright smile that only subtly touched his eyes. He turned toward the center of the Vault, and as he walked away Pava asked: "Wait! Why are you giving this to me? Won't you need it? If it has magic—if it has *power*—won't the Swath know how to use it best?"

Falthwën—Sharuyan now—offered no response as he stopped when he reached his emerald-covered crest.

2.

The six *erume* exchanged glances. Valaran's unoccupied topaz emblem hovered at the precipice of all their thoughts.

"Will this even work without her?" Peradan wondered.

"It has to," insisted Sifuran. "We have to be enough. Surely the Creator wouldn't have allowed as much to happen if our endeavor was fated to end in failure?!"

"Perhaps it would have worked were Valaran still beside us, but now? Are you certain?"

"Certain?! Of course I'm not certain!" he retorted, his eyes awash with harsh blue light. "But we've no other options! No good ones, at least! Come what may, let it never be said that I lacked the faith to follow through!"

"I'm not questioning your faith, brother!" Peradan huffed: "I'm questioning the wisdom in attempting something that requires seven of us when only six remain!"

"None of us could ever hope to replace her, nor assume her *guilt*, but I think we have to try," said Loradan. "Perhaps the six of us, buoyed by our love for our fallen sister, will be sufficient."

"Well said!" Yayan agreed with a vigorous nod. "So what'll it be? Are we gonna hem and haw for thousands of Sevens again? Or are we gonna make something happen?!"

Peradan sighed, shrugged, and, at last, acquiesced.

The *erume* waited until Heshradan bowed his head toward the symbol at the center of the Vault; when he did, the others followed suit.

He must be their…leader? Does the Great Swath even have *a leader?* Kalas wondered as he watched the ritual—rite? ceremony? whatever it was—commence.

The diamond *eru* voiced a solemn prayer; soon, the remaining stars added their unified voices to his, and the prayer became a song. Slow, reverent, and, Kalas sensed, somewhat timid, the singular melody split into six distinct parts as the *erume* found their courage and opened up their hearts and throats. Minute variations assumed greater departures from Heshradan's main theme as the song progressed. Kalas tried to listen to each part, to hear the prayer, as it were, of each *erudas* spirit, only to discover that while his ears heard six separate voices, his heart—his *kelâ*—heard just one. Neither words nor sounds approximating known language: just *music* unlike any he and all the others had ever heard.

Nïmrïk excepted.

As the harmonies swept over, under, and around and through one another, Kalas noticed unchecked tears in the old man's eyes as he tried his best not to give way to the sobs skating along the cusp of expression. The *egu* caught Kalas' stare and offered him an unapologetic smile as he wiped at his cheeks.

"Is this...is this *The* Song?" Zhalera whispered. Nïmrïk nodded before Kalas could.

"It's a part of it," said the boy. "I think. I've never heard these particular melodies, but I recognize some of the themes."

"And you hear this...all the time?"

He nodded.

"I'll admit it: I'm jealous!"

The stars' music swelled within the walls of the Vault, acquired a life all its own as it danced and tumbled over each faceted boundary and rebounded, its energy doubled, trebled, and more. Each vari-colored wall seemed to pulse in time to the Song the *erume* sang; soon, their paean transcended human perception: not because of its shifting frequencies; rather, it moved from the purely material to the immaterial.

'Spiritual vibrations,' Falthwën called them.

At the same time, the *erume* began to glow as some aspect of their shared anthem reified their aurae and summoned shafts of light from their respective symbols.

Nïmrïk and the others scanned the room as the music eclipsed their ability to perceive it. Each regarded one another with the same sense of loss as the Song's energy dissipated.

In Kalas' mind, however, as the music's power—its *soul,* perhaps —gained strength, the Song became unstable, and the Vault's walls shook with unsteady violence. He cried out, cupped his ears, and tried to drown out the noise.

"Kalas! What's wrong?!" said Zhalera. When he didn't seem to hear, she shouted.

"The Song! It's…I think it's broken! I can't—!"

Blood jetted from each nostril as his eyes rolled toward the back of his head. He screamed again. Lost consciousness. As he fell, as his hands dropped to his sides, Zhalera saw they, too, boasted bloodstains from thin streams seeping from his ears.

"What do I *do?!*" she shouted. At Kalas. At Falthwën. At the other *erume.* No one heard her.

She caught him as he slumped and dropped to her knees, scraping her scabbard on the floor.

"My sword!" she shouted, struck by a sudden thought, and pulled it from its sheath. "Sifuran said Valaran's essence is within it! Maybe it's enough?!"

At first, no one answered, and the girl hesitated. Nïmrïk came alongside her, knelt beside Kalas and said, "Only one way to know, lass! If it helps, it helps, but the boy can't go on like this!"

Her face grim, Zhalera hastened toward the empty space where Valaran should have stood. As she got closer, the invisible force of the *erumedas* song made each successive step that much more difficult, like wrestling against a pool of thick, viscous mud. She reached out her sword: just a few more inches and its point would touch the outermost band of topaz. Although she struggled with every shred of strength she could muster, it wasn't—nor would it be—enough.

"Help me! Help!" she howled within the silent Vault.

Pava rushed toward Zhalera, tried to plant her feet and push, but the polished floor provided no purchase.

"It's no use!" the cave-dweller girl panted, her feet slipping no matter how she tried to brace herself.

"C'mon, Nashmur!" said Rül as he pushed up the sleeves on his robe. "Let's get a running start! Between the two of us, I'll bet we can push through whatever it is that's holding her back!"

The commander set his jaw, clenched his fists, and looked to the farm boy for his signal.

"*Now!*" Rül shouted, and the two of them bore down on the girls.

The echo of their pounding strides alerted Pava, who leapt out of the way just in time. As one, both men collided with Zhalera. She'd been so focused on trying to reach the symbol that she didn't realize what was going on until she lurched forward and into the unseen resistance. It *absorbed* her and held her aloft as Nashmur and Rül, repelled, bounced against the floor.

Suspended in midair, she twisted for a better angle and tried to cross the emblem's threshold as she prayed aloud: "*Su pirathëthu —sethreva hwishalu!*"

Whatever power held her relaxed its grip. Against her will, she dropped her sword as she tumbled to the ground. Both she and her weapon hit the floor at the same time: Zhalera landed just outside the rim of Valaran's mark, the tip of her shimmering sword just within it.

"*Hish! Ágazhëthu!*" she exulted, eyes raised, just a moment before Valaran's gemstones exploded in a blaze of honey-colored light and energy that flung her across the room.

3.

"Did...did it work? Are we—Kalas?! Are you all right?!" Zhalera wondered as she opened her eyes and tapped the swelling bump at the back of her head. Kalas, his ears and face still streaked with his blood, cradled her in his arms. Nïmrïk and the others crowded around, now worried about *her*.

"It did!" he assured her as he ran a finger through an errant lock of hair—black as night moments ago, now a blend of lemon-tinted silver—and smoothed it back behind her ear. "The music is…fixed, I guess, and The Song in my head—it's so *loud!*—sounds…well, I don't know, but it sounds…*right*, I guess!"

"I take it back," she said as she sat up and wiped away the blood beneath his ears: "I'm *not* jealous! Not after seeing what it did to you!"

"Yeah, that wasn't pleasant. At all! It's kinda like what happened on my second Seven. Only worse! But enough about that: how are *you?* Nïmrïk said you flew through the air and landed pretty hard!"

"My head hurts. All right, my *everything* hurts, but I'm pretty sure I'm all right. It was the strangest thing, just…*stuck* in the air like that!"

"It was strange to look at," said Rül. "Creeped me out!" Nashmur and Pava agreed.

"How'd you come up with the idea to put your sword on Vala-ran's marker?" Kalas asked. "That was some pretty quick thinking!"

"I don't know. Not really," Zhalera admitted. "I remembered what Sifuran said about how she used to 'help' people, how she sometimes put a part of herself into certain things. When Falthwën made it glow, I thought he'd done something to it: I didn't realize what he was showing us. I didn't understand why he wanted me to keep it hidden, either…and then there you were: screaming, bleeding…I thought you were falling apart! I thought your ears were broken: I shouted and shouted but I don't think you heard me. I couldn't think of anything else to do."

She tried to remove the blood above his lip with a gentle swipe and only managed to smear it around. With both hands slick with sweat, she cleared away as much as possible.

"Better," she smiled as she pulled his face toward hers and kissed him.

"You're not going to slap me again?" he teased when she pulled away.

"Guys! Something's happening!" said Rül as he pointed toward the sides of the Vault where the *erumedas* colored light seemed to writhe and pounce along the walls.

"It's in time with the music," Kalas explained. "If you could hear it, you'd—"

"I can! I *can* hear it!" shouted Pava as her eyes widened with amazement. The others offered similar reactions.

"It's like before, but…now there's something else, something *under* all of it. A message, maybe? I can't understand it, but it sounds —it *feels*—like there's a thought carried through this music," said Nashmur, head cocked.

"We still have no idea what they're doing, do we?" Rül added. "Kalas: what do you think?"

"Me?! I don't know! Right now, I'm hearing—I *think* I'm hearing the same Song as the rest of you." Turning toward Nashmur, he continued: "Commander, I sense a message, too, but—"

The six *erume*—and Zhalera's sword—caught fire as their corporeal forms erupted in sheets of raging flame, as their music changed keys and crescendoed. Their song continued to build upon itself and shook the room again. This time, however, everything seemed *right*.

"That fire!" said Zhalera as its roar became accompaniment for the burgeoning chorus. "It's like a forge, when Father worked the bellows! How are they not burning up?!"

"They're stars," Nimrïk reminded her. "Thousands of times hotter than your forges. Fire itself won't hurt them!"

"Maybe *they'll* be fine, but what about *us?!*" Rül wondered as he raised an arm to shield his eyes from the rising heat and light. "It's getting *hot* in here!"

He was yelling. All of them had been, attempting to surpass the stars' volume. Rül ceased yelling when, with a blinding wash, the *erume* blinked into nothing more than fist-sized spheres of fire and rocketed toward the sky. Their bejeweled emblems cut into the floor emitted a singular pulse of energy: its pressure wave knocked everyone to the ground. The *erume* vanished, taking with them the strains of the Song.

Silence settled over the Vault.

Each remained where he'd fallen, held his breath, and looked to the infinite void high above. Looked at one another:

No one spoke. No one had anything to say.

Like a premonition, a realization whose onset is sure and sudden, a radiant pinprick pierced the black. The symbol at the center of the seven-sided room began to glow: faint, at first; then, drawing fire from the others, became too bright to behold. The skyborne gleam—no longer just a pinprick—rushed upon the floor in a column of multicolored splendor and a cascade of scintillating sparks that swirled within the Vault. Ropes of living energy emanated from the seven symbols of the Swath and sizzled toward the central marker: in the twinkling of an eye, the *erume* returned and assumed their familiar shapes. With arms extended, they concluded their overture. No longer wreathed in unconsuming flame, no longer incandescent, each focused on the roiling pillar they'd worked so hard to summon. The light...energy...*magic* proceeding from beneath their feet finished coursing toward the Vault's center. With one final blast that overwhelmed the humans' senses, the light vanished—not just the whirling construct wrought by the *erume:* every hint of illumination they'd willed into being.

Silence and *utter darkness* settled over the Vault.

"Falthwën? Heshradan?" Kalas ventured. "Hello? Loradan—?"

New light—an entirely new *kind* of light—filled the room.

Kalas gasped. So did everyone—the star-beings included.

Above the eighth symbol stood a woman—a girl?—none of them had ever seen.

"It worked!" Sifuran exulted: "It *worked!*"

Clothed in light itself, glittering like unnumbered diamonds, rubies, spessartite garnets, topaz, emeralds, sapphires, and amethysts, the girl appeared to be three Sevens, give or take a few years, but Kalas couldn't escape the sensation that she was…wholly *other* than her exterior revealed. Her skin, fairer than moonglow on windswept desert sand, radiated with luminescence all its own. Dark tresses studded with jewels and tipped here and there with touches of glimmering color fell across her back. She was looking up, toward the sky—toward the Vault's inestimable apex: when she looked around the room, surprised, she blinked her large, silver eyes once or twice, *sneezed,* and considered her new environs.

The *erume* cast their light across the Vault, and the figure, noticing them for the first time, looked from one to the next, her exquisite features rigid with uncertainty.

"My child!" said Heshradan as his peers looked to him. "Please, forgive us for what we've done! I am Heshradan, a member of the Great Swath, and we—this world!—is in desperate need!"

The others introduced themselves in kind.

Is she afraid? Kalas wondered. *I guess* I'd *be afraid if I were in her place…*

"Tell us, child, if you would: what is your name? What do we call you?"

The girl, still unsure, opened her mouth and…sang, her voice clearer than nighttime in winter. Not with words—none the *erume* understood. From the corner of his eye, Kalas saw Nïmrïk flinch.

Falthwën's face broke apart in a wide smile: "I've never heard *anything* like this before!"

The other *erume* agreed.

"This is new music!" Yayan said as she jabbed an elbow at Peradan. *"New* music!"

"You sing with such…there's so much emotion in so few notes!" added Loradan.

The girl returned a tepid smile of her own and whispered a few more notes. Her expression soured as she placed a hand to her throat, massaged her neck, and tried again to speak.

It seemed every sound she made took the form of song.

"It…*mostly* worked?" suggested Sifuran with a wry frown.

"Abarandal," said Kalas, matter-of-factly. The girl's smile turned genuine, her pearlescent teeth shining in the Vault's strange light. She stepped lightly toward Kalas, as though it mattered little whether her feet actually touched the ground. She sang a few more phrases.

"Oh! My name's Kalas," he replied as he introduced himself and the others.

"Can you…understand her?" Falthwën asked as he stroked his beard.

"Of course! Her name's *Abarandal,* and she's wondering who we are, how she got here—where *here* is?!"

"You…can *understand* her?!" repeated Loradan with a mixture of wonder and bemusement.

"Right! Like I—You say that like the rest of you can't!"

"That's *because* we can't!" said Zhalera. "It's all music to us. The most beautiful music I've ever heard, but it's just music. Yet there *is* something familiar about it…"

"Do you still doubt your place within the prophecy?" Heshradan grinned at Kalas.

Abarandal sang a new tune as she collapsed into Kalas' arms.

"They *what?!"* he gasped. "But how?! To what end? They…they think you're a part of this prophecy? That—Oh!"

"Would it be impolite to ask what it was she just told you?" said

Peradan.

"*I saw a great power fall upon the realm of men*,'" Kalas said, his brow furrowed in thought. "Maybe…maybe there *is* something to this prophecy after all…"

4.

"It's true," confessed Peradan when Kalas explained what Abarandal had revealed to him. "We called her from out of the heavens. None of us knows how long she's been waiting. Not really. Her star has never shined until tonight. And that's our fault."

"So she *is* a star. An *eru*," said Zhalera. The Vault's shifting lights glittered across her sword: she picked it up, examined it anew, then put it away.

"'Fault' is a strong word," Sifuran contradicted him. "We all know the prophecy: we've all known that at some point in history, we'd find ourselves in a situation like this!"

"So you accept that you—that *we* are nothing but chess pieces in the hands of this prophecy? That the Creator's gift of self-determination is a farce?" said Peradan, his tone full of snark.

"That's not what I said!" the sapphire star retorted.

"Even a pawn…can shift fortunes," said Kalas, conjuring the phrase from some distant memory.

"That's all academic now," insisted Loradan. "She's here—that's the important thing. I'll admit: I'm not sure what happens next! *Kathin kelësh*, according to the prophecy…but how do we—forgive me, my child!—how do we *use* that 'great power?'"

Abarandal began her song again. Even without words, everyone recognized the sense of indirection and uncertainty in her notes.

"She doesn't know," confirmed Kalas. "She has a sense that she's been…*hidden away* from the rest of creation. Set apart. To what end, she doesn't remember."

"Perhaps we can help her remember," Peradan suggested as he reached out a hand.

Tentative, Abarandal looked to Kalas; when he shrugged, she held out her own hand. When Peradan closed his fingers over hers, the young woman wrenched her hand away from the spessartine *eru* and retreated into Kalas' shoulder. She whispered something in the boy's ear.

"He was almost captured," Kalas explained. To Peradan, he elaborated: "She senses…darkness about you. I think. What she said was *anti-light*. Your close call with the *ekume* must have left its mark."

"Ah, that…that makes sense," he frowned as he looked around, his eyes narrowed.

"She'll need instruction," decided Yayan. "Someone to educate her regarding this world—even from before its cracking. We'll need—"

Before the ruby star could expound on her train of thought, spheres of darkness punctured the atmosphere within the Vault. Cacophonic riffs raked their ears as black tendrils probed the air. The noise worsened as more spheres appeared and ballooned into lightless voids.

"What's that sound?!" cried Rül as he cupped his hands over his ears.

"*Ekume!*" shouted Falthwën. "They've found us! They've breached the Vault!"

"How?!" exclaimed Loradan, Hàfilrifar in hand. "This place is inaccessible to those who don't know—"

"Don't you get it?" raged Sifuran as he drew a pair of flashing swords from some unfathomable dimension. "Someone has betrayed us!"

"*Egu!*" screamed Peradan, a wicked-looking spear as he lunged for Nïmrïk.

"No! Never!" he insisted as he stepped out of the way.

"How could it be him?" queried Heshradan as he readied his own weapon, a two-handed diamond-studded mace. "He didn't know about this place until today, he's been here this whole time, and the Vault is *sealed!*"

Undulating gouts of shadow slithered through the air, tasting it for prey and whipping at the confused *erume*. One slapped against Yayan, wrapped a tentacle around her leg and pulled.

"Not today!" she roared, severing it with her axe: after a pulse of hot red light, her attacker's appendage disappeared in a cloud of gray dust.

Other *ekume* feelers lashed out at their quarry: Loradan brought Hàfilrifar down upon too many to count; Peradan swatted more than a few out of the way; Falthwën, staff ablaze, hurled waves of destructive energy at as many flickering rifts as possible.

"Too many!" said Heshradan between blows.

An *eku* lanced a long finger toward Nïmrïk: the *egu* dodged, hunched, and, in an uncomfortable gesture that reminded Kalas of Dzharëth's final transformation, freed himself from his human skin. Now a wolf, he launched himself toward a dark star bearing down on Sifuran, grabbed it in his slavering jaws, and, with an improbable snap, broke its neck and hurled it to the ground. His foe neutralized, he bounded after another.

Nashmur had drawn his sword as well, but his efforts proved useless: every would-be strike passed through *ekume* without harm. Zhalera, wielding her ancestors' sword, held her own against the darkness.

"We've got to find a way out of here!" shouted Peradan as he scanned the Vault: "Abarandal! Follow me!"

"Kalas!" summoned Falthwën between blasts. "Protect the girl! Protect Abarandal!"

"I'm trying! My sword does nothing!"

"Protect her at all costs!" he insisted as a shadow loomed over the boy.

Kalas didn't see it until it was too late. Before the living gloom could seize him with its tendrils, Falthwën carved a quick symbol in the air and hurled it toward the boy. Kalas understood: he tucked Abarandal against his neck and rolled clear of the cleric's spell. Stunned, the *eku* seemed to shrink—if only for a moment. Falthwën rushed upon it, his staff ready for the next blow—but the creature gathered its malicious strength and came at the cleric from all sides, seized his limbs, and wrest his staff from his overworked hands.

"Falthwën! No!" Kalas screamed. Loradan turned and rushed toward Sharuyan with her sword held high.

Again, time seemed to lose momentum as the darkness whipped and slashed. Although its tentacles had seemed like nothing more than an angry antitheses of light, every lash lacerated the cleric's face, his arms and legs, his entire body. Bright white light, tinted at the edges with his signature emerald color, bled from his wounds.

"Ilmazhas!" cried Loradan as time regained its tempo.

"We'll meet again, my dearest," he insisted as his lifeforce gushed from every new injury. *"We* will *meet again!"*

With a smile devoid of sadness or regret—

Like Mother's...

—Falthwën held Kalas with his dancing green gaze. "Heal the world, my child! The *egu* wasn't wrong: there *is* great power within you! Let The Song reveal it to you! Become the light I *know* you to be! When you're 'confronted with a choice'—and you will be!—I know you'll make the right one!"

The other *erume* surrounded the *eku* that held their brother in its dark embrace: with their various weapons they hacked and slashed, but for every snaking column of blackness they felled, more sprouted in its place.

Falthwën closed his eyes and seemed to fluctuate between matter and energy, a caesura before he exploded in waves of knife-like particles of light—a cloud crackling with cleansing threads of *Sharuyandas Âsru*. When the overwhelming storm of emerald strength had burned itself out, the *eku* was gone.

Nothing remained of Falthwën except his staff.

Fighting against his rising fear and horror, Kalas made a grab for the object and willed it to produce the same fire as his departed mentor. He failed.

"Heshradan's right!" Loradan insisted as she batted at her own tears. "There are too many of them! Sharuyan was right, too: it's up to *you* to protect her! Protect them all!"

Before Kalas could defy the violet star—before he could insist that he and the others remain and help avenge Falthwën, she hurled everyone from the Vault in a dazzling blast of light and sorrow.

5.

"You're here!" whispered a familiar voice. "When Loradan returned Rül's coach to me, I had a feeling I'd be seeing you soon: but that was almost a month ago!"

"Yëlisha!" Zhalera cried and wrapped her arms around the innkeeper, careful not to upset the single lamp she held aloft.

"*Hish*, child! And it seems you've made some changes to your party?"

Kalas hadn't moved. Hadn't said a word since the lavender fronds of Loradan's *push* flickered into nothingness. Still holding Falthwën's staff, he looked around and recognized the room at Mbirin's Place where he and the others had stayed almost a month ago, according to Yëlisha.

"Falthwën—Sharuyan!—is...dead. Gone. I don't know," he mumbled. "An *eku* tore him apart right in front of us. Loradan's the one who sent us here..."

413

"*De! De!* It can't be!" she insisted as she collapsed onto one of the beds.

"Loradan and the others were still fighting. I don't know...I hope they got out in time."

"Kalas, I'm so sorry," she wept. "All of you, I'm so very sorry! Please: consider this place yours for as long as you need.

"Thank you, *shâu,*" he said with a stiff bow. "This is Abarandal, Commander Nashmur, and—"

Nïmrïk had landed behind the foot of one of the beds. Still resembling a wolf, he stood and shook himself out.

"A *rudzhegu* followed you!" she bristled.

"No, it's all right!" said Zhalera, whom Yëlisha had thrust behind her. "Nïmrïk's not like any other!"

"*Nïmrïk?!*" the buxom woman exclaimed. "You don't mean...?"

"She does, Madam Yëlisha," he answered for himself, and he told her some of the story he'd already told the others.

"For Sevens? Really?" she marveled. "And Grandmother had no idea?"

"None, I hope."

"It's *former* commander, actually," said Nashmur as he sheathed his sword. "I can't imagine the queen—uh, *regent! That* will take some getting used to! Anyway, she's...*unlikely* to suffer a traitor in her midst!"

Abarandal made a low curtsy, her shimmering vestments casting myriad multicolored sparkles along the walls.

"That's a lovely dress!" Yëlisha winked. Abarandal smiled, looked to Kalas, and uttered a few bars.

"And your *voice!*"

"She can't talk," Kalas explained. "Only sing. She says thank you for your condolences: Sharuyan was...something like a grandfather to her."

Yëlisha waved the young woman to her side and held her for a moment.

Kalas tapped Falthwën's staff on the floor with a few absent-minded clicks and wracked his brain for some idea of—

"What do we do next, Kalas?" Pava asked him. Despite their disastrous circumstances, he smiled.

"Great question," he conceded. "I…have no idea. I need to protect Abarandal—that was Falthwën's last instruction to me. From what, he didn't say. Maybe he didn't need to.

"We need information. We need education. Loradan said we roam the detritus of a broken world: Yayan said long ago they had an opportunity to prevent the world's cracking. They didn't take it because of *fear*. We can't let that happen to us: we can't let fear paralyze us like it did the *erume*."

"But we're *not erume!*" insisted Zhalera. "We—"

"That's exactly the point!" Kalas shook his head. "I'm barely past my second Seven, but I—all of us, I'd say!—have experienced fear enough to last us a thousand Sevens! I can't help wondering if the *erumedas* experiences over all those millennia might have made them second-guess themselves. I don't know what their 'opportunity' might have been, but if it was in accordance with *their* prophecy —the one entrusted to the *elume*…They way they were talking, I think Abarandal had something to do with it then, too. Or would have if they'd *summoned* her like they did beneath the Vault.

"We know she can't speak—not with words. Maybe Valaran could have given her a voice. It's doubtful we'll ever know for sure. But she can *sing!* There's meaning in her song—which, I'm certain, is a brand new movement within *The* Song! Falthwën and the others knew it: Nïmrïk, you know it too, don't you? I saw the way you listened when she first opened her mouth!"

"I do," he growled.

"'The music of creation.' 'The cord of Ilun's intent.' That's what

Falthwën called The Song. He never explained why most people never hear it—or why some do—but we *all* hear Abarandal when she sings. That's important. That's new. And *that's* what we have to understand."

"But with Falthwën…gone, with the other *erume* fighting against the *ekume,* who can possibly explain these things to us?" said Pava.

"I have someone in mind," admitted Kalas.

"Back in Lohwàlar!" Zhalera brightened.

"You're talking about Tsharak, aren't you?" said Rül. "He's old, he's been around for more than a hundred Sevens, sure, but will he know how to help us?"

"Tsharak?!" said Nïmrïk, his ears turned forward.

"That's right!" Zhalera realized. "You said you kept an eye on the boy Falthwën rescued from Kësharan, but couldn't remember his name or the name of the village where he left him. The boy was Tsharak! The village was Lohwàlar—our home!"

"And this Tsharak is still alive?! How is that possible?!" the *zhàrudzh* marveled.

"Maybe you can ask him yourself," suggested Kalas. "Yëlisha, if you'll permit it, I think we could all use a few days to get some rest. To come to terms with what's happened—and what's yet to happen."

"You know I will, young man!"

"I'd warn you that we have no way to pay for anything, but you already know that, and you wouldn't accept our money anyway."

"You learn quickly!" she teased with a wink.

"Thank you. Now, Nashmur: I hope you'll come with us? Something tells me we'll run into Shosafin sooner or later—if he doesn't run into us first! And Nïmrïk, I'd be a liar if I said I didn't see Dzharëth in you—the *rudzhegu* who killed my father—while you look…like that. But you helped us escape the dungeons under Ïsriba

—and I saw you save Sifuran: I watched you bite through an *eku* when it would have been simpler—and safer—to protect your own skin. I can't promise any other *Lohwàlarrinme* would understand if they figured out what you are, but I think Heshradan had the right idea about you. You're welcome to come with us.

"Do you mean it?" he panted, his tongue lolling from the side of his mouth as he adjusted his ears, unsure if he'd heard correctly.

"I wouldn't have said so if I didn't," said Kalas. "In a few days, we'll set out for Lohwàlar—"

"Dancer! Runner!" Rül interrupted. "The horses!"

"The what? Oh! Of course! Yes, your horses are fine! Loradan brought them with your coach! They seemed to remember this place: in fact, they seem to think they own it!" Yëlisha chuckled.

Kalas continued, "I have no idea what we'll find along the way. Maybe I'll learn how to use The Song. Maybe I'll come to understand it better. Maybe I won't. I'll worry about that later. If Ilnëshras' allies are stepping out of the shadows, if other kingdoms have their own 'Marugans,' who knows how long it'll be before everything comes undone? *Again.* The *egume* know the prophecy. They hear The Song. Parts of it, at least, and we'd be naïve to think they won't learn about Abarandal: she is the *great power* fallen upon the *realm of men.* They'll be coming for her. I don't know how, I don't know when, but we need to be prepared.

"In lots of ways, I'm still just a child who misses his mom and dad, and as much as I'd like to believe that this prophecy we've heard so much about refers to someone else, I'll trust Falthwën. I have no idea what he expects me to do, but we'll figure it out. We'll try, at least. For whatever reason, we're the ones entrusted with Abarandal's—and maybe the world's—fate.

"Let's return to Lohwàlar. Let's talk to Tsharak, figure out what we can do to prevent another cracking of the world. We have a living portion of The Song no one—neither *elu* nor *eru*—has ever heard before! Maybe it's not much. Maybe it's more than we could ever imagine. Either way, it's a start, *sàmeyahal*. It's a start."

Blake Goulette
October 2017
Holly Springs, North Carolina

Born and raised in Guilford, Maine, and its abundant woods and nearby mountains, Blake enjoys spending time with his wife, exploring the outdoors with his two boys, working with his hands, and pretending that someday he'll learn to play that guitar hanging on his wall. Today, he and his family call Holly Springs, North Carolina, home. *Beneath the Vault of Stars* is his debut novel.